Elvi Rhodes was the eldest of five children brought up in the West Riding of Yorkshire in the depression between the wars. She won a scholarship to Bradford Grammar School and left to become the breadwinner of her family. A widow with two sons, she lives in Sussex. Her previous novels include *Opal, Doctor Rose, Ruth Appleby, The Golden Girls, Madeleine, The House of Bonneau, Cara's Land, The Rainbow Through the Rain* and *The Bright One*. A collection of stories, *Summer Promise and other stories*, is also published by Corgi Books.

*Also by Elvi Rhodes*

*and published by Corgi Books*

# THE MOUNTAIN

## Elvi Rhodes

**CORGI BOOKS**

**THE MOUNTAIN**
**A CORGI BOOK : 0 552 14400 2**

Originally published in Great Britain by Bantam Press,
a division of Transworld Publishers Ltd

PRINTING HISTORY
Bantam edition published 1995
Corgi edition published 1996

Set in 10/11¼pt Linotype New Baskerville by Kestrel Data, Exeter.

Corgi Books are published by Transworld Publishers Ltd,
61–63 Uxbridge Road, London W5 5SA,
in Australia by Transworld Publishers (Australia) Pty Ltd,
15–25 Helles Avenue, Moorebank, NSW 2170,
and in New Zealand by Transworld Publishers (NZ) Ltd,
3 William Pickering Drive, Albany, Auckland.

Reproduced, printed and bound in Great Britain by
Cox & Wyman Ltd, Reading, Berks.

*This book is for Anthony,*
*with much love*

# Acknowledgements

I owe a great debt of gratitude to W. R. (Bill) Mitchell who, I daresay, knows more about the Settle–Carlisle Railway and the area in which it still runs than anyone in the world. His many books have been an inspiration and a mainstay in the writing of my novel. If I've got any facts wrong it's my error, not his.

I also, as always, thank my son Anthony for all his help in my research, and on this occasion I include my daughter-in-law, Margaret, who built me a detailed plaster model of the Ribblehead area at the time in which my story is set.

# 1

Jake Tempest (well-named, those who knew him said, for that's what he could be when he was roused) picked up his bag, swinging it aloft with ease. It was not a large bag, considering it contained his life, or as much of it, past, present and future, as he was prepared to carry around with him. It all fitted into the canvas knapsack. He liked to travel light.

In what was a gesture of thanks he rested his hand on Oggy's shoulder. Bill Ogden, the old man's name was, but everyone on the canal called him Oggy. They couldn't shake hands because the old man needed both his to bring the barge in close enough to the canal bank for Jake to jump off.

'Thanks, Oggy,' Jake said. 'It's been a real help.'

'Nay, Skipton to Gargrave's no great distance,' Oggy protested.

'It is when you're walking the rest of the way,' Jake said. 'Every little helps.'

'Aye well! If you'd nobbut come wi' me I could take thee all t'way to Liverpool. Tha could hop on one o' them big ships and sail for America, shake dust o' Skipton off thi feet proper, seeing that's what tha has a mind to do!'

Jake smiled, shook his head.

'I reckon I'll take it in easy stages, Oggy. Get a job, make a bit o' brass. It wouldn't do to land in America, and not a penny to my name. So you can wish me luck, finding work.'

The barge was within a yard of the bank now,

dead easy for Jake, who was long-legged and agile, to jump.

'You'll be all right,' Oggy said.

With a final wave of his hand Jake leapt from the barge, then fitted his bag more easily on his shoulder and walked away along the towpath.

Oggy watched him for a minute, saw him halt his stride to say something to the big horse which was towing the boat, and to run his hand along its neck, before moving on. Then he turned his attention back to the boat, manœuvring it into position to go through the locks.

The canal would turn west now. Soon they would have to go through the long Foulbridge tunnel which cut through the Pennines. He hated the tunnel, but when they came out into the daylight again they'd be in Lancashire. There'd be someone on this side, a young lad most likely, who'd lead the horse over the top, and someone a bit older to help him leg the barge through the tunnel. There always was. It was a way of earning a few coppers in hard times.

He spoke to his dog, a brown, rough-haired terrier type, now lying comfortably on the cargo of wool waste. He often spoke out loud to his dog.

'Well, Kipper, there'll be no difficulty in yon Jake Tempest finding hisself a job, an' that's for sure.'

He'd known Jake Tempest since he was a little lad. Everyone on the canal knew him. And he'd always been bonny, but now that he was grown he was as handsome a man as you'd find in a day's march. His round, childish features had firmed, so that the fine bones of his cheeks, nose and jaw shaped his face. He had thick black hair which curled over his collar, giving him a gipsyish look. They said his father had been a bit of a gipsy, though Oggy had never seen him. He'd not stayed around long.

But there was nothing of the gipsy about the lad's

eyes. They'd come straight from his mother. Bright blue, and always with a lively look in them. Oggy remembered Lily Tempest's eyes.

Yes, her son was a well-favoured man, and young with it, not more than three-and-twenty, Oggy thought enviously. Oh, he'd get on all right!

'I wonder what made him take agen Skipton?' Oggy enquired of Kipper. 'Happen a woman, I wouldn't wonder.'

If you didn't count Lily Tempest, women were the cause of most trouble in life, he reckoned. He'd certainly never have one aboard. He preferred a dog.

Jake quickly left the towpath and joined the turnpike road, turning north towards Settle, which was no more than a dozen miles from Skipton, though in all his life he'd never been there. He'd travelled much greater distances, but always on the canal. In fact he'd almost been born on the canal, on his grandfather's boat, and would have been except that his mother had left it in something of a hurry to go into hospital for his premature birth. She'd brought him back on board when he was ten days old, and for the next twelve years he'd been reared in the boat's cramped and confined living quarters.

He remembered every detail now. The short bedhole at the side of the cabin where he slept, his mother sleeping in a similar one on the other side, and his grandfather elsewhere on the barge – on deck in the summer. There'd been a highly decorated stove in the centre, with its cooking pots, and the kettle always on the boil behind the polished brass fireguard. There were tiny cupboards everywhere, narrow shelves with ornaments on lace doyleys, cushions which his mother crocheted in her spare moments. He had loved it all. They'd been happy, his mother, himself and his grandfather.

For a long time he'd thought his grandfather was

his father, until his mother told him otherwise. He'd always called him 'Pop', a sort of nickname, just as she had.

'No, love,' she'd said. 'Not that he hasn't always been the best of fathers to you.'

She'd taken both his hands in hers, looked straight at him with sad eyes.

'Your dad disappeared before you were born. I've always meant to tell you, but the time was never right. He walked off the boat one day in Leeds, and I've not seen hair nor hide of him since. But at least he married me when he knew you were on the way. I'll say that for him. So you're not a bastard.'

He'd not known what she'd meant.

'It's a child whose father didn't marry his mother, but you're not one, so that's all right.'

She'd always answered his questions truthfully.

'Don't think too badly of him,' she'd added. 'He just wasn't cut out to be a husband and a dad.'

'What did he look like?' Jake had asked.

She'd paused a minute, bringing him to mind.

'He was the best-looking man I ever saw. You're very like him − or you will be when you're older. But not in his ways. You'll make something of yourself, you will.'

'I'll never leave you,' Jake had said.

'Nor I you, love!'

So what had he made of himself, he wondered, as he walked along the road on this August morning in the year 1870.

He could still neither read nor write, though he was good at numbers. He got that from his grandfather, who'd taught him how to add up and subtract and multiply, until one day he said: 'Well, I've given thee what I know, young Jake, but now you've outstripped me. From now on, if you want to go further, you'll ha' to get another teacher.'

But there'd been no other teachers. The boat was seldom in one place long enough for Jake to get more than a few days' schooling at a time. And since he'd been with strangers, whose ways were not his ways, he'd not made much of it.

Oh well, he thought, no matter now. He'd like to be able to read and write, but there were other things in life. He knew more about nature than most boys. He knew where to find the first flowers, which of the plants growing near to the canal were safe to eat and which weren't, where the birds nested, how to foretell the weather. He knew practical things, too. He could catch, skin and cook a rabbit or a hedgehog, catch fish, and from an early age, under his grandfather's eye, he'd been able to take the barge through the locks.

When he was twelve years old life on the canal came to an abrupt end. His grandfather, whose only fault was that when he had money in his pocket he imbibed a drop too much, one night stopped off in Skipton and took on a skinful. On the way back to the boat, weaving his way along the towpath, he stumbled, fell in the water, and drowned.

'Whatever shall we do, Ma?' Jake asked after the funeral.

'I don't know,' Lily Tempest admitted. 'We can't stay on the canal, that's for sure. Oh, I can steer the boat, do the locks and all that, but I couldn't manage the cargoes. Wood, lime, gravel. It's a job for a strong man.'

'I could do it,' Jake suggested. 'I'm strong.'

'Of course you are, love,' she said. 'But you're only twelve years old, and still growing. It wouldn't do.'

'Will Dad ever come back?' Jake asked. 'If he knew about Grandad, wouldn't he come back?'

She'd smiled at that, shook her head.

'I doubt there's any likelihood of that, love. And we

haven't the slightest idea where he is. He could be anywhere in the land; or across the sea for that matter. No point in considering it, Jake. No, I'll sell the barge for what I can get. It's a decent boat, but you can bet your boots I'll not get what it's worth!'

'Why not?' he wanted to know.

'Because I'm in a hurry to sell, and because I'm a woman. I'll be offered less than if I was a man. It's the way of the world.'

It turned out exactly as she said.

'They took advantage of me,' she said. 'But never mind, love. At least I was paid on the nail, so there's a bit of cash, and I'll get a job, earn something.'

'What will you do?' he'd asked.

'There's textile mills in Keighley and Skipton,' she'd said. 'I'll get something, don't worry.'

'But Mam, you don't know anything about mills!' he'd objected.

'You're right, lad! It'll be like a foreign country to me. But I can learn. Don't fret!'

She made everything seem an adventure. When she found a menial job in the mill, and then two rooms in a house in the cheaper part of the town, she spoke as if it was exciting.

'We'll do very well here, love,' she said. 'Won't it be nice to have more space. I can show off all my ornaments!'

He had liked the cabin; it was cosy and warm. It had been a while before he'd got used to the house.

'And you shall have the bedroom,' his mother insisted. 'You're growing up; it's only right. In any case it makes sense because I have to be away to work early in the morning. No point in waking you.'

She had spent some of the money from the sale of the boat in furnishing the two rooms. All the furniture was bought cheaply, from secondhand shops, and there wasn't much of it: a bed, a sofa on which she slept, a chair or two, a table for which she made a fancy cloth from a remnant she'd bought in the market. And yet, each item as it arrived became a cause for a small celebration; buns from the baker, a fish supper, a bottle of dandelion-and-burdock.

It was the picture, however, which was the crown of all her purchases. He remembered as clearly as if it was yesterday the Saturday afternoon she came home with it. She burst in through the door, cheeks flushed, eyes shining.

'Oh, Jake! Oh, I've been so extravagant! But look what I've bought!'

She took it out of her basket and unwrapped it with the utmost care, as if it was the most delicate thing in the world.

'Just look!' she repeated. 'Isn't it lovely?'

She handed him the picture, a watercolour, framed in oak.

He took the picture from her and looked at it.

'It's a mountain!' she said.

It hadn't looked like a mountain to him. He knew how a mountain should look, he had seen pictures: triangular in shape, pointed at the top, purple in colour and with snow covering the summit. The one in his mother's picture was green and rounded, no angles, no sharp points, no snow. In shape it was like a picture he had once seen of a whale rising from the ocean.

'It doesn't look like a mountain,' he said hesitantly.

'Oh, but it *is*,' she insisted. 'It's just that it's a green mountain, an extra-high fell. Oh Jake, I *know* it was extravagant, but I shall never regret it!'

She hadn't. She had hung it on a nail on the wall by the fireplace, and every day he caught her looking at it. It was one of the few things he had brought with him from the past, in his bag, mainly to remind him of her.

*　*　*

It was getting warmer now. Pendle Hill, away to the west and over the Lancashire border, was a hazy blue in the distance. The sun, high in a cloudless sky, burned on Jake's back. He had a murderous thirst on him that only a pint of ale could slake, but thankfully there were signs of a village in the distance. He could see a cluster of houses, thin smoke spiralling from a chimney; and where there was a village there would be an alehouse.

He reached it twenty minutes later. Long Preston.

It was dark in the bar. The only window was small, set deep into the thick wall, and because the sun was so high very little light entered. After the brightness of the day outside it took him several seconds to adjust his eyes to the gloom. When he did so he saw an elderly man sitting on a bench. He nodded to him as he sat down on the bench opposite, loosing his bag from his shoulder and setting it down beside him.

A woman emerged from a door at the back of the room, a small child clinging to her skirt.

'A pint of your best,' Jake said. 'If you please!'

She made no acknowledgement, but within the minute the glass was on the table in front of him, brimful of the rich, brown liquid, crowned by a creamy collar of froth. He drank deeply, half the glass at one go, then wiped his mouth on the back of his hand.

'Good ale! And well kept!' He set down the glass and nodded his approval at the woman.

'It's my father you have to thank for that,' she said. 'I only serve it.'

And with no pleasure at all, her voice and manner said.

'Best beer for miles around,' the old man said.

Ostentatiously, he drained his glass to the last drop before putting it down.

'Then allow me to refill your glass,' Jake said. He

signalled to the woman to do so. 'And mine as well, while you're at it,' he told her, drinking down the rest of his beer.

She collected the glasses and took them away. There was a fierceness in the way she did it, resentment in every line of her body as she moved.

Jake raised his eyebrows at the old man.

'Crossed in love,' the man said cheerfully. 'Her man upped and left her three months ago. Went to sea. Since when, she hates all men. And you'll not escape, though she's nobbut just set eyes on you!'

Jake shrugged. He felt the same way about women as she did about men, but he'd not go into it, not with a stranger; not with anyone for that matter.

'No skin off my nose,' he said. 'Just as long as the beer's good.'

He glanced at the woman as she returned with the beer. She was comely enough. Her hair was thick and glossy, the colour of the corn in the fields outside. Her skin was creamy, her figure rounded in all the right places. So why had her man left her?

But her generation of women were not all they seemed, not what they promised. He'd discovered that the hard way. For all her good looks, she was probably no better than the rest of them.

She served the beer, and left them. The two men raised their glasses and drank.

'Corn's ripening well, I noticed,' Jake said.

'Aye, 'tis,' the old man agreed. 'Another week or two like this and we'll be ready to harvest. And if t'weather holds longer there'll be a second crop of hay. Beasts can do wi' that in the winter.'

They sat in silence for a while, then Jake said, 'Well, I'd best be on my way. No time to waste.'

'Where are you bound for?' the man asked.

'Settle, to start with. I reckoned I might get a job on the railway.'

'Aye, well, there's lots do. Folks have come from all over the place: Wales, Cornwall, Northumberland.'

'So I heard,' Jake said.

'The wages are better, you see. But the work's hard. They say every payday some leave, which is why they can set new men on. But I reckon you've not come far?'

'Only from Skipton.'

He had lived there for six years after he and his mother had left the canal. He had worked at what jobs he could get, not helped by his lack of education. Sometimes on the canal, sometimes in the building trade, which he learnt as he went along. His mother insisted on keeping her job in the mill, though many was the time he implored her to give it up.

'It's too hard,' he said. 'The hours are too long. I'm sure we could manage on what I earn.'

That was doubtful, and he knew it. Building work wasn't regular; when the weather was bad he was laid off. As for the canal, well, the railways were taking the cargoes more and more. He couldn't rely on steady work.

'We're all right as we are,' his mother said. 'You save what you can. Put a bit by in the bank. You never know when you might need money.'

He'd done as she'd suggested, but how many times since then had he regretted that he hadn't been more insistent that she should pack in her job, especially in that last bitter cold winter of 1866. Because, owing to the weather, he'd been laid off, she'd insisted on going to the mill when she had a heavy cold on her. In no time at all it had turned to pneumonia, and in the middle of a February night, even before he could get the doctor to her, she had died.

He had never felt so alone, so bereft, as on that day he'd followed her coffin to the churchyard. There were no other mourners, except for a neighbour. They

18

had no relatives, and had kept themselves to themselves.

Afterwards, he couldn't settle in Skipton. He deeply resented the fact that his mother had been taken from him at only thirty-six. When the spring came he moved down the valley to Keighley, and then, later, to Bradford. He didn't like either of them, they were noisy and dirty, so he came back to Skipton. It was there that he had met Vinnie. It was Vinnie who had brought him back to life.

He rose to his feet now, slung his bag over his shoulder again, and left the inn. He was conscious that the woman watched him go, though she didn't bother to answer his word of farewell.

It was hotter than ever on the road. The sun was at its zenith. Furthermore, the strong ale had made him sleepy. His limbs, his eyes, every part of him, weighed heavily. More than anything in the world he wanted to find a patch of shade, lie down in it and lose himself.

A mile further on, the village well behind him, he found what he was looking for. An ash tree grew close to the hedge which bordered the road, and on the other side of the hedge was a pasture. Through a convenient gap he went into the field, then lay down at the edge, in the shade of the tree, and, using his pack as a pillow, fell instantly asleep.

He dreamed he was with Lavinia, and everything was as once it had been. They were happy together, planning for the future when they would be man and wife. He had never been so happy.

'I've never been so happy, Vinnie love,' he said.

'Me neither,' she said.

He had taken her in his arms and was about to kiss her when, suddenly, he was wakened by the sound of a cart on the road. It took him time to bring himself

19

back into the world, to relinquish Vinnie and face the reality that she was gone. She had left him without so much as a note or a message. It was left to others to inform him that she had gone off, presumably in the early hours of one morning, with the waiter from the Cow and Calf. Everyone seemed to know with whom, though no-one knew where.

'But you must have some idea,' he'd insisted to her mother. 'She's your daughter.'

'That doesn't mean she tells me anything!' her mother said tearfully. 'She was talking about Morecambe the other day, how she'd like to go there. Happen that's where they've gone.'

Each day that followed he had waited for a line from her, an apology, an explanation. At first he knew he would have taken her back, forgiven her everything, but as the days went by his heart hardened.

'I've waited long enough,' he said to her mother. 'From now on she's out of my life and out of my mind – and I'm leaving Skipton!'

But she had not been out of his mind, he thought now, jumping to his feet. And if she had gone to Morecambe she would have travelled in this very direction. But I am not going after her, he told himself. I'll not go after any woman, ever again. The devil take them all!

Back on the road he looked ahead and saw the cart, the noise of whose iron-clad wheels had wakened him. If he put on a spurt he could catch up with it, cadge a lift. He began to run, and the driver of the cart heard him, pulled on the rein and spoke to the horse.

'Whoa there!'

'Can you give me a lift?' Jake asked.

'Depends where you're going!'

'Settle. At least to begin with.'

'Then you're in luck, lad. I'm going through to Giggleswick. Jump on!'

Jake took his place beside the driver. There was very little space; the cart was piled high behind him, everything covered by a tarpaulin. The driver flicked his whip and the horse moved forward at a steady gait.

'What are you carrying?' Jake asked.

'Household effects,' the driver answered. 'A young couple flitting from Keighley to Giggleswick. They took the train on account of the lass is seven months gone. I'm to meet up wi' 'em at the house.'

'You know Settle?' Jake enquired.

'A bit. You live there, do you?'

'No. I've never been there. I'm looking for a place to stay. You don't happen to know anyone?'

'I don't. But there's inns. The Golden Lion; the Spread Eagle.'

'I can't afford that sort of place,' Jake told him. He still had some of the money he'd saved, but he'd have to go carefully. 'A night or two's lodgings is what I want. There's bound to be something. I'll ask around.'

'You do that!'

They fell silent for a while. The road was rising now. The horse walked slowly, straining at the weight.

'I'll jump off for the hill,' Jake offered.

'I daresay she'd be pleased at that, would Polly,' the driver said as Jake got down. 'She's getting old, like me. A bit short of breath – though it's not a heavy load, as loads go.'

The country was altogether more hilly now, especially to the east and northwards towards Settle. The limestone escarpments of the hills were dazzling white in the bright sunshine. Jake watched a kestrel, its tail spread, hover ahead of them, motionless in the air, then drop with lightning accuracy to scoop up a mouse crouching at the side of the road.

A little more than an hour later they drove into Settle. At first sight it seemed, to Jake, smaller than Skipton – perhaps because the road through was narrower, and meandered. It was certainly more hilly, the cobbled streets rising sharply from the road, the market square itself on a slope. But it was every bit as busy as Skipton. And some fine buildings, he said to the driver.

'If you think this is busy, wait until you see it tomorrow!' the driver said. 'Tomorrow's market day. You'll find it hard to get a place to put your foot down then! I'll drop you here, in the market place, shall I?'

'That'll do fine,' Jake said. 'And thanks for the ride.'

He watched the cart go down the street, then stood and looked around him, wondering what would be his next move. Best to look around, get his bearings, and surely he'd find a teashop on the way. He could do with a cup of strong, sweet tea and a currant teacake. He wasn't in the mood for more ale just yet. That could come later.

He found a teashop without difficulty, and was served with a surprisingly good brew and a currant teacake as light as air, thickly spread with fresh butter.

'I'm looking for lodgings,' he told the waitress. 'You don't know anywhere, do you?'

'Permanent?' she asked.

'Oh, I don't think so. A night or two to begin with, then I'll see.'

He was in no mood to settle anywhere permanently. He had no real idea where he wanted to be, except that it was not in Skipton. It was only a chance remark made by a man in Skipton, to the effect that there were jobs in Ribblesdale to be had for the asking, which had brought him to where he was now; that, and the fact that the area had been so close to his doorstep for most of his life, and he'd never set foot in it.

'Only temporary,' he added. 'I don't rightly know where I'm bound for.'

The waitress stood there, her head on one side as

she considered the request. With no emotion, Jake observed that her hair was dark, almost black, and fell in wispy curls over her broad, smooth forehead, almost into her eyes; that her skin was clear, her cheeks pink with health. All this he noted, and brushed aside.

'Well,' she said, looking at him directly, 'I just might be able to help.'

She'd be more than delighted to do so, she thought. He was a corker! Moreover, he had a nice voice, and that was something she could never resist.

'My aunt sometimes takes a lodger or two, only temporary of course. She might well fit you in.'

'That would be fine,' Jake said. 'Where does she live?'

'Wait a minute,' the waitress said.

She left him, and went across to the other waitress who was leaning against the counter.

'Mary, will you cover my tables for a few minutes? I'll not be long.'

Mary nodded. 'What are you up to now, Sally Roland?' she asked.

'Tell you later.'

She hurried back to Jake.

'I can take you to my aunt's if you like,' she said. 'It's quite near.'

She took off her cap and apron and accompanied him out of the café, walking close beside him as they crossed the road and climbed the hill. He was a bit of all right, this one; better than anything she'd come across in Settle. She'd not yet told him she lived with her aunt, and had done for two boring years since her mother had packed her off from Leeds. He'd learn that when she'd fixed him up.

As they turned a corner she bumped against him. He had to put out a hand to steady her.

'Ooops!' she said. 'I must take more water with it! Here we are.'

She hoped he wouldn't leave Settle too soon; and if it depended on her, he wouldn't.

Her aunt opened the door.

'Why, Sally, what are you doing home at this time of the afternoon?' she asked. 'Is something wrong?'

'Not a bit of it,' Sally replied. 'Mr . . . ?'

'Jake Tempest.'

She liked that. A strong name. He looked a strong man; masterful, she wouldn't wonder.

'Mr Tempest is looking for a room, Auntie. Just for a night or two. I reckoned you might fix him up.'

'But Sally you know—'

'I must get back,' Sally interrupted. 'I don't want the sack, do I?' With a parting smile in Jake's direction, she hurried away.

Jane Sutherland watched her niece as she ran back down the hill. Now what's she up to? she asked herself. And then, as if I didn't know!

'Come in, Mr Tempest,' she said to Jake. 'Though I'm not sure I can do anything for you. You see . . .' (and as that little minx knew well) '. . . I only have the one spare bedroom, and that's taken for the moment by Mr Armitage.'

'Then I'll not trouble you,' Jake said swiftly. He turned to go. Why had the silly girl brought him here?

'But wait a minute,' Mrs Sutherland said. 'There's two beds in the room, and if Mr Armitage doesn't object . . .'

And an extra one-and-sixpence a night, she reminded herself.

'. . . And I don't suppose he will, seeing he's moving on himself the day after tomorrow.'

'I wouldn't want to disturb him,' Jake said. He was not sure he wanted to share with a stranger.

'Well, he's in his room now, so we can ask him!' Mrs Sutherland's tone was brightly confident. 'He's a very nice man. You'll find him interesting too. Knows about all sorts of things.'

Mr Armitage, summoned from his room, looked long and quizzically at Jake before delivering his verdict.

'I'll be pleased to share the room,' he said at last. 'I daresay Mrs Sutherland will make me a small reduction.'

'We'll have to see,' Mrs Sutherland said reluctantly.

'And I hope you don't snore, Mr Tempest,' Mr Armitage said. 'I shall certainly waken you if you do. I need my beauty sleep!'

'Well then, that's settled,' Mrs Sutherland said. 'Supper at seven o'clock. I'm making a nice meat-and-potato pie and me and Sally will sit down with you. You'll find this a friendly house, Mr Tempest.' And my niece will make certain of that, she thought.

Mr Armitage took Jake up to the bedroom, where the latter unpacked a few things, including his framed picture. He propped it up on a narrow shelf near his bed.

'My mother bought it,' he said in answer to Mr Armitage's enquiring glance. 'She always called it the mountain, but I was never sure.'

'Then you can be,' Mr Armitage said. 'It's a mountain, and what's more, I know it! It's called Whernside and it's not all that many miles from here.'

He picked up the painting and scrutinized it.

'It's a nice little study. Your mother made a good choice. You might make a bit if you were to sell it.'

'I don't have that in mind,' Jake said.

When, later, they went downstairs to supper, Sally was already there. She had changed into a flowered-cotton frock, and piled her luxuriant hair on top of her head, but loosely, so that it threatened to fall down at any moment. It was difficult not to look at it, though it vied for attention with the locket hanging on a silver chain which encircled her slender white

25

throat, nestling in the cleft between her round-as-apple breasts.

'You're as pretty as a picture!' Mr Armitage said with appreciation. 'Isn't she just as pretty as a picture, Mr Tempest?'

Sally, her blue eyes wide, her red mouth smiling, looked to Jake for his reply.

'Very nice,' Jake said evenly.

If Sally was disappointed she didn't show it. She felt confident of melting his ice, of weakening the resolve she saw in his face.

Mrs Sutherland dished out the steaming pie, spooning the rich gravy over the potatoes.

'Now eat it while it's hot,' she said. 'I know it's been a warm day, but I've always found gentlemen like something hot, whatever the weather.'

'You're right, Auntie,' Sally said. 'And not only the gentlemen!' She attacked her food with gusto, clearly savouring every bite.

And well she might, Jake thought. It was the best food he had tasted in many a week. He gratefully accepted the second helping Mrs Sutherland offered.

'You'll need to walk that lot off,' Sally said. 'Lucky it's a nice evening. I could do with some fresh air myself.'

The look she gave him was a bold invitation. He answered it with an equally direct look.

'I'm going to turn in early,' he said. 'It's been a long day.'

Sally's mouth continued to smile, but her eyes flashed anger. She wasn't used to this.

'But I'd be delighted to accompany you, Miss Sally,' Mr Armitage put in quickly.

'You're a real gentleman, Mr Armitage – and there aren't many of them about. But do you know, I realize I'm quite tired too,' Sally said sweetly. 'I think I'll follow Mr Tempest's example!'

As Jake lay on his bed, the light still filtering in through the thin curtains at the window, he was aware of Sally Roland on the other side of the thin wall. He also realized that she meant him to be aware. Sounds – a drawer opening and closing, shoes being dropped, a long sigh and a clear expression of relief as, he thought, she removed her stays. The bed, close up against the dividing wall, creaked as she bounced into it, and as she rolled over she bumped into the wall.

For a brief moment it felt almost as if she was in his bed, as if he had only to put out a hand to touch her, to touch her warm flesh where the locket lay. Against his will, his body responded. He closed his eyes, then opened them again quickly, and leapt out of bed.

Damn the stupid bitch! She was nothing but a whore. And if he marched in and took her now, as she was clearly inviting him to do, it would not be the first whore he had taken in the last few years. But not for a long time now. Not since the day he had met Vinnie, and with her he had never made love completely.

'Save it for when we're married,' she'd said.

And he had. And perhaps he shouldn't have. Perhaps if he'd shown her that he was a man, he'd have kept her. She wouldn't have turned to that rat of a waiter. The thought of Vinnie came between him and the woman tossing about on the bed in the next room. Was she going to come between him and every woman he'd ever meet?

He was saved from further thought by the return of Armitage from his walk.

'I daresay it might rain,' Armitage said. 'It's in the air.'

'I've decided I'll move on tomorrow,' Jake said. 'I've a notion to see this Whernside. I can put off looking for a job for a week or two.'

'But you'll get a job over that way,' Armitage said. 'They're well on with the railway at Ribblehead. And if you're going, I reckon I'll leave with you, walk with you as far as Horton and set you on your way. I've no reason for staying on here.'

'I'd appreciate that,' Jake said.

'Good. Now remember what I said. Don't keep me awake with your snoring!'

The boot was on the other foot. It was Jake who was kept awake half the night, and not by sounds from the next room, which had promptly ceased the moment Mr Armitage returned. No, it was the older man's talking. He talked until the short summer night was almost over and the dawn began to lighten the room again. And Mrs Sutherland was right. He certainly knew about a lot of things. Nature, art, landscape, literature. There was no end to it.

'My wife – God rest her soul – used to tell me I'd talk a glass eye to sleep,' Mr Armitage said amiably. He glanced across at Jake in the other bed.

'And my word, I think I've talked you to sleep!'

When they went down to breakfast, Sally had already left for work.

'Market day,' Mrs Sutherland explained. 'They have early customers in the café.'

She was surprised when both men told her they had decided to move on. Surprised, but not unduly put out. She took things as they came. It was the best way. Sally, though, was going to be furious. She'd really set her cap at the young one. Nevertheless, she passed on her niece's message, speaking to both men. It was intended for Mr Tempest, but she could hardly single him out.

'Sally said if you'd like to drop in for a cup of tea while you're in the market, she'd be pleased to give you special attention. But since you're making a start, I reckon you'll not have time for that.'

'Oh, I don't know,' Mr Armitage said. 'I daresay we might manage it!'

'But I thought . . .' Jake demurred.

'We've time enough,' Mr Armitage said. 'You'd not want to leave Settle without seeing the market, and then a nice cup of tea would see us on our way.'

Jake gave in. He liked markets, it wasn't that. He didn't want to see the girl again. In spite of the fact that he didn't even like her, last night she'd aroused feelings in him which he thought had gone for good; feelings he didn't want ever again.

The market place was thronged: rabbits, hens, puppies, a goat or two; eggs, butter; pots and pans; cures for backache, toothache, ingrowing toenails and warts. Stalls of every kind. There was scarcely room to set foot. At a point where they found themselves exactly opposite to the café Mr Armitage said: 'Well then, let's get that cup of tea, and be on our way.'

It was as if Sally had been waiting for them. She saw them the minute they came in at the door, rushed them to a table, served them with a fresh brew and thick slices of fruit cake. It was not until then that she noticed that they had what looked like all their worldly goods with them.

'We're leaving,' Mr Armitage said, following her glance. 'Got to move on!'

Sally's face fell. Though last night had come to nothing, due entirely, she told herself, to Mr Armitage's early return, she was not one to give up easily. She'd felt sure she would conquer Jake Tempest today, and now he was walking away. But she wouldn't write him off. He was far too attractive to let go.

'Well,' she said, speaking directly to Jake, 'it's a pity you're going so soon. I could have shown you the delights of Settle. But you'll come back, I'm sure of it. Everyone comes back to Settle.'

The invitation was in her eyes as well as in her words. Resist me if you can, they said.

# 2

The morning was more than half gone before the two men walked out of Settle.

'I had hoped to have made an earlier start, Mr Armitage,' Jake said. 'Though I suppose it doesn't matter.'

'Of course it doesn't! We have the whole day and the whole world in front of us. Never let time be your master. And call me Armitage,' the older man said.

It was another fine morning, not as hot as the previous day, and therefore all the pleasanter for walking. Jake remarked on it.

'It's not always like this,' Armitage said. 'And it can change in a minute. Not three weeks ago we had one of the worst thunderstorms in living memory as I was walking into Settle. Hailstones as big as pigeons' eggs! Broke the windows. Houses flooded. No traffic possible on the roads. I was soaked to the skin.'

'It looks nothing like that today,' Jake said.

'I agree! But you never can tell in these parts.'

In fact the river, on their left as they walked northwards through the dale, was full, and flowing fast.

'It's a pretty river,' Jake remarked.

'A beautiful river,' Armitage confirmed. 'The Romans thought so when they were here. They called it "Bellissima", meaning "Very beautiful". But it's seen hard times. Robert Bruce scared the living daylights out of the people in Ribblesdale with his bloody raids. And you can hear the folks hereabouts talk as if it all happened yesterday. Some of 'em are still not sure about the Scots.'

'How do you happen to know all these things?' Jake enquired. 'I never met a man who knew so much!'

'Reading. Practically everything I know I've got from reading. I always carry a couple of books in my knapsack. I hope you do the same?'

There was a short silence.

'I can't read,' Jake confessed. It shamed him. Was it somehow his own fault? Had there been a point somewhere in the past when, if he'd made a better effort, he could have mastered it?

'Good heavens!' Armitage was so astonished that he stopped in his tracks and turned to face Jake square on. 'You don't have the appearance of a man who can't read, not in the least!'

He looked intently at Jake. Put aside the fact that the young man was handsome, not badly spoken and, from the way that Sally Roland had done her best to seduce him, attractive to the opposite sex, he also looked intelligent. You could see it in the eyes; clear, alert, comprehending, though at this moment not too comfortable.

'My dear boy,' he commiserated, 'why, you're missing out on the best of life if you can't read.'

'So it seems,' Jake said, though that had not occurred to him before meeting Armitage.

'Well, I wish I had the chance to teach you,' Armitage said. 'The fact is, I'm a here-today-and-gone-tomorrow person, not reliable. But try to do something about it, boy. You don't know what you're missing.'

I wonder what *he* does for a living, Jake thought. In his own way he seems as rootless as I am. He had offered no explanation.

'I'm footloose and fancy free,' Armitage said, answering Jake's unspoken question. 'I have very little

31

money – a pittance I inherited from my mother – but my way of life doesn't need much money. As long as I can afford a stout pair of boots, a few books, paper to write on, and the price of a cheap bed, that's enough. In fact, I bless the day I gave up earning a living.'

'How *did* you earn a living?'

'I was a teacher.'

Of course! It fitted him like a glove. It wasn't only that he *had* all the knowledge, he knew how to impart it.

'And though I say it myself, I was a good teacher,' Armitage added. 'But it tied me down. I've never liked being tied down. And I've always preferred seeking after knowledge. There's no end to it. All the same, I'd like to have had a stab at teaching you to read. I've only ever taught small boys.'

They walked in companionable silence for a while but when, to the right, a high, strangely shaped hill appeared on the horizon, Armitage could not contain himself. He leapt in the air, and shouted:

'There it is! There's my mountain! Pen-y-ghent. A Welsh name, meaning 'Hill of winds', though I never did discover how it got a Welsh name. Oh, but it's magnificent! Don't you agree it's magnificent?'

'Very impressive,' Jake said. It was a strange shape, like a crouching lion.

'Like a sphinx,' Armitage said. 'You've seen pictures of the Sphinx, haven't you? And am I not right? Well, when we reach Horton, and we're not far off now, I'm going to leave you, and I'm going to walk over my mountain and down into Littondale.'

'It looks a stiff climb,' Jake said.

'Oh, not so bad! Not as high as Whernside, which is *your* mountain. But when it comes to mountains it all depends on the weather, and today it's good.'

That was an understatement. The day was

perfection. Sunny, but with an ever-present breeze which at the moment was only strong enough to nudge cottonwool clouds across a high, blue sky. In the pastures the newly shorn sheep were sharp white against the emerald green of the grass, and in the cornfields – fewer in number than the pastures, for this was sheep country, not arable – the grain was almost ready for harvesting.

'It's very good,' he acknowledged.

He felt, for a rare moment, though he knew it would not last, in harmony with the world and with the landscape through which he was walking. At peace with himself. It was a while since he had felt so.

'Well, here we are. This is Horton!' Armitage said presently. 'There's a good inn at the other end of the village. I suggest we take some refreshment before we part company.'

They walked to the point where the river made a right turn under a narrow roadbridge, and to the side of the bridge, settled in a hollow beside the road, stood the inn. Jake, ducking his head, followed Armitage through the doorway.

They were offered lamb chops, with the local cheese to follow. They ate with hearty appetites. Armitage cleared his plate, drained his tankard, patted his stomach appreciatively, then stood up.

'Well, that's it! I'll be on my way, young man! What about you?'

Jake rose to his feet and they walked out together.

'Thank you for your company,' Armitage said. 'I've enjoyed it. And I suppose I should thank you for listening to me. I seem to have talked a lot. But once a teacher, always a teacher!'

'I've learned a lot,' Jake said. 'Thank you.'

'But not as much as you will when you learn to read.'

'I hope we'll meet again,' Jake said.

'If God wills it, then we will!'

33

They shook hands, and parted, Armitage to the east, Jake continuing on the road northward. It was true, Armitage reflected as he began his climb, that he had enjoyed the young man's company, but he was not sorry now to be on his own. He was a loner, always had been. When you were walking the hills there was nothing to compare with solitude.

A curlew circled in the clear air above him, uttering its strange, mournful cry; then it dived to the ground ahead of him, so close that he could see its long, downcurved bill, its white rump. A bird of the moorlands, of open spaces; he felt at home with it.

Jake, in a way, was sorry to part from Armitage, but in another way he too was glad to be on his own again. Listening to Armitage, his head had been crammed with facts, with no time to sort them into any order. He wondered if he would ever see the man again. He hoped he might, but it seemed unlikely. They had not exchanged addresses because neither of them had an address.

The road was undulating here, rising and falling, though never dramatically. The river, which had crossed the road under the bridge at Horton, was on his right now, flowing a little less turbulently through meadows which stretched a fair way until the hills began to rise in the east. The sound of sheep still accompanied him. 'When sheep aren't eating, they're bleating,' Armitage had said.

It surprised Jake a little that there was no traffic on the road, not a solitary cart, not even a pony and trap, nor another person walking. He had the world to himself.

He thought about Vinnie. He didn't want to, but he couldn't help himself. She was in and out of his mind the livelong day. Wasn't she the reason he was taking this lonely journey?

Like a mirage in the sunlight, the vision of her

danced before him, there in the middle of the road as if she was flesh and blood, her red hair piled in curls, her green eyes dancing, though now filled with mockery. If only she'd come to him, if only she'd told him; if they'd had it out between them, he could have borne it. It was the deceit, the thought that she'd been planning this treachery even while she was in his arms, which he couldn't stomach. It ate at him like a worm at his vitals.

Sunk in his thoughts, he didn't notice time passing until it came to him that the narrow road, though not the pastures to the east, was in shadow. He raised his head and looked around him. To his left now was a great hill, and beyond that another, behind the summits of which the sun had dipped. Armitage, he thought, would have known their names, but he had no idea himself. It did seem to him, though, that by now he must be nearing Ribblehead where, so Armitage had told him, the road split, and he would have to choose his direction.

And then suddenly – he had breasted a rise in the road and taken a bend without noticing either – he saw it. He saw what he had walked all these miles for when he might have remained in Settle. It was there before him, to the north. The mountain! Not sharp-pointed, not snow-capped, but with broad slopes leading up to the wide, rounded summit. It appeared to him as though it was rising from the depths of the ocean, that one day it might, should it ever wish to do so, rise even further. Such was its power. It dominated the landscape, though, on this bright summer's day, with a benign dominance.

He could not understand his emotion on seeing it, and it didn't matter that he couldn't. Feelings of awe, wonder, satisfaction, of a goal reached (though two days ago he had had no such goal in mind) fought with each other, filled his heart and his mind.

He set his knapsack on the wall which bordered the road, and delved into it for the painting. His hands shook a little as he took it out. He looked at the painting, and from it to the scene in front of him. They were one and the same, there was no doubt about it. Indeed, the picture could have been painted from this exact viewpoint, and the colouring, too, was right. In both the picture and the real thing the afternoon sun caught the green of the fellside and tinged the tops where the green faded into browns and greys, blues and purples. Oh, what would his mother have thought? What would he have given for her to see it?

Immersed in the scene, he didn't hear the footsteps of the man approaching him along the road. Not until the fellow called out a greeting, and was almost past, was Jake aware of him.

'Wait a minute!' he called out.

The man stopped.

'What's the name of that mountain?' Jake demanded. Armitage had said the picture was Whernside, and in his heart Jake knew they were one and the same, but he had to be sure.

'Yon's Whernside,' the man said. 'I reckon you must be a stranger not to know that!'

'I am,' Jake agreed.

'Where are you bound for, then?'

Where am I bound for? Jake asked himself. In Settle he had decided, on a whim, to find the mountain of his mother's painting, and now he had found it, though he had yet to climb it, and that he knew he must do.

'I'm not sure where I'm bound for in the end,' he told the man.

'I thought happen you were after a job on the new railway,' the man said. 'There's a lot of building going on at Ribblehead, and you're not far off.'

'Then I might do that,' Jake said.

'You'll come to Salt Lake City on your left, and not long after you'll be at Batty Green. Can't miss it! You'll see the huts. Someone'll tell you where to apply for a job. Were you thinking of working on the viaduct?'

'I hadn't thought,' Jake said. 'I'll see what happens. Thanks for the information.'

Soon afterwards, on rising ground on his left, he passed a group of huts which he assumed was Salt Lake City. There was little sign of life there, just a woman with a small child clinging to her skirts. They waved as he went past, and Jake returned the greeting. And then, at a point where the road north came to a sudden halt, dividing into east and west directions, he was at Batty Green.

It was a sight which, long after he had been and gone; had arrived, stayed, and finally left, would remain with him. When the wide expanse of moorland had been reclaimed by jealous nature, he would remember the alien sight it had presented on that August afternoon.

Huts!

In the flat foreground, in the middle ground where the land began gently to rise, and on the higher ground at the far side of the moor, towards the beginnings of the lower slopes of the mountain, there were groups of huts, some large groups, some no more than two or three buildings. The huts were mostly, but not all, of a similar size, and the same low, rectangular shape. Many were whitewashed against the glare of the sun, so that they had the appearance of a crop of mushrooms which had sprung up overnight in a great green field.

He stood there, at the junction of the road, staring, and then realized he was not just seeing buildings, but that from the primitive chimneys which rose from the centre of each hut, smoke spiralled into the air, and

37

that around the nearer huts, in and out of the doorways, people were moving: mostly women and children, he noticed, and realized that the men would still be at work.

Close to the huts, dogs, hens, pigs, giving an air of permanent domesticity, foraged around for pickings.

There were tracks everywhere, flattened into the grass, churned into the mud, running in all directions, criss-crossing. Tracks along which sturdy horses pulled strange-looking carts, the like of which he had never seen before; along which men wheeled barrows, carried hods and picks and shovels; called out to each other.

Jake took a deep breath, crossed the road, and stepped into the scene.

He stopped the first man he met, a man pushing a barrow over a footbridge which spanned a narrow stream. There were small streams everywhere.

'Where do I go to ask for a job?' Jake asked.

The man set down his barrow, and pointed.

'You see that four-wheeled hut, over there? The contractor's hut. You'll find the agent there.'

'Thanks!'

The hut was no more than five minutes' walk away, over ground which, though there had been no rain for several days, was soggy beneath Jake's feet, springing with water, so that he had to take care where he trod. Four or five rough wooden steps led up to an open door in one end of the hut. Jake climbed the steps and knocked on the door. A voice growled to him to come in.

The hut was dark inside, lit only by a square window with four small panes of glass, set high in one of the two long walls. The atmosphere was stuffy, for the window was tightly shut and the stove, though not burning fiercely, was lit, with a kettle boiling on top.

What air entered through the doorway failed to reach the far end of the hut where the owner of the voice sat behind a wooden table. A brown-and-white dog, half spaniel, the other half indeterminate, lay on the floor beside the table. It raised its head at the sight of Jake, but did not get up. The man at the table studied Jake.

'I don't know you, do I?'

'I've just arrived,' Jake said.

'I thought so,' the agent said. 'I know most of the men, even though they do come and go. I've a memory for faces. What are you after?'

'A job,' Jake answered.

'Oh yes? And what sort of job?'

'Whatever's on offer. I don't mind.'

The man leaned back in his chair. There was a glint in his eye.

'I see! Well on this contract we've got carpenters, brickmakers and bricklayers, masons, engineers, clerks, stokers, saddlers, miners, labourers and navvies. And a dozen others I could mention if I had the time. So which of these various trades are you skilled in, if any?'

'Well . . .' Jake hesitated, trying to recall something in the long list to which he could lay claim.

'Where do you come from?' the man barked.

'Skipton.'

'Married?'

'No. No living relatives.'

'So, footloose and fancy free! And what did you do in Skipton?'

'Mostly in the building trade. Labouring; a bit of bricklaying. There's plenty of building going on in Skipton.'

'So why did you leave?' the man snapped.

'Personal reasons,' Jake said shortly.

Woman trouble, the man thought. He looked like

39

a man who might have the women after him. But it's not my business.

'Do you drink?' he demanded.

'Moderately.'

'You'd be wise to keep it that way. It's the curse of this place, drink is. It's where most of the wages go. If I'd any sense I'd be a publican! So what do you reckon you can do?'

'I wondered if there was an opening on the viaduct?' Jake said.

'It's mostly very skilled work,' the man said. 'They're laying the foundations and it's not child's play, I can tell you. Twenty-five feet those shafts go down to bedrock, and then six feet of concrete on top before we can start on the piers.'

'But there must be some labourers, some navvies?' Jake prompted.

'That's true, but at this moment it's skilled men we want on the viaduct. We've got all the labourers we need. Of course, come payday some will leave. It's always the way, the minute they lay hands on the money. The work's too hard, the hours too long, it's an isolated place. But it's not yet payday, so they'll stick it out.'

'So is there somewhere else I could be set on?' Jake enquired. 'I don't much mind where I go.' He didn't yet know whether he would stick it. He'd have to see.

'There's the tunnel,' the agent said thoughtfully. 'They can always do with more men on the tunnel.'

And always would, he thought, because it was a rotten job; working in the dark, or at best by candle-light; falling rocks, not enough air, and what air there was, foul. Worst of all, though, the incessant struggle to dig a way under and through the mountain for a distance of a mile and a half. But he'd not go into all that. If this man took the job, he'd find out himself soon enough.

'Where is it, the tunnel?' Jake asked.

'About two-and-a-half miles from here, up on Blea Moor. They're tunnelling under the mountain.'

It was that which decided Jake. To be working on the mountain, actually inside the mountain! They could keep the viaduct!

'If there's a job for me there, I'll take it,' he said without hesitation.

'Then report there in the morning,' the man said. 'Ask for Isaac Hargreaves.'

'Thanks,' Jake said. 'I'll do that. And can you tell me where I can get a bed for the night?'

'Let's see. If you're going to try for the tunnel, you'd be best looking for a place close by it. Jerusalem, say – or Nazareth.'

'Jerusalem? Nazareth?'

'Shanty towns – or the beginnings of them. Not many huts at Nazareth, as yet; but there will be.'

While the agent was speaking, there was a knock on the door and a man entered. He was tall, powerfully built, dressed in dark trousers and unbuttoned waistcoat, his shirtsleeves rolled up over muscular arms. He wore a black, brimmed hat, and in his mouth a clay pipe was clamped.

'Ah, Seymour!' the man behind the table greeted him. 'You're just the man I want. This young fellow here . . .' He turned to Jake. 'What did you say your name was?'

'Jake Tempest.'

'Right. He's going to try for a job in the tunnel and he'll need somewhere to stay. Your wife takes in a lodger or two, doesn't she?'

'That's right,' Seymour said. 'We live at Nazareth,' he told Jake. 'I'll point you the way.'

He had a short conversation with the agent, then went outside with Jake.

'Keep ahead,' he said, 'the mountain on your left.

In fact, follow the tramway, then you can't go wrong. It goes up to the tunnel.'

He pointed towards the lowest part of the valley, where men were working on the viaduct. Jake glimpsed the tramway, where a light engine pulled trucks.

'Tramway?' Jake queried. 'Any chance of a ride?'

Seymour shook his head.

'I doubt it. Supposed to be for goods only. But if you keep clear of the bog it's not a bad walk. You'll come first to Sebastopol and Inkerman, and about three-quarters of a mile on you'll reach Jericho. Nazareth is the same distance again. Anyone there will tell you which my hut is.'

'I'll be off then,' Jake said.

'Right! And you can tell my wife I'll be late home. We're working while the daylight lasts.'

Jake struck out towards the viaduct area, picking his way. If it was all going to be like this he'd need some stouter boots. He wondered what the people here did for shops. His question was partly answered as he passed through Sebastopol and Inkerman – he didn't know which was which – and observed a pedlar going from hut to hut, and a cart delivering milk.

As the ground rose, there were fewer huts, fewer carts, horses, people. But for the noise of the tramway, it was almost tranquil. Flowers grew abundantly in the grass, cropped short by the ubiquitous sheep: buttercups, daisies, Herb Robert, the small, bright yellow tormentil carpeted the ground; and in the strange circular hollows, completely symmetrical, which he had noticed all along his walk, and which he knew to be shakeholes, meadow cranesbill abounded.

He stopped, and watched a hare dodging around in a particularly large hollow, in and out of the ferns. If it saw him, it gave no heed.

Presently he came to another settlement. He spoke

to a woman sitting at the door of a hut peeling vegetables.

'Is this Jericho?'

'It is,' she said. 'Who would you be wanting?'

'Nazareth,' Jake said.

'A bit further up,' the woman said.

Nazareth, when he reached it, surprised him. There were fewer than a dozen huts, built on both sides of the tramway, which passed through the middle of the settlement, presumably on its way to the tunnel. The huts were uniform in size and appearance, freshly whitewashed, tidy around the outside, one or two with lace curtains at the small windows. It was quite different from Sebastopol and Inkerman, even from Jericho: cleaner, tidier, civilized.

A girl sat on the grass outside one of the huts, weaving a daisy chain. She looked up as Jake's shadow fell on her.

'Hello,' he said. 'I'm looking for the Seymours' hut. Do you know which it is?'

'Over there,' she said. 'The other side of the tramway track. The middle one.'

He knocked on the door.

'Come in please!'

It was a woman's voice, but low-pitched. He stepped into the hut.

The woman stood behind the table, her hands deep in a bowl of dough. She stopped her kneading for only a brief moment while she looked at him.

'Yes?'

'Mrs Seymour?'

'That's right.'

She was tall, so that she had to stoop over the baking bowl, but while she regarded Jake she stood to her full height. Her eyes, meeting his directly as if in appraisal, were brown, flecked with yellow: cool, but not hostile. Her hair was brown also, but deep with colour, like the leaves of a copper beech. Or even more, like a chestnut newly escaped from its husk, Jake thought. Rich and glossy. Her face was pale, her dress was black, and she wore a white apron. So why, he thought, did this combination of sombre hues result in an impression of someone alive with colour?

'Your husband sent me,' he said. 'I'm looking for lodgings, hoping to get a job on the railway.'

She finished kneading, turned the dough over in the bowl, smooth side uppermost, covered it with a cloth and set it closer to the stove to rise.

'You would have to share,' she said. 'I don't have much room. This is the living-room, and it's exactly as you see. The room at one end is mine and my husband's, and the one at the other end I let to lodgers.'

'How many would I share with?' Jake asked. He didn't like the sound of it.

'One only, at the moment, though there are three beds in the room, so it could be two. Would you like to look? The other man is out at work. He works in the tunnel.'

He followed her into the room. There were three narrow beds set close together, one chest of drawers, a shelf over the head of each bed, and various hooks on the wall. There was no room for a chair. It was, however, clean and fresh-looking, with colourful checked blankets on the beds.

'How much do you charge?' he asked.

He thought the sum she asked was on the high side, and she read that in his face.

'It's the usual,' she said. 'And if you get a job you'll earn good wages, as much as eight shillings a day if you're lucky – depending on what you do. Why else do you think men come from all over England to this benighted spot?'

'I suppose so,' Jake said. He had not discussed

money with the agent, and was agreeably surprised at the wages.

'All found,' Mrs Seymour added. 'I do your washing, and I'll feed you well. Ask anyone.'

'Well then, if you'll have me,' Jake said.

'This will be your bed,' she said. 'Mr Mahoney has the one against the wall. You must sort out the drawer space with him.'

'Thank you. I'd like a wash,' Jake said.

'The men wash in the back. It's only yards away. If you choose the right place it can be quite private. It saves carrying the water.'

'Mr Seymour said I was to tell you he'd be late home. They're working while the light lasts.'

A slight frown line creased Mrs Seymour's forehead. She knew what it meant. When they'd worked as long as the light allowed, the next step would be the alehouse. There was no shortage of alehouses.

'Then we'll not wait till he comes for our dinner,' she said. 'It'll be ready in an hour.'

Jake found the spot in the beck he reckoned his landlady had intended. A steep outcrop of bank overhung the stream, so that he was able to strip off his clothes and bathe without fear of being over-looked. The water was fast-flowing and icy cold, and stung sharply against his flesh; but when it was over, and he was dressed again, he felt invigorated: a new man, all his fatigue washed away.

Back in the hut, the air was filled with the delicious smell of mutton stew. He realized how sharply hungry he was. Another man sat at the table, waiting. He was small and dark, with a black beard and an untidy moustache.

'This is Patrick Mahoney,' Mrs Seymour said. 'Your room mate.'

'Pleased to meet you,' the man said.

Even aside from his name, there was no need to

45

announce his nationality. His soft voice, his accent said it all.

'I'm from Cork,' he added.

'And since you're both here, I'll serve the dinner,' Mrs Seymour said. 'It's a hot meal on a hot day,' she apologized as she filled the plates with the thick stew, topped with dumplings.

Soon after the meal was over the Irishman went out.

'Will you be coming with me, then?' he invited Jake. 'It's a few beers I'm after.'

'Thank you, I won't,' Jake said. 'I reckon I'll turn in early. It's been quite a day.'

'Suit yourself.'

'And I have a pile of ironing,' Mrs Seymour said. 'So if you've finished at the table, I'll get on with it.'

It was a dismissal, Jake thought; not unkind, but quite brisk.

'Then I'll say goodnight, Mrs Seymour.'

In the bedroom, he lay on the bed, listening to the soothing sound of the beck. What would tomorrow bring, he wondered. Would he get a job? And, just before he fell asleep, where was Vinnie? What was she doing?

Some time afterwards – it was pitch dark – he was wakened by the sound of someone coming into the hut, singing; and then his landlady's voice asking for silence. He had thought the singer must be the Irishman but, his eyes now used to the darkness, he saw that Patrick Mahoney was in his own bed. He had slept so deeply that he hadn't heard him return.

' 'Tis Himself!' Mahoney mumbled. 'One over the eight! But at least he sounds cheerful with it.'

# 3

It had taken a long time for Jake to get to sleep again after Seymour's return. At first it had been Seymour who had kept him awake. He paid no heed to his wife's pleas to be quiet, but continued to laugh and sing and talk. Although the two bedrooms were separated by the living-room, the walls were thin, the doors flimsy – the huts were, after all, only temporary – and there was no shutting out the sounds. Fortunately, when Seymour came to the end of his song and lowered his voice to talk, his words were indistinct. Only his cajoling tones came through, and from his wife there was silence. Minutes later, and abruptly, Seymour too fell silent.

The interruption, though perhaps no longer than twenty minutes, left Jake wide awake. He tossed and turned, flung off the blanket because he was too hot, then gave up the effort to find sleep, and lay on his back. The night was less dark than it had been and the square of sky, seen through the window, hinted at a rising moon, but the silence of the night was intense. All that disturbed it was the beck, which sounded faster and more furious than it had in the daytime. Thank heaven, Jake thought, that the Irishman didn't snore. He was sleeping as peacefully as a baby.

Eventually, though not before the sky was already lightening with the new day, Jake turned on his side, pulled the blanket around his shoulders, and at last fell asleep.

When he wakened the room was bright, Mahoney's

bed was empty, and there was a smell of bacon in the air. He jumped out of bed, pulled on his shirt and trousers, and went into the living-room. Mrs Seymour was clearing dirty dishes from the table. She looked up and smiled at him.

'Good morning! I hope you slept well, Mr Tempest?'

'It seems as if in the end I slept too well,' Jake said. 'You've finished breakfast!'

'The men have,' Mrs Seymour said. 'They left a while ago. They make an early start, especially Will. He has a two-mile walk to work.'

She moved across to the stove, where thick rashers of bacon were cooking in a black iron frying pan.

'I can only give you one egg with your bacon,' she said. 'The hens aren't laying well, but there's fried potato.'

'It smells good,' Jake said. 'I'm sorry to give you the trouble of cooking a second breakfast just for me.'

'Oh, it's not just for you,' she said. 'It's for the both of us!' She moved aside the sizzling bacon, tilted the pan, and dropped two eggs into the pool of fat. 'I always wait for mine until the men have gone to work. It's my bit of peace.'

'Then I'm sorry to disturb you,' Jake apologized.

'That's all right,' Beth Seymour said. 'How do you like your egg?'

'Turned over, fried on both sides,' Jake said.

'A ruin of a good egg,' she said. 'But if that's what you want!'

She dished up the food and put the plates on the table, then she paused before sitting down.

'I hope you'll not find me rude, Mr Tempest. What I meant when I said it was my time of peace was that I always read when I'm having my breakfast. I don't get much chance otherwise. And I'm nearly at the end of the book. I want to finish it. Do you think that's very rude?'

'No,' Jake said. 'Don't mind me.'

'Thanks.'

She took a book from a shelf, sat down at the table and opened it.

Nothing more passed between them. Jake watched her, fascinated, though not so much by the fact that she was reading, but because, while seeming never to move her eyes from the book, she ate at a steady pace through the contents on her plate. Then she stretched out a hand and, without looking, took a slice of dry bread and mopped up every vestige of fat. Simultaneously with the last mouthful she reached the end of the book, giving a deep sigh as she closed it.

Then she came quickly back to earth.

'Why, Mr Tempest, you've only half-finished!' she cried. 'Is everything all right?'

'Delicious!' Jake said quickly. 'My mother always complained I was a slow eater.'

It was untrue, but he could hardly tell her that he'd been busy watching her instead of getting on with his bacon.

'You'll have another cup of tea?'

He hesitated. It was time he left. He was going after a job, wasn't he?

'Well . . . if *you're* having one.'

He observed her again as she went to the stove and poured water from the kettle into the large brown teapot. She wore a blue cotton blouse this morning, with the sleeves rolled up high, showing her strong arms as she manœuvred the heavy kettle. Strong arms, but not coarse; rounded and shapely, with fine skin, lightly freckled; slender wrists. Her hands looked capable, an unusual mix of square, practical-looking palms and long, tapering, artistic fingers.

'What were you reading?' Jake asked.

'*Wuthering Heights* by Miss Emily Brontë. Of course it's not the first time I've read it. It was given to me by a woman I worked for before I was married. Oh, it's so romantic, isn't it?'

She seemed not to notice that he didn't reply.

'I could read all day,' she confided. 'The same lady who gave me this book was a member of a circulating library. She would lend me any books I cared to read. I've read all Mr Charles Dickens. I cried like a child when he died earlier this year. I do truly mourn him!'

She brought the teapot back to the table and poured two cups, then she picked up the book, and ran her hand over the cover as if it was a live and cherished thing, before replacing it on the shelf.

'Do you read much, Mr Tempest?' she asked.

'No,' he said.

He changed the subject.

'I should be away. I have to see a man name of Isaac Hargreaves. I'm hoping he'll have a job for me.'

This time yesterday he hadn't been all that sure whether he wanted a job hereabouts, or whether he'd move on somewhere else. Now, he thought he'd be disappointed if he didn't get one.

'I expect he will have,' Beth said. 'I don't know him. He probably lives up at Tunnel Huts. They're always wanting men in the tunnel.'

It was her turn to observe him as he sipped his tea. He couldn't be in that much of a hurry, the way he was making it last. She didn't mind. As soon as he'd gone she'd set to, and it would be all go until the men came home in the evening.

He was good to look at, a cut above a lot of the men who worked on the railway. But no doubt, if he stayed, he'd fall into their ways, he'd soon be as rough as the rest. She'd not been here long, but she'd already seen it happen; to her Will for instance. She saw the change in him, much though she loved him.

'Which way do I go?' Jake asked.

'It's simple. Follow the beck, which means you'll

keep the cutting on your left. Where the beck crosses the cutting – they've built an aqueduct there – you'll see the mouth of the tunnel. It's not more than three-quarters of a mile, all told. The Tunnel Huts settlement is right by it. You'd perhaps have been better looking for lodgings there. No distance to walk at all.'

'I reckon I'll be all right here,' Jake said, smiling. 'Better not to live right on top of the job.'

'That makes sense,' Beth agreed.

'Then I'll be off.' He pushed his cup away. 'I'll just put on a clean shirt, and I'll be away.'

'Hand me your dirty one,' Beth said. 'And anything else that needs washing.'

'Thanks. Shall I fetch you some water before I go?'

'It's all right,' Beth said. 'I do the washing in the beck. It's the best way. Good luck!'

He walked out of the hut into another fine, warm morning. A group of children, including the girl he had spoken to yesterday, were playing a skipping game; two dogs lay stretched out in the sun and the sound of a baby crying came from one of the huts. Down by the beck, a woman washing clothes called out to him.

'Good morning! You're new here!'

'Good morning,' Jake said. 'Yes I am.'

Again there were no men around. The answer to that was quickly made plain. They were all working on the line, or in the deep cutting at the approach to the tunnel. Steep, rocky hillsides climbed up on either side of the narrow strip of land along which, when it was levelled, the railway would run until it plunged into the darkness of the tunnel, inside and through the mountain itself.

He stopped to survey the slope of the land. It rose steeply in front of him, yet they would have to keep the line as level as possible if the engines were to haul the trains at any sort of speed, and this was to be a fast line, fifty miles an hour. But Armitage, that fount of all knowledge, had told him that the maximum gradient they could allow, even though the ground climbed all the way from Settle to Blea Moor, was one in a hundred.

'And that's as steep a gradient as you'll find any-where in the country,' he'd said. 'No wonder they call it the Long Drag! Which means,' he'd added, 'they'll have to sink some pretty deep shafts from the top of the tunnel, to get down to near-level ground.'

Jake missed Armitage. He could have done with him right now. There were so many things he'd like to know, all of which Armitage would no doubt have learned from reading the newspapers. Also Armitage could have told him something about the book Mrs Seymour had been reading.

Mrs Seymour herself, Jake reckoned, probably knew a lot. She had a lively air about her. Not that he had any intention of asking her questions. Rather than ask a woman, he would keep his ignorance to himself. There were ways of finding out things if he kept his eyes and his ears open.

There was a hut on a piece of levelled ground at the end of the cutting, and to that, walking now along a narrow path at the base of the rock, he made his way. As he reached it a man came through the doorway.

'Excuse me,' Jake said. 'I'm looking for Mr Isaac Hargreaves.'

'Then you've struck lucky,' the man said. 'I'm him! What would you be wanting?'

He was a tall, lanky man with a narrow white face. Black bushy eyebrows met over the bridge of his nose and curled upwards at the ends, in exactly the same manner as did his luxuriant dark moustache. His voice was harsh, rasping. Somehow it went well with his face.

I'd not want to get on the wrong side of him, Jake thought.

'A job,' Jake said.

'What sort of job?' Hargreaves demanded. 'We've got mainly miners, bricklayers and labourers in the tunnel. Which of those jobs can you do?'

'I'm not a miner,' Jake admitted. 'But I can do labouring, or a bit of bricklaying.'

'You can, can you? And where've you worked before?'

'Skipton. But I don't carry references.'

Why had it never occurred to him to do so, he wondered. Because he'd left in a huff, that was why. 'But I can give you names.'

'You needn't bother,' Hargreaves said. 'I don't go much on references. Pack o' lies more often than not. Are you as strong as you look?'

'Stronger,' Jake said.

'You'll need to be. It's hard graft in the tunnel, and tunnel's what I'm offering you.'

'Then I'll take it!'

'Have you got lodgings?'

'In Nazareth, with a Mrs Seymour. There's a Patrick Mahoney lodges there, works in the tunnel.'

Hargreaves spat on the ground, though whether by need, or habit, or to express his opinion of the Irish, or of Mahoney in particular, it was impossible to tell.

'Six shillings a day,' he said.

'I was told it might be as much as eight shillings,' Jake said. He thought he had the measure of this man. Stand up to him or he'd walk all over you.

'Well you were told wrong,' Hargreaves said. 'Happen seven shillings a day when you're worth it, if I find out you can lay bricks well. Right now, how do I know you can do it at all?'

'You can try me. But if I lay bricks satisfactorily, I'll look for eight shillings. Anyway, I've heard the

Midland Railway Company are generous employers on the Settle–Carlisle.'

He had heard nothing of the sort. All he knew of the Midland, and again it was Armitage who had told him, was that they desperately wanted this line to bridge the gap between Settle and Carlisle in order to give them access to Scotland. They'd gone to parliament for permission to build it.

Hargreaves grunted.

'Generous is not the word I'd use. They have to pay over the odds to get men to work here. Mind you, what they *do* do is look after your welfare. Before they've done there'll be more amenities on Batty Green and Blea Moor than ever you saw in Skipton. Come on, then. I'm going to take you up to number one shaft. They're short of men there.'

He set off at a brisk pace in the direction of the tramway which climbed up the steep side of the moor. Jake followed, a pace behind.

'Jump on,' Hargreaves said. 'It's not encouraged but it'll save time.'

The tramway was carrying containers of building supplies.

'Before we had the tramway, all this stuff had to be pulled up the slope by donkeys, poor devils,' Hargreaves said.

They jumped off again at the entrance to number one shaft. The ground was piled with stone and rubble which had been dug and hauled up out of the mountain. A winding engine, which worked the metal cage-like contraptions which brought up the rubble and took down men and supplies, stood empty at the entrance to the shaft. Another engine stood a few yards away. Hargreaves climbed into the empty contraption and Jake followed him.

'What's the other engine for?' he asked.

'It pumps water out of the mountain, when

necessary, and blows air to the men down there – always necessary. Have you never been down a mine?'

'Never!' Jake said. He had never fancied it.

'Oh, well. It's a bit like that at the moment. You'll soon get used to it.'

They were descending slowly, deep into the ground. The cage jerked and swayed in a disconcerting manner.

'How far down?' Jake asked.

Hargreaves shrugged. 'Maybe ninety yards, give or take a bit.'

Jake was thankful when the cage came to a halt on solid ground.

'Out you get!' Hargreaves said.

Two things struck Jake simultaneously. One was the noise: pickaxes, hammers, chisels, spades; men talking, one man singing in a sweet, true tenor voice. And every single sound hit against the black limestone and grit walls of the inside of the mountain and bounced back again, doubling itself.

The other thing was the lighting, the only source of which was candles. They were balanced on jutting rocks, in crevices, wherever there was space enough to take a candlestick. The glow from each one of them penetrated only a short way before it was swallowed up in the thick blackness, and its role taken up by the next one. Jake had never experienced such darkness nor seen so many small sources of light.

'A pity man can't see in the dark,' Hargreaves said, following Jake's gaze. 'It costs upwards of fifty pounds a month to light this tunnel. A fellow would be rich on that!'

At the spot where they stood, at the bottom of the shaft, the tunnel was brick-lined, and the arches completed. As far as Jake could see, it was so in both directions for a distance of several yards, though not all the arches were completely bricked and the ground was not properly levelled.

'Follow me,' Hargreaves said.

He took Jake several yards down the tunnel and introduced him to a man laying bricks.

'Tempest starts as a labourer,' he said. 'You'll know where he's needed most. He'll be on day shift to start with.' He turned to Jake. 'Might as well start at once, now that you're here. This is Bill Thornton. Below ground you answer to him. He'll tell you what you need to know.'

He walked away. Jake's last sight of him was as the cage ascended, bearing him away from the darkness to the daylight.

The rest of the day was unlike any other Jake had spent in his life. Bill Thornton quickly set him on clearing rubble and sending it up the shaft. Each time he sent the container on its way aloft, he wished he was the man at the top, receiving it and piling the contents onto the spoil heap. Would he get a turn at that, he wondered. He hoped so.

The darkness confused him, and the candles, casting flickering shadows, dazzled him. He found himself stumbling over the rough ground. At one point he tripped over a lump of rock and fell heavily, tearing his trouser leg and hurting his knee.

'You'll get used to the dark,' Thornton said shortly. 'You'll develop cat's eyes, like the rest of us. Even so, you'll always have to watch out. If you get injured, let me tell you, if you're off work, you'll earn nowt. There's a Settle and Carlisle Sick Fund, but what a man gets from that won't keep him in beer and tobacco, and since you've hardly been here ten minutes, you'd get nowt anyway.'

'I'm not planning to go on the sick fund,' Jake said. His knee hurt quite badly, but he would say no more about it. He'd not risk losing his job on the first day.

It was a little later, moving a few yards down the tunnel, that he heard Patrick Mahoney's voice. Though he couldn't yet see him, he was presumably hidden in the gloom some yards away, there was no mistaking the accent. He walked towards the sound, and Mahoney spotted him first.

'Why, 'tis yourself!' he said. 'So they put you on number one shaft. Are you all right, then?'

'I am,' Jake said. His knee was hurting like hell, but never mind that.

Presently a whistle blew, and everyone stopped working on the instant and began to move towards the shaft.

'Dinner time,' Mahoney said.

Three at a time, they climbed into the cage and were raised to the surface. Jake blinked, and held up his hand to shade his eyes as he stepped into the strong sunlight. Most of the other men were already sprawled out on the grass a few yards away from the shaft entrance, and it was not until he saw them take out their tins, unwrap their bundles, open their water bottles, that he realized he had brought no provisions at all with him. He had not given it a thought.

Patrick Mahoney, sitting on the ground beside him, opened his jock tin to reveal a thick beef sandwich, a piece of cheese, a slab of fruitcake. Suddenly, Jake was ravenously hungry.

'You've not brought your jock?' Mahoney asked.

'No. I didn't think of it. I suppose I reckoned if I got a job I'd be told to start tomorrow.'

'Herself must have thought the same. She'd not be letting you leave the house without your food. She's a good provider, Mrs Seymour.'

Jake tried not to look at Mahoney's food. He could feel the saliva gathering in his mouth.

'Well, you'd best be sharing mine,' Mahoney offered.

57

He took out his knife and meticulously divided everything into two.

'I can't do that,' Jake protested.

'And you can't work the rest of the day on an empty stomach,' Mahoney said. 'Come on, let's be having you. There's enough for the both of us. The trick is to eat it slowly. I found that out a long time ago.'

No food, Jake reckoned, had ever tasted so good, and no water so refreshing as that he drank from the Irishman's bottle.

'Meself, I'd rather it was a pint of ale,' Mahoney said, 'but we're not allowed to drink on the job.'

Jake, his hunger eased, lay back on the short-cropped grass and squinted up at the blue sky, then closed his eyes. He was on the point of falling asleep when another whistle sounded. The men rose slowly to their feet and went back to work, down into the darkness. Jake had not noticed it in the morning but, after the sweetness of the high hill, the air in the tunnel smelt foul. Fresh air, he knew, was regularly blown into the tunnel, but it was clearly not enough. There was also another smell which, though he had noticed it earlier, he could not identify.

'Gunpowder,' Mahoney informed him. 'The miners were using it this morning, before you arrived. It's the only way to blast some of the rock. Nasty stuff, gunpowder!'

The afternoon passed slowly, though he was kept hard at work on the same job. There seemed no end to the amount of rubble to be moved. He said so to Thornton.

'And every bit of it needed,' Thornton answered. 'What we take up out of the tunnel will be used to help build up embankments further along the line, or happen on the foundations of the bridges and viaducts.'

Jake was thankful when the time came to knock off.

He was used to manual labour, but nothing as hard as this. His back was breaking and his knee grew more painful by the minute. Also, it had bled. There was a damp, sticky patch on his trouser leg.

When at last they emerged from the tunnel, like animals coming out of their holes, he thought, the men on the next shift were grouped at the entrance, waiting to descend.

'We work around the clock,' Thornton explained. 'Every day except Sunday. You might say it's a rush job, except it can't really be hurried. It's bloody hard work, and bloody slow. If we open up three or four yards a week we've done well.'

A few yards from the entrance to the shaft the two men parted company.

'I live at Tunnel Huts,' Thornton said. 'Very handy!'

A short distance down the track Patrick Mahoney, whom Jake had not seen as they came off the shift, caught up with him.

'And how did your first day go?' Mahoney enquired.

'All right, I suppose, Mr Mahoney,' Jake said. It was the most he could say. He had hardly *enjoyed* it, it hadn't been what he expected; but then, what did I expect? he asked himself.

'The name is Pat,' Mahoney said. 'No formalities. Except, of course, to the bosses. Watch out for Thornton, he can be awkward.'

'I thought he seemed all right,' Jake said.

'Ah well, perhaps 'tis so. Perhaps 'tis because you're not Irish. The Irish are not popular on this railway. I don't know why. But then, did the English and the Irish ever get on?'

Jake didn't answer. He had met with the same feeling in Skipton, but he'd never taken sides, he wanted no part in it.

'You're limping,' Patrick observed.

'I fell. Gave my knee a bit of a knock. It'll be

59

all right once I can get back and attend to it.'

At a point where they should have turned left to reach the Seymour hut, Patrick said: 'I'll be loving you and leaving you for now. I'm going down to Batty Green. Tell Mrs Seymour I might be a bit late for supper, but perhaps she'll be kind enough to save a bite for me.'

He gave no further explanation. Perhaps he has a woman on Batty Green, Jake thought. But when he passed the message on to Beth Seymour, she smiled.

'His glass of ale holds more attraction than food. It's the same with most of the men, and you can't blame them. They do hard, backbreaking jobs, in all kinds of weather, and they deserve their pint. The only trouble is, they never stop at one or two. They lose count, don't know when to call a halt.'

She was sitting on the grass outside the hut, peeling a mound of potatoes. She had undone the buttons on the high neck of her blouse, against the day's heat. Around the long column of her throat she wore a necklace of red glass beads which glowed like rubies in the light from the sun. The sun also picked out the lights in her brown hair, turning them to flecks of gold.

'Do you not drink, Mr Tempest?' she enquired.

'Oh yes! At the moment it's too far to go. If you don't object, the name's Jake.'

'It's a nice name,' she acknowledged. 'There's water in the jug in the house if you fancy a cold drink.'

'Thanks!'

What he did fancy was a good wash, better still a bath. He felt dirty from tip to toe and, despite the fact that it had been cold in the tunnel, sweaty. He was not sure, however, that it was a good time to bathe. There were too many people around the huts now, and he would be in full view. But a wash he must have, and he must see to his knee.

60

It was not until he started to move towards the hut that Beth Seymour noticed his torn trousers, and the bloodstain over his knee.

'Good heavens!' she cried. 'Whatever have you done to yourself?'

'It's nothing much. It'll be as right as rain when I've bathed it,' Jake said.

He went past her and into the hut, where he drank two full mugs of water. Then he went into the bedroom in search of his towel and some soap. It was obvious that in his absence it had been swept and tidied, both beds neatly made. A clean-washed vest and socks, a newly ironed shirt, lay on the bed. He felt ashamed that he'd left his part of the room in such a mess, but that was one of the things living alone did to you. You didn't care.

As he looked around the room he realized what was missing. He had not hung up his picture of the mountain. It still lay on the chest of drawers where he had left it last night. He would see to that when he'd cleaned himself up.

He gathered up his spare pair of trousers, his clean underwear and shirt, and made his way to the beck.

'I'll have a look at your knee when you come back,' Beth called after him. 'It might need a bandage!'

The ice-cold water of the beck – he was to learn that however hot the sun, however long it shone, the water on the moor, in the beck and in the many small streams which sprang from the ground, was always cold – refreshed his body while sharply stinging his knee. But there was no great damage: an inch-long cut, and some grazing around it, but his trousers had prevented the gravel embedding itself in his flesh. It would heal soon enough.

He dried himself, and dressed, then washed his blood-soaked trousers in the beck. When he got back to the hut his landlady had gone inside. He held up the wet trousers.

'Where can I hang them?'

'There's a line at the back,' she said.

When he came inside again she said, 'If you'll sit down and roll up your trouser leg, I'll take a look at your knee.'

'There's no need . . .' Jake protested.

'Better to be on the safe side,' she advised. 'It's a dirty place, the tunnel, or so I'd think. If you've got a cut you should have it covered. You wouldn't want it to get worse.'

Her tone was cool, matter-of-fact, as if he was a child. He sat on the chair and, kneeling in front of him, she rolled up his trouser leg. When she saw the cut and the grazing she gave an involuntary gasp.

'Why, it's quite nasty! It must have been really painful. I reckon it needs some disinfectant and a bandage.'

The stinging of the icy beck water was nothing compared to the pain of the disinfectant, which she dabbed on his knee abundantly. Then she covered it with a folded square of cotton, and started to bandage it. She was deft and sure, and at the same time gentle. Those practical-looking hands, Jake thought, as he watched her tying the bandage, had not lied.

She tied the last knot, cut off the ends of the bandage, then, lifting her head, leaned back and smiled up at him.

'There! That's better!' she said.

'Thank you. Thank you very much!'

A shadow blocked the light from the doorway. Jake turned his head and saw William Seymour standing there.

'I see my wife's making you feel at home!' Seymour said.

Beth Seymour rose to her feet, still smiling.

'Jake had a slight accident at work, in the tunnel. I was putting a bandage on. You're early, Will. I didn't expect you so soon.'

He grunted.

'Nevertheless, I'm pleased to see you,' she said. 'Supper won't be long.'

Jake rose to his feet.

'Thank you very much, Mrs Seymour,' he said. 'It's much more comfortable.' He turned to her husband. 'Your wife's a clever nurse.'

'Oh, she's clever at lots of things,' Will Seymour said. 'You'll find that out.'

'Well if you'll excuse me, I have a few things to do,' Jake said. 'Oh, by the way, may I hang a small picture on the bedroom wall? And if I may, could you give me a nail and lend me a hammer?'

Will Seymour rummaged in a box, then handed Jake the hammer and nail. Beth Seymour was busy at the stove.

# 4

'Remember, both of you,' Beth said as she served breakfast to Jake and Patrick – Will had left earlier – 'I'll not be in when you get home today. I'll leave you a meal, but it will be cold.'

'And where would you be going, Mrs Seymour?' Patrick enquired pleasantly.

Beth stood with her hands on her hips, gazing at him.

'Patrick Mahoney, where do you think I'd be going?' she demanded. 'Where do I go every Saturday afternoon?'

'Oh, it's Saturday, is it?' Patrick asked. 'Do I ever know the day of the week, working under the ground like a mole? And then, aren't Saturdays and Sundays all the same to us? Doesn't the Company like us to work our shifts through the weekend, no interruptions to the work?'

Jake ate his breakfast while looking from one to the other of them. They did a lot of sparring, but it was all good-natured.

'So you're taking the market tramway down to Batty Green to spend your man's hard-earned money,' Patrick said. 'Is that the size of it?'

'You know it is,' Beth answered.

Every Saturday afternoon the empty trucks made a special journey from Tunnel Huts to Batty Green, stopping at the different shanty towns to pick up those who wanted to make the trip, which in practice was all the women and, if the weather was halfway decent, the children as well. It was an uncomfortable journey, everyone jammed together, standing in open trucks which swayed perilously on the downhill run; but it was even worse on the return journey, everyone laden with shopping baskets, possibly livestock, a hen or a rabbit. And there were always those on the homeward journey who had taken more than a drop too much and were boisterous, abusive, or just plain sick, however the drink took them.

'I wouldn't miss it for the world,' Beth said. 'It's a nice change.' In spite of which way it goes, she thought; by which she meant that some Saturdays Will would return with her, help to carry the baskets, but on other Saturdays he would be persuaded by his mates to stay on in the inn, arriving home any old time. Thankfully, the long walk back in the cold, pitch darkness did something towards sobering him up before he reached the hut.

'You need to watch out,' Beth frequently warned him. 'A man could be drowned falling into one of those shakeholes, if he happened to be drunk, and if it just happened to have water in the bottom!'

A few months ago a man *had* been drowned, in just such conditions. It struck fear into the hearts of the wives, but it seemed not to bother the men one bit.

She'd never in her life seen anything like the shakeholes, and no-one knew how they'd happened. Lost in the mists of time, they said. They were scattered over the moor at irregular intervals, circular holes in the ground, ranging in size from no more than a couple of feet across, and shallow, to wide enough and deep enough to swallow a house. The trouble was that since the grass grew to the very edge, or over the edge, you didn't always see the near ones.

'You should carry a lantern,' she advised.

His reply was always the same. 'I don't need a lantern. I can see well enough.'

'Are you going to buy anything special?' Jake asked now.

Beth thought for a minute.

'Not that I know of. But there *will* be something, and I'll recognize it when I see it. I shall buy the newspapers of course. Anything I can find to read.'

He had not yet admitted that he couldn't read, although he'd been living there two months now. He'd have to come out with it, though. He was running out of excuses for not borrowing any of the few books his landlady offered him, or reading the *Craven Herald* and the *Lancaster Guardian* which she brought back every Saturday from Batty Green. Both Patrick Mahoney and Will Seymour could read, though the former only haltingly, stumbling over the long words. Jake felt himself the odd man out. His inability to read had never bothered him much until he'd met Armitage, and now there was Beth Seymour.

'To be truthful, we don't want for much up here, do we?' Beth said. 'Burgoyne & Cocks bring provisions from Settle up to Jericho and Tunnel Huts, and some of what *they* don't sell, the pedlars bring right to the door at least once a week.'

'Mr Burgoyne and Mr Cocks must be making a small fortune,' Patrick Mahoney said.

'I daresay,' Beth agreed. 'But where would we be without them? They're like manna from heaven! No, what I go to Batty Green for every Saturday afternoon is the change of scene. To get away from you lot!'

The fact that traders came from Settle, and up the steep hill from Ingleton, and set up what was almost a market, was a bonus. And it was there that she found the items which made the hut more of a home: a vase, a cushion, a tablecloth, a calendar.

Mahoney rose from the table.

'Time we were off,' he said. 'Don't bother to do me

66

a meal. I'll be going down to Batty Green myself. I'll get a bite there.'

'Very well. And what about you, Jake?' Beth asked.

'I might do the same thing. I'll see how the spirit moves me!'

His knee, which for a week or two had prevented him undertaking the five-mile return trip to Batty Green, was now quite better. All that remained of his fall was a scar.

'Well, I'll make something for all of us when we get back later,' Beth promised.

Or for those of us who do get back, she thought. If Patrick Mahoney met up with his fellow countrymen, he'd make a long night of it, probably take the Sunday off work. It wouldn't be the first time. It was in the lap of the gods what Will would do. He didn't work Sundays, and often stayed in bed until noon.

As for Jake Tempest, she never quite knew. He'd been lodging with her for two months now and she felt she knew him not much better than she had in the first week. He'd volunteered little of his past life, except that when she had admired the painting of the mountain which he'd hung on the bedroom wall, he'd spoken of his mother. She wondered why, at twenty-three, he wasn't married; why some woman hadn't captured him. Yet, though he kept himself to himself, he wasn't unfriendly. He was always polite, and helpful. It was just that he kept this distance between them when she would have liked to get to know him better.

She went to the door and saw the two men off to work.

'I might see you both on Batty Green!' she said.

She watched Patrick and Jake stride out across the moor, then turned back into the house. She made her own breakfast, then took down her book from the shelf. She was re-reading *Pride and Prejudice* by Miss

Jane Austen, which she had bought herself before she and Will came north, while they were living in Surrey. In those early days of their marriage, Will had taken pride in her love of books, had encouraged it. Now he seemed to resent it.

'You always have your head stuck in a book,' he complained. 'That's no comfort for a man at the end of a hard day's work.'

So now, to save argument, she only read when he was out of the house. In the evenings, if he was not down at Batty Green with his pals, they sat opposite each other, she with her mending or knitting, he falling asleep.

But this time at breakfast was her own. There was no-one to stop her, or even to complain. With a sigh of contentment she found her place in the book and simultaneously lifted a forkful of breakfast to her mouth.

She loved this book. She felt she knew every character intimately, and though she admitted that Darcy was devastatingly attractive, old Mr Bennet was her clear favourite. The story spoke to her of a life of which she knew nothing at all; balls, parties, high-born people. It was, in a way, a fairy story. She devoured every word as avidly as she devoured her breakfast.

Breakfast over, she reluctantly replaced the book, then fed the hens, did some washing and hung it out to dry. After dinner, with her shopping bags and baskets over her arm, she set off to walk down the hill to Jericho, where she would pick up the market tram. When she arrived, a group of women and children were already standing by the track. It being a fine day, no-one had elected to stay at home.

By now she knew most of the women, and was on good terms with them. Jericho was mostly families. The single men, and the more available women, tended to live on Batty Green, closer to whatever entertainment was on offer. The Jericho women were, on the whole, decent, hardworking souls who had accompanied their husbands to this outlandish spot so that, for the time it took to build the railway, they could be sure of money in their purses, the wherewithal to feed and clothe their families. For that, and because it would only be temporary, they were prepared to tolerate the isolation and, above all, the terrible vagaries of the weather.

'Good afternoon, Mrs Seymour,' a woman called out. 'Another nice day!'

'It's been a nice week, Mrs Hobson,' Beth said.

'It won't keep up,' Mrs Hobson said. 'We're halfway through October and up here the winter starts early in November. You weren't here last winter, were you?'

'We came in April,' Beth said. 'It was still cold. There was plenty of snow on the tops.'

For weeks she had been unable to get warm, except in bed, cuddling up to Will. It was so different from her home, where, though there could be snow, the winters were short and reasonably mild. She had left behind trees everywhere, trees coming into leaf, or even in blossom. The daffodils had been almost over, but tulips and wallflowers were bursting their buds. Here on Blea Moor, there were no trees. She badly missed them. The flowers came later than in Surrey and grew close to the ground, sheltering from the wind which blew day and night.

'Then you've got the worst to come,' Mrs Hobson said. She did not believe in looking on the bright side. It led to disappointment.

'You get used to it.' The new speaker was a small, neat woman, carrying a baby, and with three more children in tow. She spoke with good humour.

'But you're north-country bred, Mrs Drake,' Mrs Hobson pointed out. 'You come from Northumberland.'

69

'I suppose that helps,' Mrs Drake acknowledged. 'Up there, we reckon folk are soft in the south – no offence meant of course!'

The tram was in sight now, descending the hill, the trucks, still mostly empty, swaying alarmingly. They would be steadier, Beth consoled herself, when they had the weight of people in them.

The women sorted out their children, gathered them together, and everyone climbed into the trucks.

'Let me take the baby, Mrs Drake, while you see to the other children,' Beth said.

She could perhaps more usefully have offered to deal with the older children, but she wanted to feel the baby in her arms. Three years she and Will had been married, and never a sign of a child. Every month she hoped, and every month her hopes were dashed. And she wanted not just one child, but several; four, five, six. She herself was the youngest of six children. All her brothers and sisters were dear to her, though there was not one who hadn't protested when she'd announced she was going to marry Will Seymour.

'It won't work,' her eldest sister had said.

'Susan is right,' her brother Tom had said. 'It won't work!'

'It's all very well for the rest of you to talk,' Beth had protested. 'You're already married, all of you.'

She didn't ask them why it wouldn't work. She didn't want to hear. Nevertheless they told her, all of them, separately and together.

Tom summed it up.

'He's just not your type. You're chalk and cheese!'

She had wavered when Tom spoke, but not for long. Though she loved Tom more than anyone in the family since her parents had died, she loved Will more.

'I'm sorry you don't like him, but I love him and I'm going to marry him. So it's no use saying any more.'

And she still loved him. She had found out that he was moody, but she could bear his bad moods because his good ones were magic to her. She couldn't understand why she hadn't conceived. She wanted to consult the doctor, but Will would have none of that.

'Do you think I don't want a child?' he demanded whenever she pressed him. 'Of course I do! Every man does. But if the Lord chooses you to be barren, then I shall bear it, and so must you. It isn't as if I reproached you!'

Mrs Drake handed over the baby. He was well wrapped up in a wool shawl and bonnet, but when Beth held him in her arms he freed his hands and pulled at her bodice. She held out a finger and he grabbed it, fastening his own small fingers around it in a firm grip.

'He'll do well,' Mrs Hobson remarked, watching him. 'He'll hang on to whatever comes his way.'

'I'd sooner not bring all the children,' Mrs Drake said, 'but I do it as much for their sake as for mine. They get fed up, being around the house all day. They'd be better if they could go to school.'

'They say they might start a school,' Mrs Hobson said. 'But if they do, it'll be on Batty Green because that's where most people live.'

'Then it'll be no use to us,' Mrs Drake said. 'It's a two-mile walk, in all weathers. Snow all winter, and even in the summer it's boggy underfoot. The bairns wouldn't be safe.'

'It's a shame,' Beth said. 'When they get to a certain age, children need school.'

'And their poor mothers need them to go to school!' Mrs Drake spoke with feeling.

'I heard you were a teacher,' Mrs Hobson said to Beth. 'Is that right then?'

'Yes and no,' Beth said. 'I worked for a lady, a Mrs Carmichael, who ran a small private school. I helped her with the children, but I couldn't claim to be a proper teacher.'

The tram set off with a jerk, then wound its way down the hillside, stopping at Inkerman, Sebastopol and Belgravia. It was now completely full. When they'd first come to Ribblehead Beth had wanted to live in Belgravia. It was a cut above the other shanty towns. The huts were not quite so close together, and some of them had porches, which not only looked nice, but were a protection against the weather. Belgravia would also have been handier for Will's work on the viaduct. Unfortunately there hadn't been a free hut.

When they reached Batty Green everyone climbed out. Beth, who had kept the baby throughout the journey, reluctantly handed him back to his mother.

'He's lovely,' she said.

'You should have one of your own,' Mrs Drake said. 'I reckon you have a way with you. But you can't have this one, even though he was a bit of an afterthought. There's six years between him and the next one. I don't know why. Nature's very mysterious, and that's a fact!'

'I'll look out for you on the way back,' Beth said as they parted company.

For a moment she stood still and looked around her. The place was thronged. She reckoned everyone from Tunnel Huts to Salt Lake City, on the Settle Road, was here, as well as those who had travelled from Settle and Ingleton to serve them. There were hawkers, cheapjacks, a stall for household goods, another offering boots and shoes; greengrocers, dairy produce, bakers' goods. There were also horses, carts, donkeys, hens, rabbits. Everything except a bookstall, Beth thought. Sometimes she was lucky enough to find a book on the secondhand stall.

Where should she start?

The answer was easy. First of all she must buy the

two weekly newspapers before the newsvendor sold out. She handed over threepence and put the papers safely in the bottom of a shopping bag. She would like to read them this very minute, cover to cover, but they must be saved, and read at leisure. She must make them last.

The arrangement with Will was that they would find each other somewhere in the crowd. Unless overtime was called for, and it often was, he finished work at one o'clock on Saturdays, so he should be around by now. Except, she thought, that the minute they downed tools, he and his mates would make the inn their first stop, and he might well still be there. More likely than not.

She was surprised therefore, and almost jumped out of her skin, when she felt his hand on her shoulder, heard his voice in her ear.

'I've been looking for you. I saw the tram come in.'

'I went to buy the newspapers before they sold out. Where shall we go next?'

He shrugged. 'Up to you, lass!'

'So we'll go to the bakers. I'd like to buy a nice cake for Sunday tea.'

'*You* can bake a cake,' Will protested. 'Better than any of this bought stuff.'

'I know I can. I just thought I'd like something I hadn't made. Something fancy!'

There was a wonderful display of cakes, fancy bread and pastries. Beth spent several minutes considering it, trying to decide what to buy.

'Can I help you?' the assistant asked.

Beth looked up into the face of a very pretty girl; black hair, a flawless complexion and bright eyes.

'I'm sorry,' Beth said. 'There's so much choice!'

'Then make up your mind, love,' Will urged. 'Can't you see the young lady's busy?'

73

The assistant treated him to a beaming smile.

In the end, Beth chose an iced sponge cake, with buttercream through the middle and walnuts on top, four custard tarts, and a fruit malt loaf. The assistant wrapped them carefully.

'They won't be easy to carry,' Beth whispered to her husband, 'especially the custard tarts.'

Will smiled at the girl.

'Do you think we might leave them here until we're ready to go home? We've other things to shop for, and there's such a crush.'

'Certainly, sir! You can come back any time you like.' There was the faintest, but decisive, emphasis on the word 'you'.

'My word, she's a bit of all right!' Will said to Beth as they moved away.

'So I noticed,' Beth said. 'I'm sorry if I cramped your style. All the same, I'll make certain I go back with you when we collect them.'

They moved around slowly, inspecting each stall in turn. Beth bought a green glass vase, which would look well on the dresser, a new white handkerchief for Will, and a shoulder of lamb which was going cheap because it was nearing the end of the day. And then, to her great delight, on the secondhand stall she found a book of poems: *Sonnets* by William Shakespeare. It was small, not more than three inches across, bound in brown leather with gold decoration on the spine, and it had clearly been much used. She caught her breath with pleasure at the sight of it. She opened it at random, and began to read: 'Shall I compare thee to a summer's day? Thou art more lovely and more temperate.'

She read the words in a half whisper. Oh, it was wonderful; she had to have this book! But it was marked at a shilling, and that much she could not possibly spend.

'Oh, come on!' Will grumbled. 'Surely you don't need another book?'

'But I do, Will! I do! Do you think he would take ninepence?'

'Just *ask* him! Either leave it be, or ask him.'

'Will you take ninepence for this?' she asked the stallholder.

'The binding alone's worth a shilling, lady,' he protested.

'It's very worn,' Beth said. 'And I'm afraid ninepence is all I can afford.'

He pondered.

'Go on then,' he said reluctantly. 'Though I'm a fool to meself and I'll never make a decent living.'

He wrapped the book in a scrap of paper, and she tucked it into her pocket so that nothing in her basket would soil it.

'Let's be moving,' Will said. 'We can't spend all afternoon here. We must go and collect the cake and things.'

'But it's not time for the return tram,' Beth said. 'We've an hour yet!'

Without answering, Will strode off towards the bakery stall. Beth hurried after him. In fact, she was too happy with the purchase of the book to mind much about anything else.

They stood in front of the bakery stall, waiting their turn. The same girl was serving, though now at the other end of the counter. She really was attractive, Beth thought, but in a bold sort of way.

The girl finished serving and moved towards them. She raised her head, looked straight over Beth's shoulder, and cried out in surprise.

'Why, it's Jake Tempest, I do declare!'

Beth and Will spun around, and there he was.

'Don't say you've forgotten Sally Roland!' the girl said. 'I wouldn't believe you if you did!'

Will grinned at Jake.

'You're a dark horse!' he said. 'So introduce us to your friend!'

'I'll introduce myself,' Sally said. She could see Jake Tempest's reluctance and she wasn't letting him get away with it a second time. 'I'm Sally Roland. I live in Settle, with my aunt. Mr Tempest stayed in the same house. We got on very well!'

'I hope your aunt is well,' Jake said non-committally. He hadn't seen her as he approached the stall, or he'd have made off at once.

'In the best of health,' Sally replied. 'So, are you working on the railway here?'

'Not here,' Jake said hurriedly. 'Further up. I'm seldom here.'

Damn the woman! He wanted nothing to do with her. Yet who could deny her attraction? It was so obvious. And apparently so to all the customers waiting to be served. They were drinking in every word.

'Well, we must change that, mustn't we?' Sally said pleasantly.

Beth nudged Will.

'We should pick up our things and make a move,' she said. 'We're holding things up.'

'No hurry!' Will said.

'I'll walk with you, carry some of your parcels,' Jake said hastily. If he had wanted something from the stall, he no longer remembered what it was. All he wanted now was to be off.

'It's interesting you should find a friend here,' Beth said as they moved away.

'Not a friend, exactly. I lodged one night in her aunt's house before I came on here.'

'Oh!' Beth said. 'I thought you knew each other quite well!'

'I'd say you've got a foot in the door there!' Will said, grinning. 'Who knows what could happen if you

76

played your cards right? She's a corker, and no mistake.' He seemed unusually cheered by Jake's encounter with the girl.

Beth gave her husband a sharp look. Personally, she had thought the girl was common, not at all right for Jake Tempest, but she'd keep quiet. It was none of her business.

'Then as Jake's here to give you a hand with your baskets,' Will said, 'I'll leave you for a while and wet my whistle. I'm as dry as a bone!'

'Oh, but—' Beth began.

He didn't wait to hear her objections.

'I'll meet you at the tramway, ride home with you.'

Beth stared after him, then turned to Jake.

'I'm sorry! There's no need for you to be carrying my parcels.'

'It's no trouble,' Jake said. 'But we've three-quarters of an hour before the tram leaves. What would you like to do? Or have you not finished your shopping?'

'I've quite finished,' Beth answered him. 'Do you think we could walk over and see what they're doing on the viaduct? Although Will works on it, I know next to nothing.'

'Me too,' Jake admitted. 'I'd like to take a look.'

They left the vicinity of the stalls, crossed the dirt track, and walked westwards. In the wide valley over which the viaduct would be built the ground was flat, cropped short by sheep and horses, trodden down by feet. But it was uneven, and made more so by its bogginess. It was difficult to know where to walk.

'I'll go first, pick out the firmest bits,' Jake offered. 'You try to follow in my footsteps.'

It was not easy for her. He had a long stride and was not hampered by skirts around his ankles. More than once she was marooned on what seemed to be the only dry bit of land around, and he had to turn around and take her hand, helping her across as best he could.

Nearer to the viaduct, wooden planks had been laid down to make an easier passage.

There were large heaps of stones and rubble at intervals along the ground, stacks of wood in varying lengths, and piles of bricks. The bricks, Beth knew because that much Will had told her, were made at the brickworks erected no more than half a mile away along the valley, made from the clay which lay under the peat, and mixed with ground shale. Jake picked a brick from a heap.

'They're good and strong,' he said. He knew a bit about bricks.

'Will said they make thousands a day,' Beth told him.

'They'll need them,' Jake said. 'They're wanted in the tunnel as well as on the viaduct.'

The building of the viaduct, which they had now reached, was still in the early stages. Much of the work, so far, had been in digging and lining the deep foundations. Twenty-four great arches, built on massive piers, fashioned from black marble, would eventually carry the new railway line eighteen feet above the valley beneath. So far, only three piers were beginning to rise, and they still had a long way to go before they reached the springing, where the arch would start to turn.

'I wonder how long it will take,' Jake said.

'Will reckons a few years yet,' Beth replied.

'And does he plan to stay to the end?'

'Oh, I think so! What about you?'

'It's too early to decide,' Jake said.

They walked forward, past the line of the viaduct. Beyond them, to the west, the view was dominated by Ingleborough, etched black against the late afternoon sun.

'That's much more my idea of a mountain,' Jake said. 'Evenly sloping sides, climbing to a peak at the top – except that in this case it looks as though the top has been sliced off.'

'And so neatly done,' Beth said. 'From here it looks completely flat.'

'It will be even more like a mountain when there's snow on it,' Jake remarked.

Beth laughed.

'You won't have to wait long for that! Six weeks, or even less. Anyway, shouldn't we be moving? I wouldn't want to miss the tram – and Will will be waiting for me.'

Will was not waiting, nor had he turned up when the tram was due to leave. Beth looked across the green – the crowd had thinned by now – hoping to see him hurrying towards her. In her heart she knew it was a forlorn hope. He had undoubtedly fallen in with his friends and there would be no telling what time he'd reach home. Nor was Patrick on the tram, but then she didn't expect that.

'He's no doubt been held up,' she said to Jake. 'He'll be very disappointed.'

He wouldn't be at all, but she had to say something, make some excuse for him, however lame. Jake made no reply.

The tram chugged slowly up the hill.

'It's best to stay on until Tunnel Huts,' Beth remarked. 'Then we can walk down the hill instead of up.'

Jake took most of the parcels. How could she have managed without him, she wondered. When they were inside the hut she made a pot of tea, buttered two currant teacakes, and the two of them sat down at the table. It was peaceful. Jake Tempest was a peaceful man to be with – though did that make him sound dull, she wondered. He was far from that.

She picked up the book of sonnets from the table, fingered through it.

'Do you like poetry?' she asked.

'I don't know much,' Jake admitted. 'In fact hardly any.'

She turned to her favourite sonnet, and began to read aloud: 'Shall I compare thee to a summer's day? Thou art more lovely, and more temperate.'

Then, suddenly, she put the book down and pushed it across the table towards Jake. She had a sudden notion to hear him read. He had a good voice, deep and clear.

'You read it!'

His face reddened. His eyes met hers, and there was panic in them. She couldn't understand it.

'What's wrong?'

'I can't,' he said.

'Then read something else. Anything!' She thought his objection was to the particular sonnet, that perhaps it was too personal, too intimate.

'You don't understand. I can't read! I can't read at all!'

She stared at him in disbelief; not that it was unusual for a person to be unable to read, but because it seemed wrong for him. He was intelligent enough.

'I'm sorry,' she said. 'I didn't realize. Would you like me to read the rest out loud?'

He nodded. She read the sonnet through to the end. They looked at each other without speaking. Then Jake said, in a quiet voice:

'I'd like to be able to read. I'd like to read what you've just read – out loud.'

'Then you shall,' Beth said. 'One day you shall. I shall teach you to read.'

# 5

It was long past dark when Will Seymour arrived home, steady enough on his feet, but with a carefulness in his speech which signalled that he was not totally sober. Jake saw the flash of anxiety and annoyance in Beth's face as her husband came into the room, and then it was gone, and only a slight tightness in her voice when she returned his greeting betrayed her feelings.

'I've kept your supper hot, Will. Sit down and I'll serve you.'

Is she being polite for my sake? Jake wondered. He would make his excuses and go to bed as soon as he could; but not immediately; that would be too obvious.

'So you didn't wait for me?' Will grumbled.

Beth had put the pan back on the stove and was stirring the contents.

'We did for quite a while,' she said evenly, not turning around. 'But we were hungry. Don't worry, this will be ready in a minute or two. It's not long since we finished.'

Will sat down heavily, his elbows on the table. He gave Jake a cold stare.

'Well at least my wife didn't lack for company,' he said.

'No. And I was glad of Jake on the way home,' Beth said pleasantly. 'I don't know how I'd have managed everything otherwise.'

'Was it my fault if the tram left early?' Will demanded. 'I was there at the right time.'

Beth didn't reply. It was patently untrue, the kind of excuse a small boy would make, and that was so often the way he behaved now. He used not to be like that. It was this place, the strain of his job, which had changed him. She had learnt to deal with him by showing the patience she would have given to a child. She would not make things more difficult for either of them by arguing.

She filled his plate with stew, and set it before him. He ate without speaking. It was an uncomfortable silence. Will himself, when he had cleared his plate, was the one to break it.

'So what *did* you do to pass the time?'

'Oh, I had lots of jobs to do,' Beth said. 'When I'd done them, I read.'

Jake said nothing, thankful that the question had not been put to him. What Beth had *not* said was that she had read aloud, to him. Sitting opposite him at the table, she'd read, quietly, yet with the passion they merited, several of the poems from her newly acquired collection. He had watched as well as listened; observed the way the light from the lamp burnished her hair, noted the expressions on her face as she spoke the lines, for all the world as if she were living them.

For Jake there had been something about the evening which had made it unlike any other he had ever known. And if anyone had told him that an evening spent listening to someone reading poetry would be charged with magic, he would have laughed out loud.

'I suppose you didn't see Patrick on your travels?' Beth asked her husband.

'Neither hair nor hide of him. If you ask me, we'll not see him tonight.'

'I daresay you're right,' Beth said. 'Poor Patrick! He seems to live another life from the rest of us.'

'Poor Patrick my foot!' Will said. 'He's typical of the Irish – born to trouble, they are.'

'But not always of their own making,' Beth suggested. 'You heard about it yourself, we read it in the newspaper, how Irishmen in Settle were threatened, told they had to leave the town. But after the fight, when it came to court, it wasn't the Irish who were found guilty, it was the English!'

'Then why are the Irish always at the centre of any fight?' Will demanded. 'Tell me that!'

'Because they're picked on, that's why!' Beth said sharply. She had meant to stay calm, and here she was, flaring up.

'Nonsense! You're too soft,' Will said.

Yet wasn't it one of the reasons he had always loved her, because she was tolerant, saw the best in everyone, including in him? She had not changed from that; she was the same tender, loving woman she had always been. It was he who had changed, and he knew it.

Why? he asked himself. Why do I pick on her? Why do I go against her all the time?

She was the last person in the world to deserve such treatment, yet he seemed not to be able to help himself. He felt churned up inside, always at war with his own person, and therefore with everyone else.

It had not been like this in Surrey. They had lived in near-tranquillity there, content with their smallholding, both of them working on it; they never made much money but he knew now, looking back, they had been happy.

If they were not now, the blame was his. He would do better.

He rose to his feet and went around to the other side of the table where Beth was sitting. Suddenly he had urgent need of her, he wanted to show her his love, to atone for his churlishness. He placed his hands on her shoulders and bent to kiss the back of her neck.

'Please, Will!' Beth's face flamed.

'Not in front of the lodger, eh?' Will said, smiling. 'Well, I'm sure he'll understand.'

'I'm just off to bed,' Jake said quietly. 'I said I'd go in to work in the morning, Sunday or no Sunday.'

'And so are we,' Will said. 'Going to bed, I mean.' He pulled Beth to her feet, and put his arm around her.

'I'm sorry I was so bad-tempered,' Will said when they were in the bedroom. 'I don't know what comes over me. You don't deserve it.'

'That isn't what matters,' Beth said. 'What matters is that I don't understand it. You've changed, Will. I don't want you to change. I loved you the way you were. Can't you tell me why?'

'I hardly know myself. Perhaps we should never have left Surrey.'

He had wanted to leave Surrey because, although they were happy with each other, Beth's family did not approve of him, and they made that plain. He was not, in their eyes, successful, and never would be.

And then there had been the other cloud in their sky, that Beth did not have children. He had tried to come to terms with that, but it had not been easy, and he was not sure that he had done so. A man wanted sons to follow after him. It was the most natural thing in the world.

'We agreed it would be a good thing to leave,' Beth reminded him. 'We agreed a change of scene, of work, would do us good.'

They had agreed, but she had only paid lip service. It wasn't what she'd wanted, but Will saw the chance of good money, a way to succeed in a new place. It hadn't worked.

'Is it the job?' she asked now.

'Partly.'

The job was hard going, harder than anything he'd

84

ever done in his life. Also, he hadn't envisaged himself being forever a labourer, but by now he had been forced to accept that that was what he was, and would be all the time he worked on the line. His skills lay in tilling the land, in husbandry, in looking after a few animals. They were of no use to him in building a railway.

'Should we leave?' Beth asked uncertainly. 'Should we try somewhere else?' Where they would go, what they would do, she couldn't imagine, but she would try anything to make Will happy.

'No!' Will said firmly. 'We'll stay where we are. I'll stick it out. I won't be beaten!'

It was because so many of the men had found the job so hard, the land inhospitable, yet resolved to stick it out, Beth thought, that they drank so much. Will had never been a heavy drinker until they had come here, and now drink was changing his character. She watched its effects every day, but could do nothing. It was a subject which Will would never discuss. To mention it at all threw him into a rage.

Jake went to bed, though not, for a long time, to sleep. Long after he had heard the Seymours go to their room he lay on his back staring into the darkness, his thoughts ranging far and wide.

He thought of his mother, then of Vinnie; from Vinnie, by no logical route, to Armitage. Where was *he*? From Armitage it was a reasonable step to Sally Roland, and today's encounter with her. In spite of the fact that he had no liking for the girl, the memory of her blatant sexual charms disturbed him against his will. He pushed the thought of her away, turning over on his side to escape her. But it was when his thoughts turned to Beth Seymour that he really clamped them down, refused to give them form or shape. Would it have been better if he'd found lodgings at Tunnel Huts? Was it too late to do so?

But now wasn't she going to teach him to read? And there was more than one reason why he would not lightly give that up.

When Jake wakened next morning he saw that Patrick Mahoney's bed was empty, hadn't been slept in. He yawned, then rose, glanced at the painting of the mountain, as he did every morning, picked up his towel and left the hut for his morning wash in the beck, closing the door quietly behind him. No point in disturbing anyone, he was quite capable of making his own breakfast and packing up something to eat at midday.

There was a keen nip in the air as he went across to the beck, and when he slipped off his shoes and walked into the shallow water near the bank he gasped at the coldness of it. If he had been half asleep before, he was suddenly wide awake now. He washed quickly, and hurried back to the hut.

When he opened the door the smell of bacon met him, and the sight of Beth at the stove.

'Won't be a minute! Nearly ready!' She spoke quietly. Jake guessed Will was still asleep.

'You shouldn't have got up,' Jake said. 'I can manage.'

'I know. But I was awake,' she said. She had not slept well. Will's lovemaking, which had started gently, had in the end been rough, demanding. When it was over, and he was immediately deep into sleep, she was left bruised in body and confused in mind. It seemed on his part no more than hunger and lust, which left her unsatisfied. He no longer spoke of the child he had also wanted; and what would a child be like, she wondered, conceived in such circumstances? But she *did* love Will, she was sure of that.

'I heard you leave the house,' she said to Jake. 'It's really no trouble.'

She flipped the egg over, fried it on the second side,

slipped it onto the plate, and served him. Then she poured him tea, and a cup for herself, and sat down at the table.

'Is it cold out?' she asked.

'Yes,' Jake said. 'And the water's like ice.'

'Before long it will be frozen over in the mornings. You'll have to bring water in at night, and wash in the bedroom.'

'It'll be warmer,' Jake said, mopping up his plate with a piece of bread. 'And by the way, Patrick didn't come in.'

'I thought he hadn't. I'd have heard him,' Beth said. 'I hope he's all right.'

'I expect he will be.' In the short time he had been there, Jake had developed quite an affection for the Irishman. 'Time I was off,' he said.

'I've packed your jock tin. When I go down to Batty Green this afternoon I'll see if I can find out about Patrick.'

'Batty Green?'

'There's a Mission service. There won't be many more outdoors this year with the weather getting colder, but they say they'll have finished building the Mission hut in a few weeks now, then we'll be under cover.'

'It's a long way to go,' Jake said.

'But worth it. You should try it.'

'I don't think it's in my line,' Jake admitted.

When he had left for work, Beth took down her book and started on another chapter. Will might well be another hour or two before he rose. By reading slowly, and carefully rationing herself to a very few pages each day, she still had the last two chapters left. What she would do after she reached the end she dreaded to think. There were the newspapers, of course, but that was not the same. Nevertheless, she steeled herself to close the book with the last chapter

87

saved for another day. And now she had the sonnets. Perhaps she would learn some by heart.

She thought about how she would teach Jake to read. She had very little experience even with children's reading – that had not been one of her duties at Mrs Carmichael's – and none at all with a grown man. How would she set about it?

Will came in from the bedroom.

'I'm ready for my breakfast,' he said.

'It won't be long. Patrick didn't turn up.'

Will shrugged. 'It doesn't surprise me.'

'I thought I'd make some enquiries when I went down to the Mission this afternoon,' Beth said.

'You'd be better doing nothing of the kind. Leave it be. It's not the first time he's done this.'

'I know,' Beth acknowledged. 'I just have a feeling . . .'

'If you *must* go all the way to Batty Green, be content with your hymn singing. Leave the man to stew in his own juice.'

Beth said no more. Will's brief, gentler mood, when they'd first gone into the bedroom last night and had actually talked to each other, had passed. She would do what seemed best to her.

Walking down to Batty Green, she caught up with Mrs Drake and her two eldest children, and fell into step beside them until the children skipped ahead.

'I left the baby and the little one with their dad,' Mrs Drake said. 'These two like to come, and at least they learn something more than I can teach them.'

'How old are the children?' Beth asked.

'Emily's eight, Tom's seven and Ada is six. They should all be at school, and if I'd had my way they would have been. I didn't want to come here, you know. It's like living on the edge of the world. But you have to follow your husband, don't you? And he has to go where the work is.'

88

Her words about the children fanned a spark in Beth's mind, a spark which Mrs Drake herself had ignited yesterday when they had spoken on the same subject, and had been kept alight by Jake's admission that he couldn't read. Could *she* teach these children – not just Emily, Tom and Ada, but a few more from Jericho and Nazareth, even two or three from Tunnel Huts? She would have to keep it to a small group, she couldn't manage a large one. In fact, she didn't know that she could do it at all. She would have to give it more thought. And there was Will. What would he have to say? Quite a lot, no doubt.

'A nice crowd gathered,' Mrs Drake observed as they neared Batty Green. 'Though mostly women and children, as usual.'

There was a scattering of men; a few dogs wound in and out among the crowd, and hens pecked away at the ground on the fringes of the grass. On a raised knoll an upturned beer crate had been placed for the Missioner, and nearby a man with a concertina was practising hymns.

'I daresay some folks are curious to set eyes on the new Missioner,' Mrs Drake said. 'I am meself.'

'New Missioner?' Beth queried. 'What's happened to Mr Tiplady?'

James Tiplady was the man appointed by the Bradford City Mission and the Midland Railway Company to look after the spiritual needs of the workers and their families on this section of the line. He was an extremely popular young man, much respected. Beth felt a pang of disappointment that he was gone.

'Nothing's happened to him,' Mrs Drake said. 'He's just gone back to Bradford for a few days. This fellow's to take his place in the meantime.'

The Missioner came out of Mr Tiplady's hut and crossed towards the crowd, who gave way for him as he walked to the hillock and climbed onto the beer crate. He was a tall, fair-haired, lively-looking man. And he had a nice smile, Beth thought.

'We're going to start with "All things Bright and Beautiful",' he announced in a loud, clear voice, 'because it's a beautiful day. We don't have enough hymn books, but it doesn't matter because you all know it. So sing up everyone!

'Now,' he said when that was over, 'I'm going to read you the story of a small boy called Samuel, and how God called to him, though at first he didn't think it *was* God.'

He found the place in the bible, then suddenly, as if the thought had just struck him, he raised his head and looked around the people in front of him.

'I have a better idea,' he said. 'Why not one of you? Raise a hand, anyone who will volunteer to read the passage!'

Not a hand was raised.

'Oh, come on! I don't believe this!' the Missioner said. 'Someone out there must have the courage!'

Mrs Drake nudged Beth.

'You can read, Mrs Seymour! Go on, have a go!'

Shall I, Beth wondered? It was a lovely story, one of her favourites.

'Come along! A lady would read this very well.'

'He could charm the ducks off the water!' Mrs Drake said. 'I wish I was a good reader. I'd be up there quick as a flash!'

In a sudden rush of enthusiasm, hardly knowing what she was doing, Beth raised her hand.

'Ah! A brave lady!' the Missioner said. 'Please come forward!'

She did so. The Missioner stepped down from his box, helped her onto it, and handed her his bible.

'Here you are,' he said. 'First book of Samuel, chapter three, verse one.'

For a second, before she began to read, Beth raised

her eyes and looked at the crowd in front of her. What am I doing? she thought. I must be mad! Then she lowered her eyes to the book and began to read. And as always when she read, she was quickly transported into the story.

When the reading was over they had a hymn, then prayers, then another hymn.

'I really enjoyed that,' Mrs Drake said when the service was over. 'I do like a good sing. It fills the lungs.'

As the crowd began to disperse, the Missioner sought out Beth.

'That was a brave thing to do, and you did it well,' he said. 'Do you live on Batty Green?'

'No,' Beth answered. 'I live in Nazareth. It's further up, near to the tunnel.'

'I don't know it,' he admitted. 'Do you have any special difficulties there?'

'We do,' she said. Then in a rush – she hadn't meant to talk about it, any more than she had meant to read the bible in front of all those people – she told him about the lack of schooling for the children.

'I know we're getting a school on Batty Green,' she said. 'But that won't be any use to *our* children. They desperately need something not only to occupy them, but to educate them. They can't even learn to read, or to count.'

'But you read very well,' he said firmly. 'Why can't you teach them? A few children together, including your own.'

'I have no children,' Beth said. 'I'm like Hannah, waiting a long time for the Lord to send her Samuel.'

'And in the end He did,' the Missioner reminded her. 'But in the meantime, couldn't you do something for these other children? We should always use what gifts we have.'

'I'll think about it,' Beth promised.

'Write and tell me what you think,' he said. 'The City Mission at Bradford will find me. Mr Tiplady will be back here soon, and I know he'll be interested, but I'd also like to hear what you decide. And if there's anything I can do to help . . .'

'I really will think about it,' Beth repeated.

'Remember what you read today,' the Missioner advised. 'Don't ignore the call!'

'Right now I want to look for my lodger,' Beth said. 'He didn't come home last night. Not that it's the first time, but as I was coming down here . . .'

She broke off, and they both turned their heads at the sound of fierce shouting across the Green. A group of men was leaving the alehouse, or more likely they were being thrown out, since a fight was already in progress.

'Trouble!' the Missioner said.

He set off at a run towards the scene, Beth following close behind. The last thing she wanted was to witness a fight, but she couldn't stand aside, any more than the Missioner could.

She was horrified by what she saw. This was certainly no fair fight, one man matched against another, though even that she would have hated. Here, a single man was the target and he was being assailed by two others while a circle of onlookers, most of whom had poured out of the alehouse at the prospect of an exciting spectacle, stood around shouting encouragement, cheering and booing. Such was the confusion that it took Beth a second or two to recognize the man at the centre of the fight.

'It's Patrick!' she cried. 'It's Patrick Mahoney! Somebody do something or they'll kill him!'

He had no chance at all. He was hemmed in by the two men, who rained blows upon him from all sides, to his head, his body and his arms. And then he was tripped and fell face down, and one of the three, a big man, kicked him in the side, then jumped on his back and repeatedly bashed his face into the ground. Patrick's screams died away. He was silent, but still the man on his back kept at him.

With no thought for her safety, or what action she could possibly take, Beth started to run forward. The Missioner grasped her by the arm and tried to pull her back.

'No!' he ordered. 'Leave it to me! There's nothing *you* can do!'

She ignored him, broke away from him and ran to confront the smaller of the two men. Possessed of a strength which her intense fury gave her, her fists flailing, she pummelled him hard, and then, in a moment of inspiration, she raised her leg and kneed him in the groin.

'Take that, you brute!' she yelled.

He turned away with a howl of anguish. For a moment she was horrified by what she had done, though not repentant. He deserved it. She began to walk towards Patrick, and as she walked a sharp stone flew through the air and caught her a stinging blow on the back of the head.

'And you take that!' the man shouted. 'You bloody cow!'

She put her hand to the back of her head, and when she brought it away it was smeared with blood. But there was no time to think about it now. She would say nothing. In any case, she was probably more angry than hurt.

The Missioner, with a superhuman effort, had dragged the bigger of the two men off Patrick.

'Get back!' he shouted. 'Can't you see the man's unconscious? Do you want to finish him off?'

'Irish pig!' the man said. 'It's no more than he deserves, and the rest of his lot! I'd be glad to do it!'

'And be hanged for murder?' the Missioner said. 'I'd see to it that you were, make no mistake!'

The man spat on Patrick's prone body, and left. By now the crowd had joined in a free-for-all, fists flying, blows landing without discrimination on whoever happened to be in the way.

Beth went on her knees beside Patrick. Troubled that, face down, he was unable to breathe, she turned him onto his back. She gave a loud cry when she saw him, turned dizzy and sick with shock at the sight of his injuries.

The Irishman's face was covered in blood and mud. Blood oozed from a cut above his swollen right eye, trickled from his battered nose. The skin around his cheekbone was livid; his lips were split and bleeding, as were his gums where two front teeth had been knocked out.

'He's coming to!' the Missioner said, kneeling down beside her.

He examined the injured man carefully.

'I want to make sure you can be moved,' he told Patrick. 'I'll try not to hurt you.'

Patrick gave no sign that he had heard. The Missioner turned to Beth.

'I'm no doctor, but I doubt he's broken any bones. We'd better get him into Mr Tiplady's hut and see what we can do.' He looked up at the people standing around. 'Two or three of you help me to carry him.'

When Mr Tiplady's housekeeper came to the door she gave a scream at the sight of the bloodstained figure.

'Why, whatever's the matter?' she cried. 'What in the world has happened to the poor man? Bring him in at once!'

'A fight,' the Missioner said. 'We'll lay him on the sofa and then attend to him.'

'You must give me time to spread it with a sheet,

94

and a towel or two,' she said firmly. 'I have to answer to Mr Tiplady for the condition of that sofa.'

'Then do it quickly,' the Missioner instructed.

The housekeeper covered the sofa and Patrick was lowered onto it, then she brought bowls of water and she and Beth between them started to bathe his wounds.

'Just look at his hands, poor thing!' the housekeeper said. 'His knuckles are all bruised and bleeding.'

While she tended to his hands, Beth saw to his face, gently wiping away the congealed blood, staunching the cuts which were still bleeding. He stank of liquor, but perhaps it was as well that he was full of alcohol, Beth thought. It might act as an anaesthetic against his pain.

'Should we send someone for the doctor?' the housekeeper asked.

The Missioner considered.

'I don't think we need to,' he said in the end. 'In the time it would take someone to get down to Ingleton and bring the doctor back, I think we'll find he's rather better. He's a little improved already.'

'He is,' Beth agreed, though that was partly because she had cleaned the dirt off. All the same his injuries were nasty. He must be in pain.

Patrick now tried to smile his thanks, but his mouth was too stiff and swollen. Then he attempted to sit up, but fell back immediately, too dizzy to move.

'Oh, Patrick,' Beth said ruefully, 'how in the world am I going to get you home?'

'I can manage that,' the Missioner said. 'I have my horse. If I can borrow a light cart I daresay we can make him comfortable in the back. I reckon the sooner he's in his own bed, the better.'

'He's going to have a cup of tea first,' the house-keeper said. 'We all are. And while I'm making it,' she said to the Missioner, 'someone in the contractor's

95

hut might tell you where you can borrow a cart.'

The Missioner untethered his horse and led it the short distance to the contractor's hut, from which he returned fifteen minutes later with the horse hitched between the shafts of a light, high-sided cart. The housekeeper had found a narrow mattress and a pillow which, when they were fixed in the cart, made a comfortable enough bed for Patrick. Beth tucked a rug around him.

'We'll soon be home,' she said. 'Try to sleep.' She wondered how he had got himself into all this, but now wasn't the time to ask him.

The Missioner helped her onto the front of the cart, then jumped up himself and took the reins.

'How far is it?' he enquired.

'Between two and three miles. Not all rough going, but you'll have to watch out for the boggy places or you'll get a wheel stuck.'

'Perhaps I should have borrowed a bog cart,' he said. The bog cart, instead of having wheels, was fixed onto a drum-like, revolving cylinder, far less likely to sink into the marshy ground.

'I think we'll be all right,' Beth said. 'We're a light enough load.'

'And I'll take it slowly,' the Missioner promised.

Though he drove slowly, and the horse picked its way carefully, it was a bumpy journey over the rough track. Beth twisted around a great deal of the time, keeping an eye on Patrick, who now lay with his eyes closed, breathing stertorously, and from time to time uttering a low moan, though that was more a result of the pain of his injuries rising to the surface, Beth thought, than the roughness of the ride.

'Thankfully,' she said to the Missioner, 'I think he's on the verge of sleep most of the time. I do wonder, though, whether we should have sent for Doctor Stokes.'

'Then if you are still uneasy when he's been put to bed, I will ride down to Ingleton and ask the doctor to call, though I daresay it will be tomorrow before he does so.'

'Of course,' Beth agreed. 'It would be dark by the time you reached Ingleton. Except for a grave emergency I wouldn't expect the doctor to ride so far out on the moor at night.'

When the cart drew up at the Seymours' hut, Will appeared in the doorway.

'What's this?' he said sharply. 'My wife being driven home in style? Are you not well then, that you can't manage on your own two feet?'

'I'm quite well, thank you, Will,' Beth said. 'This is not for my benefit. It's poor Patrick. He's been badly beaten up. He's lying in the back of the cart and we'll need your help to get him to his bed.'

Will turned his attention to the Missioner.

'And who might you be?'

'I'm Alan Crossland. I'm the Missioner here while Mr Tiplady's away.'

'He went to Patrick's rescue,' Beth explained, 'then kindly borrowed a cart to bring him home. Otherwise I don't know what we'd have done!'

'Left him where he was,' Will said. 'Some drunken brawl he was in, I don't doubt.'

'I'm afraid so,' the Missioner admitted.

'Never mind that now,' Beth interrupted. 'We must take Patrick in. It's turning cold and he should be in bed. I don't think he can walk, though.'

'Why not?' Will demanded. 'Has he broken both legs?'

Beth gave him a sharp look. His remark was totally unnecessary.

'Not either leg,' the Missioner said. 'But when he tries to stand, he keels over. I think the cause might be a blow to his head.'

'Then he should be in hospital, not here,' Will grumbled.

'I'm hoping he'll be all right after a good rest,' the Missioner said. 'All the same, I *will* ride down to Ingleton when I leave here, and inform the doctor. In the meantime, Mr Seymour, will you help me to carry him into the house?'

'Is Jake not home?' Beth asked. 'He could give a hand.'

'He's not,' Will said.

But as they were lifting Patrick out of the cart, Jake appeared.

'Good heavens above!' he called out. 'What's happened? Here, let me give a hand!'

When Patrick had been carried inside it was Beth and Jake who, between them, put him to bed. He was drowsy, and seemed hardly to know what was happening to him. Although his cuts had almost stopped bleeding, new bruises had appeared on his face and hands, and both his ears were purple and swollen.

'The fight didn't last long,' Beth told Jake. 'You wouldn't think he'd be so badly knocked about – but there were two of them onto him. Anyway I'm not going to bathe him again yet. We'll let him sleep.'

It was when she bent over the bed to tuck in the bedclothes around Patrick's shoulders that Jake saw the matted hair, sticky with blood, on the back of her head.

'You're hurt!' he cried out. 'The back of your head! What happened?'

'It's nothing. A man threw a stone at me. If you knew what I'd done to him,' she added primly, 'you might say I deserved it!'

'I can't believe that,' Jake said. 'Are you quite sure you're all right?' He looked at her anxiously. 'You look pale.'

'I'm quite all right,' Beth assured him.

The truth was, her limbs were shaking and she didn't know how to control them. She would be glad to sit down, but she couldn't let the Missioner go without offering him refreshment. So when she went back into the living-room and saw that Will had at least put the kettle on she was grateful.

'You'll take a bite to eat, and a cup of tea?' she invited the Missioner.

'Or something stronger?' Will suggested.

The Missioner waved away Will's offer.

'Tea will be fine.'

'You've signed the pledge, I suppose,' Will said in a sour voice.

The Missioner shook his head.

'Though James Tiplady has told me more than once that drink is the biggest problem of the men building this line. It worries him a great deal.'

'And it'll take more than him to cure it!' Will said. 'What do you expect? Hard, dangerous work, a hellish climate in a godforsaken country; no comforts – most of the men don't bring their wives. Drink's the only thing.'

'It will be better when the Mission hut is finished,' the Missioner said. 'It won't only be used for services. We'll be able to have concerts, recitals, readings; something for everyone.' Though I suppose as usual, he thought, it'll be the women and children who'll attend. It will take more than a concert to keep the men out of the inn.

'I must say, Mr Seymour,' he said, 'your wife is a remarkably courageous woman.'

'My wife is too impulsive,' Will said. 'She rushes into things which are none of her concern.'

'We must be thankful that some people do,' the Missioner said. He drained his cup, and stood up. 'I must go now.' He turned to Beth. 'I'll return the cart

99

and then ride down to Ingleton and have a word with the doctor.'

'Thank you,' Beth said. 'Thank you for all your help, Mr Crossland.'

'And don't let all this make you forget about the reading business,' he said. 'It's very important. If there's any way I can help, let me know.'

He jumped onto the cart and set off down the hill.

'Reading business?' Will said when they went back into the hut. 'What does he mean?'

Beth was annoyed that the Missioner had mentioned the subject. Except where Jake was concerned, she had not yet decided what she would do; and if she did decide in favour of teaching the children, she wanted to tell Will in her own time, seizing the right opportunity. With him in his present mood, now was definitely not the moment.

'Nothing, really.' She spoke in an offhand manner, busying herself with making a meal.

'How can it be nothing if he said it was very important?' Will persisted. 'Whatever it is, I've a right to know. I am your husband, in case you've forgotten the fact!'

'Don't be silly, Will!' Beth said mildly. 'You know perfectly well I keep nothing from you.'

That was not totally true, she thought uncomfortably. She had said nothing to Will about teaching Jake to read. In fact, she had thought of not mentioning it at all if she could manage to do it in secret. It would only cause trouble. Will was so insanely possessive these days.

'Come on then,' Will said impatiently. 'What's it about?'

'Oh, it's just that I was wondering whether I'd try to teach a few children to read. There's no hope of them getting any schooling here, so it would be good for them, and an interest for me.'

'And I suppose when you'd settled everything the way you wanted it you'd have graciously informed me.'

'It's not like that at all,' Beth said. 'Of course I'd have consulted you first. I just haven't had time, that's all. The subject only came up this afternoon.'

'You can put it out of your mind, then,' Will ordered. 'You're a married woman, with a husband to look after and a house to run. You don't need any other interest. As far as that goes, you don't need lodgers. I'm quite capable of providing for both of us.'

He glowered at Jake.

'I'll go and take a look at Patrick,' Jake offered. He was not going to be drawn into this. It would be easier for Beth if he wasn't.

'And that's another thing,' Will said when Jake had left. 'You had no business to bring Patrick Mahoney back here. This isn't a hospital and you're not a nursemaid!'

It was too much for Beth. She'd tried to keep her temper, but she'd try no longer. She banged down the pan she was holding, and turned on her husband.

'This is Patrick Mahoney's home,' she said furiously. 'While he pays his way and behaves properly, he has every right to be here. If you think I'm going to turn him out when he's in trouble, then you can think again, Will Seymour. As for teaching the children to read, I wasn't sure what I'd do, but now you've made up my mind for me! I shall do it, and nothing you say can stop me!'

She was amazed at herself, and in her heart a little frightened. She had never, ever before spoken to Will like this.

'You'll do what I say,' Will thundered. 'I'm your husband and you'll obey me!'

'I'll obey you when you're reasonable,' Beth

retorted. 'I will *not* obey you when anyone can see you're totally wrong!'

He took a step towards her, and raised his hand. She faced him defiantly. She knew he was going to hit her, but there was no way she would retreat. The flat of his hand caught her on her cheek, and the weight of it sent her stumbling backwards against the table. Will dropped his hand and looked at her, horrified. What had he done? What had come over him? He saw the exact marks of his fingers, red on her cheek, and thought he would never forget them as long as he lived.

Jake rushed into the room.

Beth and Will were staring at each other as if frozen to the spot, Beth with her hand to her face, her eyes bright with tears. It was crystal clear what had happened.

Jake rounded on Will.

'How dare you strike your wife! Don't you know what she's been through today?'

'Keep out of this,' Will snarled. 'It's none of your affair!'

'If you so much as lay a finger on her again, I'll make it my affair!' Jake was white with anger.

'Please Jake!' Beth pleaded. 'Please don't make things worse!'

Will turned to Beth.

'I didn't mean it! I don't know what came over me!' He took a step towards her.

'Don't touch me!' she cried. 'Don't touch me!'

Without another word, he turned and ran out of the hut, slamming the door behind him.

# 6

The sound of the door slamming reverberated in Beth's ears; its ferocity shook the glass in the window frames. In her heart, below her anger, there was fear and consternation; she wanted to run after Will, to bring him back, to heal the awful wound which had so suddenly opened between them; but anger was uppermost and her body was incapable of taking the step. She cradled her cheek in her hand, still smarting from the blow. He had never before laid a finger on her. What had she done to provoke him to this?

She had forgotten Jake's presence until he spoke.

'Are you all right?'

'I shouldn't have let him go. I should have stopped him.'

'Do you want me to go after him?' Jake asked.

'No. It could only make things worse.'

'Whatever you say. I'm sorry if I've already done that.'

'And when he comes back, it might be kinder if you weren't here,' she said nervously.

'I couldn't have stood aside, Beth!'

Jake's voice was calmer than his thoughts. He was not concerned with being kinder to Will, far from it. He could willingly have wiped the floor with him, and knew he would have done so had the man gone an inch further, but for the moment he would do whatever was best for Beth.

'Sit down,' he said. 'I'll get you a drink. And I don't

mean a cup of tea. I'll pour you some of that whisky Will offered the Missioner.'

When Jake gave her the whisky, she gulped it, and promptly spluttered and choked.

'Oh! It's so strong!'

Jake smiled. 'You're meant to sip it slowly.' But the *contretemps* with the whisky had lightened the atmosphere just a little.

'Perhaps you should go to bed now,' he suggested. 'If you drink the rest of the whisky I poured you it will help you to sleep.'

'Oh, no!' Beth said quickly. 'I couldn't possibly. No, I shall wait until Will returns. Though please don't think you have to keep me company at all.'

'I'll stay for a while if you don't mind,' Jake said. 'I'm not at all sleepy.'

They sat in silence for a while, a silence both awkward, and at the same time intimate. There could never be the same distance between them again.

'I couldn't help but hear that you were arguing about teaching the children to read,' Jake said presently. 'I didn't try to listen but I couldn't help hearing.'

'Don't apologize,' Beth said. 'You could hardly fail to hear. It's I who should be sorry, not you.'

'If it's going to make for further difficulties, and I think it will, then you should give up the idea of teaching me,' Jake said.

Beth studied him intently.

'Do you want to learn to read? Really *want* to?'

'Of course I do,' Jake said. 'I want to very much.'

'Then you shall,' Beth said. 'You must leave me to work out how, and when, but teach you I will. What's more, if their parents want it, I shall teach those children. I'm quite determined and I know it's right. My husband will have to get used to it, which I'm sure he will.'

'There's something else I must ask you,' Jake said. However difficult it was, it had to be said.

'Yes?'

'Would it be better if I left Nazareth? If I found lodgings at Tunnel Huts? Perhaps you and Will would be better on your own?'

His question took Beth by surprise, and her reaction to it even more so. It had not dawned upon her, until now, how much his presence in the house meant to her, how much she would miss him if he left. She preferred not to think about why this was so, but it was the truth; and perhaps, she thought, that was the very reason why she should agree to his suggestion. She pushed the thought away from her.

'Oh no!' she said quickly. 'There isn't the slightest reason for you to leave here – unless it's your wish, of course. Besides . . .' she searched around for a reason to give for wanting him to remain '. . . besides, we wouldn't be on our own, would we? There's Patrick. I might really be glad of your help with Patrick. I'm not at all sure how he's going to be.'

It was a flimsy excuse. There was no reason to suppose that Patrick would not be perfectly fit in a very short time, nor that she would not be able to deal with him until he was.

'I'd be glad to do that,' Jake said. 'But if the time comes when . . .'

'If it does I will let you know,' Beth promised. 'You know, Will is a good man, really. His bark is worse than his bite. What you saw tonight was not the real Will, not the man I love. I think the job is getting him down. Working on the viaduct is not easy. It's not work he's used to.'

'I suppose not,' Jake said.

And working every day in the tunnel was no bed of roses, he thought. There were many times when he envied Will, and all those others who worked in the open air instead of in the black bowels of the earth. But he had chosen the tunnel, he had accepted the challenge, and he wouldn't go back on it.

He changed the subject.

'Do you know how Patrick came to be in the fight?' he asked. 'I know he's wayward, he's a law unto himself, but I wouldn't have put him down as a fighting man. He's easygoing.'

'I know nothing,' Beth said. 'It was all so quick, everything happening at once. But I do remember the worst of the two men who were setting about him, the one Mr Crossland went for. I shan't ever forget him. And if anything happens to Patrick . . .' she broke off.

'Nothing will,' Jake said. 'He'll be all right.'

'I know,' she said. 'But if anything did, I'd track that man down and I'd see that he was punished, even if it meant I had to testify in court.'

'Don't worry,' Jake said. 'It won't come to that. If the man thinks he's hurt Patrick badly, he'll probably leave the neighbourhood. What about the one who hurt you?'

'I couldn't remember him,' Beth admitted. 'I went at him so hard, I didn't even look at his face.'

The time crept by until it was almost midnight.

'You really should go to bed,' Jake said.

'No. I'll wait a little longer,' Beth said. 'But you should go. You've an early start in the morning.'

'I daresay you're right,' Jake agreed. 'I'll go. But call me if you need me.'

An hour later, most of which time Beth had spent looking out of the window watching for him, Will had not returned. It was a dark night and he had no lantern with him, nor had he been wearing a coat, and by now the ground was white over with frost, and he had had a cold on him for the last two days. She moved the lamp from the table into the window, so that he should see it. There were no lights left in the huts in Nazareth; everyone went to bed early, on a Sunday night especially.

She picked up her book of poems but it was impossible to concentrate. They made no sense. She poked the fire in the stove into a blaze, walked restlessly around the room. In the end she could bear it no longer. She must go and search for him, though where she didn't know, other than down the rough track towards Batty Green; or perhaps higher up, towards the tunnel.

She put on her cloak, lit the lantern, and left.

It had been Jake's firm intention to stay awake until he heard Will Seymour return, but after his long day in the tunnel, nature took over and he fell asleep. When he wakened, he thought it was Patrick, moaning a little in his sleep, who had roused him, and then, coming to slowly, he realized that he had heard the outer door being closed. He waited for voices and for footsteps, but there were none. No-one had come in; someone had gone out – and it must be Beth.

He sprang out of bed and ran into the living-room, saw the lamp set in the window, saw that her cloak was gone from the hook by the door and the lantern from its usual place on the shelf. He looked out of the window, but there was no sign of her. The night was as black as ink, no moon, no stars. He must go after her! He left the hut – if there was a spare lantern he had no idea where it was – and hurried down the track.

So which way shall I go? Beth asked herself. And could she do any good at all, searching for Will like this? But she had to, she couldn't have sat quietly at home waiting, not after the manner in which he'd rushed out of the house, the wild look he'd had on him.

He would be more likely to go down the hill towards Batty Green than uphill towards the tunnel, she thought. It was the way he normally went; on the other hand, he hadn't been normal. Even so, she'd take the downhill track.

Against the velvet darkness of the night the light from the lantern did not reach far ahead, but hopefully it was far enough to keep her from walking into a boggy patch of land. She made for the tramway track. If she walked as near as possible to that she should be reasonably safe. Her eyes were already getting used to the darkness. Over to her right she could now distinguish the great mass of Whernside, brooding over the moor.

Jake, though Beth did not know it, was not far behind. Guided by the glow from her lantern, he had spotted her quickly but, he decided, he would not catch up with her. He would remain a short distance behind, but close enough to see that she came to no harm. When she met up with Will, it would do no good for him to be on the scene. When that happened, and once he could be sure that everything was all right, that she was safe, he would make his way back to the hut and be in his bed before they arrived home.

The moor, Beth thought as she walked, was a frightening place at night. Where could Will be? Was she even looking in the right direction? Supposing he had hurt himself? Supposing he had stumbled and fallen, as she herself almost had on the uneven ground a moment ago – would she even see him unless he was directly on the track?

She began to call his name.

'Will! Will, where are you? Where are you, Will?'

Her voice cut through the darkness. Jake, hearing her cry, wanted to catch up with her, to comfort her. He began to hurry towards her, but before he had taken more than a few steps there was an answering sound; not words, but a groan. Though faint, it was unmistakable.

Beth stood still, frozen to the spot, frightened by the sound. Just supposing it was not Will? In that case who might it be, what would happen? She called out again.

'Will! Is that you, Will? Where are you?'

The answering cry was again faint, but now she knew it came from her left, away from the tramlines. There was still no telling whether or not it was Will.

'I'm coming!' she called. 'Hold on! I'm coming!'

She moved in what she hoped was the direction of the voice, though no further sound came. Jake, keeping her lantern in sight, moved behind her. Every few yards she called again, straining her ears for an answer, but none came. The ground was more difficult now, wet and boggy, with tussocky grass which, in the darkness, made it difficult to proceed.

'Will!' she cried. 'Are you there? Where are you? Please answer!'

She swung the lantern around in an arc, but could see no-one, though she was sure the voice had come from this direction. Then as she swung the lantern yet again she saw, with horror and dismay, that she was in an area of shakeholes. As far as the light reached, there they were, all around her, waiting to entrap her. It was a miracle they had not done so. She had no doubt now that that was what had happened to the owner of the voice. And she was convinced that it was Will.

'Please answer, Will!' she cried again as loudly as she could. 'Please call out! I'm trying to find you!'

This time there was a reply, a definite call, but too faint to tell for sure where it came from, though it seemed to be straight ahead.

'I hear you,' she shouted. 'Keep calling. I'm coming to find you!'

Gingerly picking her way – it was impossible to hurry across the treacherous ground – she moved forward in the direction of the voice, which she was now sure was Will's. When she found him it was clear why he had fallen into the shakehole. Tall grass grew all around its rim, concealing its size and depth. Had she not been moving cautiously, she might well have fallen into it herself.

It was not safe to stand too close. Carefully, she lowered herself to the ground and lay face down, then inched forward until she could see over the edge. She held her lantern at arm's length, shining its light into the depths of the hole. Then she saw him.

It was Will all right, lying ten feet down, in six inches of water. He lay on his side, with one leg bent up towards his body. Only because he was against the side of the hole, where the ground sloped upwards a little, was he able to keep his face clear of the water.

'Oh, Will,' Beth cried. 'Oh dear, dear Will!'

'Hurt my back,' he said. 'Can't move.' His words were indistinct, as if he had no strength in him.

'Oh Will, how am I going to get you out?' Beth said. 'I'll have to fetch help!'

'Be quick,' he mumbled. 'Very cold. Very cold.'

'I know, my love. I'll be as quick as ever I can. I'll knock someone up in Jericho. Oh Will, hang on, my love. I won't be long. But I'm sorry, I'll have to take the lantern. It's not safe otherwise.'

She did not hear Jake coming up behind her. When she rose to her feet and turned around and saw the figure of a man, though not who it was, she screamed.

'It's all right!' Jake said. 'It's me!'

'Oh! Oh Jake! Oh, I'm so glad . . .'

It was not the moment to ask how he came to be there, only to thank God that he was.

'He's down in the bottom,' she said. 'He's lying in the water. Oh Jake, what shall we do?'

'Give me the lantern,' Jake said.

He took the lantern and peered down the hole, and then around all sides of it.

'We're coming!' he shouted. 'Hang on!'

He turned to Beth.

'We must get him out, and as quickly as possible. He must be very, very cold.'

'How can we move him?' Beth cried. 'How can we get him up? He's hurt his back, I don't know how badly.'

'We'll find a way. We must.'

Jake swung the lantern again, carefully studying the inside of the dark hole.

'The ground slopes a little on the side where he's lying,' he said. 'That's how he's keeping his head above water. I want you to light my way with the lantern while I get down there and lift him out.'

'Oh Jake, I don't see how you can!' Beth protested. 'Shouldn't one of us go to Jericho and get more help?'

Jake shook his head.

'It will take too long and there's no time to waste. He's lying in ice-cold water. We must get him out as quickly as possible.'

He called down the shakehole. 'It's Jake. I'm coming! Don't go to sleep, Will! Stay awake!'

If he lost consciousness he would be a dead weight, impossible for one man to carry or drag up the steep slope.

It was not too difficult to descend, and to his great relief Jake found a narrow ledge not far above the place where Will's head rested. If he could get him onto the ledge, he thought, it would get him out of the water and give them both a short breathing space while he worked out the rest, how to get from there to the top. If he couldn't do it, then they would have to stay on the ledge while Beth went for help. But that was a last resort; the night was bitter.

'You're going to be all right,' he said to Will. 'I'm going to turn you on your back then I'm going to put my arms under your armpits and pull you up onto the ledge.'

Will gave a loud cry of pain as Jake began to move him.

'I'm sorry to hurt you,' Jake said. 'I'll be as careful as I can.' But Will Seymour was a heavy man and it was only possible to get him onto the ledge by giving a tremendous heave.

Will could not contain his shouts of pain as he was moved. But at least he was now fully conscious, Jake thought, and would be able to follow instructions, though what those should be he hardly knew himself. It seemed an insurmountable task. Should he, after all, have gone for help instead of attempting the rescue himself? But he knew it would have been too great a risk. If Will had lost consciousness he might well have slid into the water. Which, though shallow, was enough to drown a man if he turned face down.

'We can't do it!' Will said faintly. 'It's impossible.'

'We can do it!' Jake's voice was firm. 'Though I'll need your help, as much as you can possibly give me. It isn't a sheer drop on this side, it's a slope; steep, but still a slope, with one or two near-level shelves. I'm going to continue to hold you under the arms, and I'm going up backwards, dragging you with me. It'll be painful for you, but it could work. And if it doesn't, we'll try something else.'

But what else? How could he carry Will, even on his back, and at the same time climb the slope? And had Will enough strength left, in that case, to cling onto him?

'We're coming up!' he called to Beth. 'Make sure you lie flat on the ground, and don't lean over too far with the lantern. I'll need the shallowest slope and any ledges, and it won't be easy for me to see them because I'm coming up on my back. I want you to guide me when you can.'

'I'll do that,' Beth said. She was trembling with fear. 'Oh, Jake! Oh, Will!'

Jake dug his heels into the ground as well as he could, and thanked heaven that it was soft, then with every ounce of strength in his body he began to prise himself up, dragging Will with him, stopping every few inches to catch his breath and renew his strength.

Afterwards, he found out that it had taken no more than a quarter of an hour to reach the top, and safety, but it had been the longest fifteen minutes of his life. The moments when he thought they would not make it, that the two of them would slide back into the water, had each one been an eternity.

'And now I *shall* have to go to Jericho and get help to carry him back,' Jake said to Beth when they were safe on top again. 'If we were to attempt to do it on our own we might do great harm to his back.'

He laid Will, who was shivering violently, on the ground. Beth wrapped him in her cloak then sat on the ground beside him and cradled his head in her lap. His face was contorted with pain. She took his hands in hers and rubbed them, trying to bring him warmth, then she stroked his face.

'Oh Will, love, I wish I could do more,' she said. 'But don't worry, we'll have you home soon.'

Jake took off his jacket and put it around her shoulders.

'Oh no!' she said. 'You need it yourself.'

'I can keep warm by walking,' Jake said. 'You'll freeze to death, sitting here. But I *will* have to take the lantern, because we're off the track. Otherwise it will take me twice as long.'

'Of course you must.'

'I'll be as quick as I can,' he promised.

Will fell asleep almost as soon as Jake had left. He was icy to the touch and Beth wondered whether it was wise to allow him to sleep when he was so cold. Nevertheless, she decided to let him do so. At least he would feel his pain less, though she could tell from the spasms which contorted his face that the pain was haunting his dreams.

Sitting there in the darkness, she wondered how long it would be before help arrived. She tried everything she could to make the time pass more quickly, though she could concentrate on nothing for long. She made herself think about the book she had been reading earlier in the day; she thought about the Missioner, then about Patrick Mahoney. Was Patrick all right? He was alone.

What she refused to dwell on – she resolutely pushed it away whenever it came into her mind – was her quarrel with Will, and the fact that he had struck her. It was her fault, it must be. She had driven him too far.

And now she was growing sleepy herself. Though she knew she must not allow herself to drop off, only the fact that her feet were so cold, and that the weight of Will's head on her lap was uncomfortable, kept her awake until, suddenly, she saw the lights of lanterns bobbing in the distance and, as they came nearer, heard the sound of voices.

There were three men with Jake. They had brought blankets, a can of hot soup, and a door on which to carry Will. Gently, Beth wakened Will, and made him drink some soup. Then the men wrapped him in the blankets, laid him carefully on the door, and began to carry him home. Beth put on her cloak and, taking Jake's arm, followed them.

It was not until Will had been carried into the hut and laid on his own bed that Beth remembered Patrick again. She looked at Jake.

'Patrick?' she queried.

'I've looked in on him. He's all right,' Jake assured

her. 'In fact, he's asleep. He looks as though he hasn't moved since we put him to bed.'

'Thank goodness for that!' Beth said.

Jake was not so sure. It seemed not quite normal that Patrick should sleep so deeply. Even through all the disturbances of Will's homecoming, with so many people walking about the house in the middle of the night, he had not stirred. But at the moment Will Seymour was the more urgent matter.

In spite of the fact that his soaking wet clothes had been replaced by dry ones, his bed heated by a stone hot-water bottle, plus a brick which Beth had heated and wrapped in a piece of flannel, and that blankets were piled upon him, he remained cold. He had stopped complaining about his back, indeed he was now too lethargic to complain about anything.

'I don't like it,' Beth worried. 'He seems so unresponsive.'

'I think we must rouse him,' Jake said. 'I think we must force some hot drinks down him.'

'I reckon he needs the doctor,' one of the men from Jericho said.

'The doctor is coming tomorrow, to see Patrick Mahoney,' Beth said. 'But I don't know when. I can't be sure he'll come early. I wish I could.'

'It's three o'clock in the morning, there's not much to be done now,' the man said. 'What I will do is walk down to Ingleton before I start work, and tell the doctor it's urgent. I work on the viaduct, so I go in that direction.'

'I'd be greatly obliged if you'd do that,' Beth said. 'And thank you, all three of you, for what you've done.'

'We'd best get off, then,' the man said. 'Not long 'til morning.'

'You had better go to bed, Jake,' Beth said when the men had left. 'Get some sleep in what's left of the night, before you have to be up again for work. I'll sit with Will.' They were standing together by Will's bedside.

'I could stay with you,' Jake offered. 'We could take it in turns to catnap.'

'No!' Beth was emphatic. 'You've done enough.'

'Then promise you'll call me if you need me,' he said.

'I promise!' She stretched out her hand and touched his. 'Jake, I can never thank you enough. You've saved my husband's life.'

Have I, Jake asked himself as he went to bed. Had Will's life, in fact, been saved? He was not so sure.

When Jake had gone, Beth continued to sit by Will. She took each of his hands in turn in her own and chafed them gently, trying to bring back the warmth, but with little success. Then she took off her long skirt and climbed into bed beside him, curling her body against his cold one, trying to give him all the warmth that was in her.

Jake rose early next morning, but when he went into the living-room Beth was already there. She had stoked up the stove, and the kettle was singing.

'How is he?' Jake asked. 'Is he warm again? And what about you?'

Her face was pale, with dark shadows of fatigue around her eyes and fine lines of worry marking her smooth forehead.

'Will's not only warm again,' she said. 'Now he's burning hot. He has a fever on him.'

'I'm sorry to hear that,' Jake said. But he was not surprised, not after what the man had gone through. And they still didn't know how long he had lain in the shakehole.

'And you?' he repeated. 'How are you?'

The kettle was boiling; he made the tea.

'I'm all right,' Beth said. 'I just hope the doctor comes soon.'

She was surprised that she felt as wide awake as she did. She had slept little, trying to remain as still as possible in case her movements should disturb Will, or cause more pain to his back. By the time morning came the heat from his body had been more than she could bear; she had had to get up.

'What about Patrick?' she asked Jake. 'Poor Patrick, I keep forgetting him.'

'I think he's all right,' Jake said, but there was doubt in his voice. 'His cuts have bled a bit during the night.'

'Then I'll go and bathe them in a minute,' Beth said.

'No,' Jake said. 'I'll do that. You have enough on your plate. He was awake a few minutes ago, so when I've drunk my tea I'll see to him.'

The truth was that he was worried not so much about Patrick's cuts and bruises, which would heal with time, as about the fact that he seemed confused. His words were slurred, and nothing he said made much sense.

He saw to Patrick, who, even before Jake had finished bathing him, fell into another sleep. When Jake left him Beth had gone back into her bedroom. He knocked on the door and she called to him to enter.

'I'm off to work now,' he said. 'Are you sure you'll be all right? Would you like me to stay?' He stood at the foot of the bed, looking at Will. He didn't like what he saw. The man's face was flushed a dusky red; his breathing was short and rasping.

'I'll be fine,' Beth said. 'You must go to work.'

It was a fine, bright day as he walked up to the tunnel, the morning sun shining on the face of Whernside. There was still an early morning nip in the air. It was the kind of day when he would have liked to have stayed on top, not gone down into the darkness of the tunnel. In any case, he was not happy about leaving Beth with the two sick men.

# 7

Before taking his place in the queue to go down into the tunnel, Jake sought out Mr Hargreaves.

'I'm reporting for Patrick Mahoney,' he said. 'He can't come to work today. He's poorly.'

'Poorly?' Hargreaves queried. 'So what's the matter with him?'

Jake hesitated.

'Well, not exactly poorly . . .'

'Then what?'

'He's been in a bit of an accident,' Jake said. 'He's a bit cut up, a bit fuzzy in the head. Not fit to work in the tunnel. He should be all right in a day or two.'

Hargreaves gave Jake a long, hard look. 'Has he been in a fight? Is that it?' he asked suspiciously.

'Don't ask me,' Jake said. 'I wasn't there. I don't know the details.'

'No doubt he was drunk,' Hargreaves said.

'I know nothing about that. As I said, I wasn't there. But he's not suffering from a hangover. He's poorly. The doctor's coming up to see him.' If only it was as simple as a hangover, he thought.

'It had better not be a hangover,' Hargreaves was sharp and sour. 'We have a reputation here, on the tunnel job, of turning up regularly on a Monday morning in a fit condition to work. Never mind the other sites; we're different.'

'Yes, sir,' Jake said. 'Well, if Patrick isn't here himself tomorrow, which he might well be, I'll be sure to let you know what the doctor says.'

'Do that,' Hargreaves said. 'And remind Mahoney, no work no pay. No help at all if he's brought it on himself.'

'I'll tell him,' Jake said. He wouldn't, of course.

He walked away, climbed into the cage, and was lowered down the shaft into the tunnel. The tunnel was progressing at a steady rate, so that when he reached the bottom he had a longer walk underground to where he was working. He was still on general labouring jobs, endlessly moving stones up to the surface, from where they would be taken away to build up embankments on other parts of the line, nothing being wasted. He had been promised that when there was an opening he would be given a trial on the bricklaying, and he looked forward to that. He would feel then that he was really helping to build the tunnel, that there would be a part of it he could look at when it was finished, and say, 'I built that!'

It came into his mind that Patrick was a bricklayer, and that perhaps if Patrick was off work for a little while Mr Hargreaves might allow him to step into that job. Then he quickly put away the thought as a strong feeling of guilt swept over him.

To Beth's great relief, Doctor Stokes arrived at ten o'clock in the morning. He was a short, stocky man, well matched to his broad-backed horse.

'I gather the patient was injured in a brawl?' he said. 'That's what the Missioner told me.'

'Oh no!' Beth began. 'It wasn't . . .' Then she recollected herself. She was so concerned about Will that she had forgotten for the moment that it was not her husband the doctor was here to see, but Patrick Mahoney.

'So where is he, then?' the doctor asked. 'Let's be seeing him.'

'I'm sorry. This way, Doctor.'

She led him into Patrick's bedroom.

Patrick lay on his back, his usually pleasant features disfigured and distorted by his injuries, his hands, outside the bedclothes, purple-bruised and swollen against the white counterpane. His eyes were open, and staring, though at what it was impossible to tell.

Doctor Stokes turned to Beth.

'I thought you said he hadn't been in a fight?'

'I didn't mean Mr Mahoney. Of course *he* has. It's obvious isn't it? It's my husband who wasn't in a fight.'

The doctor stared at her.

'This is somewhat confusing, Mrs Seymour. What has your husband to do with it?'

Beth explained.

'In fact, Doctor,' she finished, 'I'm very anxious you should look at him when you've finished with Mr Mahoney.'

The doctor bent over Patrick.

'Well man, you've made a real mess of your face,' he said. 'But that will heal, given time. I'll give your landlady some crystals and she'll dissolve them in water and bathe your face – and your hands. How do you feel in yourself?'

Patrick seemed to reply, but his words were jumbled, making no sense. It was not even certain whether he was speaking to the doctor, or rambling to himself. Whatever it was, it seemed to distress him until, on the instant, he closed his eyes and was asleep again.

Gently, the doctor ran his fingers over Patrick's head, exploring the scalp under the matted hair. Then he raised the man's eyelids and looked closely into each eye. Patrick gave no sign that he felt any of it. This done, the doctor looked at Patrick intently for several seconds, then he straightened up and walked out of the room, Beth following him.

'What do you think, Doctor?' she asked. His careful, silent examination of Patrick had unnerved her.

Because her attention had been on Will, where Patrick was concerned she had thought only of his cuts and bruises, nothing more. Now she felt sure there was more. It showed in the doctor's manner.

'He's had a blow to the head. A considerable blow, I'd say, as if he'd been kicked. There's a nasty swelling. Did he lose consciousness?'

'For a short time,' Beth said.

'I thought so. The man's concussed, though how badly it's impossible to tell as yet.'

'Oh no!'

Beth felt stricken with guilt. Since the moment Patrick had been brought home and she had helped to settle him in bed, she had not been near him; moreover, she had given him no more than a passing thought.

'I'm very sorry,' she said. 'You see, it was the other things happening. So what are we to do, what can *I* do? Ought he to be in hospital?'

'I think not. For the time being he's better off where he is,' the doctor said. 'The journey to the hospital would do him no good at all. So unless he gets worse . . .' He left the sentence unfinished. 'But are you able to look after him, that's the question.'

'I hope so,' Beth said. 'He's my lodger, and he has no family of his own.'

'There's not a lot you can do,' Doctor Stokes admitted. 'Just keep an eye on him, keep him quiet. He could recover quite soon.' Or not, he thought. 'And now I'll take a look at your husband.'

His face was grave as he examined Will, listened intently to his chest. He turned to Beth. 'You say he hurt his back.'

'Yes. It's been giving him a great deal of pain,' Beth said. 'In the lower part.'

The doctor turned down the bedclothes and tested the movement and feeling in Will's leg. Though he did not open his eyes, or speak a word, Will winced with pain when his left leg was touched.

'At least the feeling's there,' the doctor said. 'That's a good sign. But I'm afraid we'll have to inflict more pain because there's no way we can leave him lying so flat. Your husband has double pneumonia, Mrs Seymour. I'll need a few more pillows or cushions to prop him up.'

'I'll get them at once,' Beth said. 'But won't it hurt his back, to be raised so?'

'It will,' the doctor admitted. 'But the pneumonia is what matters now. We must do everything we can for that! Did he have a cold on him before he went out?'

'He'd had one for several days. He hadn't thought it was serious.'

The doctor studied Will again, then left the bedroom, motioning Beth to follow him.

'I have to tell you, Mrs Seymour, that your husband is very ill. Also, that he will get worse before he's better. He has a high fever, and such is the nature of the illness that over the next few days it will mount to a crisis. If he survives the crisis, he will recover. We must pray that he does so.'

The room spun around Beth. She grabbed at the nearest chair, and felt Doctor Stokes pushing her head down between her knees. Then her head cleared, and she sat up.

She's a pretty thing, Doctor Stokes thought, but now she was white with anxiety; and with good reason, more than she realizes.

'Do you know how long he was in the shakehole, in the water?' he asked.

'I don't. He doesn't seem able to tell me anything. I think he set out to go to Batty Green. It could have happened on his way there, or not until his way back.'

'So he could have been in the water half an hour, or as much as three hours?'

'Oh Doctor, he could! And it's all my fault!' Beth cried out in anguish. 'If he dies, I'll have killed him!'

Doctor Stokes put his hand on her shoulder.

'Then we shall have to make quite sure he doesn't die, my dear. And if you nurse him well, it will be you who has saved him. You can do more than I can.'

'It's all my fault,' Beth repeated. She was not to be comforted.

'And why is it your fault?'

'I provoked him,' she said. 'We quarrelled. He ran out of the house. It's all my fault!'

'No!' Doctor Stokes said. 'It is not your fault. All married couples quarrel. You can't take the blame for everything, so dry your eyes. And tell me, are you going to be able to look after two men? Do you know anyone who could help you?'

'I don't,' Beth said. 'I have a lodger, but he works in the tunnel during the day, though I know he'd keep an eye on Patrick at night.'

'Well, that's a help. It's your husband who'll need the most attention.'

'But I'll manage,' Beth said. 'There's no two ways about it. I'll manage! I'll do all that's needful.'

'I'm sure you will,' the doctor agreed. 'But you must also contrive to look after yourself. Take rest whenever you get the chance, and see that you eat well. You must keep up your strength or you'll be no good to anyone.'

'I will,' Beth promised.

'Then I'll be here tomorrow.'

Beth saw him to the door, and watched while he mounted his horse and rode away. Then she squared her shoulders, took a deep breath of the clear air, and went back into the house, back to Will. He had slipped sideways from the pillows and was no longer propped up. As carefully as she could, fearful of hurting his back, she righted him. The heat came off his body as if from glowing coals. When she touched his face, his skin was hot and dry, his lips blackened and cracked.

She fetched water and bathed his face, trying to cool him down. Throughout it all his eyes remained closed, his breath short and rasping. Sharp fear swept through her. Whatever the doctor might say, it was her fault. It had been that last sentence, 'Don't touch me' which had sent him out of the house, perhaps to his death.

'Will,' she begged. 'Will, come back to me! Please open your eyes! Please look at me! Say you forgive me.'

It was impossible to tell whether he had even heard her.

Tears ran down her face and splashed into the basin of water as she carried it back into the living-room.

When a knock came at the door she snatched up a towel and hastily dried her eyes.

Mrs Drake stood on the doorstep.

'I've come to see if there's anything I can do. My husband was one of the men who helped to carry Mr Seymour back, though of course you weren't to know that. He was the one who went down to the doctor this morning.'

'Oh, please do come in,' Beth said. 'I can't thank your husband and the other men enough. We could never have managed without them.'

Mrs Drake, stepping into the house, waved the thanks aside.

'There's half-a-dozen others in Jericho who'd have done the same. And I daresay in Nazareth for that matter. It just so happened that your lodger knocked on our door first.'

'Even so, what they did was wonderful.'

'So how is your husband?' Mrs Drake asked. 'My man said he didn't look too good.' Her husband had said more than that. He'd said he wouldn't take bets on Will Seymour's recovery.

'He's not good,' Beth acknowledged. 'He has double pneumonia. The doctor says there's not a lot to be done, apart from nursing.'

'Well, I'm here to offer help,' Mrs Drake said. 'Whatever you need.'

'But you have your children to look after,' Beth said. 'How can you spare the time?'

'Don't let that worry you, pet. I can make arrangements about them. People are very neighbourly. You find that out when there's trouble.'

'So it seems!' Just the sight of Mrs Drake, small, plump, homely, lifted a little of the weight from Beth, made the world seem less dark. 'And I'm grateful. You see, it's not only Will. I have Patrick to look after.'

'Patrick?'

Beth explained.

'My other lodger, Jake Tempest – it was he who got Will out of the shakehole – will help with Patrick when he can, but he works in the tunnel, at present on the day shift, so he doesn't have much time to spare. He has to get his sleep.'

'And you look as though you could do with a good night's sleep,' Mrs Drake said. She had quickly observed Beth's tearstained face, the droop of her shoulders.

'I didn't get much last night,' Beth admitted. 'But it doesn't matter. Anyway, I wouldn't want to leave Will.'

Mrs Drake nodded.

'I'm sure he mustn't be left, but you can't do it all, pet. Now, if you'll pardon me taking the liberty, I'll make us both a cup of tea; I could do with one, and you look as though you could. And while I'm doing that, why don't you go back to your husband. I'll give you the nod when the tea's ready, then you and I can have a chat.'

Ten minutes later she put her head around the bedroom door.

'I've poured,' she whispered. 'Will I bring it in here, or not?'

Beth glanced at Will.

'What do you think of him? He seems to be fast asleep.'

Mrs Drake crossed to the bedside. The poor man looked terrible, and that was a fact. It was a look she had seen before, when her father had had pneumonia, but she wouldn't say anything about that, or its outcome, to Beth Seymour. Anyway, this man was young and presumably strong. Her father had been pushing sixty. Gently, she laid a hand on Will's forehead.

'He's certainly got a high fever,' she said. 'I think we should moisten his poor lips again before we have our tea, then perhaps we can leave him be for a few minutes.'

While they drank their tea, Mrs Drake put forward her suggestions for helping out. Her soft yet firm north-country voice, her fund of common sense, were balm to Beth's troubled spirit. She recognized that in Elsie Drake she had found what she had always had until she'd come to live here, and what she'd sorely missed: a friend of her own sex.

'In the first place I'll take all the washing, including the bedding,' Mrs Drake said. 'You've no time to bother with that.'

'It's extremely good of you . . .' Beth began.

'Not a bit of it,' Mrs Drake said. 'It can go in with mine. And I'll come for two hours every afternoon to let you get a bit of rest. Also, if you want any messages done, my Jack will do them. He has to go down to Batty Green every day to work, so it'll be no trouble.'

'It's unbelievably kind of you,' Beth said. 'I wish there was some way I could repay you.'

'Oh, I'm sure there will be one of these days, but for now don't even think about it, hinny.'

'I'd be grateful if you'd take a look at Patrick while you're here,' Beth said. 'Would you mind?'

'Not a bit!'

He was sleeping deeply, snoring a little.

'My goodness, he's a bit of a mess!' Mrs Drake said.

'He should have his face bathed again, but it seems a pity to disturb him.'

'Quite right! Never disturb a sleeping patient. Well, I hope he won't give you too much trouble. You've got enough on your plate.'

'I'd better get back to Will,' Beth said.

'And I'll be off, but I'll be back at two o'clock sharp.'

Back in her own bedroom Beth found Will less tranquil. He was half awake now, tossing around, and had thrown off his bedcovers. Quickly, she drew them up again around his shoulders, but when she tried to tuck them in he lashed out at her, trying to push her away. She was amazed at his strength, but observing the dusky redness of his face and the glassy brightness of his wide-open eyes, she realized that his strength came from his fever.

'Hush, love! Lie quiet.'

She spoke softly, and as calmly as she could, though there was no calm in her. She stroked his burning, dry hand with her own cool one, and in the end she had the relief of seeing his eyes close and his limbs quieten down.

She fetched her mending basket, and sat on the chair by his bedside. She darned socks and sewed on buttons, but it was impossible to concentrate; too many thoughts were chasing around in her head. After a short time she laid the work aside.

She thought, for the first time since the doctor had

left, of what her position would be, because of Will's illness. There had been no time to consider it until now.

There would be no money at all coming in from him, nor indeed from Patrick. She had a little saved, though not much, and she doubted if Patrick had a penny piece to his name. It was the pattern with most of the men who worked for the Company; they earned good money and spent it as fast as they got it. Indeed, many of them ran out of money long before the next payday was due, in which case they subbed from the Company, and were thus always in debt. She didn't know that Will did so. He never told her how much he earned, or what he spent it on. He gave her her housekeeping money, and that was it. But Patrick, she suspected, was another matter. She would not be surprised to learn that he owed the Company.

What would she do when the money ran out? But wasn't it wrong of her to think about that now, with Will lying so desperately ill? Never mind the money, Will was all that mattered!

Even more resolutely did she push away the thought which had flashed into her mind for a brief second, the question which asked, 'What will you do if he dies?' She would not answer that.

The wedding-present clock which had pride of place on the dresser was striking two as Mrs Drake knocked at the door.

'Oh, I'm so pleased to see you, Mrs Drake!' Beth said.

'Call me Elsie. How is he? How are they both?'

'Patrick is sleeping. Will is much the same. He's calm at this moment but he has these restless fits, and he's as hot as fire.'

'Well, you can leave him to me for a bit,' Elsie Drake said. 'I'll see to him. And I've brought a couple of lemons. I thought you might not have any, and there's nothing better than home-made lemonade for a fever. Well sweetened to restore strength. It wouldn't do Patrick Mahoney any harm either.'

'I'll make it,' Beth said.

'No you won't! I'll do what's needful. You lie on the sofa here and do your best to get a couple of hours' sleep. Don't worry, they'll both be looked after.'

'I know they will, Elsie,' Beth said. And she would have no difficulty in sleeping. She was dog-tired.

'I'll waken you at four o'clock with a cup of tea,' Elsie Drake promised. 'And you're not to make a single move before then, otherwise I might as well not be here.'

'But what if . . . ?'

'If you're needed, I'll fetch you. And that's a promise!'

Beth lay on the sofa, a cushion under her head and a rug spread over her, and was asleep within minutes. Afterwards she wondered, guiltily, how she could have slept, knowing Will's desperate state.

It was half-past four when she opened her eyes. Elsie stood in front of her, a cup of tea in her hand.

'I hadn't the heart to waken you earlier,' she said. 'You were well away.'

Beth sat up quickly.

'How is he?'

'About the same, I'd say.'

'And Patrick?'

'Sleeping. So you can concentrate on your husband.'

In fact, Elsie thought, Will was, if anything, worse, but she wouldn't say so. There was nothing more to be done about it.

'Doctor Stokes warned you he'd be worse before he was better,' she said as cheerfully as she could. 'So you mustn't be alarmed if that happens. The doctor will be here tomorrow, and if you need me at all, send

Jake Tempest down to fetch me. I'll come at once.'

When Elsie Drake had left, Beth went first to look at Patrick. He was still asleep. Was it natural to sleep so much? she wondered.

She went to Will, gently laid her fingers against his cheek. It was burning.

'I'm going to bathe your face again with cool water,' she said. 'Then I'll give you another drink of lemonade.'

He made no reply, his eyes remained closed as she bathed his face. Has he missed me? she wondered. Did he even know I wasn't here, that it was someone else?

'Now drink your lemonade, love,' she said, holding the cup to his lips.

He turned his face away, silently refusing it.

'Come on, Will,' she said. 'You've got to drink if you want to get better.'

Did he want to get better? He seemed beyond caring about anything.

'Oh, Will darling, please try!' she begged. 'For my sake!'

With the minimum co-operation on Will's part, she managed to get some lemonade down him, though as much ran over his chin as into his mouth. She needed a feeding cup with a spout. Now, he seemed exhausted again.

'I'll straighten your pillows,' she said. 'Then I'll leave you in peace.'

He said nothing, but she saw the anxious look in his eyes, and he stretched out a hand and grabbed her wrist, his hot fingers burning her skin.

'Oh, I'll not leave you, love!' she assured him. 'I'll sit right here beside you while you try to sleep.'

She was too anxious to read, or to occupy herself with mending or knitting. Instead she sat, hands clasping and unclasping, trying to control the thoughts which whirled around in her head. It was wicked, she knew it was, to think that Will might die, yet however often she pushed it away, the thought came back, strong, unbidden, and with it a yawning, black future; as dank, as dark, as cold as the deepest shakehole. She had been no more than sixteen when her brother had first brought Will home, and from that first hour he had filled her life. However difficult he had become, she could not envisage a life without him.

And I mustn't do so now, she admonished herself. I must be positive. She would will him to recover and to live. Whatever strength was in her, she would give to him. He would feel it flow from her, fill him. She would save him. 'Please God!' she prayed. 'Please God!' She had no more words, but if God was any good at all, if He was all-knowing, He would know what she wanted.

It was a relief when she heard the door open, and Jake's tread in the house. When he came into the bedroom she put her finger to her lips.

'He's just fallen asleep,' she whispered.

Even in sleep, the shocking sound of the sick man's breathing filled the house. It spoke of pain, Jake thought, with every indrawn breath.

'How is he?' he asked quietly. 'What did the doctor say?'

She motioned him to go into the living-room, and followed him. She gave him the doctor's verdict.

'He says we must expect him to get worse until the crisis comes. After that . . .'

Her voice failed her. She turned away, trying to hide the tears which had sprung into her eyes and threatened to fall.

Jake stood by the table watching her, her head bent, one hand raised to cover her eyes. Her hair was escaping from its coil on the top of her head, falling untidily around her neck. Compassion welled in him. He wanted to take the step forward which separated them, to hold her close against him and let her cry on his shoulder; but he could not do that.

'I'm sorry,' he said.

Beth took a deep breath, then lifted her head to face him.

'Doctor Stokes was worried about Patrick, too. I mustn't forget Patrick. He has concussion. He's been beaten about the head.'

'And what's the treatment?'

'Nothing really. Keep him quiet, let him rest. The doctor will be here again tomorrow.'

'Then I'll go in and see him,' Jake said. 'After that I'm here to do anything you want doing.'

'I'm sorry your tea's not ready,' Beth apologized. 'It wasn't possible today.'

'It's no matter,' Jake said. 'I can make a meal for both of us. Since she had no daughters my mother saw to it that I knew how to cook. Simple things, nothing fancy.'

'Thank you,' Beth said. 'That's very kind. Everyone's kind. Mrs Drake came. She was wonderful. She's going to come each afternoon for two hours, to give me some rest. Did you know it was her husband who helped to carry Will home, and went to see the doctor this morning?'

'Yes, I knew. I saw Mrs Drake when I knocked them up. I'm glad she's coming. She's a nice woman.'

'I must go back to Will,' Beth said.

He was awake.

'I'm going to give you another drink of lemonade, love,' she said. 'The more we get down you, the better.'

She tried to hold his head steady while she gave it to him, but the liquid still dribbled out of his mouth. He seemed too weak to deal with it. She set the cup down, then, hearing Jake back in the living-room, she went to speak to him.

'I'm sorry to ask you before you've even had your tea, but would you go down to Mrs Drake's and see if you can borrow a feeding cup?'

'Right away,' Jake said.

Mrs Drake opened the door to him with one child in her arms and another standing close behind her. Two more children sat at the table, drawing. She welcomed Jake warmly. He explained his mission.

'Come in,' she said. 'I've got just the thing.'

From the cupboard she brought out a white china cup, shaped like a small teapot, but without a lid. It had a fine, curved spout.

'I used this when my dad was bad,' she said. 'I'm surprised Beth doesn't have one.'

'Perhaps she's never had to deal with illness,' Jake said.

'Poor lass! Well, she's got plenty on her plate now,' Mrs Drake said. 'It's as well she's got you.'

'And you.'

'Now, will you stay and have a bite with us?' she invited. 'It'll be ready in a minute, and there's plenty.'

'Thank you, I'd better get back. Besides, if I make a meal it might persuade Beth to eat.'

'You're right,' Mrs Drake agreed. 'Well, just wait a minute, I want to get a few things together.'

She bustled around, and finally put a filled basket on the table.

'There you are! I was going to bring this with me tomorrow, but if you'll carry it, so much the better.'

When Beth unpacked the basket she found a loaf of newly baked bread, six eggs, a jar of lemon curd, a pat of butter and an apple tart.

She looked up at Jake with the first smile he had seen on her since Sunday.

'Oh Jake, it's wonderful! Not so much for what's in

133

the basket, as for the fact that she thought of it at all!'

'I know. I think you've found a true friend there, Beth.'

When Doctor Stokes came next day he examined Will carefully, then stood by the bed, not speaking, his face grave.

'How is he, Doctor? Please tell me!' Beth begged.

He shook his head.

'I'd be deceiving you if I said anything other than that your husband is still critically ill. I'd do you no service. He has pneumonia in both lungs, and there's little I can do for him. As I said before, it comes down to good nursing, and God's will.'

'But he's young! He's strong! Surely that counts for something?'

'It should,' the doctor agreed. 'Pneumonia is called "the old man's friend", but I've seen time and time again how fiercely it can strike the young.'

'Then what more can I do? Please tell me,' Beth implored.

'Watch over him. Get every drop of fluid down him you possibly can. See that he's moved as often as possible; it's harmful for him to stay in the same position all the time. But you must get someone to help you with that, even more for his sake than for yours. It won't be easy on him.'

'I'll do all that,' Beth promised. 'But what else? Surely there must be something else I can do?'

'If you believe in God,' Doctor Stokes said, 'then pray. It can do no harm. It might even work where all else fails.'

He looked in on Patrick.

'His cuts and bruises are healing,' he pronounced. 'Otherwise he seems much the same.'

'He was rational for a short time last evening,' Beth said. 'But he has no memory of what happened. He was puzzled as to why he was here.'

Doctor Stokes nodded.

'That's not unusual. He might never remember what happened before he was concussed. And it could all be a long job. Keep an eye on him, but concentrate on your husband. If nursing Mr Mahoney in addition proves too much for you, then let me know, and I'll see what can be done.'

Afterwards, looking back on it, Beth wondered how she had come through the week which followed. And if it had not been for Jake and Elsie Drake, she thought, she could not have done so.

It was they who between them moved the sofa from the living-room into the bedroom so that Beth would be able to lie down, and perhaps snatch some sleep, during the nights.

'While I'm here in the daytime you can rest in the armchair in the living-room,' Elsie said.

Between them, Jake and Elsie took on every household chore. Jake fetched the water, cleaned out and stoked the stove, made most of the meals: gave an eye to Patrick when he could. Elsie did every bit of washing and ironing, and most of the housework. And they both, in turn, and in accordance with the doctor's orders, helped to move Will at regular intervals, doing it with the utmost care and compassion.

'I shall never be able to repay either of you; never, ever,' Beth said.

As for what Beth did, aside from sitting hour after slow hour with Will, watching his fight against the consuming fever, hearing his noisy breathing, she prayed. She prayed as she had never prayed in her life before. She importuned God, she railed at Him, she begged Him. She bargained with Him: 'Spare Will and I'll work for you for ever. I'll always be on your side!' But they were the kind of bargains she had made with God when she'd asked Him to send her a child. They hadn't worked then.

On the Friday evening – it was the fifth day of Will's illness and he showed no sign of recovery, quite the reverse – Jake said, 'I know you must be needing things from Batty Green. I could go down tomorrow afternoon, if you like.'

'I don't like to trouble you,' Beth said.

'It's no trouble,' Jake assured her. 'In any case, I need new boots. The bad weather will be here any time now, and what I have aren't strong enough to stand it.'

'Well it's true there are things I need,' Beth said. 'Flour, salt, butter, meat, for a start. So yes, I'd be grateful.'

'Then make a list,' Jake said.

When Beth had written the list she took her purse from the dresser drawer and counted its contents. There was Jake's money to come, of course, but there would be nothing from Patrick and Will, and perhaps not for some time. And there would be the doctor's bill. Doctor Stokes had refrained from forecasting how long Will, if he survived the crisis, would be incapacitated. 'We must take a day at a time,' he'd said. She knew it would be several weeks. It was too soon to break into her small savings so there was nothing else for it, she must start at once to make economies.

She went back to the table and studied the list again. Jake watched her as she struck off one item after another.

'I really don't need all these things,' Beth said lightly. 'I don't know what I was thinking of!'

'If you don't mind me saying so . . .' Jake hesitated; he had already discovered that Beth Seymour was a proud woman. '. . . Well, I was thinking, it's possible the Company owes your husband a bit since last payday. I know you can't get down to see anyone, but I could ask the contractor, if you like. If they wouldn't let me have it, then the clerk could bring it up here to you.' It was not an easy area to speak about to her. There was also the possibility that Will Seymour owed money to the Company; there might be little, if anything, to come.

'I'd appreciate that,' Beth said. 'It would be best if the clerk could bring the money here to me. In fact, I'd like a word with him.'

That was not strictly true; she just didn't want Jake to know how short of money she might be.

'I'll try to arrange that,' Jake said. 'And I was thinking, now that Patrick's off work, I could pay a bit of his money each week, say ten or fifteen shillings, and he could pay it back to me when he's earning again.'

'Oh no!' Beth began.

'It would be between him and me,' Jake interrupted. 'I can't trouble him with explanations now, he wouldn't take it in, but if I could I'm sure it's what he'd want.'

'No!' Beth repeated. 'It's good of you, but Patrick is *not* your responsibility. I'll manage without his money until he gets better.'

'He's not really your responsibility.'

'Oh yes he is! He's my lodger. This is his home, and as far as I know he has no other, so I'll stand by him as long as it's necessary.'

'Well, if you change your mind . . .'

'If I do, I'll tell you,' Beth promised.

# 8

'You'll have to hurry, Jake, or you'll miss the tramway.'

Beth's voice was tight with anxiety. She didn't want him to go, she didn't want to be left alone, but he had to. They needed the supplies he had undertaken to bring back, aside from the fact that he was going to buy much-needed new boots.

She would not have Elsie Drake's company this afternoon. Elsie's husband was working, so that she herself would have to go down to Batty Green to buy in, *and* take the children. Saturday was the one day when neighbours were not free to help; they were all flocking in the same direction and would all return burdened.

'I'm just leaving,' Jake replied. 'And I won't hang around for the tram back. I'll walk it. I'll be as quick as I can.'

'Your time's your own, Jake,' Beth reminded him.

All the same, she would be glad to see him back. She was so nervous. She wanted to be with Will every minute of the time, of course she did, but sitting there, watching him grow steadily worse, was frightening beyond anything she had ever known. Thankfully, the doctor was due at any time. He rode up from Ingleton every day and, though he said little, it was a comfort to know that he was keeping a watch over Will.

'You won't forget the newspapers, will you?' she asked Jake. They were now an extravagance, a luxury she could not afford, but she was prepared to make do with less food for herself in order to have something to read.

'They're on the list,' Jake reminded her. 'I won't forget.'

He hurried down to Jericho and caught the tram by the skin of his teeth. Elsie Drake was already aboard with her children, and he went and stood by her.

'How is he today?' she asked.

Jake shrugged.

'No better. No better at all! Worse, if anything.'

'Poor man! He can't go on like this, can he? It's not humanly possible. And poor Beth, too. It's a miracle the way she's coping.'

'It's with your help,' Jake said. 'I don't know what she'd do without it. All the same, I reckon she's near the end of her tether.'

He had watched Beth every day for the past week, reluctantly left her every morning to go to his work, hurried back at the end of the shift. He had seen her grow paler, the shadows under her eyes deepen. She moved around the house as if she was trapped inside a bad dream which was sapping her strength.

'I worry about her,' he said to Elsie.

He worried, too, about Will Seymour, and about Patrick, but most of the time about Beth.

Elsie looked up at him. It was not just his words, but the note of his voice, which startled her.

There's a man in love, she thought, if ever I saw one! But did he know it? And did Beth Seymour know it, or was her whole mind centred on Will? As well if neither of them did; it was not the time for complications, it was not the time for Jake Tempest to have to leave. Right now, and who knew for how long, Beth needed him. That much was certain.

The tram shuddered to a stop at Batty Green. Jake helped Elsie out with the children before they parted company.

'See you on the way back!' Elsie called.

'I'm walking!'

Batty Green was, as always on a Saturday, crowded. Jake pushed his way through the throng towards the newspaper seller, and from there to the stall where he hoped to find the boots he was looking for. Most Saturdays, he'd been told, a shoemaker from Settle set up shop on Batty Green, and did a good trade.

Sally Roland, standing behind Burgoyne & Cocks's stall and not at the moment serving, looked across, though quite at random and with no particular interest, towards the shoemaker's stall. She gasped at the sight of Jake standing there, looking intently at boots while waiting his turn. Her employer did not know it – he had thought she was being unusually obliging – but she had volunteered to work Saturdays on Batty Green in the hope that she might set eyes on Jake Tempest. She had not been able to get him out of her mind, which was unusual for her since her motto was 'love 'em and leave 'em'. He had presented a challenge which she would not ignore.

She turned to the other woman serving on the stall.

'Call of nature,' she said quickly. 'Be back in a minute!'

And it *was* a call of nature, she thought, as she picked her way towards Jake. Nothing had ever called more clearly to her than the nature of this lovely man. He looked even better than she'd remembered, which was unusual. She'd found the reality seldom lived up to the dream, but in his case it did. He was taller, his shoulders broader, his legs longer, his features more finely cut.

He didn't see her as she moved quickly towards him. She took him by surprise, thrusting her arm through his. He felt the softness and warmth of her even before he turned his head and found her blue eyes looking up into his, her red mouth curved in a smile.

'Surprise, surprise!'

She clung tightly to his arm and moved closer to him, so that there wasn't a hair's breadth between them.

'Good afternoon, Miss Roland,' Jake said.

'I hope you're pleased to see me!'

He wasn't especially pleased to see her, but neither, he realized to his surprise, was he entirely displeased. She was certainly the brightest thing he had set eyes on this past week. She wore a blue wool costume – the day was chilly – buttoned up to her throat, but still showing every curve of her body, and above its neckline a frilly white ruff framed her face. On her head, in accordance with a rule laid down by her employers for anyone who was serving or selling food, she wore a white mobcap with black ribbons. If it was meant to cover her hair, it failed. Her black curls sprang from underneath it, corkscrewing down her neck, falling over her broad, white forehead. She was a pleasant sight, Jake acknowledged.

'Miss Roland, is it?' she pouted. 'We're very formal today! And you haven't said you're pleased to see me!'

'Of course I am,' Jake said politely. 'You're looking very well.'

'Is that all?'

She knew she was being too forward, but she judged it was the only way with this man. He escaped too easily, and she didn't intend to let him escape again if she could help it.

'You look charming,' Jake said. It was no less than the truth.

'Then you can treat me to a cup of tea,' Sally said. 'One of the huts is serving tea. Did you know that?'

'No, I didn't. But I'm in a hurry. I have to get back. I also have to buy some boots. I'm sorry!'

She gave no sign that she was annoyed by his

coolness, and when he made a move to free himself, she clung to him more tightly than ever.

'Oh, it won't take but a minute! And I'm cold, and quite desperate for a hot cup of tea!'

She began to pull him gently, but with persistence, in the direction of the tea hut. 'I promise we won't be long,' she said.

The hut was presumably a family home on other days of the week, but now the main room had been almost cleared, and set up with a large table in the middle and one or two at the sides. It was quite busy, but they found a small table and Jake ordered tea.

'And a piece of gingerbread,' Sally begged. 'I just love gingerbread!'

When, without thinking, he laid his hand on the table, she covered it with her own. It was at this moment that Elsie Drake walked in with her brood, and they took their places at the centre table. The moment she sat down she saw Jake, hand-in-hand with a girl she knew she'd seen before somewhere.

Jake looked up, and felt himself redden at the sight of Elsie's frank stare, though she was not to know that it was annoyance, not guilt, which made him do so. He snatched his hand away from Sally's, and gulped down the rest of his tea.

'I'm sorry. I definitely must go. I have to get back.'

'Why the rush?' Sally asked. 'We could have a good time together.' She laid her hand on his sleeve.

Jake shook his head. The sight of Elsie Drake had brought Beth back into his mind. She was, he knew, worried and frightened, waiting for his return. He could have shaken this pretty little flirt by his side for keeping him even for five minutes, though in fairness, he reminded himself, she couldn't know the circumstances. He must have seemed as rude to her as she was irritating to him.

Nevertheless, he stood up.

'I'm sorry, I must go.'

He spoke to Elsie Drake as they passed her.

'I'm on my way back,' he told her.

'But Jake, I thought we were going to choose some boots for you?' Sally said in a clear voice.

He said nothing, but walked out of the hut, Sally following. He had not yet done Beth's shopping. He would have to walk back with Sally, since most of the things on the list were to be found on Burgoyne & Cocks's stall.

'I'll leave the boots for now,' he said. 'I don't have the time.'

'That's sensible,' Sally agreed. 'You'll do far better, coming to Settle for your boots. Eli Drummond only brings a small selection up here. *And* he charges more.'

'Settle's a long way on Shanks's pony,' Jake said. 'I'll take my luck here another time.'

'Oh, you don't need to walk it,' Sally said quickly. 'There's always some cart or other going in either direction. Or you could come back with me on a Saturday night, stay at my aunt's, and fit yourself up with boots on the Sunday. Eli would open up for you.'

Jake strode up the moorland track as fast as the slope and the weight of the shopping would allow him. He was annoyed that he had wasted time dallying with Sally Roland over tea when he had intended to hurry back to Beth. Nor had he bought his new boots, which he was going to need before long. It would be November next week, and here, on the high moor, the bad weather would come early. It would be boggy, even snow-covered, underfoot. The brightness had already gone from this late October day. Not many weeks now before he would be coming home from work in the dark.

He reached Nazareth. From a short distance away

he saw a man leave the Seymours' hut, mount his horse, then come towards him down the track. It could only be the doctor. He raised a hand to halt him.

'Excuse me stopping you, Doctor. I saw you leaving the Seymours' hut. I'm one of their lodgers, Jake Tempest. I wonder if you'll tell me how you find Mr Seymour? I'm very worried about him.'

'And with good reason,' Doctor Stokes said. 'Mr Seymour is a very sick man.' He didn't usually give bulletins to someone who wasn't close family, but this man seemed genuinely concerned. Also, Mrs Seymour had told him what a great help her lodger had been to her.

'I think the crisis must come tonight, or tomorrow,' he said. 'He can't go on much longer.'

'What can I do?' Jake asked.

'You can support Mrs Seymour,' the doctor said. 'She's going to need all the help she can get. She shouldn't be left alone at this stage. I haven't told her in so many words, and nor should you, but it's likely that her husband will die.'

'I'll be there,' Jake said. 'I won't leave her.'

'Good man. I'll be back tomorrow, then.'

When Jake went into the hut, Beth's face lit with relief at the sight of him.

'Oh Jake, I'm so glad to see you! Will . . .'

'I spoke with the doctor just now,' Jake interrupted. 'He told me. But at least—' He broke off. How could he say it? How could he say, as he almost had, that at least, if the doctor was right, by tomorrow Will could have turned the corner? They both knew that, just as easily, Will could have died.

They faced each other, saying nothing for fear of saying the wrong thing. It was Beth who spoke first, with words that were nothing to do with what was in her heart.

'Did you get everything?'

144

'Everything on your list.'

'And your boots? Did you get those?'

'No, I . . . didn't see what I wanted. I'll have to try next week.'

'I'm sorry. Did you see Elsie?'

'I travelled down with her.'

He would say nothing about seeing her in the tearoom, though he was aware that she might do so. Not that it mattered, it was easily explained, but now was not the time. He felt annoyed with himself that he should feel guilty, then put it out of his mind.

'I must go back to Will,' Beth said.

Jake nodded agreement.

'I'll look in on Patrick, and then I'll make a meal.'

Beth shook her head.

'Not for me. For you and Patrick – but I couldn't.'

Patrick was awake, and looked better than he had all week. He spoke hesitantly, but his words made sense.

'The doctor came to see me. Have I been badly then?'

'Since last Sunday,' Jake told him. 'You were in a fight. You were injured. Don't you remember?'

Patrick's face creased with the effort to do so.

'I don't remember a fight. What was it about?'

'That's what we'd like to know. Don't you recall being in the inn?'

Patrick scratched his head.

'Not at all, at all. Haven't I all these things in my head, and going round and round, or maybe they're just dreams. But nothing about a fight.'

'Well, don't worry about it now,' Jake said. 'It might come back to you later, but it's no matter if it doesn't. Just get well!'

'Oh, I will,' Patrick agreed. 'I am well. Just a bit tired for the moment. But is Beth all right? She came in with the doctor. She looked peaky.'

'Will is seriously ill with pneumonia. I'll tell you more later. Why don't you go to sleep now, and when you waken I'll have your tea ready.'

Patrick gave a deep sigh. He was tired again. He couldn't be bothered with all this. He closed his eyes, and was asleep almost before Jake reached the bedroom door.

For Beth, though the week through which she had just lived seemed like a year, the hours through which she sat at Will's bedside following the doctor's visit were an eternity. Time ceased to exist.

She was aware that from time to time Jake brought cups of tea, which she sipped briefly, then set aside; that when it was dark, he lit candles in the bedroom, two at the head of the bed and another on the table next to the sofa. For several stretches of time he sat with her, neither of them speaking, and at one point she was dimly aware that Elsie Drake came into the room, stayed a while, then left. But all these happenings were outside the world in which she was living.

That world was confined to herself and Will, to the small area of the bed in which he lay propped up against the pillows, and the sofa on which she sat, watching for any sign, hearing no sound but his breathing.

Not until afterwards did she realize that she had sat there for more than six hours, and that at some time after midnight – one of the few things which came through to her was the clock in the living-room striking twelve – she had fallen asleep.

It was three o'clock in the morning when she wakened with a start. She was aware at once that something was different, that something had happened. To begin with, the sound of Will's breathing no longer dominated the room. Also, the candles at the head of his bed had burned low. In her half-awake

146

state the two differences came together and made one. She gave a loud cry.

'He's dead! He's dead!'

She would have flung herself on his body had not Jake seized her from behind and led her, shrieking, from the bedroom. He was saying something, but she didn't want to hear it.

'Why didn't you waken me?' she cried. 'Why did you let me sleep? How *could* you?'

He turned her around to face him, held her by the shoulders and shook her.

'Beth! Beth, listen! Will is *not* dead! He passed through the crisis and now he's asleep. He's going to be all right! Do you understand?'

Beth stared at him for a second, and then his words sank in, and when they did she burst into tears, a flood, a torrent, her whole body shaking, all the hours and days of strain and fright pouring out of her.

Jake folded her in strong arms and held her close against him, stroking her back. Not thinking about it, hardly knowing what he was doing, except that he wanted to comfort her, he kissed her on the top of her head. Then he put a finger under her chin, raised her head – her face was wet with tears – and kissed her full on the mouth, hard and long. He was filled with desire for her; with his mind and his body, he wanted her.

She was compliant in his arms, so soft and yielding. Then she stirred, and he realized that she was returning his kiss with a passion which matched his own.

'Oh Beth!' he said. 'Oh Beth!'

Perhaps it was the sound of his voice which brought her to her senses. She pushed him violently away and stared up at him in shocked confusion.

He dropped his arms to his side, stepped back.

'I'm sorry! I'm sorry! Oh Beth, I meant only to comfort you!'

That was how it had started out, but not, for him, how it was now. Now he knew – and how had he not recognized it before? – that he was in love with her, with this woman whose husband had all but died, and who lay asleep, and still so ill, only a few feet away from them.

With an effort, Beth calmed herself, spoke quietly. 'It's all right, Jake. It was the heat of the moment for both of us, nothing more. We'll forget it.'

Oh no, Jake thought, I won't ever forget it! It had happened in the heat of the moment all right, but for him that moment was one of blinding truth. It would never leave him.

'I'm going back to Will,' Beth said. 'And you should go to bed now, get a few hours' sleep. Oh, Jake, how shall I ever thank you for all you've done for me?'

She reached up and kissed him gently, on the cheek; a kiss which a sister or a friend might have given.

Jake said nothing. He could not trust himself to speak.

'Good night, Jake,' Beth said. 'I must go to my husband.'

She went into the bedroom, and closed the door behind her. The sound of the door closing pierced Jake to the heart. It was a symbol of where he stood. She was where she belonged, and he was forever outside that door. He sat down at the table and buried his head in his hands. It was almost four in the morning and his life seemed as dark as the night outside. What would he do? How could he stay here, seeing her every day, watching her go through that bedroom door and close it behind her?

The windows were squares of daylight before he rose from the table and went to his bed, resolved on only one thing, that he would leave Nazareth. He would tell Beth before the new day was over, and he would tell her why. To declare his love, hopeless though it was, would be his one and only indulgence.

Doctor Stokes was at Nazareth early on Sunday morning. Beth, looking out of the window, saw him riding up the hill and rushed outside to greet him. He was as jubilant as she was at her news. He was also surprised. He had not expected to find Will Seymour alive, but that he would keep to himself.

'Then let's have a look at your good man!' he said, following Beth into the house.

'Yes,' he said when he had examined Will, 'yes, he has turned the corner. And you can take the credit, my dear. Your nursing has done more than I could ever have done.'

'I can't take all the credit,' Beth said. 'Not by any means. I couldn't have done it without the help Mrs Drake and Jake gave me.'

'That's as may be,' the doctor said. 'I grant you've been fortunate there, and I hope that's going to continue. Your husband has turned the corner, he's on the right road, but there's a long way to go yet. A slow recovery is best in the end, and that's what you must aim for. Don't let him rush at it.'

'Oh, I won't!' Beth promised.

'Good, nourishing food: calves' foot jelly, beef tea, gruel, broth. A glass of ruby port every midday wouldn't go amiss, as soon as he can take it.'

'I'll see he gets all that,' Beth said. Somehow she would.

'And in a day or two, when he's stronger, I shall want to take a look at his back. Has he complained much?'

'He's hardly spoken,' Beth said. 'He's been too ill to talk. But I can tell that it's been paining him. I see it in his face.'

'Well, we must see what can be done,' the doctor said. 'And now while I'm here I'll take a look at your lodger, see how he's getting on.'

He found Patrick awake, and lucid, though his speech was hesitant.

'I'd like to get up, Doctor,' he said.

'You can do so tomorrow,' Doctor Stokes said. 'But don't rush at things, take it easy.'

'When can I be going back to me work?' Patrick asked. 'I'm needing the money, so.'

'I don't doubt it,' the doctor agreed. 'You work in the tunnel, don't you?'

'That's right.'

'Then we'll consider it in another week. It's too soon to say.'

Elsie Drake arrived within minutes of the doctor's departure. She had hurried from Jericho full of apprehension. When she'd left Nazareth late last night she wouldn't have given a row of pins for Will Seymour's chances, but now the minute she came face-to-face with Beth, she knew everything was all right. It didn't need words to tell her. Beth's shining eyes did that. She opened her arms wide, and Beth rushed into them.

'Oh, Elsie. Isn't it wonderful!'

Elsie nodded. It was all she could do. There was a lump in her throat the size of a hen's egg, and it wouldn't let the words get out.

'Well,' she said when her voice returned, 'what he'll need now is a nice blanket bath, and his bedding and nightshirt changed. He'll have been in a right sweat. I'll give you a hand.'

Between them the two women did all that was necessary, but though they were as gentle as they could be, Will winced with pain when he was moved.

'I'm sorry, Will love,' Beth apologized.

He nodded his head briefly; he was too weak to talk.

'You'll feel all the better for it,' Elsie said, smoothing the last crease out of the counterpane. 'I daresay you'll fall into a good sleep now, a natural sleep.'

When Elsie had gone, Jake was left alone in the

living-room with Beth. Will had, as Elsie had forecast, fallen into a deep sleep.

'Please come and sit down, Beth,' Jake said. 'I have to talk to you.'

She was ready to sit down. She suddenly realized that she had had practically no sleep – nor, for that matter, had Jake.

'What is it Jake? I'm terribly tired.'

'I'm sorry. You must be.' Now that the time was here, he didn't know how to begin.

'What is it, Jake?'

He plunged in.

'I'm going to leave Nazareth.'

She stared at him, uncomprehending.

'Leave Nazareth?'

'I must, Beth! I have to.'

'But why? I don't understand. You've said nothing of this before. I thought you were happy.'

'I was.' But had he been? Hadn't there been this longing, undefined, unacknowledged, almost from the first?

'Then what? Is it the job? Is it the tunnel?'

'Oh Beth, it's none of that! Don't you know what I'm talking about? Don't you know that I'm in love with you? Surely you felt that, just a few hours ago? I thought then, just for a minute, that you felt the same way about me.'

She stared at him.

'But Jake, it wasn't like that! It was the relief of it all. Who else would I turn to but you? Not just because you were there, but because it was *you*. Whatever else happened was in the heat of the moment. You know that.'

'No!' he contradicted. 'For you it was, though I didn't think so at the time. For me it was real. I thought for the moment it was the same for you, but I was wrong.'

'It couldn't be, could it?' Beth said quietly. 'I'm a married woman. I love my husband. I thought he'd died, and suddenly he was alive again.'

'And I discovered I could love a married woman,' Jake said. 'And I know I'll go on loving you. So you see why I have to leave?'

Beth jumped to her feet, walked to the window, and looked out.

'I can't bear it!' she said.

Her voice was muffled, he could tell she was crying and he longed to go and comfort her, but it was impossible. He gripped the table, willing himself not to move, not to go near her.

She turned around and faced him.

'What will I do without you, Jake? Especially now. You're my best friend and I need you. I can't love you as I love Will, but I love you as a friend. I truly do. Won't that suffice?'

'You don't know what you're asking,' Jake said roughly.

'I think I do. And I'm still asking it, Jake. Please don't leave me! Not while Will is ill. I beg you!'

They looked at each other, long and hard, each searching the other's heart. Jake was the first to speak.

'Then I'll stay until Will is on his feet again.'

It had not occurred to either of them, and did not until much later, so that it was never part of either Beth's request or Jake's decision, that without him there would be no money at all coming into the house. What they had asked, and given, though painful to both of them, was too deep for that.

'Beth!'

It was a faint cry from the bedroom, the first time for several days that Will had had the strength to call out.

'I'm coming!' Beth cried.

A few minutes later Jake tapped at the bedroom door.

'I'm going for a walk,' he called softly.

He had to get out of the house. The room was full of emotion, it hung in the air, almost tangible. He had to have time and space to clear his thoughts. He had to be able to breathe.

Beth looked out of the bedroom window and watched him leave, his shoulders hunched, his hat pulled down, his coat collar turned up against the cold. He walked away with long strides; thankfully, Beth thought, not out of her life – or at least not yet. She could not have borne it.

# 9

Over the next two weeks Will's chest improved remarkably.

'It's no more than I'd expect, now that the worst is over,' Doctor Stokes told Beth. 'He's a strong young man. What we have to look out for now is his back.'

'It's giving him a lot of pain,' Beth admitted.

'He'll need rest. And massage would help. I don't suppose you know how to do that?'

'I've no experience,' Beth said. 'But perhaps if someone would show me . . .'

'You have to know what you're doing, but there's a woman living in Jericho who's gifted that way. If she'd give your husband one or two treatments, then perhaps you could learn something.'

'I'd certainly like to.'

There was more than one reason why Beth would prefer to do it herself. First and foremost, she wanted to help Will. She could not shake off the guilt which his condition aroused in her, reminding herself constantly that if she had not driven him into leaving the house on that night he would not be in his present pain. When he vented his ill-temper on her, when he grumbled, as he did much of the time now that he was getting better, she bit back the retort which sprang to her lips, stifled the resentment she too often felt, telling herself that it was no more than she deserved.

Also, by now she was desperately short of money. How could she afford to pay for treatment? During the first week of her husband's illness the wages clerk had brought what was owing to Will: a sum of three pounds, seven shillings and sixpence. There would be nothing more until Will could resume work. All she possessed was what remained of her meagre savings, and Jake's regular money. There was nothing yet from Patrick, and there was still the doctor's bill to come. She dreaded that.

Doctor Stokes, reading her thoughts, as he so often did on similar occasions with his patients, said: 'There's no point in me continuing to come, Mrs Seymour. Rest, and good food, is the quickest way to get your man back to work, though I can't say how soon that might be. In any case, November is a treacherous month. He mustn't venture out too soon.'

'I'll see he doesn't,' Beth promised. 'And you'll let me have your bill?'

'In due course,' the doctor said. 'In due course.' He would delay it as long as he was able. 'Your friend, Mrs Drake, will no doubt know the woman I mentioned.'

'I'll speak to her today,' Beth said. 'And what about Patrick Mahoney?'

'I'll take a look at him before I leave,' Doctor Stokes said.

Patrick was lying in his bed. He sat up quickly as the doctor came into the bedroom.

'So how are you?' Doctor Stokes asked.

'Sure, I am much better. 'Tis just my headaches. But I want to go back to work on Monday.'

Doctor Stokes was dubious. You could never be totally sure with a patient who'd suffered a head injury. It wasn't straightforward, you couldn't see into the head. He would have been happier if the Irishman hadn't worked in the tunnel. It was not the place for a man with his problems. However, there was nothing he could do about that.

'Very well,' he said reluctantly. 'But don't overdo it. And come to see me if need be.'

In the afternoon Elsie Drake came, as she still did most days, though sometimes now with her youngest child, Joe.

'You don't mind, do you?' she'd asked the first time she'd done this. 'The other three are all right, but it's not always easy to find somewhere to leave the baby.'

'Of course not!' Beth had told her. 'Anyway, he's a good little soul. I like having him here!'

Now, she held out her arms to Joe, who came readily to her. Beth held him close, enjoying the feel of the child in her arms, his softness and warmth, the sweet smell of his skin and hair.

'The doctor says Will needs massage,' she told Elsie. 'He says there's a woman in Jericho who does it.'

'That's right. Phoebe Grange. They say she's excellent. Not trained, but with a natural gift.'

'Do you think she'd charge much?'

Elsie looked up at the anxious note in Beth's voice.

'I don't know. I shouldn't think so. I expect you're finding things a bit difficult, aren't you?'

'Very difficult.' She hesitated. 'To tell you the truth, I don't know how much longer I can manage.'

It was a relief to tell someone. She couldn't bother Will with it; how the good food she was providing and the extras like the bottle of port she had managed to buy were eating away at the money. It would only make him worse-tempered. She was too proud to tell Jake, and there was no point in saying anything to Patrick. But Elsie was a friend. She couldn't help, but at least she would sympathize without spreading it around.

'I wish I could think of a way of earning some money, but I can't. There's nothing I can do,' she said. 'Or at any rate nothing that people want.'

'Oh, but you're wrong there!' Elsie said quickly. 'You can read. You talked about teaching the children to read. There's a skill not all that many folks have.'

Beth looked doubtful.

'It's true I intended to give it a try. It got pushed aside by Will's trouble. It was never my intention, though, to make money from it. I don't know that I'd like that.'

'Stuff and nonsense, Beth!' Elsie protested. 'Not that you'd make a fortune, of course, but I'm sure people would be only too pleased to pay what they could. I would, for one!'

Joe had grown suddenly heavy in Beth's arms as he fell asleep against her shoulder. She sat down in the nearest chair, easing the child's weight against her.

'Oh Elsie, how could I take money for teaching your children to read!' she said. 'Think of all you've done for me!'

'That's different,' Elsie said. 'That's no more than one neighbour helping another. You'd do the same for me!'

'But you *did* it!' Beth argued. 'Where would I have been without you?'

'Well, if you're going to teach my children to read then I'd want to pay my whack,' Elsie's mouth set in a stubborn line. 'For a start, it might cause awkwardness with others if I didn't. I reckon everyone has to be the same.'

'In fact,' Beth said, 'even aside from the money, I'd quite like to do it. It would give me something else to think about.'

Her days now consisted entirely of the demands of the household and of Will's and Patrick's illnesses. It was not that she was unsympathetic to either of them, but she would dearly like to turn her mind in another direction.

'Of course I'd have to see what Will thought,' she said. 'I doubt he'd like it.'

'Put the plain facts before him,' Elsie advised. 'Men

have their theories, and that's all very well, but sometimes they have to be made to look at the facts.'

Beth sighed. It had never been easy to make Will do anything he didn't want to do, and it was getting increasingly difficult, but Elsie was right. Somehow, though she didn't look forward to it, she'd have to make him face the situation, if only because things couldn't continue as they were.

'I'd best be off,' Elsie said. 'Think over what we've said. I'm sure you'd get half-a-dozen children, more if you wanted. For a start, Phoebe Grange has a couple who ought to be at school if there was anywhere for them to go.'

Beth watched Elsie set off down the path towards Jericho, then she went back into the house and closed the door. It was a chilly day, with a sneaky wind.

I *will* do it, she thought! I'll do it for the money, and I'll do it for myself! Moreover, she would tackle Will that very afternoon. There was nothing to be gained from putting it off, and in any case she'd like to have it settled before Jake came in from work.

When she looked in on Will he was asleep, though stirring a little, as if ready for waking. She returned to the living-room and prepared a tray of tea, and when she took it into the bedroom he was awake. He lay flatter now that his chest was so much better, but she saw his grimace of pain as he moved awkwardly in the bed.

'I've brought us both some tea,' she said. 'Can you manage with an ordinary cup, or would you like your feeding cup?'

'I don't want the feeder,' Will snapped. 'I'm tired of being treated like a baby.'

'I'm not treating you like a baby,' Beth said patiently. 'I just want to do what's most comfortable for you, Will love.'

'If that's what you want, then help me to sit up, so

158

I can drink like a man. And another thing, I'm sick of drinking tea! When am I going to get a glass of ale?'

Beth didn't answer. She was too busy trying to help him into a better position. He cried out in pain as she did so.

'Not like that, stupid!'

The words cut her like a whip, but she contained her anger, telling herself that it was the pain which made him like this.

'I'm sorry if I hurt you,' she said quietly. 'I'm doing my best.'

He grunted, then with Beth's help he eased himself onto his side, propped himself on one elbow, and with sharp impatience took the cup from her. He was filled with frustration and anger, careless of what he was doing, so that when he raised it to his lips he spilt half of it. The hot liquid soaked the sleeve of his nightshirt and slopped over his hand. He gave an angry cry.

'Now look what you've made me do!'

'I did not—'

She swallowed the rest of the sentence, fetched a towel and a clean nightshirt, and with great care helped him to change.

'Now you can lie down to ease your back, and I'm going to pour you some fresh tea into the feeding cup so that you can drink it in comfort. It doesn't matter how it looks because there's no-one but me here to see you.'

She sat beside him while he drank the tea.

'Doctor Stokes says it would do you a lot of good – for your back I mean – if you had some massage treatment. There's a woman in Jericho – Elsie knows her – who's apparently good at it.'

'And how can we afford to pay for such treatments?' Will asked. 'I'm not daft, so don't think I am. I know there's nothing coming in except for your fancy lodger, and I'm not having *him* paying for me!'

Beth took a deep breath. His attitude was exactly what she'd expected it to be, but she'd have to drum some sense into him. Finding the right words was not easy.

'What I want above everything, Will, is for you to be better—'

'Do you think I don't?' he interrupted. 'Do you think I enjoy being a useless lump?'

'Of course you don't. I know that. And if the doctor says massage might quicken your recovery, help your pain, then somehow or other you must have it.'

'So you can wave a magic wand, can you?' His voice was heavy with sarcasm.

'Not a magic wand,' Beth said. 'But I know a way I can make a bit of money.'

'So what is it?' He was all suspicion. 'I warn you, I'll not take charity from anyone, and I forbid you to borrow money.'

'I've no intention of doing either of those things.' Somehow she kept her voice calm and even, though inside she was shaking.

'You remember I had the idea of teaching some of the local children to read? I know I hadn't thought of doing it for money, but in fact I could. Oh, I know I wouldn't earn much, but it would make a difference, not only to pay for your treatment, but to help to keep us going. And the sooner you're better, the sooner you'll be back at work and earning your wages again. We'll be back to normal.'

She faltered. There was nothing more to say. And deep inside her she recognized, with great surprise, that to go back to what had been normal was not any more what she wanted. She wanted more, something extra, though she didn't know what, and in Will's present frame of mind it was certainly not to be mentioned.

Will's face was as dark as thunder, and in his eyes

she saw the hurt he was feeling. Why couldn't he understand that she wanted to help? Why did he make demands on her, yet feel diminished when she tried to do something?

'I don't like it,' he said presently.

'I know you don't, Will. I didn't expect you to. But admit that it makes sense. And what alternative is there?'

She waited. It seemed an age before he spoke, as if he had dismissed the whole thing, then he said: 'Have it your own way, then!'

It was a grudging permission, given without the slightest encouragement, but at least it was permission.

'Think on, only until I'm earning again,' he added. 'You'll stop it at once, then.'

Beth didn't answer. How did he think she could break off halfway through teaching the children to read, just to satisfy his pride? But she'd face that problem when it arose. In the meantime she'd move quickly, before he changed his mind.

'Then, first things first, I'll go down to Jericho tomorrow morning and see about your massage. The sooner the better. Then I must go to Batty Green to see Mr Tiplady about some books.'

It was Mr Crossland, the regular Missioner's stand-in, who had offered help with the project, but it would be only polite to ask through Mr Tiplady.

'And who's going to look after me while you're gallivanting here, there and everywhere?' Will grumbled. 'What happens to me when you're off teaching these children?'

'I promise you won't be neglected,' Beth assured him. 'For a start, I needn't go anywhere to teach the children. They can come here.'

'A houseful of noisy kids isn't going to help me to get better,' Will said.

Beth caught her breath. She wanted to shout at him,

161

to scream. He was clearly going to make her fight every inch of the way, but fight she would, and she'd win. She'd try not to show her frustration, and she certainly wouldn't give in. She was going to do this, she'd not go back on it.

'Well, it'll have to be one thing or the other,' she said reasonably. 'Either I go to them, or they come to me. But you can make the choice, Will. Whatever you say.'

She would rather by far go to the children. She longed to get out of the house. She admitted to herself, and was ashamed of the fact, that she would be glad to get away from Will for a few hours a day. Of course, he wouldn't let her. She could guess which choice he would make, and she'd have to abide by it.

'I can't start until I get some suitable books,' she said. 'So I must see Mr Tiplady as soon as I can.'

Will turned his head aside and closed his eyes. The subject was closed. I would have liked a glimmer of encouragement, Beth thought; just a glimmer. But since there was none to be had, she'd be thankful for the least possible discussion. Silence was preferable to grumbles.

'Do you want anything?' she asked Will.

His eyes remained closed, he didn't answer, though she knew he was awake.

'Then I'll make a start on the supper,' she said.

Jake would be home in less than an hour. The thought lightened her heart. Almost without noticing it happening – and she would not allow herself to acknowledge it for fear she might feel she must bring it to an end – his return from work had become for her the high point of each day.

She dreaded the day when he would leave, though it had not been mentioned again since he had declared his love for her. Why could they not be just the very best of friends? Special friends. She pushed away the question of what the situation did to Jake, so great was her need of him.

When he came into the house he brought something of the outside world with him, enlarging her world, which seemed otherwise to be bounded by two sick men. He would talk about the happenings of the day; it didn't matter that they were trivial rather than dramatic. His anecdotes about the men with whom he worked were such that she almost felt she knew them. Most of all, she never needed to look at Jake to judge what sort of a mood he was in, what his temper was. He was unfailingly pleased to see her, and she him.

She peeled onions, carrots, a turnip, and added them to the stock in the large pan. There was precious little meat in the stew. Yesterday the butcher's old horse had dragged a small cart up the hill, all the way from Ingleton to the huts, as it did twice a week, but she had only been able to afford a bit of scrag end and two pennyworth of bones. The butcher, though, had been generous with the bones. There was quite a bit of meat left on them, so it would be a tasty meal and, as well as seeing to Will, she would ensure that Jake got his share of what meat there was. After all, he was paying his way, and he did the hardest job of any of them.

But never mind, she thought, her spirits lifting, when she started to earn a bit from teaching the children, they'd celebrate with mutton chops!

When Jake came into the house Beth was standing at the stove with her back to him. He paused in the doorway, watching her. Though she was busy at her task, her head bent, her hands occupied, there was, as always, a stillness about her which never failed to attract him. It was not the stillness of inaction, but rather of an inner strength which had no need of fuss. She inhabited her own world with confidence. Seeing her, he had an almost overwhelming urge to put his arms around her, to turn her around to face him, to enter her world.

He had opened the door quietly, so that she had not heard him, but now the cold blast of air reached her and she turned around.

'Jake! You're home!'

There was a world of welcome in her voice and in her face. What wouldn't I give, Jake thought, to have the right to this welcome every day of my life; for the brightness of her face and the shine in her eyes to be exclusively mine?

'I'm sorry if I startled you,' he said.

'I was deep in thought.' She had been thinking of him, though she wouldn't tell him that. 'It's blowing cold, isn't it?'

Jake turned and closed the door.

'It's straight from the north, and nothing in the way to stop it. It wouldn't surprise me if we had snow! What sort of a day have you had?'

'The doctor came,' Beth said. She told him what Doctor Stokes had suggested about the massage treatment. 'So I'm going to look into it tomorrow morning. But there's also something else.' Eagerly, she told him about her plan to teach reading.

'You sound excited,' Jake said.

'Oh I am!' she admitted. 'And of course when I start to teach the children, I'll also start to teach you. I haven't forgotten my promise.' She was fearful of what Will would say about that, but she wouldn't be put off. She would do it.

Before Jake could answer, Patrick came in from the bedroom. He was fully dressed, his hair combed, and he looked more cheerful than Beth had seen him for a long time, more like his old self. Except – the thought struck her suddenly – that he had lost weight. She chided herself that she had not noticed this before. Almost all her concern had been for Will.

'My word, Patrick, you're looking better!' Jake said.

'Oh I am, I am!' Patrick said quickly. 'Hasn't the doctor given me the sack, and I'm going back to work on Monday morning!'

He felt better than he had at any time since the fight, about which, tease at his brain though he might, he could still remember nothing. But no matter, he was cured. Providing his headaches didn't come back he was as good as new.

'That's good news!' Jake said. He hoped he sounded more sure of it than he felt. At this moment the Irishman sounded fine, but in Jake's experience he could change his mood in an instant. Since the fight you never knew where you were with him.

'And there'll be a job for me to go back to,' Patrick said. 'Isn't that so?'

'Of course!' Jake replied.

In fact, during Patrick's absence he had been promoted into his job, and he had enjoyed the bricklaying, as well as earning more. Would he now have to go back to the labouring? But the tunnel was coming on fast, so perhaps there'd be bricklaying for both of them. He said nothing of this to Patrick.

'I'll have a wash,' he said to Beth, 'then I'll lend you a hand.'

He fetched soap and his towel and went outside. He still washed in the stream, though not for much longer, he thought now, as the icy water tingled on his skin. Winter was too close.

On the following morning, after Jake had left for work, Beth saw to Will, then said: 'I'd like to get down to Jericho as soon as I can to see Mrs Grange. If she'll agree to come, then the sooner the better. Will you be all right?'

'I'll have to be, won't I?' Will said. 'Too bad if I need anything!'

'Patrick's here,' Beth pointed out. 'I'm sure he'll see to you if need be.'

'I don't want that mad Irishman looking after me,' Will grumbled. 'For all we know he's not right in his head!'

'Oh, I'm sure he is,' Beth said. 'He's going back to work on Monday.'

It was the wrong thing to say. She realized that as soon as the words were out of her mouth, and the expression on Will's face confirmed it.

'I suppose you think I don't want to get back?' he said fiercely.

It was what he wanted most in the world, and not only for the money. There was no sense of purpose in his days now, lying here like a clod, afraid even to turn over for the pain it gave him. He missed his work-mates, longed for the easy banter that flew between them on the job, for the drinking in the inn when the day's work was over. He needed men's company, and Beth didn't seem to understand that. At the beginning of his illness, when he was too ill to benefit from it, his mates had walked up the hill to visit him. Now when he needed their company, no-one had been near him for more than a week.

'Do you think I enjoy lying here?' he persisted.

'I know you don't, Will,' Beth said. 'That's why I'm anxious to get Mrs Grange here as soon as ever I can. I'll be back as quickly as I can, and with any luck she might come with me.'

Beth called first at Elsie's hut. The baby was asleep in its wooden cradle which stood near the hearth. The three other children sat on the floor, mildly bickering among themselves.

'Sit down and I'll make a cup of tea,' Elsie said. She turned to the children. 'Either go and play in the bedroom, or shut up!' she ordered. 'I can't hear myself speak. I'm sorry,' she apologized to Beth. 'They get fast what to do, and it's too cold for them to be out on the moor.'

'I can't stay,' Beth said. 'I've left Will.'

'A cup of tea won't take a minute,' Elsie argued. 'The kettle's on the boil. So did you put it to Will about the reading lessons? What did he say?'

'He agreed,' Beth answered. 'Well, no, that's not quite true. He didn't agree. He didn't like it at all, but he said I could go ahead. But more urgent, he did agree to the massage, and it's my belief that once he feels a bit better, the easier he'll be to deal with. So if you'll tell me where Mrs Grange lives I'll go and have a word with her.'

'Drink your tea, then I'll walk across with you,' Elsie offered.

Phoebe Grange was not at all what Beth had expected. For no good reason – as she admitted to herself when she thought about it afterwards – she had expected, when her knock at the door was answered, to see a comfortable, motherly-looking sort of woman, a penny-plain lady with strong, capable hands dedicated to healing the sick. Mrs Grange was twopence-coloured and, from the top of her golden hair, which was rolled into at least a score of rag curlers, by way of her flowered sateen dressing-gown, to the thin soles of her pink, pom-pommed mules, as fancy as anything Beth had ever seen.

She stood with one slender hand on the door-knob, the other raised to her face, her long, delicate fingers resting against her smooth cheek. The fact that it was eleven o'clock in the morning and she was clearly not long out of bed took nothing away from her gaudy appearance. She was like an exotic butterfly.

She held the door no more than half open, but behind her Beth glimpsed two children. The younger, a girl of about six years, wore only a vest, which came halfway down her thighs. The boy, a year or two older, wore trousers, but no shirt.

Elsie spoke first.

'I hope we haven't come at an awkward time, Phoebe, but Doctor Stokes recommended you to Mrs Seymour here.'

'Then you'd better come in,' Phoebe Grange said. She turned to the children. 'Go and get dressed before you catch your deaths.' She yawned. 'We've only just got up,' she added unnecessarily.

'So Doctor Stokes recommended me, did he? Well, I *am* going up in the world! I get plenty of recommendations for one thing and another but not usually from the doctor! So it can't be what I think.' There was a glint in her eye as she looked at Beth. 'So what can I do for you? You look fit enough to me.'

'Oh, it's not me, it's my husband,' Beth said. She explained about Will. 'Perhaps if you could give him two or three treatments, then maybe I could learn to do it. You see, I'll be honest with you, I couldn't afford many.'

Mrs Grange raised her finely arched eyebrows.

'So you plan to learn my skills and take my customers, do you?'

'Oh no! Nothing's further from my mind,' Beth assured her. 'It's like I said—'

Mrs Grange's mouth curved into an enchanting smile, revealing a row of pearly-white teeth.

'Don't worry! I didn't mean it. I doubt you could do it, not unless you're a natural. Oh, you could learn the movements, but you have to have the gift. I have the gift. My mother had it, and her mother before her.'

She sounded supremely confident without being in the least boastful.

'Well, I'll see what I can do. Where do you live? Shall I come this afternoon?'

'That would be wonderful,' Beth said. 'I live in Nazareth.' She hesitated. 'You haven't told me how much you charge, Mrs Grange.'

'Call me Phoebe. It's more friendly. We'll talk about money later. First off, I'll need to see what I can do. I can't help everyone, you know.'

'What did she mean about recommendations not usually being from doctors?' Beth asked Elsie as they walked away.

Elsie laughed.

'She's the one some women go to when they find they're pregnant once too often. Me, I wouldn't touch that with a bargepole, and I don't suppose you would either!'

'It doesn't seem as though I'll ever need to,' Beth said bleakly. Sometimes she thought the world was peopled with women who had more babies than they wanted. She didn't understand why some cruel fate had decided that she, who had looked forward to and would have welcomed half-a-dozen children, should be barren.

When she told Will that Phoebe Grange was coming to give him a treatment that afternoon he frowned.

'I don't know that I want some old woman mauling me about,' he grumbled. 'What good can she do?'

Beth opened her mouth to put him right, then thought better of it. He had a surprise coming to him, but let him find out for himself.

At half-past two, without waiting for her knock to be answered, Phoebe Grange walked into the hut, entering like a summer breeze, cheering up the dull November day; a scented breeze at that, since she moved in a cloud of spicy, musky perfume. Without waiting to be asked she took off her cape, revealing a bright green blouse, lavishly trimmed with braid and fringing, which closely moulded her curving bosom and neat waist. When she removed her bonnet her

169

hair, elaborately coiffured, shone like gold. All those rag curlers, Beth thought, had not been in vain.

'To work,' Phoebe Grange said briskly. 'Take me to your husband!'

When she followed Beth into the bedroom Will's eyes opened wide. He clutched the sheet and pulled it up around his chin.

'So, Mr Seymour,' Phoebe said, standing by the bed, smiling down at him, 'I gather you're in a bit of pain?'

Will nodded. He opened his mouth to explain, but no sound came. Phoebe took hold of the sheet and without ceremony pulled it down as far as his knees.

'I'm going to roll you over onto your side,' she said. 'And we'll have to have your nightshirt off first, otherwise I can't get at you, can I?'

Beth stepped forward to give a hand.

'Can't you just roll it up?' Will's voice was no more than a whisper.

'We'd best have it off,' Phoebe said firmly. 'I need to find just where the trouble is or there's no point, is there? And don't be embarrassed, Mr Seymour. You're not the first man I've seen mother-naked, not by a long chalk.'

She ran practised fingers up and down the full length of his spine. His head was turned away from her but, standing by the other side of the bed, Beth saw the colour spread over his face and down his neck. Even his ears glowed red. Poor Will, she thought! She had never seen him embarrassed before. He had always made himself out to be a ladies' man, more so than she'd appreciated sometimes.

Phoebe bent over the bed, her expression intent, her fingers probing into Will's back until, suddenly, he gave an involuntary jerk and a loud cry.

'Ah! Good! Found it! There's the trouble!' Phoebe sounded as pleased as Punch at Will's yell of agony. 'Now we know where we are! No! Don't hold yourself stiff, Mr Seymour. I can do much more if you just let go; don't fight me.'

Beth turned away to hide a smile she couldn't quite suppress. Poor Will! At this moment he couldn't have fought a day-old kitten. She had never seen him so powerless, so subjugated to someone else's will, and a woman's at that.

She composed herself, and turned back again to watch what Phoebe Grange was doing.

'I think you'd be most use, Mrs Seymour, if you were to go and put the kettle on,' Phoebe said. 'I'll be finished in fifteen minutes and I'm sure we could all do with a cup of tea then.'

It was a clear dismissal. I'm not to be allowed to learn her secrets, Beth thought.

To the accompaniment, from the bedroom, of sharp cries and groans from Will and encouraging noises from Phoebe Grange, Beth set about preparing the tea. Patrick hurried in from his bedroom and stood open-mouthed.

'What in the name of all the saints is she doing to the poor man?' he demanded.

'Making him better,' she said. 'At least I hope so.'

'Then I'll be going out for a walk,' Patrick said. 'I would not like her to be starting on me!'

'Don't go too far,' Beth warned. 'It's cold.'

For fifteen minutes the sounds came from the bedroom, then gradually subsided. When all was quiet again Phoebe Grange came into the living-room.

'My word, I'm ready for that cup of tea!' she said. 'And so is your man. The poor fellow's quite exhausted! But men are such babies, aren't they?'

'I haven't looked after a sick man before,' Beth confessed. 'They seem so strong when they're well. At least Will does.'

'They're all alike,' Phoebe said dismissively. 'But we

wouldn't like to be without them, would we?' She winked at Beth.

'So what can I do for him?' Beth asked.

'Nothing really. You haven't the knowledge, so you could make matters worse, and you wouldn't want that, would you?'

'Of course not,' Beth agreed. But how am I going to pay her? she asked herself.

'I'll need to come every day for at least a week,' Phoebe said. 'And if it's the money you're worried about, then you can pay me a little bit at a time. I don't do it for the money, though God knows I need it, same as we all do, especially when we have kids.'

'There's something I might be able to help with where your children are concerned,' Beth said. 'I'm thinking of starting a reading class – reading *and* writing probably.' She explained what she had in mind. 'I'd have to charge,' she said. 'Especially while Will's not in work. But perhaps in your case we could do a deal.'

'Sounds all right to me,' Phoebe said. 'I don't hold with too much book learning, but the Lord knows I'd be glad to get my two from under my feet a bit. I've other fish to fry.'

'I have to wait until I get the books,' Beth said. 'Then we'll make arrangements.'

When Phoebe had left, Beth went in to Will.

'Are you feeling better? Did she do you good?' she asked.

'She half killed me!' Will moaned. 'I daresay my back's black-and-blue.'

'I'm sorry, love. But did she do you some good?'

'She might have,' he admitted. 'When's she coming again?'

'Tomorrow. And every day for a week.'

Will said nothing to that, but Beth reckoned his face brightened at the thought.

Next morning, to Will's annoyance, Beth went down to Batty Green to seek out the Missioner.

'You're never at home,' Will grumbled.

She said nothing. To answer back was to start another argument and she had no stomach for it. She had too much on her mind.

She found Mr Tiplady at home, and explained the situation to him, including the fact that until Will was earning again she would have to charge for the lessons.

'Mr Crossland said he felt sure the Bradford City Mission would help,' she said. 'I thought if *you* were to write to him it would be best – if you approve, that is.'

'I approve most heartily,' Mr Tiplady said. 'It will be a wonderful thing for the children, *and* for their parents. As I daresay you know, we'll be opening a school here in the spring, but of course that won't be much use to anyone as far away as Jericho and Nazareth. So you tell me what you'll need and I'll write to Mr Crossland today.'

'I need first readers,' Beth said. 'I could do with about nine if they're to have a book each. And I had thought I might try to teach them to write at the same time. I don't quite know how that would work out, and I'd need slates and slate pencils.'

'And a blackboard and easel,' Mr Tiplady said.

'I suppose so.' It sounded a great deal. 'I couldn't pay for these things all at once,' she said.

'We'll think about that later,' Mr Tiplady assured her. 'And the moment I hear from Mr Crossland I'll walk up and let you know.'

From Batty Green back to Nazareth Beth walked on air. In spite of the dullness of the day, of the wind in her face, never had the distance seemed so short, or the going so easy.

In the afternoon, and every afternoon for the rest of the week, Phoebe Grange came to treat Will, and

173

each day, though he complained to Beth after Phoebe had left at the torture she had put him through, he was a little better.

'We'll soon have you on your feet,' Phoebe said as she left Will on the Sunday afternoon.

On Monday morning Patrick went to work. Jake accompanied him, and Beth watched out of the window as the two men walked away over the moor towards the tunnel.

Things are looking up, she thought. Things are definitely looking up.

# 10

At the end of that first day of Patrick's return to work he and Jake were in the first cage up the shaft to the surface. Getting out, they stood for a moment with the others, greedily breathing in the fresh moorland air. It was what all the men did when they came up out of the tunnel, especially those who were not miners by trade, not used to working underground. But half-a-dozen deep breaths and they were restored, all except Patrick Mahoney, who continued to gulp in the air as if he could never get enough of it.

'So how did it go, your first day back?' Jake asked as the two of them set off to walk back to Nazareth.

Patrick shook his head, said nothing.

I don't need to ask, Jake thought. He was well aware that for Patrick it had not gone well. They had worked close together on the same side of the tunnel, each with their own labourer – to Jake's relief he had been kept on as a bricklayer – and to Jake, it had seemed an average sort of day, neither worse nor better than any other.

'First day back,' he said now. 'You'll soon get used to it again.'

It was not that Patrick had expressed his un-happiness in so many words, but he had been uncharacteristically silent, he who had the Irish gift of the gab, who always had something to say for himself.

'That I will not,' he replied. 'I will never get used to it again!'

How could he explain what the ring of the miners'

sledgehammers as they battered with such force against the hard rock did to his head? How could he describe, and to whom could he confess, the terror which swept through his body, so that his insides seemed turned to water, at the roar of the explosions in neighbouring parts of the tunnel where they were using gunpowder? And you never knew when the explosion was going to come. You waited for it, apprehensive, not knowing, and when it did come you wanted to throw yourself down on the ground and bury your head in your hands to shut out the noise.

You couldn't do that, of course. You had to keep the panic inside yourself. If you didn't, if you were the cause of spreading it, you'd be out on your ear. He hoped no-one had noticed him, though the foreman had never been far off, always on the prowl.

Jake had noticed. He had observed a number of things. When the other men had taken up a song, or whistled a tune, Patrick, though he was known to be a fine tenor, hadn't joined in. He hadn't laughed at the jokes which flew back and forth, though formerly he would have been the first to crack one. And after one of the explosions Jake had seen rivers of sweat running down his ashen face. He was also aware that these signs had not gone unnoticed by the foreman.

Deliberately, as they walked now down Blea Moor, picking their way around the bog, he changed the conversation, turning his head to where, on the right, the great mass of Whernside was silhouetted against the darkening sky.

'I never did climb the mountain,' he said. 'It was one of the first things I meant to do when I came here, and now I reckon it'll have to wait until the spring.'

The days were getting shorter. Already he was going to work in the dark, and soon night would fall before they came up from the tunnel. He would see daylight only at the weekend.

'I wouldn't mind going on the night shift before long,' he said to Patrick. 'I'd still be going to and from work in the dark, but at least there'd be a few hours of daylight to enjoy – when I wasn't sleeping.'

Patrick didn't answer. He hoped that Jake's shift wouldn't be changed, not unless his own was changed to match. If anything had kept him on an even keel today it had been the close proximity of Jake. Jake had looked after him with great care through his illness, and today he had realized that he still needed him. Not for ever, of course – he would pull himself together – but for now.

He seems a thousand miles away, Jake thought. They were almost at Nazareth now, and walked the rest of the way to the Seymours' hut in silence.

Entering, they met head-on with Phoebe Grange, who was on the point of leaving. She nodded briefly to Patrick, whom she had seen on a previous occasion, and turned her full attention to Jake, giving him the benefit of her charming smile.

'I haven't met this gentleman before,' she said to Beth. Not for one second would she have forgotten such an attractive man, even though at the moment he was in his working clothes and his face was liberally smudged with dirt.

'Mr Jake Tempest, Mrs Phoebe Grange,' Beth said. She deeply envied Phoebe's self-confidence. 'Mr Tempest lodges with us. Mrs Grange has been giving Will a treatment. She's just leaving.'

Phoebe held out her hand. Jake extended his, painfully aware that it was exceedingly grubby from his day's work, ashamed when he saw his dirty fingermarks on her gloves, to which she paid no heed at all.

He was totally unprepared, on a November day in Nazareth, for the sight of anything as exotic as this woman. With her fashionable clothes, her feathered and flowered tiny hat tipped forward on her golden curls, her voluptuous figure, she would have drawn immediate attention in Settle or Skipton, even in Bradford or up-to-date Leeds.

'I'm later than usual today,' Phoebe said. 'But ten minutes earlier and I'd have missed you.' Her eyes were on Jake. They told him she would have regretted that.

Beth broke in.

'So I'll see you tomorrow, Phoebe. I'm glad you're pleased with Will.'

Phoebe nodded.

'He's doing very well. As I promised, we'll have him up tomorrow. And by the way, I might be a little late again!'

Her parting smile included them all. When Beth had closed the door behind her she looked at the two men, who stood rooted to the spot.

'A sight for sore eyes!' Patrick said with awe.

Jake pulled himself together, grinned at Patrick.

'Well at least she's cheered you up,' he said.

'I must get on with my chores,' Beth said. 'I've no time to waste.'

Jake looked up at the edge in her voice.

'I'll give you a hand,' he said gently. 'I'll fetch the water first, then I'm yours to command.'

He always would be. No bird of bright plumage could compare to Beth Seymour.

When Jake and Patrick returned from work next day it was to find Will sitting in his armchair in the living-room, Phoebe Grange and Beth hovering around him.

'Well, this *is* a surprise!' Jake said. 'It's good to see you up. How do you feel?'

'I feel all right,' Will said. 'From now on I'll be up every day.'

He spoke defiantly because defiance was what he

felt. He was full of anger against the pain in his back. It thwarted him at every turn. He wanted to be fit and well, and back at his job, but almost every movement he made was a reminder that this was still a way off. Dressing – he had refused to sit in the living-room in his nightshirt – and walking through from the bedroom, even with the help of a woman on each side of him, had called for a major effort. He was as exhausted after it as if he had climbed Whernside. Now, the sight of Jake and the Irishman coming in from a day doing man's work, earning money, did nothing to soothe his feelings.

'You'll be up a bit each day only if you behave yourself!' Phoebe said. 'And I said a *bit*, not all day. And remember, you're to wait until I'm here to help you!'

The severity of her words was softened by her merry smile, and the pressure of her hand on his shoulder as she stood beside the chair. She was a woman-and-a-half, this one! She had done him good from the moment she'd first walked into the bedroom, dressed to the nines, even before she'd laid a finger on his body. And did she know, Will wondered, what her massage did to him, apart from easing the pain in his back? Did she guess at his feelings as her warm hands moved across his body with such delicate yet firm strokes? Did she know that she made him feel a man again, with a man's desires so strong that he wanted to pull her into the bed with him?

He suspected she did. There was something in her look, something in the occasional slap she gave him, ostensibly part of the treatment but really reproving him for what he had neither said nor done but only thought about. She could read a man's thoughts, he was sure of it.

But now, though she kept the pressure of her hand on his shoulder, she was smiling at Jake Tempest, who stood in the middle of the room, tall, strong and healthy, effortlessly dominating the space simply by his presence.

'I'll do whatever you tell me to, Phoebe,' Will said. 'Anything!'

'That's what I like to hear,' she said. 'And I think it's time you went back to bed. You've been up long enough. Mustn't overdo it on your first day! Perhaps you'll give a hand, Mr Tempest?'

'Certainly,' Jake agreed.

'My wife can do that,' Will objected. He wanted no favours from Jake Tempest.

'Of course I can,' Beth said.

'No need, Beth,' Phoebe said, 'since Mr Tempest is here. He's a big, strong man.' She looked directly at Jake, her voice and her eyes full of approval.

Between them they raised a reluctant Will to his feet and led him back to bed. If she *can* read a man's mind, Will thought, she'll know I'm not liking this. And what about Tempest, what was *he* thinking as Phoebe stood close by him, the two of them looking down on him as he lay helpless in bed?

'I'll be off now,' Phoebe said. 'I'll be back tomorrow afternoon.'

Was she speaking to him, Will asked himself, or to Jake Tempest?

Jake followed her out of the room; Beth saw her to the door.

'How do you think Will's doing?' Beth asked.

'He's doing well, I'm pleased with him,' Phoebe said, 'though he'll need a few more treatments before he's fit to go out, let alone return to his job.'

'I want him to have whatever he needs,' Beth said. 'But you still haven't told me what you charge.'

'Oh, don't worry about that at the moment,' Phoebe said. 'Didn't we agree you'd teach my kids to read. We'll see how it works out.'

Beth saw Phoebe out, watched her walk away, then turned back to Jake.

'Phoebe's so clever. There's nothing I can do for Will that she can't do better.'

'I wouldn't say that.'

He wanted to tell her that just by being herself she was a hundred times better than Phoebe Grange, attractive though that lady undoubtedly was, but it was yet another of the things he couldn't say to her. He recognized the kind of woman Phoebe Grange was. Once upon a time he would have fallen for it.

'Where's Patrick?' Beth asked.

'Gone to lie down. He has a headache.'

'Has it been a bad day?'

'No. Just average for work. But he doesn't seem to be settling in too well.'

Patrick had been as nervous as a cat all day, right from the moment at the start of the day when they'd gone down the shaft into the tunnel. The cage had swayed, which was not uncommon, they were used to it, but Patrick was clearly frightened. He clutched fiercely at the man standing next to him, all but knocking him off balance.

'What the hell do you think you're doing?' the man demanded.

'I didn't do nothing! You pushed into me!' Patrick said.

'You're a fool and a liar, Mahoney,' the man said.

'I did no such thing!'

Patrick put up his fists. There was a wild look in his eyes.

'No man calls me a liar and gets away with it!' he cried.

Jake had gripped Patrick by the arm and physically restrained him. Fighting while in the cage, or anywhere in the tunnel, was a sackable offence, and there was no shortage of witnesses to the fact that Patrick had started it.

'Calm down!' Jake said. 'Let it go!'

The cage reached the bottom of the shaft, and the man whom Patrick had threatened got out and walked away, saving the situation, though, it seemed, only for the moment. As he walked off he called out over his shoulder, 'I'll see you on top, Mahoney, when we come off the shift. Don't think I won't!'

Halfway through the morning Jake had gone along the tunnel to seek him out.

'Let it go, will you? You know Patrick Mahoney's not himself. He's been ill.'

'He's a menace,' the man said. 'He shouldn't be working in the tunnel. But I'm not spoiling for a fight. It's up to him, not me.'

The strange thing was that by dinnertime, when they ascended the shaft, the cage totally steady on this occasion, Patrick seemed to have forgotten all about the morning's incident. He faced the other man with a blank expression and apparently no remembrance of it.

'Is he going to be all right?' Beth asked anxiously.

'I wish I knew! Not if he goes on like this.' He would do all he could to protect Patrick. He liked him; there wasn't a nicer man alive when he was in his right mind, but there was only so much he could do. The rules were strict, perhaps more so in the tunnel and on the viaduct than on other parts of the line.

'At any rate, Will seems better,' he said to Beth.

'Oh, he is, thanks to Phoebe!' And better in health than in temper, Beth thought.

The next day two things happened.

The first was that, early in the afternoon, an official from the Company rode up from Batty Green to see Will. Beth opened the door to him.

'Mrs Seymour?'

'That's right.'

'My name's John Pennington. I'm from the Company. I've come to enquire about your husband, to see him, in fact.'

Beth's heart lurched. A *frisson* of fear went through her. Though his words were polite enough, there was something in the man's voice which told her that this was no ordinary social call. Moreover, it was one she had been expecting and dreading for a week or two now. She could guess what it was about.

'Please come in,' she said. 'Take a seat. My husband's in bed, he was just taking a nap. Can I help, Mr Pennington?'

John Pennington took a seat at the table, observing the worried look on the face of the young woman who sat down opposite him. This was a part of the job he did not like, but he had no option, it was one of the duties he was paid for.

Beth waited.

'Well, Mrs Seymour,' Pennington said, 'I've been asked to see your husband, to enquire how he is and, not to put too fine a point on it, when we may expect him to be back at work. So I'll need to speak to him; but before I ask you to wake him, perhaps you can put me in the picture.'

It was often easier to get a straight story from the wife. Nervous she might be, but she didn't try to pull the wool over one's eyes, to bluff him, as the man sometimes did. He'd not make a judgement, though, until he'd seen Seymour for himself.

'So how is your husband?' he enquired.

'Oh, he's much better in himself!' Beth spoke with all the cheerfulness and confidence she could muster. 'He's made a very good recovery from the pneumonia. It's just his back, now. You see, he injured it when he fell down the shakehole.'

'I see. And what does the doctor say? When did he last see him?'

'Oh, Doctor Stokes is very pleased with him! He doesn't need to see him much now. He recommended some massage, and Will's having that every day. It's doing a lot of good.'

'That must be costing a bit,' Mr Pennington said.

'I can manage it,' Beth said quickly. 'I have an arrangement with the lady who does it. Anything to get Will better as soon as possible. He can't wait to get back to work.'

'And the fact is, Mrs Seymour, we can't wait to have him back. At least, we can't wait much longer.'

'He's not being paid,' Beth said quickly.

'I know. It's not just that. There's also the question of this hut.'

'I've been paying the rent. At least . . .' She faltered. 'Until the last week or two. But I'll make up the arrears as soon as I can!'

'And it's not only that, Mrs Seymour,' Pennington said. 'You see, these huts are only for the occupation of someone working on the line. And if your husband isn't going to be fit to work . . . I'm sure you understand.'

'Oh, but he is!' Beth urged. 'Quite soon! He just needs a little longer!'

'It's a question of how much longer, Mrs Seymour. The Company's a reasonable and fair one – I'm sure you'll agree – but it's not a charitable institution.'

Beth flushed, tried not to show her anger.

'Mr Pennington, the last thing my husband has ever wanted is charity! He's a proud man and a hard worker, as I'm sure anyone will tell you.'

He nodded.

'I don't dispute that. The question is, will he be *able* to work, especially on the viaduct? And when? If it's not to be soon, then we'll need to replace him, and whoever takes his place will need somewhere to live. It's what the huts are for, and we don't have any spare for people not employed by the Company. That's the brutal truth, Mrs Seymour.'

However just it was, he hated what he was saying. He felt personally guilty for the deep anxiety in the woman's face.

'You realize I have two lodgers?' Beth said. 'They have to live somewhere, have to be looked after.'

Pennington nodded.

'I shall bear that in mind. But I don't have to tell you that it's not as difficult for a single man to get lodgings in some other hut, thus releasing this for a family. If it should come to that,' he added. 'If it comes to it.'

Silence fell. What else can I say, was the question in both their minds. John Pennington was the first to speak.

'And now, I'm afraid, I have to see your husband for myself.'

'Of course.'

Beth rose to go into the bedroom to Will, but at the same moment he called out.

'Who's there? Who is it?'

'I'm just coming,' Beth called back.

She turned to Mr Pennington.

'You've told me everything and I've taken note of it. I'll explain it all to Will later. Can I ask you not to upset him more than you need?'

'Of course.'

A minute later he stood beside Will's bed.

'So how are you, Mr Seymour? How are you getting on?'

'Very well,' Will said. 'Very well indeed! If you'd called later this afternoon you'd have seen me up, walking around.'

'Is that so?' Pennington turned to Beth.

'Oh yes, it is!' she confirmed. 'And he'll be up each day from now on.'

Pennington chatted with Will for a few minutes, then rose to his feet, made his farewells, and followed Beth back into the living-room.

'I've made up my mind, Mrs Seymour,' he said. 'Of course the final decision isn't up to me, it's for the Company to say, but what I shall suggest is that we do nothing until the end of the year. It's the middle of November now, so it allows a few weeks.'

'Thank you. Thank you very much.'

'And I hope your husband continues to improve.'

When he had left she sat down; she had to, her legs were trembling. What will we do if we lose our home? she asked herself. Where will we go? One thing was certain, in spite of what she had said to Mr Pennington she would not speak to Will of that possibility. He had no need of a spur to goad him into recovery. To get back to work was what he wanted most in the world. The question was, and she knew it had been in her heart long before Mr Pennington's visit, *would* he recover? Would Will ever again be fit enough to do his job? But it was a question she must keep locked inside her.

'Beth! What are you doing? Come here!'

Will's voice was firm and strong, and for once he sounded reasonably happy. Beth took a deep breath and went into the bedroom.

'Well, that was all right, wasn't it?' Will said. 'It was good of him to pay me a visit.'

'Very civil,' Beth said steadily.

'I reckon so. When is Phoebe coming?'

'She'll be another hour yet.'

'She does me a lot of good, you know.'

'I do know.'

What was more important than ever now was that Will should have as many treatments as he needed.

186

Somehow, somewhere, she would find the money. Could she, she wondered, confide in Phoebe Grange, tell her it was vital that Will should be cured, and soon? She didn't know Phoebe well, or how discreet she was. And did she herself wish to hear, if that was what Phoebe had to tell her, that a complete cure was impossible?

'Well, what about a cup of tea while we're waiting?' Beth was glad to have Will, with his mundane request, break in on her uneasy thoughts.

Fifteen minutes later when they were drinking the tea, there was another knock at the door.

'It'll be Phoebe!' Will sounded pleased.

'I don't think so, Will.' Phoebe would have walked straight in. She didn't stand on ceremony.

When Beth answered the door James Tiplady, the Missioner, stood there. His horse, the same strong Fell pony which had brought Patrick Mahoney back on that awful Saturday afternoon, was tethered near by.

'Good afternoon, Mrs Seymour,' he said pleasantly. 'May I come in? I've got something for you!'

He deposited the bundle he was carrying on the table, opened it up, and took out nine books, nine slates and a box of slate pencils.

'There!' he said proudly. 'How will *that* do? And don't think the blackboard and easel have been forgotten. I couldn't manage them on my old horse, but I've persuaded the fellow in charge of the tramway to bring them up. He'll deliver them to you tomorrow.'

Beth cried out with excitement.

'Oh, Mr Tiplady, this is wonderful!' She picked up a book and examined it. '*My First Reader*. It's *exactly* what I wanted! And illustrated, too!' Her face clouded. 'The only thing is,' she said hesitantly, 'that though I did ask for nine of everything, I'm no longer sure that

I can afford so many. Nor am I sure that I'll get nine pupils.'

'Oh, you'll have no difficulty in getting the pupils!' James Tiplady was full of confidence. 'And there's even less difficulty about paying. Everything you see here, plus the blackboard and easel, is a gift from the Bradford City Mission.'

Beth stared at him.

'I can't believe it!'

'Well it's true. According to Mr Crossland, the people at the Mission are most interested in what you're going to do. And I think you'll find if you have other needs for the job, they'll meet them.'

'But that's most tremendously generous,' Beth said.

James Tiplady nodded agreement.

'Yes. The people of Bradford *are* generous. And how is your husband?'

'He's improving, but it's slow work,' Beth replied. She had a sudden urge to tell him about Mr Pennington's visit, and the worries it had caused her. Perhaps he could do something? Perhaps he would put in a good word with the Company?

She decided against it. After the wonderful gift he had just brought her it was too much to ask for more, though if the worst came to the worst, she thought, Mr Tiplady was someone she could turn to.

'Shall I have a word with him?' James Tiplady asked.

She showed him into the bedroom. Will was civil to him, but no more. She felt ashamed of his lack of response to the Missioner's friendliness. She was relieved when Mr Tiplady left after ten minutes' one-sided conversation.

'Why did he come?' Will asked. 'Why did you ask him in? You know I'm not one for parsons.'

'As a matter of fact,' Beth said, 'he didn't come to see you. He came to see me. He brought me the reading books and the slates.'

188

'Oh, *that*! You're determined on that nonsense, aren't you?'

'I am,' Beth kept her voice steady. She would not let it be the subject of another argument.

'Well just remember, the day I'm back at work is the day you give it up!'

She was saved from replying by the sounds of the door opening, and Phoebe's quick step in the house. She stood in the bedroom doorway, radiant in yet another colourful outfit, blue and green with touches of red. She cheered up the drab day. Like a bird of paradise or a summer butterfly, Beth thought. Certainly she cheered up Will. For the first time that day a smile spread across his face.

'So, Will, are you ready for me?'

The bantering note in Phoebe's voice sparked off a reply from Will.

'I'm always ready for you!'

'Shall I give you a hand?' Beth offered.

'Ta, love,' Phoebe said, 'but I think we can manage, eh Will?'

'Then I'll leave you to it,' Beth said.

For the next half-hour grunts and groans, interspersed with laughter, came from the bedroom. Phoebe was still smiling when she came back into the living-room.

'You certainly do him good, and in more ways than one,' Beth said. 'It's the first time I've heard Will laugh in weeks.'

'Poor man! It's not easy to laugh in his situation,' Phoebe said.

'I know. He's desperate to get back to work. He's a frustrated man.'

'And I daresay you're just as desperate for him to do so?'

'As a matter of fact, yes,' Beth admitted. 'Though I wouldn't want him to overdo himself.'

She made a sudden decision, and as a result told Phoebe about Mr Pennington's visit. 'So when do you think . . . ?' she concluded.

Phoebe shook her head.

'I don't know. Not yet, love. When I do know I'll tell you. Now shall we go and get that husband of yours out of bed – though to my mind, if his back would let him, he'd sooner get the two of us *into* bed!' Phoebe laughed heartily at the thought. 'He's a frustrated man in that direction all right! I'll have to do something about it before he goes off pop!'

Beth blushed. Phoebe always spoke so openly, but though there was usually a *double entendre* in her words, there was also an honest vulgarity which robbed them of offence. More often, what she said left Beth feeling that if there was a fault it was her own, that she was a prude.

Once again, Phoebe was still there when Jake came in from work. This time he came alone.

'Why, Mr Tempest, fancy seeing you!' Phoebe said. 'We do keep running into each other, don't we? Now if you like I could give you a nice massage, take all the weariness of the day's work out of you!' Her tone was teasing, though with just enough undercurrent to make it clear that she was ready if he was.

'Thank you, Mrs Grange,' Jake said. 'Actually, I'm feeling fine.'

'Some other time,' she conceded. 'Or place!'

'Where's Patrick?' Beth broke in. 'Is he all right?'

'He's gone down to Batty Green.' Jake's tone was even, but the look on his face warned Beth not to ask any more questions.

Will picked up the look, not intended for him.

'If he's in trouble, he needn't come here. And if he comes back drunk, he'll not be let in!'

'Oh, I don't think you need worry,' Jake said. 'As it happens, when I've tidied up and had a quick bite,

I'm going down there myself. I'll meet up with him and see he's all right.'

You're worried about him, Beth thought. There's more to it than you're letting on. But she wouldn't ask, not while Will was in the room. Patrick was like a red rag to a bull to him. As for Jake, sometimes she thought Will hated him. She couldn't understand why. It hadn't been like that in the beginning.

'Now, Will, time you were back in bed!' Phoebe said.

Between them, the two women saw him back to his bed.

'You're certainly walking better today,' Phoebe said. 'We'll have you up longer tomorrow, walk you around the house a bit.'

Since Jake had gone to his room she did not linger, but as soon as she had left, Jake reappeared.

'Is there something more about Patrick?' Beth asked.

Jake hesitated, then said, 'He hasn't been himself all day. He's been behaving strangely, talking wildly. He's been picking quarrels with the other men, threats flying through the air from both sides. Now he's marched off to Batty Green in a nasty, pugnacious mood. I don't like it. I'm worried what might happen.'

'What will you do?'

'Go after him. He wouldn't hear of me going with him but he can't stop me following.'

'What about your supper? It'll be another half-hour.'

'I'd rather not wait. I'll take a sandwich, eat it on the way,' Jake said. 'It's dead certain Patrick will have gone to the alehouse, and if he has a drop too much, goodness knows what sort of trouble he'll get into! And if he's in a fight, and the foreman hears about it, he'll lose his job as sure as God made little apples. If that happens, he'll not get another anywhere on the line.'

'Patrick's a changed man,' Beth said unhappily. 'He was the mildest of men when he first came here.'

Jake, as he had expected, discovered Patrick in the alehouse. It was crowded to the door but there was no difficulty in finding him.

It was his voice which gave him away, his fine tenor voice singing 'The Minstrel Boy'. A small man sat beside him, accompanying him on the concertina, and a group of men stood around, listening.

'Thy songs were made for the brave and free, They shall never sound in slavery!'

There was a moment's silence when the song ended before the applause broke out.

'Give us another!' a man cried. 'Give us "Sally Gardens"!'

Patrick and the accordionist duly obliged, and then with another and another. The Irishman sang of his homeland, of its history, of its people. Jake, standing on the edge of the group, watched and listened in amazement. This was not the Patrick he had known today. There was no belligerence, no quarrel, no turmoil in this man. How could it happen, this lightning change of mood?

When Patrick finally stopped singing, the pints of ale lined up beside him, and beside the accordionist. Both men grinned with pleasure.

'Thirsty work!' Patrick acknowledged.

When he was drinking his third pint – in no time at all – Jake pushed through towards him.

'That was grand,' he said. 'I'm leaving now. It's getting late. Shall we walk back together?'

Whatever Patrick said, Jake decided, he would go along with. He would stay by his side. There was no way he was going to leave him here, drinking. It was a relief, therefore, when Patrick said, 'I'm ready!'

The November moon was all but hidden in the heavy mist. Lights in the huts around the Batty

Green area penetrated the damp darkness for a short distance, but once they had left the settlement behind it became difficult to see more than a yard or two ahead.

'We'll stick by the tram track. That's the safest way to avoid the shakeholes,' Jake said.

Carefully though they picked their way, there was no escaping the bog. Time after time one then the other sank ankle-deep into the mud, yet it was the same clay which, on a dry day, hardened to such an extent that the men working on it could break it only with a pickaxe.

'A hell of a climate,' Jake said.

' 'Tis indeed,' Patrick agreed. 'And I'm thinking I'll be leaving it for a better.'

'Leave?' Jake was astonished. 'But why? Where would you go?'

'Where else but back to Ireland?' Patrick said. 'As to why . . . I've come to it that I can't manage my life here. I can't think straight for long. At this minute, sure, I'm fine, but the devil gets into me before I know it. It's not me, you know. 'Tis the devil himself. There's no holding him!'

'You'll improve,' Jake assured him. 'You'll get better.'

Patrick shook his head.

'The devil is powerful here. I'd be safer from him back in Ireland with my own folk. I have a mother and sisters in Cork. Did I ever tell you that? They'd look after me.'

Perhaps he was right, Jake thought. It was too hard a life, working in the tunnel, for all but the strongest.

'When would you go?' he asked.

'One day soon. A day when God seemed on my side, when He would walk with me.'

'I would miss you,' Jake said.

They were almost at Nazareth now. The small shanty

town was dark as they walked into it, the only light was that which shone ahead of them from the Seymours' hut.

When Jake had left, Beth made the meal and took Will's plate into the bedroom.

'This is the last time I have my supper in bed,' Will said. 'From now on I'll be up for it, see if I'm not!'

'Good!' Beth said. 'I hope you will be.'

'Phoebe's doing me the world of good,' he said. 'She's a remarkable woman, that one.'

'She certainly is,' Beth agreed. 'Now you eat your supper before it goes cold, and I'll go and get mine.'

What she longed for most of all at this moment was an hour's peace and quiet. The day had seemed one long bustle, one happening after another. She was eager to look at the readers Mr Tiplady had brought, which she'd not had time to examine in any detail. She wanted to work out her plan of campaign, decide which parents she might approach, and how she would set about teaching the children.

Book in one hand, she ate her meal, hardly tasting her food. When she had finished eating she began to make notes. There was so much to think about, to decide. Seldom had an evening passed so quickly.

Immersed in what she was doing, she didn't at first hear Will call out. It was the demanding note in his voice which told her that he'd done so more than once.

'I'm coming!' she called. Reluctantly, she put down her notes and went into the bedroom.

She could hardly believe the sight of Will. He was a stranger, sitting up in bed, his face flushed, his eyes glittering, for all the world as if he had a fever.

'What ever is it, Will?' she asked. 'What's wrong?'

'Come to bed!' His voice was hoarse. 'Come to bed at once.'

'To bed? Why, is it late? The men aren't back.' She wanted to be there when they returned. She wanted to know about Patrick.

'Damn the men!' Will shouted. 'It's me you're married to. I'm ordering you to come to bed!'

'Very well,' Beth said quietly. 'If it's what you want.' She didn't understand his mood, but clearly she must try to placate him.

She crossed the room and began to make up her bed on the sofa.

'Not there!' Will shouted. 'You've slept on the bloody sofa for the last time. You're my wife and I'm your husband and you'll sleep in my bed or I'll know the reason why.'

A chill fear crept into Beth, but she would not show it. 'But you *do* know the reason why,' she spoke as calmly as she could. 'I sleep on the sofa because of your back. I don't want to do anything to hurt you.'

'I'll decide that,' he said. 'I'll show you what hurt is,' Will said. 'You've never known that, have you, but by God you will!'

Ice-cold waves ran down her body. She stood rooted.

'Come here!' Will commanded. His voice was hoarse and angry. There were round, crimson spots of colour on his cheekbones.

This is a nightmare, Beth thought. It's not real. She felt sapped of strength, unable to do anything of her own accord. With halting steps she approached the bed and when she was within arm's length he leaned forward and jerked her towards him.

'No!' she cried. 'No, Will! What are you doing?'

He had finished with words. As he grasped her she felt his breath hot on her face, rasping in her ears. He fumbled with the top button of her blouse, but when it wouldn't yield to his clumsy fingers he took hold of the material with impatient hands and tore the garment from her as if it had been no more than tissue paper. She was astonished at the strength in him.

He pulled her further onto the bed, pushed her on her back and pinned her there. Then he lifted her skirt, tore off her undergarments and came down on top of her.

It was when the searing pain and the deep, deep humiliation of what he was doing to her became more than her flesh and spirit could stand, that the whole world blotted out in a merciful blackness.

When it was all over, and he lay asleep and still, as if he was unaware of what had happened, she crept out of the bed. She tasted the blood on her lips, where he had bitten through the skin, and felt it trickling down her chin. Her body was an enormous, throbbing bruise.

She staggered into the living-room. All she knew, and the need consumed her, was that she must wash herself. She must scrub herself from head to foot. No matter how much it might hurt. She must scrub away the deep disgust.

Not seeing clearly, she tripped, and fell to the floor. She did so at the same moment as Jake, followed by Patrick Mahoney, came into the house. She lay there before him, unable to move, looking up at him like a frightened animal.

# 11

For a second, Jake stared at Beth in horror and disbelief, then he dropped to his knees beside her, enfolded her in his arms and held her close.

'My darling! My darling! What is it? What's happened?'

No words came from Beth. She gave a small whimper, like a frightened child seeking comfort, and finding it in his arms. She could think no further than to stay there for ever. Jake, sensing her deepest need, continued to hold her against him, murmuring endearments.

'You're safe now,' he said gently. 'I'm here. Hush now!'

But as he continued to hold her, as she looked up at him, he saw more clearly the state of her; her bleeding lips, a bruise on her neck, and another, red and purple against the white skin of her breast; her clothes torn from neck to hem. There was no doubt in his mind as to what it was she had suffered.

Anger flooded him, anger so fierce, so strong, that his body trembled with it. How could this have happened? Had someone broken into the hut and attacked her? But as fast as that idea came into his mind, he dismissed it. It wasn't so. In a way, it would have been preferable to know that the act had been perpetrated by a frenzied stranger. As it was . . .

'Who did this to you, Beth?'

He tried to keep his voice calm, not to alarm her further, but Beth heard the anger in it, felt the trembling in his body. She didn't answer him. In the silence while Jake waited for her reply they could hear Will's deep snores from the bedroom.

'It was him. It was Will, wasn't it?'

Beth nodded.

Beside himself, Jake gripped her hard.

'I'll kill him!' he said. 'I'll beat him to a pulp and then I'll kill him!'

His voice went into Beth like a steel blade. She pulled herself away from him.

'No!' she protested. 'No! I can't bear any more! Please don't do anything, Jake. Go to bed. Leave me.'

'How can I?' Jake demanded. 'How can I leave you like this?'

'You must,' Beth begged. 'It will be worse for me if you don't, if he finds you and Patrick here.'

He had forgotten that Patrick was there. The Irishman had stood by silently, saying nothing.

'Please!' Beth implored.

Jake considered for a moment. It went against his every instinct to leave her like this, but perhaps she was right – and it was her choice.

'Very well,' he said reluctantly. 'I'll do so, but only because you ask it. It's not what I want to do, and I'm not sure it's right. In any case, I must bathe your face first.'

Without being asked, and without a word, Patrick fetched a basin of water and a cloth. Gently, with the utmost tenderness, Jake bathed Beth's face, and the bruises on her neck and chest. Only by the greatest effort did he contain his anger as he did so. And when Beth winced with pain at the cold water on the sore places, the pain shot through him also.

It was not until the bathing was over that Beth realized to what extent her clothes were torn and how immodestly she was exposed to the two men. Hastily she tried to pull the two halves of her blouse over her breasts. Without a word, Jake fetched her cloak from its hook by the door, and wrapped it around her.

'You must keep warm,' he said, as if that was the only purpose of the cloak.

'Thank you,' Beth said. 'Please go now. Please leave me.'

'Promise me you won't go back into that bedroom,' Jake said.

Beth shuddered.

'I can promise that.'

'And you'll call me if you want me? I'll leave my door open.'

'I will.'

He kissed her gently on the forehead, then left her, Patrick preceding him into their bedroom.

When the men had gone, Beth sat for several minutes wrapped in her cloak, her head leaning back against the chair. She was weary beyond belief, unutterably tired, but then, rising above the weariness, the strong, irresistible desire to wash herself, to cleanse herself thoroughly from top to toe, rose in her. There could not be even the beginnings of sleep, for which she longed, until she had done that.

She stirred the fire into life, then fetched clean water and put the bowl on the table. She would have liked to have plunged into the fast-running waters of the beck where it was deepest, or failing that to have filled the tin bath, but the first was impossible, and as for the bath, she had neither strength enough to carry it in from where it hung on its nail outside, nor water enough to fill it. The bowl would have to do.

She took off her cloak and the rest of her clothes, then systematically she washed every inch of her body, lathering the flannel well with the red carbolic soap.

When she came to the washing of the most private parts of her body, the secret places which until tonight she had yielded to Will in such love, and which now she never would again as long as she lived, she held her breath against crying out with the stinging pain of it. Yet the very act of washing, of using the strong, coarse soap, cleansed her in more than a physical way. The greater the pain, she told herself, the more I am cleansed. For it was not sexual love, or an excess of it, or anything at all to do with love, which had happened to her. It was violence. She was washing away violence.

When it was done she dressed herself in clean clothes which she had ironed that afternoon and left on the clothes-horse to air. Then she put on her cloak, picked up the bowl of water from the table, and went out of the hut. There she flung the tin bowl and its contents as far as it would go. Never again would she have it in her house. The bowl bounced against an outcrop of stone, the sound reverberating in the still night.

Back in the hut she picked up, with the firetongs, the garments she had been wearing earlier, and fed them to the fire. When they had been reduced to blackened shreds she took the poker and beat the shreds into ashes.

That done, and the last vestige of her torn and stained garments destroyed, she wrapped her cloak further around her, sat down in the armchair, and prepared for sleep. She turned the lamp low, but did not put it out. She knew that, for the moment, she couldn't bear to be in the dark.

Weary though she was, sleep was slow to come. She tried to pray, but the familiar prayers she normally said – thanks for the day past, hope of blessings for the day to come – she could not bring herself to utter. Where had God been when she needed Him? There were too many questions in her head.

'What shall I do?' she asked herself. 'What shall I do when tomorrow comes? How shall I live?'

In the men's bedroom Patrick and Jake prepared for bed quietly. It was a time when, usually, they talked, but what was on their minds now was not for discussion.

'Do you think anything will happen?' Patrick ventured anxiously. 'Do you want me to stay awake? I can, you know.' He was yawning heavily.

'No,' Jake said. 'You get your sleep. If I'm needed I'll waken all right.' He had, in fact, no intention of falling asleep until he was sure Beth was settled.

Though she moved quietly, he heard the sounds as she washed herself. Then when he heard the outer door open he was startled, and jumped out of bed to go after her, but was relieved to hear her come in again before he could do so. With his whole heart he longed to go in to her, to take her in his arms and comfort her.

When he wakened in the morning his first feeling was one of guilt that he should have slept at all. Quickly, he went into the living-room.

Beth was asleep, fallen sideways in the armchair, her head on a cushion. She was pale. Her eyelids were swollen and there were dark circles beneath her eyes. Her lips, though no longer bleeding, were still bruised and swollen. Looking down at her as she slept, he knew he had never loved her more; also that there was little he could do to help her. He went back to his bedroom, where Patrick was stirring.

'She's asleep,' he said. 'You get off to work. I'll stay until she wakens. No use two of us being absent.'

But when he had dressed, and went back into the living-room, Beth was awake.

'I'll stay with you,' he offered. 'I'd like to.'

'No,' Beth said. 'I'd rather you went to work. I have to face Will and it will be better if I do it alone.'

'But what if . . .'

'I'll be quite safe,' Beth interrupted. 'He wouldn't touch me. If he tried I would run out of the house, go to Elsie. He can't run after me.'

'You promise?'

'I promise.'

'When I get home from work,' Jake said, 'I want to talk to you.'

Jake and Patrick had not been gone long when Will called from the bedroom.

'Beth! Beth, come here!'

She was washing the breakfast dishes. Slowly, she straightened up, took a towel and dried her hands, meticulously attending to each finger in order to prolong the act. She didn't know how to face him.

'Beth! Beth!'

There was no escape. She put down the towel and walked slowly to the bedroom, standing in the doorway, not wanting to set foot inside the room.

Will was sitting up in bed. He looked at her, then stared at her. She knew what he was seeing, she had seen it in the mirror. He was seeing the swollen mouth, the bruises, the deadness of her eyes. She continued to stand there, not speaking, observing the red tide creep up his face, seeing the mounting horror in his eyes as he saw what he had done.

'I'll get your breakfast,' Beth said, turning away. The words came awkwardly because of the stiffness of her mouth.

'No, Beth! No! Come here!'

Without answering, she left the bedroom and began to lay his breakfast tray. When she took it in to him and placed it on his bedside table he stretched out a hand to touch her. She stepped back quickly, out of his reach.

'Beth, I'm sorry! I'm sorry! What else can I say?'

She felt no emotion as she saw the tears spring in his eyes.

'What can I say?' he repeated. 'Beth, please say you forgive me!'

'Don't say anything.' She was amazed at the flat calm of her voice. 'There's nothing to be said. And don't ask me to forgive you. It's not possible.'

'Please, Beth,' he pleaded. 'I don't know how it happened. It'll never happen again. Can't we make a fresh start?'

'Yes,' Beth said. 'We must make a fresh start, that's for sure. But don't expect it ever to be the same. It won't be. I'll look after you. I'll make your meals and keep your house. But I will never share your bed again. Never!'

'Beth! Don't be hard on me! I didn't mean it!'

'But *I* mean this. I mean every word of it. If you so much as lay a finger on me I shall go to the police. Now please get on with your breakfast. I want to clear away. I have things to do.'

She fought back the tears until she was in the living-room, but then she could do so no longer. Sitting at the table, she buried her head in her hands and let them flow.

How can I go on? she asked herself. Day by day to the end of my life? Yet what else could she do, where else could she go? What alternative had any woman to a bad marriage unless she was rich, and therefore independent? But there must be a way, there must be something. There must be someone who could advise her.

She thought of Mr Tiplady. He was a minister of God, wasn't he? There to help people. He would listen to her, treat her kindly. But in the end, she thought, he would remind me of my marriage vows, 'for better or for worse'. Well, she didn't need to be reminded.

She dried her eyes. That's it, she thought. The crying is over. I have to go on. The mainspring of her life, her marriage, was broken beyond repair, but there were other things, even in her small world, and she would concentrate on those.

The sight of the children's readers, still piled on the table, gave her the first ray of hope. The sooner she started on that job, the better. She would begin by going down this very morning to see Elsie.

And then she remembered the state of her face. How could she let herself be seen by anyone, looking the way she did? How could she explain it? For she had no intention of telling the truth. She was too deeply ashamed, even though common sense told her the shame was not hers. It couldn't be helped that Jake and Patrick knew, but she could trust them to tell no-one, nor would she allow them ever to speak of it to her.

Any idea that she may have had of not showing herself until her face was healed came to nothing half an hour later when there was a knock at the door and Elsie Drake walked in, carrying the baby, and with the three other children at her heels.

'It's freezing cold out there!' she said, closing the door firmly behind her. 'If it doesn't snow before the day's out my name's not Elsie Drake! I reckon we—'

She stopped short, catching sight of Beth's face.

'Why, what in the world . . . ?'

'I tripped over the rug and fell against the corner of the table,' Beth said quickly. 'So clumsy of me!'

Elsie continued to stare at her. It didn't ring true. How could falling against the table give her that mouth, and the bruise on her neck? Also, she was ghastly pale.

'Fell against the table?'

'That's right.'

Beth's look was defiant. It was plain that Elsie didn't believe her, but it was all she was going to get.

Elsie read the look. It said, 'Ask me no questions

and you'll get no lies!' Even though she'd just told a whopper.

'Well, I never!' she said. 'Now, a bit of zinc ointment's what you need. I use zinc ointment for just about everything from a sore finger to a broken leg.'

'I don't have any,' Beth said. 'I'll get some next time I go down to Batty Green – if I'm not completely better before then.'

'Which brings me to what I came for,' Elsie said. 'I wondered if you'd mind the children while *I* went down to Batty Green. There's a few things I need – and I'll bring you some zinc ointment, or anything else you want. I don't want to take the children in case it starts snowing.'

'I'd be glad to look after them,' Beth said. 'You know that.'

Elsie Drake looked at Beth closely.

'Are you sure you're all right? You look washed out.'

'Quite all right, thank you, Elsie. I'm a bit tired. I didn't sleep well, that's all.'

'Well it takes it out of you, not sleeping. Don't I know it with four kids!' If that was Beth's story, she'd let her stick with it, but when did falling over a rug give that look in the eyes?

'I wanted to see you,' Beth said. 'The reading books have arrived for the children. I reckon I'll be ready to start on Monday, if I can get the children together.'

'You can have my three any day,' Elsie said. 'And I reckon the same will go for Phoebe's.'

Phoebe! I'd totally forgotten Phoebe, Beth thought, and she'll be here this afternoon. She'd managed to deceive Elsie about her appearance, or at least to stop her asking further questions, but would she be able to do the same with Phoebe? Phoebe Grange was a woman of the world; candid, outspoken, pulled no punches. And if Phoebe guessed the truth, how far would she spread it?

'I reckon Mrs Parker would let her two come,' Elsie said, breaking into Beth's thoughts. 'That would be seven to start with – and a lucky number at that!'

'I think I could manage seven,' Beth said. 'And we'll have to decide just where I'll teach the children: here, or in one of your houses. With winter almost on us we have to think of the weather.'

She would like, very much indeed, to be able to hold the classes in some house other than her own, for the simple reason that it would take her away from Will for a spell. Will, though, was the reason why that would be difficult to do. He was still unable to get around without help, so how could she leave him for even a few hours each day?

'I've brought a bottle for the baby in case he gets fractious, though I don't suppose he will,' Elsie said.

Beth held out her arms.

'Give him to me then. I'm sure he'll be no trouble at all.'

The feel of the baby in her arms, held close against her breast, was balm to Beth's spirit.

'I'll be off then,' Elsie said. 'I'll try not to be long.'

'No need to hurry,' Beth assured her. She was glad of the children's company. Apart from welcoming them for their own sakes, they would be an effective barrier between herself and Will.

When he heard the door close behind Elsie Drake, Will called out again.

'Beth! Beth!'

Beth went reluctantly, standing in the doorway with the baby in her arms. She looked at Will without speaking.

'What's happening?' he asked.

'I'm looking after Elsie's children while she goes to Batty Green.'

He looked a sorry sight. He had not had a wash and he needed a shave. The bed was unmade, in the same state as when she had run away from it last night. She knew she should do something about these things, it was her duty, but she could not. She couldn't bear to go near him, let alone to touch his flesh with hers. She was aware that a little later Phoebe would arrive and she would not expect to see Will in his present state, but there was nothing she could bring herself to do about it.

The baby fell asleep, growing suddenly heavy in Beth's arms. She left the bedroom and laid the child on the armchair, blocking him in with another chair so that he couldn't roll off.

'Now you three,' she said to the other children, 'come and sit to the table. I have something to show you.'

She gave them each a slate, a slate pencil and a reader, then found the place for them in the books and pointed to the picture.

'What's that?'

They all knew the answer.

'A cat!' they said in unison.

'And you see that, underneath the picture. A word. What does *that* say?'

Only Emily could answer.

'It says "cat", Mrs Seymour.'

'Indeed it does. Did you know, or did you guess?'

'I guessed,' Emily admitted.

'Then you guessed well. It's always worth while having a guess.'

It was terrible, Beth thought, that at eight years old Emily could only guess at the word. But I shall change all that, she told herself – and the thought gave her the first lift of the day.

'Well now, I want you to do something you'll be able to show your mother when she gets back from Batty

Green. I want you each to draw a cat on your slate. You can copy the picture in the book, or you can draw any cat you like.'

It was clearly seven-year-old Tom who had the artistic talent. He drew a large, fearsome-looking cat with long whiskers while Emily and Ada painstakingly copied the cat from the book.

'Very good,' Beth said when they had finished. 'Now, can any of you write words?'

'No, Mrs Seymour,' they chorused.

'Well, you're going to,' Beth said. 'Look at the book and just draw the word "cat" under your picture. Watch me first.'

On a slate of her own she showed them, carefully forming each letter in turn. Again, Tom got the hang of it quickly but the girls' efforts were less sure.

'That's splendid,' Beth said. 'You've all written and read your first word. Now, if you turn your slates over to the other side we'll do something even better. I want you to draw a picture of yourself. If you like you can go and look in the mirror, and then draw what you see.'

'I can't do it,' Ada said.

'Then I'll help you. Bring your slate and stand by me and I'll draw you. Let's see . . . you have a round face, long, curly hair with a ribbon bow, and big eyes. A beautiful blue, but I can't put the colour in with a slate pencil.'

And I am no portrait artist, Beth thought as she drew on Ada's slate. But Ada seemed satisfied.

'Now *you* can draw in your dress,' Beth said. 'It's got stripes so that's easy.'

The drawing of the self-portraits took a long time, and much squeaking of slate pencils, which set Beth's teeth on edge.

'Now this is the exciting bit,' she said. 'I'm going to show you how to write your own name. Copy what I do on my slate and put it under the picture on yours. And be thankful your mother gave you all short names!'

The time flew by. Tom, carried away, wrote his name several times, all around his portrait.

'That's very good,' Beth said. 'They're all very good. Another day I'll show you how to write your last names. People who can't write their names have to put a cross, but you'll be able to sign your own names for the rest of your lives.'

They were still at it when Elsie returned. They shouted at her as she came in at the door.

'Look what we've done! Just look!'

Elsie gazed at the slates in astonishment. 'I wouldn't have believed it!' she said. 'It's wonderful. And so quick!'

'I don't suppose every lesson will go as well, but we've made a good start,' Beth admitted. 'And the baby has slept through it all.'

'Well, we'd best get off,' Elsie said. 'It's started to snow. Here's your zinc ointment.'

When Elsie and the children had left, Beth took Will's dinner tray and left it on his bedside table. She did not stay and talk with him, as she sometimes did, while he ate it, but left immediately.

Later in the afternoon there was a knock at the door and Phoebe walked in. She stopped dead halfway across the room.

'What in the world . . . ?'

'I tripped over the rug and fell against the corner of the table,' Beth said. The lie came more easily the second time, though she doubted, from the look on Phoebe's face, whether it was any more convincing than it had been for Elsie.

'Well, you certainly fell hard,' Phoebe said. 'And how's Will?'

'About the same. He'll be pleased to see you. Will

you excuse me if I leave you to it? There's something I have to do urgently.'

'Of course,' Phoebe said.

In the bedroom, Phoebe stared at the state of the bed, and of Will himself. He was slumped down in the bed, his hair unkempt, his chin and jowls blue with a day's growth of beard. The bedclothes were every which way, and on the table close to him lay the congealed remains of his dinner, of which he seemed to have eaten very little.

Something had gone badly wrong. Beth Seymour had always been meticulous in her care of her husband, and of his surroundings. Phoebe had never seen him like this.

And it has something to do, she thought, with the state of Beth's face. Not for a minute had she believed the tale of falling against the table. So what had he done that his wife was not going near him? More worldly, more experienced with men than either Elsie Drake or Beth, Phoebe guessed what he had done. Hadn't something like it happened in her own life? Didn't she have a child whose father she had never seen again, to prove it?

She had been well aware, when she had been treating him, of Will's desires, and of his frustrations. She'd perhaps added to them. She had had a certain sympathy with him, but she could never condone what she now felt sure he had done to his wife. If a woman gave herself willingly, in marriage or out of it, that was one thing. She understood that well enough. If she was taken by force it was quite another. However, she concluded, I'm here to treat his back, not to sort out his marriage.

'So!' she said. 'You've decided to grow a beard?'

'It looks like it,' Will grunted.

'Or have you changed your mind? Would you like me to shave you?'

'Beth usually helps me,' Will said. 'She's been too busy. Did she say anything?' His tone was nervous.

'What about? Oh, you mean her face? Only that she'd tripped over the rug and fallen against the table. Dangerous things rugs can be.'

So at least Beth had not given him away, Will thought. He was not to be further humiliated.

'Well, since Beth's busy I'll clean you up and tidy your bed before I give you your massage,' Phoebe said.

If you hadn't massaged me the way you did, Will thought, if you hadn't played on my feelings, none of this might have happened. But, he soon found out, it was to be different this afternoon. Her hands moved over his body in a brief, competent and impersonal manner.

'I'll get you out of bed on my own today,' Phoebe said when she had finished. 'I think you're mending fast. The sooner you get back to work the better. For today I'll walk you round the bedroom and the living-room, and you can try a bit of it on your own. I reckon you're not quite as helpless as I thought you were.'

Will gave her a quick look. Was she getting at something? But he wasn't going to ask.

She was correct in her estimate of his walking. He managed it much better than he had hitherto. When, in the living-room, Phoebe suddenly said, 'Now you do the next bit on your own,' he did so, though clinging onto the furniture for support.

Beth sat at the table, poring over her books, not even pretending to watch Will. Passing close by her he put out a hand and would have used her shoulder for support, but she twisted away and went to do something at the other side of the room.

So I was right, Phoebe thought. This is a pretty kettle of fish.

'Sit in here for a minute,' she said to Will. 'I'll make

your bed before you get back into it.' She spoke pleasantly, though all three of them knew it was not her job to do it. Beth followed her into the bedroom.

'I'll do it,' Beth said. 'It's up to me.'

They faced each other across the bed, met each other's eyes.

'I can see you're busy with your books,' Phoebe said mildly. 'I don't mind doing it this once. And while I'm at it, shall I change the sheets?'

Without a word, Beth went to the drawer and took out fresh sheets and pillowcases.

'I must tell you, and I reckon you'll be glad to hear it, your husband's improving fast,' Phoebe said. 'But now he needs to be got out of bed twice a day, and walked around the house. And he should stay up for longer. He needs to get his muscles in trim if he's to get back to work.'

'I'll see to it,' Beth said quietly. 'Not today, but I will from tomorrow.'

She would too. Tomorrow she would make a fresh start. She would look after him as well as she was able, neglecting none of his needs except one; but sleep with him she would not. That was over. She would share the bedroom, sleeping on the sofa. She had no wish for others to know the state of her marriage. It was strange that she had no fear that Will would molest her again.

'Oh, Will,' she cried in her heart, 'what has it come to that I use the word "molest" about my husband?'

'Then I'll leave you to it, and thank you,' she said to Phoebe.

Phoebe changed the bedding, found Will a clean nightshirt, then brought him back and helped him into bed. He tried to catch hold of her hand but she pulled away from him.

'Don't think I've no sympathy, and don't think I don't understand,' she said. 'I know. I'm not daft. But if ever I hear or see that Beth has fallen over the hearthrug and bashed into the table again, there'll be trouble. She's too good for that, and you know it.'

'I didn't mean . . .' Will began.

'We'll not discuss it further,' Phoebe said. 'I'll see you tomorrow.' She patted his hand briefly and was gone.

# 12

When Jake and Patrick emerged from the candlelit tunnel in the early evening of the November day, expecting to meet the darkness of the moor, it was to discover a white world. Snow covered everything; every hillock, every depression, every tuft of winter vegetation. As yet there was no great depth to it, and for the moment it had stopped falling. The air was still and frosty, without wind, so that there were none of the deep drifts in which a man could easily lose his way. The moon was rising, too, and later on the moor would be as light as day. Already there was no need of the lanterns the men carried.

'Did I not say 'twould snow?' Patrick demanded. 'Did I not tell ye so?'

Snow was another of the things he disliked in this alien country. At home on the west coast of Ireland, where – so clever men said – the Gulf Stream came all the way from America, without getting cold, to warm the waters offshore, there was scarcely any snow.

'Didn't I foretell it?' he repeated.

'You certainly did,' Jake said. 'And I agreed with you.'

Jake was used to snow. Here in the North of England, and especially on the high moor and on the fells, it came early and stayed long. It would not be as bad in the valleys. There they could hope for days, even weeks, when it might melt away, filling the streams and rivers; but here, once it fell to any depth, it would remain until the late spring.

At the moment the snow was of little consequence to him. His mind was, and had been all day long, on Beth. He had not wanted to leave her and he was anxious to be back, therefore he set off at a good pace, which Patrick found difficulty in matching.

'Will ye slow down!' he begged.

Jake did so.

'I'm sorry,' he said. 'I'm in a hurry to be back.'

It was not that he thought that anything worse would have happened to Beth; if that had been in his mind he would never have left her, no matter what she'd said. It was simply that he wanted to be with her, to comfort her in whatever way he could.

'No, *I'm* sorry,' Patrick said.

He'd almost forgotten. Things went in and out of his mind so quickly these days. Sometimes they never came back at all. But now he remembered the sight of Beth when they'd come back from Batty Green last night, and her face when he'd fetched the water for Jake to bathe it.

'If 'twas not that the man is half-crippled already,' he said in an angry growl, 'I would take him out and tear him limb from limb, so I would!'

Jake said nothing. When he thought of Will Seymour his rage knew no bounds. If I started on him at all, he thought, I would kill him. And what good would that be to Beth, her husband dead and me in prison, or worse?

But he would take her away from him. On that he was determined. Plans had run through his head all day long as he had laid the bricks in the tunnel, and before the day was over he would put them to her.

When they reached the hut Phoebe Grange was on the point of leaving. There was no sign of Will, so presumably he was back in bed.

'Why, Mr Tempest!' Phoebe exclaimed, 'I haven't

seen you for a day or two. How are you? You're looking fine!' She made no attempt to conceal her admiration.

'I'm very well, thank you.'

Jake's tone was terse. Given any encouragement, Phoebe Grange would linger to chat. He didn't want that. He wanted to be with Beth who, pale and subdued, stood behind Phoebe, every bit as anxious for her to leave.

'That's good! Is it still snowing?'

'Not at the moment,' Jake said. 'Though that isn't to say it won't come down heavily any minute.'

'Oh well, a few flakes of snow won't hurt me,' Phoebe said. 'I'm warm-blooded!'

Patrick brushed past her to the bedroom, and Jake followed. It was the quickest way to get rid of Phoebe. When he heard the door close behind her he returned to the living-room and went towards Beth. He would have taken her in his arms, but she turned away.

'Supper's on,' she said quietly, standing at the table with her back to him. 'It will be ready as soon as you are.'

Jake took the one step it needed to bring him close to her. He put his hands on her shoulders but she was rigid under them, steadfastly facing the other way.

'Don't turn your back on me, Beth,' he said quietly.

With gentle force he turned her around so that she was facing him.

It was the expression in her eyes which hurt him. Her face was already healing, though it would be some days before it would be back to normal, but as for her eyes, it was as if the light which had once glowed so brightly behind them had been extinguished. They were dull, empty, almost colourless.

'Beth, I've got to talk to you.'

He kept his voice low, glancing at the bedroom door, not knowing whether Will was awake or asleep.

Beth followed his glance.

216

'He's asleep,' she said. 'He always sleeps after his treatment. But it makes no difference, there's nothing to be said.'

'Oh yes there is!' Jake contradicted. 'And you must listen to me.'

'Whatever it is, I don't want to hear it,' Beth said.

'You're going to.'

Her body was facing his, but she turned her head away. She didn't want to listen to him or to anyone else. She wanted to be left alone. Couldn't he understand that?

'Beth, you must leave him! You can't stay here. Come away with me. I'm not sure where we'd go, what we'd do, but there'd be something. I could get a job further up the line, on another contract. Appleby, even Carlisle. They wouldn't know us there. It would be a fresh start.' The thoughts and plans which had whirled around in his head all day long poured out of him. Beth turned to face him again, shook her head, interrupted him.

'Please stop!'

'I won't stop,' Jake said. 'Not until I've said what I have to say. I love you, Beth. I'd look after you, I'd make you happy. I'd never harm a hair on your head, or let any hurt come to you.'

'Please stop!' she repeated. 'It's impossible.'

'It's not impossible,' Jake urged. 'We can do it.'

'No!'

'Why not? Don't say you don't love me, because I wouldn't believe you. But even if you do say so it doesn't matter. I've enough love for both of us; and one day you will, I know you will.'

'No!' Beth said. 'I'm married to Will. I made promises . . .'

'And what about *his* promises?' Jake demanded. ' "With my body I thee worship." Didn't he promise that? Is that what he did?'

Beth felt the blood drain away from her face. She thought she would faint.

'For pity's sake stop it!' she cried. 'Do you think I don't know?'

He was caught by the agony in her voice. He had wanted to bring her comfort and instead he had caused her anguish. He dropped his hands to his sides. He had never felt so helpless.

'I'm sorry,' he said. 'I've been clumsy. I've said it the wrong way; I've chosen the wrong moment.'

'Please, Jake!' Her voice was softer. 'There isn't a right moment for what you've just said to me. It can't be done.'

'Then promise you'll remember it, and if you change your mind . . .'

'I won't change my mind.'

Nor, Beth thought, would he ever know how near she had come to losing herself in the shelter of his arms, to going with him wherever he wanted to take her.

'It might be best if *you* went,' she said. 'It might make it easier for all of us.'

Jake shook his head.

'Not as things stand. I couldn't leave you like this. I have to stay, but I won't trouble you. I'll be here if you need me, if you change your mind.'

'I shan't do that,' Beth said. 'Go and get ready for supper.'

He collected a jug of water, took it into the bedroom and poured it into the bowl. When he had washed he changed out of his dirty working clothes into clean ones.

'I'm hungry!' Patrick said. 'It smells good.'

They sat at the table, Patrick eating heartily, Jake and Beth trying to give the appearance of doing so. Beth had taken a tray in to Will, wakened him, and waited until he began to eat it. From now on she must

218

do everything that was to be part of her normal life; a new kind of normal life, but she had to go forward. She would not look back. There was a deadness inside her, but perhaps it would change, and if it didn't, no-one would know.

'I had a piece of news,' Jake said.

In view of what he had had to say to Beth, he had put it aside. Now that she had turned him down he had to give it. Patrick and Beth looked up at him.

'I'm going on to nights,' Jake announced. 'Starting next Monday.'

Astonished, Patrick stopped eating, his fork halfway to his mouth.

'No-one said anything to me about changing on to nights. 'Twas never mentioned.'

'It's not the whole shift,' Jake said. 'Just a few, mostly brickies.'

'Not me, then?'

'No.'

'But who will I work with?' Patrick asked anxiously.

'I suppose with whoever takes my shift,' Jake said. 'Don't worry. You'll be all right.'

Patrick's reaction to the news was exactly what Jake had feared. Without telling the Irishman, when the foreman had sent for him to tell him of the change-over, Jake had at once asked if Patrick couldn't also change, so that they could continue to work together. The foreman had refused outright.

'He's a liability on the day shift,' he said. 'He'd be worse on nights.'

'But I'll be there to look after him,' Jake promised. 'I'll see he's all right.'

'You won't have time,' the foreman said, 'because the other thing is that I'm putting you in charge of a small group of bricklayers. You won't have time to wet-nurse Mahoney. You'll have enough with your own job and supervising the others. And since it's promotion, and more money, I take it you'll not refuse it. Even if you do, you can't have Mahoney.'

Jake had said nothing of this to Patrick. Time enough when it had to come out. It had all, to Jake, been of less importance today than Beth.

Patrick put down his fork, pushed his plate away. What would he do? How would he manage? Jake was his rock and stay. Jake understood how he was, noticed quickly when he was in difficulty.

'Then I shall leave,' he said. 'I'll go home to Ireland.'

'Don't say that,' Jake begged. 'Give it time. I'll still be here. Beth will be here.'

'No, I'll go home,' Patrick said. 'I had it in mind anyway. Didn't I tell you so, and wasn't it only yesterday?'

He rose to his feet and went to the bedroom. He had a headache coming on. Jake stood up to follow him but Beth put out a hand and drew him back.

'Not just yet, Jake. Let him be alone.'

'He thinks I've let him down,' Jake said.

'Well, you haven't. It's better for him to go home, we both know that.'

They were quiet for a while, hardly speaking. How can everything change so much in just twenty-four hours? Beth asked herself.

After a while, Jake broke the silence.

'So I'll be here during the day,' he said. 'Part of the time I'll be in bed, and for the rest I'll try not to get under your feet.' I would rather be here at night, he thought. I want to be here to protect her if need be.

'I shall have the children here,' Beth said. 'I start on the lessons next week. And it might be easier for *you* to start learning when you're here during the day – though I'm sure you wouldn't want to mix in with the children.'

Whatever he decided, it wouldn't be easy with Will

around, as he would be more and more. But she wouldn't let him stop her. She'd promised Jake to teach him to read, and she'd not break her promise.

If the weather was halfway decent, Jake thought, he'd take some of the walks he'd promised himself and never got around to, but if the snow really came down that wouldn't be possible. He would have to get out, though. How would he sit for so many hours in the same room as Beth, feeling as he did about her? And how would he endure Will?

A week later Patrick Mahoney left, quietly and without fuss, his few belongings carried on his back. He was ready to quit the house when Jake came in from the night shift.

'I'll walk down to Batty Green with you,' Jake said. 'Or a bit further if you like?'

'I'll be glad of your company so far,' Patrick said. 'I'm hoping to get a lift on a cart from Batty Green – if not to Settle, then to Ingleton.' It was not a long way from Ribblesdale to the west coast of England, and from there he'd get the boat home. It would be good to be home. His mother would be glad to see him.

'Neither of you is setting foot outside this door without a good breakfast inside you,' Beth said firmly. 'So you can both sit at the table and I'll serve you.'

At Batty Green the two men went into the alehouse and had a last pint of beer together. Patrick, Jake thought, would have stayed for another and another, but he dissuaded him. In any case, there was a cart almost ready to leave for Settle.

'I'll never forget you!' Patrick said.

'Nor I you,' Jake replied.

He stood there, waving, until the cart was out of sight, then he went back into the alehouse.

Will, so much improved was he, had started to get up towards the end of the morning, to stay up for his

dinner and return to bed for his treatment, which
Phoebe gave him after she had made him walk around
the hut. He could have managed without so many
treatments now, she said, but as the children were
there five days a week for their lessons, and she usually
came to collect them afterwards, she said she might
as well do it.

'At this rate,' she said to Will, 'we'll have you back
to work after Christmas – weather permitting.'

'It can't come too soon,' Will said. 'I'm fed up, stuck
in here!'

He had never wanted the children in the house, and
now that they were there he didn't like it. He didn't
like the attention they had from Beth.

'You wait on them hand and foot!' he grumbled.
He was sitting in the most comfortable armchair, close
to the warmth of the stove, a cup of tea at his elbow.

'Is there anything you want?' Beth asked patiently.

'No,' he admitted. 'Not at the moment.'

'Well, then! And when there is something, I'm right
here.'

She knew very well – they both did – that he couldn't
fault the care she gave him, the way she kept his house,
made his meals, attended to his person. She was
pleasant, she was civil, she was ever-helpful, but he
would have given up a large slice of that in exchange
for the warmth which existed between her and the
children. He listened to the greetings when they
arrived in the morning, to their laughing and chatter-
ing throughout the day, to their quips and jokes,
occasionally to their tears. Beth was in the middle of
it all, enthusiastic, interested.

'Are you saying I neglect you for the children?' she
asked when he grumbled about it.

'I'm not saying that. You just seem to be having a
good time with them, and I'm out of it.'

'That's because you keep yourself out of it. You

won't take any interest, you won't even learn their names,' Beth said. 'So what do you expect?'

'I never wanted you to do it,' Will said.

'We need the money,' Beth said. 'It isn't much, but it does help. You know that's why I started it. You ought to be pleased that I find it rewarding in other ways also.'

He was not yet up when Patrick left for the last time, and Patrick did not go in to him to say goodbye.

'Good riddance!' Will said when Beth told him the Irishman had gone. 'The sooner we get rid of the other one, the better!'

'We'll not be getting rid of him,' Beth said. 'Not if we want to pay the rent and eat.'

'The minute I'm back at work, he goes!' Will threatened.

'Perhaps you're right,' Beth said in a calm voice. 'Perhaps that would be best. We'll discuss it at the time.'

Did it occur to Will, she wondered, to ask himself why Jake stayed at all when he was so rudely treated by the man of the house? Apparently it didn't.

And then the hut door opened and in came the children, all seven of them, and all in the care of eight-year-old Emily Drake, who shepherded them every morning. It was only because it was dark by the time they left in the afternoon that one of the mothers came to take them home.

A blast of cold air blew into the hut as they streamed through the door. But, thought Beth, welcoming them with a wide smile, they bring enough warmth to heat the whole house.

'Wipe your feet on the mat,' she said. 'But before you take off your caps and coats I want to show you something.'

'What is it, Mrs Seymour?' Emily asked.

'Turn around, all of you,' Beth instructed, 'and look

at the wall by the door. What do you see that's new?'

Tom saw it first.

'Hooks, Mrs Seymour. They weren't there yesterday!'

'Quite right!' Beth said. 'Mr Tempest kindly put them up, and at just the right height for you to hang your outdoor clothes. Tell me how many there are. Start by the door and count along the row.'

'Seven, Mrs Seymour,' Emily said.

'That's correct. Now you can each choose a hook, hang up your things, then come to the table and I'll tell you what we're going to do.'

At the table she gave them each a strip of paper and a wax crayon.

'Now first of all you're going to print your name on the paper, just your Christian name, and in your very best printing, then we'll fix them up over the hooks so you'll each have your very own. Don't rush. Do it carefully.'

Tom Drake was, as usual, the first to finish.

'I've done! I've done!' he cried.

'And so you should have,' Beth said. 'Yours is an easy name.'

'I haven't finished mine,' Clarissa Grange said.

'And I can't remember how to do mine,' her brother admitted.

'Well, Clarissa's is the longest name and Aubrey's is the most difficult,' Beth acknowledged. 'I'll give you a hand.'

Trust Phoebe Grange to give her children fancy names, she thought. It's quite in character.

'Jane and Bertie, you can do yours, can't you?' she asked. Jane and Bertie Parker, children of Elsie Drake's neighbour, had learnt to write their names before they came to the class, though not to read. But they were apt pupils, there'd be few difficulties with them.

'Shall I draw a pattern around mine while I'm waiting?' Tom asked.

'If you like,' Beth said.

In a way, Tom would be the most difficult pupil simply because he was the brightest. He had known no more than the others on the first day but, in addition to his artistic talent, he soaked up knowledge like a sponge. It wouldn't be easy to keep him occupied.

He was a handsome boy, she thought. He had a face a painter would want to put on canvas; oval, fine yet strong-featured, clear, olive-skinned. He had an exotic, foreign look about him – not the least bit like either of his parents. As she studied him, thinking that he was the kind of son she would like to have, he looked up from his drawing and caught her eye. His own were dark, and sparkling with intelligence. They exchanged smiles.

Beth was surprised, too, by the rapidity with which Jake was learning to read and write, though why she should be surprised she didn't know. He was an intelligent man. It was just that, like the children around the table, he'd not until now had a chance. Now he worked every spare minute at it. When he came in from the night shift he washed, changed his clothes, ate his breakfast, and was ready to start when the children arrived.

'You don't have to sit with the children,' Beth said. 'I'll give you separate lessons.'

'It's all right,' he said. 'I'm happy to do that. After all, we're at the same stage at the moment – at least me and Tom are.'

'Well, it's good for them to see a grown-up learning,' Beth said.

After an hour or so Jake would close his book and take his things into the bedroom. He had to get his sleep, he pointed out. Beth was aware that he timed his day so that he would not still be having his lesson when she broke off to help Will to get up, and that he would be out of sight when Will took his place in the living-room. So he slept, or worked at his reading and writing in the bedroom, until halfway through the afternoon when Will went back to bed for a spell. Thus the two of them managed to meet each other only for supper, after which Jake usually went down to the alehouse at Batty Green until it was time for him to go to work.

He grew to enjoy the company at Batty Green, though he had to keep a watch on how much he drank. If he turned up the worse for it he'd be barred from working in the tunnel, let alone being in charge of other men. What he hated about going to Batty Green was leaving Beth with Will.

Weekends were the worst times for him. The children, whose weekday presence made the hours go quickly, did not come in at the weekend, and as Saturday was Jake's night off it meant that he was at Nazareth from the time of his return from work on Saturday morning until he went back on Sunday night. Will, who was improving with every day, was up most of the time. There was no getting away from him. It was not that there were open quarrels between the two men, but Will was truculent, sniping. Jake, for Beth's sake, held himself in check against the jibes.

On a Saturday morning in mid-December Will was at his most awkward. He had breakfasted in bed and risen soon afterwards – he was capable now of getting up without Beth's help. When he came into the living-room, Beth and Jake were at the table eating breakfast. Jake, between mouthfuls, was reading aloud from the book which lay open in front of him.

'Very good!' Beth said. 'You really are coming on, Jake. I'm going to write to Mr Crossland to ask him for a couple of more advanced readers. You and Tom are both ready for them.'

'Quite a cosy little scene,' Will said. There was a wealth of ill-feeling in his voice.

Beth looked up.

'Come and sit down, Will. I'll pour you another cup of tea.'

'Oh, I wouldn't want to interrupt,' Will said.

Jake rose, pushed back his chair.

'I've finished.'

'Don't go,' Will said. 'Read to us! What is it then? The cat sat on the mat? The cup is on the table? Oh no, table's a long word, isn't it? But never mind. With all the attention my wife gives you you'll soon be able to read long words.'

Jake picked up the book and snapped it shut.

'Jake is doing exceptionally well,' Beth said steadily. 'He can be proud of himself.'

'Hooray!' Will said, clapping his hands.

Jake went into his bedroom and gave vent to his anger by flinging the book from one side of the room to the other, where it fell on the floor behind the bed. He didn't mind the taunts to himself – they were childish and deserved to be ignored – but he couldn't bear it that Beth had to suffer the indignity of them. Once again he wondered whether he should leave, find other lodgings. That shouldn't be too difficult. Yet not only did he not want to leave Beth, he didn't want to cut himself off from the new world which even his elementary reading had opened up for him. He was greedy for more. He wanted to take it in in great gulps.

Presently he went back into the living-room. Beth was busy cutting out letters which the children would assemble into words on Monday morning; Will sat, unoccupied, in his chair. Jake broke the silence between them.

'I won't be in for my dinner. I'm going down to Batty Green.'

'Oh!' Beth said. 'I thought . . . but you will be back for supper?'

'I'm not sure,' Jake said. 'If I'm not, don't bother to save me any.'

'We won't!' Will said.

As Jake emerged from the warmth of the hut, the cold was biting, the air frosty under a clear sky. The gain was that with the temperature so low, the snow, where it had been trodden, lay as hard as iron underfoot. It was possible to stride out, and this Jake did, pulling his hat down over his ears, muffling his neck and chin in his scarf. It was the wrong time of the day for the tram to Batty Green, but it didn't matter. He needed exercise, the more vigorous the better. Even more he needed, for a while, to put a distance between himself and Nazareth.

The snow was kind to the moor, forgave what men had done to it. It softened and blurred the mean-looking huts, the pieces of machinery, the spoil-heaps of rubble which had been taken out of the tunnel and the cutting. Since it had stopped falling, blotting out the landscape, the men were back at work in the cutting and on the viaduct. There was no time to be lost. On his right as he walked, the white peak of Whernside stood magnificent and strong against the sky. The sight of it put his frets and troubles into perspective. There was nothing, he thought, that the mountain had not seen in its long history.

Reaching Batty Green his first stop was at the café. The keen air had made him hungry and he ordered meat-and-potato pie. When he had followed that with a plate of jam roly-poly and washed it down with a mug of tea, he left, and walked around the Saturday market. It was disappointing that, though there was money in his pocket, there was nothing he wanted to buy. He hesitated at Burgoyne & Cocks's stall, wondering whether he would buy biscuits to give to the children on Monday, but in the end he decided against it. Even so small a thing could be taken the wrong way by Will Seymour.

Sally Roland, he noted, was not serving on the stall. He wondered why.

When he walked into the alehouse he had the answer. There she was, drinking port-and-lemon in the company of a man whom Jake recognized as a regular.

When Sally saw Jake she smiled, and called out to him in a ringing voice.

'Why, just look what the cold's brought in! If it isn't the handsome stranger himself!'

She moved up on the bench to make room for him, and when he sat down she leaned close to him, her body soft and warm against his, her heady perfume assailing his nostrils. Jake made no attempt to move away from her. Suddenly, surprising him, her warmth was what he needed.

'What would you like to drink?' he asked her.

'Well,' she said, 'by rights I should be going – in fact I shouldn't be here in the first place!' She laughed merrily at the thought. 'I escaped from the stall at the insistence of this gentleman here. He thought I looked in need of something and he was quite right. I've been slaving away all morning. I'm quite worn out!'

'You don't look it,' Jake said.

She looked as fresh as a daisy and as pretty as a rose. Though she wasn't his style, he told himself, there was no denying that she was attractive, and not least because she was so full of life, exuding vitality from every pore.

'So what's it to be?' he asked.

'Well, since you're so pressing,' Sally said, 'I'll have another port. It warms you up, port does; and it's cruelly cold behind that stall.'

They sat a long time, Sally with a third glass of port, Jake with as many pints of ale. Why not, Jake thought? It was warm, the company was congenial – though the man who had originally brought Sally into the inn had wandered off.

'He knows when he's outclassed,' Sally said. With one finger she delicately stroked the back of Jake's hand, and when she looked up at him her eyes were as soft as velvet, the pupils wide and dark. There was a moment of silence between them and then it was broken by a man who came into the inn and made straight for Sally. Jake recognized him as an assistant who worked on the stall.

'If it's all the same to you, miss, and if it wouldn't be interrupting anything, it's about time you got back to work! We'll be packing up soon. If you don't come we'll be off to Settle and you'll be left behind here.'

Sally Roland sighed.

'What's the world coming to when a girl can't have a few minutes to talk to an old friend?'

'A few hours more like,' the man said. 'Well I've told you, we'll be off soon!' He turned and marched out.

'I'd better go,' Sally said mournfully. 'He can be awfully mean. He might tell on me. Not that I'd mind being left here – if the conditions were right, that is.'

Jake went with her to the door, watched her walk across to the stall. She'd passed a bit of time, and pleasantly too. He felt grateful to her. He went back to his seat and ordered more beer. There was nothing to hurry back for.

The following Friday there was a hitch with the bricklaying in the tunnel, which made it necessary for Jake and two of his men to go in to work on Saturday afternoon to make up for it. It was late in the evening when he reached home. He was not sorry to have been away. Will had been at his most unpleasant all week and Jake doubted if today would have been any different.

'There's a letter for you, Jake,' Beth said as soon as he entered. 'Elsie Drake brought it. She said a young woman at Batty Green asked her to deliver it to you.'

She knew who the young woman was since Elsie had lost no time in telling her.

'It was that hussy from the bakery stall,' Elsie had said. 'No better than she should be, I'd say. I'd advise him to steer clear of that one! I was in two minds whether I'd deliver it.' But she *had* agreed to do so, if only because she hoped to learn later what was in it.

Jake opened the letter. He looked at it long and hard. There was no way he could read it. What made it worse was that it was in Sally's scrawling handwriting, not in clear print as in the reading book.

'What is it?' Beth asked. 'Not bad news, I hope?'

'I don't know,' Jake confessed. 'I can't read it. Only the odd word here and there.'

'Oh Jake! Do you want me to read it for you?' Beth offered.

He handed her the letter. There was nothing else he could do. She read it aloud in her soft clear voice: 'Dear Jake, Am pleased to tell you Mr Armitage is coming here for Christmas and he would like to see you. My aunt says to tell you you will be welcome. You can have a lift on the cart from Batty Green on Christmas Eve. Yours truly, Sally.'

Will listened with interest.

'What a good idea!' he said.

As she handed the letter back to Jake Beth's heart plummeted with disappointment. She wanted him to be in Nazareth for Christmas. She would not enjoy it without him.

'What shall you do?' she asked.

'I'll have to think about it,' Jake said.

# 13

On Monday Jake had still not decided what he would do about Sally Roland's invitation; how he would answer it, which he must do soon. Of course he wanted to see Armitage, there was no doubt about that, but, equally, he didn't wish to be away from Beth at Christmas. Yet what right had he to be with her? None at all. And would his presence help the situation between man and wife, or would it simply make matters worse?

Monday was not an encouraging day. When Jake arrived home from work Will was, unusually, already at the table, drumming his fingers while he waited for breakfast which Beth was preparing at the stove. The aroma of frying bacon filled the room.

'He's here!' Will called out with ill grace as Jake entered. 'Perhaps we can eat! I'm starving.'

'It won't be more than a few minutes,' Beth promised. 'Good morning, Jake! Did you have a good night?'

'Very good,' Jake replied. 'Everything went well. I'll just wash my hands and face. I won't be long.'

When he returned his breakfast was already on the table. Will had started on his.

'A fellow at work gave me the piece of rope I've been wanting,' Jake said towards the end of a meal which had drifted into silence because it seemed there was no topic on which Will could be pleasant. 'It's all I needed to finish off the sledge.' He had been making the sledge for a couple of weeks now.

'I thought it might be a good idea to go down to Jericho and bring the children back on it. It won't take them all, but the four smallest could ride. It isn't easy for them, walking in the snow.'

'Rubbish!' Will said. 'Pampering them, that's what it is. When I was a child we walked in the snow.'

'We also sledged,' Beth said. 'And we didn't often have snow like they have it here. I approve of the idea, Jake, though it won't be easy, pulling four up the steep bits.'

'Oh, our hero won't baulk at that!' Will said nastily. 'Showing off his strength!'

Jake gritted his teeth.

'I had thought,' he said to Will, 'that I could take you on the sledge down to Batty Green – if you can face the cold, that is. You could have a drink, it would make a change.'

'And you'd pull me back, would you?' Will said truculently.

'That's right.' He could manage that. Will had lost a lot of weight during his illness.

'No thank you,' Will said. 'When I go down to Batty Green it'll be on my own two legs, not carted around like a baby!'

Jake shrugged.

'Please yourself.'

He rose from the table and went into his bedroom, where he was working on the sledge. In better weather he would have been able to work outside, but now his bedroom was his refuge. He was not welcome in the living-room. Fifteen minutes later he had fixed the rope, and was ready to leave to collect the children.

'Like a bloody Saint Bernard dog!' Will grumbled as Jake left. 'Anyway, why do we have to have the kids in this weather, coming in with snow on their boots, dripping all over the floor? Why can't they stay at home?'

Beth, who had been standing in the doorway watching Jake set off on the new sledge down the hill towards Jericho, thinking how much she'd like to be on it, closed the door with a bang and whirled around to confront her husband.

'When did you ever care about the state of the floor, Will Seymour?' she demanded. 'When did you ever have to do anything about it? And why are you so horrid to everyone? To the children, to me, to Jake Tempest. You never have a pleasant word. So why?'

'If you can't see the answer to that, you must be bloody blind!'

'Well I can't! So tell me! And I don't like your language.'

They faced each other, two angry people. Will gripped the arms of his chair. Why am I like this? he asked himself. Why is it I resent the children? And why do I hate Jake Tempest – which I do?

'Tell me! Tell me why!' Beth persisted.

He knew the answer. He'd spent more time thinking about it than he'd ever been given credit for, but it was so difficult to admit it in words.

'Tell me!' Beth repeated.

'Very well, I will! It's because you belong to *them*. You belong to those kids and to that man.'

There was more to it in the case of Jake Tempest. Jake knew what had happened on that night. Oh, he might not have been told, he didn't suspect Beth of that, but he knew all right. He would always know. And every day he stands in judgement of me, Will thought bitterly.

'You don't belong to me any more,' he said.

'I look after you,' Beth said. 'I do everything I can for you.'

'I know. But it's not what I want, not all I want. You don't belong to me.'

'I don't belong to anyone,' Beth said. Her voice was tight.

'You used to! You were mine once! You were all mine!'

Beth heard the anguish in his tone, but she could not say what he wanted to hear.

'I belong to myself,' she said.

Nor was that what she wanted. Desperately, she desired to belong to someone. It was unbearably lonely not to. During the day she had the children, and she was happy with them, but at the end of the day they went back to their homes and parents, where they *really* belonged. As for Jake – well, it was better not to think about Jake. She simply thanked God that he was there.

'Beth,' Will said suddenly. 'Can't we go back to where we were? I'll try to do better, I really will.'

Beth shook her head.

'We can't do that. We can't go back.'

'Why can't we?'

'You know why!'

'Then can't we make a fresh start? Can't we begin again?'

'I don't know,' Beth said. How can we, she thought. But how could they continue to live like this? It was slowly eating away the life from both of them. In the silence which followed they continued to look at each other, trying to find the right words. It was Beth who spoke first.

'You're right! We have to make a fresh start. We can and we must. We can't go on as we are, nor can we mend everything at once. But at the very least we could try being decent to each other! *And* to the rest of the world.'

'I'll do that!' Will said eagerly. 'Oh, Beth, I'll do anything! But being agreeable to each other is not all I want, and you know it. We are man and wife.'

'It's all I can give you,' Beth said. 'At least for now.'

He didn't hide his disappointment; he couldn't.

'It *is* a start.' It was Beth who was pleading now.

'Very well,' Will said, though reluctantly. 'I'll try to be patient.' He didn't know how he would manage it, but he would try.

'It's almost Christmas,' Beth said. 'Season of peace and goodwill. At least let's get through Christmas decently.'

'And who knows what the New Year will bring?' Will felt suddenly hopeful. He wanted to put his arms around her, but he knew he mustn't attempt it. He must go slowly; he would win her back, but it could only be little by little.

He stretched out his hand and took hold of her wrist, pulling her closer to his chair. Beth, though she tried not to, flinched at his touch, but she steeled herself not to jerk her arm away.

Then, to her relief, she heard the children shouting outside the hut, and in the same instant the door burst open and they trooped in, Jake with them. Will's hand was still on Beth's arm as she stood beside him. She knew at once that Jake had taken in the scene. When he looked at her, and she returned his look, she saw disbelief in his eyes.

It was seeing Will's hand on Beth's arm, and the pleased look on Will's face, as though he had won a prize, and the fact that Beth stood there, not attempting to escape, which decided Jake to accept Sally Roland's invitation. The rest of the day confirmed him in his decision. Though there was embarrassment in Beth's manner, he sensed a difference in her relationship with Will. It was notable also that Will treated both him and the children with unusual civility. Why would he do that? Why the sudden change?

Before he went to work at the end of the day, when the children had left and Will was back in bed, Jake said: 'I've made up my mind, Beth, I *will* go to Settle for Christmas.'

'Oh, Jake!' Beth looked at him in consternation. 'I'm disappointed. I'd hoped we'd have a good Christmas here.'

'I daresay you will,' Jake said. 'But I don't think you need me.'

'Oh, but you're wrong,' Beth said. 'As for the rest, as for anything else . . .' she hesitated, 'it's not what you think.'

For one brief moment Jake's self-control deserted him.

'Oh Beth, how *can* you? How *can* you?'

'I've told you, it's not what you think,' Beth repeated. 'It's just that . . . I have to make an effort.'

'Don't try to explain,' Jake said. 'You don't have to. If things are . . . improving . . . then I suppose I have to be pleased for you.'

He was not being honest with himself. He was not pleased. How could she do it? How could she let Will touch her? He thought of the night he had seen her lying on the floor, bruised and bleeding, her clothes torn from her body. This new thing, whatever it was, would not work and, in his heart, did he want it to? One thing for sure, however; he didn't understand women. It seemed to him he never had.

On Christmas Eve Beth gave the children a party. She had baked mincepies and gingerbread men, and in the afternoon Elsie and Phoebe joined them and everyone played games; Nuts in May, Kneel on the Carpet, Blind Man's Buff. Jake agreed to be 'blind man' and Beth tied a scarf around his eyes so that he could see nothing as he clumsily tried to catch the children. It was Phoebe Grange he caught, and there was no difficulty in guessing who she was, both from the feel of her and her scent.

'No trouble in catching *her*,' Elsie muttered to Beth. 'Every move he made, she stood in front of him!'

Will could not take part in the games, but he watched. It seemed to Jake that he watched Beth the whole time, his eyes hungrily following her every move, though he kept himself in check and said nothing untoward.

This is no place for me, Jake thought. Let me get away. He would go down at once to Batty Green, and if Sally wasn't ready to leave, then he'd wait in the alehouse until she was.

As soon as the game ended he said: 'I'll have to go. I mustn't miss the cart.'

'We'll all have to go soon,' Elsie Drake said. 'It's almost dark already.'

'The children can borrow the sledge over Christmas, if they want to,' Jake said.

'Can I be the driver?' Tom asked.

'I suppose so,' Jake agreed.

Tom was certainly the most skilled at it. He knew which way and how far to bend when taking a corner. He knew which leg to put out, and when. He was as skilled with the sledge as with everything else he did, yet, surprisingly, not one of the other children resented his superior skills. He was far too popular for that.

Jake stood in the doorway.

'Well then,' he said, 'I'm off! Merry Christmas everybody!'

It was Beth's eyes he sought, as she stood at the back of the room. In them he saw the longing he felt in his own heart. Why am I going, he asked himself? Why am I leaving her? I'm a fool!

When he reached Batty Green Sally was not yet free.

'I'll not be more than a half-hour,' she said. 'We've nearly sold up. You wait at the Welcome Home and I'll join you there.'

It was the better part of an hour before she appeared. Once, he left his seat and went to the door to look for her. The short December day had already given way to night. Lanterns and flares lit the area around the green and Burgoyne & Cocks's stall was still at work, with a straggle of last-minute customers waiting to be served. Jake returned to his place.

'I might as well have another tot of rum while I'm waiting,' he said to the landlord. It would be his fourth, and the landlord, full of seasonal goodwill, was doling out generous measures. But what did it matter, Jake asked himself. He was not driving the cart.

Sally came at last, fresh and bright, no sign on her that she had been at work from early morning.

'Here I am!' she announced cheerfully. 'I hope you're going to buy me a nip of something before we set off. I need something to keep the cold out. It's perishing out there!'

'Then come close to the fire and get warm before we leave,' Jake suggested.

He ordered a drink for her, and for the driver of the cart who had followed her in.

'But we mustn't linger,' the driver said. 'The horses are rarin' to go, and I'll not be sorry to see my own bed, I can tell you.'

By the time they left Ribblehead and set out on the road to Settle the moon was rising, though what gave even more light than the moon was the covering of snow. It shrouded everything; fields, barns, hedges, near and distant hills. Pen-y-ghent brooded like a huge white animal over the broad valley beneath. Leafless trees stood out stark and black against the whiteness.

When he had last travelled this road, Jake thought, on his way to look for a job on the railway, the fields, even the high slopes of the fells, had been dotted with sheep, shining white in the sunshine. Now they had been brought down and were just discernible, concentrated near the farm buildings, close at hand for feeding and where an eye could be kept on the pregnant ewes.

'Have you thought,' Jake asked Sally, 'that in the south, where it's coats warmer than here, they'll be birthing their first new lambs at Christmas? We shall have to wait until the beginning of April, when the new grass comes through.'

Sally yawned. 'No I haven't,' she admitted. 'I don't give a lot of thought to sheep.'

'It's a whole new world down south,' Jake said.

'It's a world I'd like to see,' Sally said. 'I'd like to go to London. Things happen in London. Nothing ever happens here.' But something would over Christmas if she had her way.

She pulled up the rug which she was sharing with Jake, and underneath it she cuddled closer to him, settling her head against his shoulder.

'Oooh, I *am* cold!' she said. 'My poor hands are numb. Can't you warm them?'

Jake took her hands in his, first one and then the other, and began to chafe them.

'Mmmm!' Sally murmured. 'That's better!'

'Here,' the driver said, 'we'll have a little drink. Keep us all warm!' He took a flask from his pocket and handed it around.

'I shall be tight!' Sally giggled.

It was almost midnight when they reached Settle. Sally had fallen fast asleep, leaning heavily against Jake. The driver stopped the horses at the end of the narrow street which led to Sally's aunt's house. Mrs Sutherland was at the door to greet them.

'I thought you were never coming!' she said.

When they stepped into the house Jake looked around, expecting to see Armitage. There was no sign of him.

'Has Mr Armitage gone to bed?' he enquired.

'Mr Armitage?' Mrs Sutherland said. 'What—?'

Sally interrupted quickly.

'Oh, Aunt Jane, don't say he hasn't shown up!'

'Shown up?' Mrs Sutherland looked nonplussed.

'Anyway, we need a nice cup of cocoa,' Sally said. 'I'll help you to make it.' She grabbed her aunt's arm and dragged her into the kitchen.

'What's all this about Mr Armitage?' Mrs Sutherland demanded. 'Who said he was coming?'

'Why, surely *you* did, Aunt Jane?' Sally was wide-eyed.

'I said no such thing, and you know it! What are you up to, Sally Roland?'

'But I was sure you said Mr Armitage was coming here for Christmas! Oh dear, I expect you said it would be nice *if* he came.'

'As far as *I* remember – and since I'm not yet in my dotage I remember quite well – Mr Armitage's name has never passed my lips. All you said to me was that Mr Tempest was at a loose end and wondered if he could come for Christmas.'

'Oh, I *have* got it wrong!' Sally was the picture of contrition. 'Auntie, please don't give me away. Can't we leave it that he just hasn't turned up? Who knows, he might do so.'

'And why would he do that, without a word of warning?' Mrs Sutherland asked.

'Well . . . well, because it's the kind of thing Mr Armitage might do. Oh, please don't say anything. Jake will be so cross if he thinks I've made such a stupid mistake!'

'Mistake, is it?' Mrs Sutherland said. 'You could have fooled me! But since he's here, and there's no getting back to Ribblehead until after Christmas, I'll keep quiet – though for his sake, not for yours. I wouldn't want to make him feel uncomfortable.'

All the same, she thought as she poured the cocoa, and since it was Christmas Eve added a tot of rum to each cup, someone should warn him. But how could *she* do it? The silly girl was her niece, her sister's child. She was fond of her sister.

The minute he had finished his cocoa Jake stood up.

'If you'll excuse me, I'll be off to bed. It's a pity about Mr Armitage. Perhaps he'll arrive tomorrow.' There was something strange about it, he thought, but he was too tired to work it out now. Also, he had drunk too much.

Mrs Sutherland took a candlestick from the sideboard, lit the candle and handed it to Jake. 'The same room, Mr Tempest. Sleep well!'

Sally yawned, stretched her arms wide.

'I must go to bed too,' she said. 'I'm dead beat. Merry Christmas, all!'

She preceded Jake up the narrow staircase and at the door of her room she turned around and faced him, holding her candle so that its soft light lit up her face beneath her cloud of dark hair, adding even more brightness to her eyes.

'Is it good night then, Jake?' she said softly. 'Suddenly, I'm not tired.'

'I am,' Jake said. 'Good night, Sally.' He brushed past her and went into his room.

Five minutes later he had blown out his candle and was in bed. He lay on his back and watched where the moonlight crept around the gaps at the sides of the window blind, lighting up a corner of the wall. For a moment he was wide awake, his thoughts as clear as crystal. He thought of Blea Moor under the snow, of the hut at Nazareth and, beyond and above all, of Beth Seymour. Heart, soul and body he longed for her. Why had he been such a fool as to leave her to come to Settle, even for Armitage?

Hers was the last face he saw, superimposed over everything, her eyes looking directly into his, before he was suddenly pitched and drowned in an ocean-deep sleep.

At first, less than an hour later, he was scarcely aware of it when Sally climbed into his bed. The feel of her soft, naked flesh, the curves and hollows of her body against his, had the quality of a dream, a dream in which she led him, guiding his movements, and he simply obeyed. It was not until her hands began to explore his own body, at first slowly and then with increasing urgency, and always with expertise, that he emerged from the dream into reality.

It was too late. He had awakened with a desire, the strength of which consumed him. His whole body, joined with hers, impelled him, goaded him, towards one end. He was hardly conscious of her except as, at one and the same time, fuelling his need with her own swift crescendo and, finally, in a burst of a thousand shafts of light, fulfilling it.

'Beth!' he cried out. 'Beth!'

Sally, lost in her own fulfilment, did not hear him, or perhaps didn't care. She had got what she came for.

Jake left Settle immediately after breakfast on Boxing Day.

'Must you go so soon?' Sally asked. She was still half asleep and would have liked to have stayed in bed, preferably in Jake's bed. But there would be other times. She was certain of that.

'Yes, I must,' Jake replied. 'I have to work tonight, and since there's no cart going to Ribblehead today, I need an early start.'

On a visit to the inn on Christmas Day he had managed to arrange a lift as far as Horton, but from there, the greater part of the journey, he would have to walk. He was not sorry to be leaving. He would have liked to have done so on Christmas Day itself, but out of politeness to Mrs Sutherland, to whom he could not offer a reasonable explanation for such a premature departure, he stayed.

No mention was made between himself and Sally as to what had occurred on Christmas Eve. It might almost not have happened except that, throughout Christmas Day, Sally exhibited a new-found proprietorial manner towards him – a hand on his arm, a turn of speech – which did not go unnoticed by her aunt. But when she went to his bedroom door that night, she found it locked.

'Jake!' she called softly. 'Jake, it's me!'

There was no answer. No matter, Sally thought. There was no way he could hold out against her for ever.

As Jake walked the long road to Ribblehead, thoughts raced around in his mind. He thought of Sally Roland, and what had happened between them on Christmas Eve. The memory didn't perturb him unduly, much of it still seemed dreamlike. Nor was it, he reckoned, an isolated experience for her. She was no novice, he could swear that. It was no more than an episode in which he had given her what she wanted. Or rather, he thought, she had taken it.

He dismissed Sally from his mind and thought about Armitage. For what mysterious reason had he not shown up? The memories of Armitage crowded in as he tramped the road they had walked together. I liked him, he thought, I wouldn't have reckoned he'd have let me down.

And where was Patrick Mahoney? Hopefully he was in Ireland, safe with his family.

Most of all, though, Jake thought about Beth, and his thoughts quickened his step. He had surprisingly little feeling of having been unfaithful to her, for whatever had happened to his body, no other woman had for a single second entered his mind. It had been

Beth, all Beth. His one vivid memory was of how he had called out to her. In his own way, in his heart, he had been faithful to her.

It was dark before he reached Ribblehead, and when he walked over Blea Moor the snow had started to fall again. When he reached Nazareth and saw the light in the hut it was like coming home. Never mind that nothing would be ideal, that he was returning to a situation he had been glad to leave only two days earlier; Beth would be there.

In the week after Christmas Mr Pennington, the Company representative, called again.

'I'm glad to see you looking so much better, Mr Seymour,' he said. 'What we want to know now is just when you'll be back to work. It's been a long time . . .'

'And don't think I'm not aware of that,' Will interrupted.

'The Company's been very patient,' Mr Pennington said, 'but there is a limit, and it's my duty to tell you that we're fast approaching it.'

Beth felt sick with fear at his words. To her mind, though he was greatly improved, Will was not yet fit to return to work; but if he didn't, would they lose the house?

'As a matter of fact, I'm fit enough right now,' Will said. 'And eager to go!'

'But with the weather taking such a turn since Christmas,' Beth interrupted, 'I've heard all work's at a standstill, except in the tunnel.'

Elsie Drake's husband, and Phoebe's husband who worked in the cutting, had both been laid off. Since Boxing Day there had been another foot of snow, and strong winds had caused drifts too deep to dig through. Even in the tunnel, Jake said, the snow had blown down the shafts. And to get to and from the tunnel was a hazard in itself.

'That's true,' Mr Pennington conceded. 'But the minute the weather improves . . .'

'Then you'll see me back on the job,' Will promised.

'We'll leave it at that, then,' Mr Pennington said. 'I trust you'll not let me down.'

'I'll not do that,' Will spoke with confidence.

'You'd think he'd have something better to do than come here in this weather,' Beth said when Mr Pennington had left.

The fresh snow had taken its toll of everything. It was impossible for the children to get to and from Nazareth, even with the help of Jake's sledge. Once or twice Beth had managed, with difficulty, to get to Jericho, but aside from that the reading lessons had come to a standstill. Jake had benefited from that, since Beth had been able to spend extra time with him. He had forged ahead with both reading and writing.

But no lessons for the children meant no money from them, and there was very little left in Beth's purse. That was balanced, in a way, by the fact that there was hardly any food to be bought. It was a week now since supplies had come from Settle or Ingleton.

'It's a good thing I laid in all I could afford to,' Beth said anxiously. 'I don't know what we'd do otherwise. In any case, what we have won't last long.'

The worst thing, she thought, would be if she ran out of flour.

'As long as I have flour,' she said, 'I can make some sort of bread. There won't be much nourishment in it, but it'll help to fill us. And the potatoes are nearly finished, and what few *are* left are going bad.'

There had been no milk for several days. She wished she had done the same as some others on the moor, and kept a goat. When the spring came, if ever it did, she would consider that.

It was mid-February before the weather improved

and the desperately needed supplies came through to Ribblehead. News that there was food to be had spread like wildfire.

'I'll take the sledge down to Batty Green,' Jake offered. 'I can bring back goods on that.'

'Bring back anything you can lay hands on,' Beth said. 'Spend what money we have. If there's one thing we've learned it's that food is of more use than coins in a purse.'

Jake went first to Burgoyne & Cocks's stall, joining the throng of people waiting to be served. When at last it came to his turn Sally Roland stepped forward to attend to him. He had been observing her while he waited. She looked pale and tired, she had very little chat for the customers, which wasn't like her. But no wonder, he thought; there were so many of them, impatiently pressing to be served.

She attended to his purchases, handed him his change, then said: 'I've got to see you! I'll be in the Welcome in half an hour. I'll sneak off. Mind you're there!'

'What is it?' Jake asked. 'Is something wrong?'

'You can see I'm too busy to talk now,' Sally said. 'I'll see you later.'

He was waiting when she came in.

'You look cold,' Jake said. 'What would you like to drink? A hot toddy?'

Sally shuddered.

'Lemonade, nothing more. My stomach won't take it.'

'I'm sorry to hear it,' Jake said. 'What caused that?'

She gave him a hard look.

'You did!' she said. 'You caused it. I'm pregnant!'

Jake stared at her in horror.

'Don't look at me like that,' she said. 'It takes two to make a baby. And you helped to make this one all right. We hit the jackpot first time!'

'Are you quite sure?' he said. 'Couldn't you be mistaken?'

'Of course I'm sure!' Sally snapped. 'You'd be sure if you were sick every morning and felt like death the rest of the day!'

'I'm sorry!' He couldn't think of words to say.

'I'm sure you are,' Sally said. 'So am I. But sorry won't mend it and there's only one thing will. You'll have to marry me. I'll be forced to tell Aunt Jane any day now, and if I tell her I'm in the family way and there's no husband in sight, she'll turn me out of the house, lock, stock and barrel! You wouldn't want your bairn to be born in the workhouse, would you?'

# 14

At the end of February Will Seymour was able to return to his job, as were all the men working on the viaduct. The weather was still cold, though not quite so bitter, and the wind, ever-present at Ribblehead, though it had hardly abated in strength, had changed to a thaw wind from the west. It was now possible to clear the area around the viaduct of the deepest snow so that work could begin again – greatly to the relief of the men, who had been too long without wages.

To Will, there were several new faces, but that didn't surprise him. On every part of the line men came and went, finding the work too hard and the weather impossible to bear. He was pleased, therefore, to find that Joseph Clark, whom he had known from the beginning, was still there.

'My word,' Will said, 'it's come on by leaps and bounds since I was last here!' He nodded towards the viaduct.

'How long is it you've been away, then?' Joseph asked.

'Four months. You couldn't see anything above the ground then. Everything was in the foundations.'

'Sure, foundations are what count in life,' Joseph said soberly. 'Without strong foundations, what can stand against the enemy?'

Joseph, Will noted, had not lost his turn of phrase which made his utterances sound as though they were straight from the scriptures.

'The enemy in this case being the weather,' Will said. 'Well, you're right there, Joseph!'

Now, the piers of the first few arches, built from huge blocks of black limestone, had risen as far as the 'springing', the point at which the arches would begin to curve.

'I reckon Mr Farrer must have made a fortune from all the limestone on his land,' Joseph said. 'A gold mine under his feet!'

At the point where the arches turned, limestone gave way to bricks, made from local shale and clay at the brickworks which had been set up close by on Batty Green.

'They reckon the brickworks can turn out twenty thousand bricks a day if need be,' Joseph said. 'And they *will* be needed before the viaduct and the tunnel are done.'

The wooden scaffolding which had surrounded the piers while they were being built had been dismantled, moved along the line of the viaduct to support new piers. These first few, merging into their arches, now stood silhouetted against the winter sky; tall, independent, strong, and seemingly indestructible. Will felt a lump rise in his throat as he gazed up at them. Dear God, how he had missed all this! No-one would know the half of how he felt. But now he was back where he belonged! From now on everything would get better.

The thought of Sally's pregnancy pressed down on Jake like a heavy black cloud, a cloud which would not go away, which would at any moment break on his head and drown him. He knew what he must do, he had known from the moment she'd broken the news. Without loving her, and while loving another woman, he must marry Sally Roland. It was the right thing, the only thing, payment for a brief pleasure which he could hardly recall. There was no escaping it and he didn't intend to try to.

In the week since it had happened he had relived that scene in the inn a hundred times.

'You'll have to marry me!' she'd repeated, almost in hysterics. 'I'm not bearing a bastard child – and you know it's yours, you can't deny it!'

'I'm not denying it. I will marry you.' He'd spoken quietly, hoping she'd do the same.

'You promise? God's honour?'

'I promise!'

She'd relaxed immediately, and at once begun to make plans.

'I'll tell my aunt the minute I get home. First off there's the date – it'll have to be soon! And then all the other arrangements.'

She'd prattled away fifty to the dozen. In his numbed state he'd hardly heard any of it. She could arrange what she liked and he'd go through with it because he had to.

That had been a week ago, a week in which, whenever he thought about it, which was most of the time, he envisaged a hopeless, loveless future stretching before him – for he doubted that Sally, in spite of her eagerness to be married, had any more love for him than he had for her. And now it was Saturday again, and she would be at Batty Green, and he must see her. There was no avoiding it. It wouldn't be fair to her and also, if he were to do so, it was inevitable that she would seek him out at Nazareth.

This he could not allow to happen for the simple reason that he had not yet told Beth. For the whole week he had, insofar as it was possible while living in the same house, avoided her. He had spent hours in his room, ostensibly at his reading practice. He had taken long walks, in spite of the weather. He had jumped at the offer to work a few hours' overtime in the tunnel. What he had not been able to avoid was sitting down to meals with Beth and Will, though he had never felt less like eating.

Now, he pushed away his dinner plate and rose from the table. Beth broke off eating and looked up at him.

'Why, Jake, you've hardly touched your dinner! Is it not to your liking?'

'It's fine,' Jake said. 'I'm not very hungry.'

'You've been picking at your food all week,' Beth said. 'Is there anything wrong? Do you not feel well, is that it?'

It was the perfect moment to tell her. Will was at work, the children didn't come on a Saturday, her concern was obvious, but he couldn't bring himself to do it. How could he possibly begin to say the words?

'I'm all right,' he said. 'A bit tired. It's been a hard week.'

That at least was true. With the beginnings of the thaw the snow on the hills had begun to melt, over-flowing the streams which ran down the moor. Most of the week they had been working in several inches of water in the tunnel.

'I've one or two things to do,' he said, 'and then I'm going down to Batty Green.' He would tell her the minute he returned, when he'd seen Sally again. He promised himself he'd put it off no longer.

He went into his bedroom, closed the door behind him, sat on the bed and put his head in his hands. What a mess he was in! What a mess!

Sunk in his thoughts he hardly noticed time passing, nor did he hear the knock at the door of the hut. It was only Beth's tap on his bedroom door, and her voice calling out, which roused him.

'Jake! There's a visitor for you!'

The surprise in her voice might have warned him, but it didn't. When he walked into the living-room, there, standing by the table, a broad smile on her pretty face, was Sally Roland.

'I thought I'd pay you a visit!' she said brightly. 'I've never been to Nazareth, never seen where you live. So the boss gave me an hour off for good behaviour, I cadged a lift on a cart, and here I am! Oh Jake, I've got such a lot to tell you!'

Beth, standing between them, looked as stupefied as she felt. Sally, seeing her expression, gave a peal of laughter.

'He's not told you! I can tell he hasn't! Jake, you are a naughty boy not to have told your landlady!'

'Told me?' Beth queried.

'Why, that we're to be married,' Sally announced. 'There! What do you think of that?' There was a smile of pure triumph on her face.

Beth stared at Sally. It was impossible. She didn't believe it. Yet there was no doubting Sally's utter certainty. Beth switched her look to Jake. He was staring at her, and the expression on his face confirmed everything Sally had said. But there was no triumph in him. He was the picture of abject misery, his eyes pleading with her as his gaze was locked in hers. She felt the blood drain from her face, felt herself go cold.

For a moment Sally did not exist. She and Jake were the only two people in the room.

'Why?'

Beth's lips framed the word, but no sound came. She started to tremble, and desperately hoped it didn't show. She put out a hand to the table, to steady herself.

But what right have I to feel like this? she asked herself. I have no right at all. I'm a married woman. Jake is a free man. There is no way we can mean anything to each other.

Yet that was manifestly not true. He meant the world to her, and she knew that she did to him. Nevertheless,

253

she told herself firmly, he is free to marry whoever he chooses, and I am not.

But why Sally Roland? She knew at once that this girl would never make Jake happy, nor he her.

Stop it, she told herself. It isn't your business. She took a deep breath and forced herself to speak.

'Congratulations! And now I'm sure you must have a great deal to discuss so I'll leave you to it. If you'll excuse me, I have jobs to do in my bedroom.' She was amazed at the steadiness of her voice.

She went into her bedroom, closing the door firmly behind her, and lay on the bed, face down on the pillow, her hands tightly clenched.

'I can't stay,' Sally said. 'I've got to get back to the stall. I thought you'd come back with me, and then when I've finished work we can meet in the Welcome Home. I've so much to tell you!'

'I can't come now,' Jake said. 'I've things to do. I'll be down by the time you finish.'

He had to speak to Beth. There was no way he could leave the house without seeing her alone.

'There'll be a tramway down quite soon,' he said. 'You catch that and I'll follow.'

Beth heard the outer door open and close, and then there were no more voices. They have both left, she thought. She was mercifully alone, and now she could let the tears flow. At first she didn't hear Jake when he knocked on her bedroom door.

He knocked again, urgently.

'Beth! Please! I must talk to you!'

There was a moment's silence before she came to the door. She looked him straight in the face, then walked past him into the living-room, sat in the armchair, leaning her head against the sheepskin which draped the back of it. Her face was as white as the sheepskin but her eyes, though red-rimmed, were now dry.

'Why?' she said. 'Tell me why.'

'She's having a baby.'

'And you . . .' It was difficult to speak. 'You're the father?'

'Yes. But there's more to it, Beth . . . It was the only time . . . Never before, nor since.'

He wanted to tell her that it was she, and only she, who had been in his mind. Sally Roland had had nothing to do with it.

'I don't want to hear any more,' Beth's voice was quiet, but firm. 'I hope . . . I hope you will be happy.'

'You know I won't!' Jake cried. 'How can I be happy without you – or you without me?'

'You mustn't say these things,' Beth said wearily. 'I'm a married woman and you are about to be a married man.' And a father, she thought; and *she* is to have your child, and I am never to have a child. She wished he would go away. Suddenly, she was unbearably tired.

'When will you leave?' she forced herself to ask.

'I'm going down to Batty Green shortly,' Jake said.

'I don't mean that. When will you move out?' She wanted it to be soon; she couldn't bear to go on seeing him every day.

'I don't know. I haven't thought about that,' Jake confessed.

'It will have to be before you're married.' There was no way he could spend even one night under her roof, married to Sally Roland. Surely he understood that?

'I understand,' Jake said, reading her thoughts. But did she realize what it had been like for him all this time, seeing her go into the bedroom with Will, and even more so now that they were on better terms? 'I understand that only too well,' he said.

'I know you do,' Beth acknowledged. 'So the sooner you go, the better for both of us.'

'I don't know where,' Jake said, thinking out loud.

'The Company might rent you a hut,' Beth suggested. 'Or perhaps someone at work might know of something. If you'll allow me to ask her, Elsie Drake might help. There's no spare room in her house, but she knows a lot of people.'

How can I do this? she thought. How can I sit here, calmly discussing how he can most conveniently go out of my life? She was not calm inside. She felt sick – sick in her stomach and sick at heart.

'Then please ask Elsie,' Jake said. 'I'd be grateful.'

In the event, she saw Elsie Drake on Monday morning when she brought her children and Phoebe Grange's.

'Well, that's a right turn-up for the book!' Elsie said. 'I'm astonished – though having a slight acquaintance with Sally Roland I shouldn't be. She's been after him quite a while. I fancy she knows how to play her cards, that one!'

Beth, settling the children to their work, said nothing.

'Have you thought of having them here?' Elsie asked. 'You'd get twice the price for the same room, with the two of them.'

'It's out of the question,' Beth said sharply. 'Will wouldn't countenance it. Especially now that he's back at work. He never wanted lodgers.'

'Well, I'll ask around,' Elsie said.

The answer came later that same day when Phoebe Grange arrived to collect the children.

'I hear your lodger's wanting a new berth – a double berth at that! Well here's one who'll be more than willing to accommodate him – and his new wife of course, when he gets her. And I've got the room.'

'What will your husband say?' Beth asked. She did not like the thought of Jake living in Phoebe's house. But it has nothing to do with me, she reminded herself.

'Oh, he's easy enough!' Phoebe said. 'He'll not mind. When would Jake want to come?'

'*If* he decides on it,' Beth said. 'And that's up to him . . .'

'I'd make him very comfortable!' Phoebe interrupted.

'I'm sure you would. *If* he decides on it, then I daresay the sooner the better, though you'll have to ask him. He's taken two days off work to go to Settle. He'll not be back until tomorrow night.'

'Making arrangements for the wedding, I expect,' Phoebe said.

'I daresay,' Beth's voice was stony.

It was decided between them that Jake and Sally should be married in Settle on a Saturday in March. Sally, half-serious, put forward the idea that they should have a gipsy wedding. It was little more, as far as she knew, than jumping hand-in-hand over a broom laid on the ground, or some said laid on a fire.

'It would be fun,' she giggled. 'Though what if my skirt touched the broom and gave me away?'

'What do you mean?'

'If the bride's skirt touches the broom as she jumps, it shows she's not a virgin.'

'We're not marrying over the brush,' Jake said firmly. 'Since we're doing this for the sake of the child, I want to be sure it's legal.'

'The gipsies reckon it's legal,' Sally said.

'We're not gipsies. We'll be married in front of the registrar!'

Though Jake was adamant about this, in every other detail – what she should wear, what he should wear, the choice of the wedding ring, where they should spend the two-day honeymoon she insisted on (she chose Skipton as being the liveliest place they could afford) – Sally had her own way. Though Jake did his

257

best for her sake to show interest, his heart was not in it. Only when he thought of the child did his hopes rise a little. The child was to be the salvation of this unsought marriage.

Accepting the fact that Jake must be close to his work, Sally agreed to lodge with Phoebe Grange. 'For the time being,' she said. 'Though we *will* want our own place sooner or later.'

She had given up her job with Burgoyne & Cocks a week before the wedding, and after their short stay in Skipton, stopping only briefly to see Aunt Jane in Settle, she returned with Jake to Jericho, where she settled down to being a married lady.

What came as a shock and a surprise to Sally was Jake's total ineptitude in the marriage bed, especially in view of their lovemaking on Christmas Eve. True, she had taken the initiative then, and she did so now, but with no success whatever. In the end, it was always he who turned away from her, leaving her angry, humiliated, frustrated.

'You're no man!' she stormed. 'You're worse than useless!'

'I'm sorry,' he said in a quiet voice.

He had not willingly humiliated her. He could not help it that he had no desire for her and that, in the end, her very presence in his bed, the warmth and voluptuousness of her body, were anathema to him. When he turned away from her it was with relief.

'It's very strange,' Phoebe said to Elsie Drake. 'I mean, I can't help noticing what goes on – or in this case what *doesn't* go on! After all, I live in the same house, and we all know how thin the walls are!'

'You are awful, Phoebe,' Elsie protested. 'I daresay it's because she's pregnant. You know how strange women can be when they're pregnant.' It was inconceivable to either woman that the failure could be on Jake's part.

258

'Oh, I do!' Phoebe agreed. 'With my first I was always craving for kippers! Any time of day or night I fancied kippers, and actually I hate the things. But I never went off bed. After all, it's the one time you can have as much as you want without worrying you'll end up in the family way.'

'That's true,' Elsie said. To her way of thinking, Phoebe had a one-track mind. And she must know something I don't know, she thought, or how would she have only two children?

'No,' Phoebe mused, 'there's more to it, but I can't fathom what it is.'

When Phoebe took the children to the Seymours' hut the next day, Beth said: 'I'll only be able to have them for the morning tomorrow. In the afternoon Mr Tiplady's having a party, and I'm invited. I'm to meet Miss Herbert, the new schoolteacher at Batty Green. She comes from Nottingham. You know they've opened the school there?'

'I've heard,' Phoebe said. 'But she'll do no better with the children than you have with our little lot. It's a miracle how they've come on – and especially young Tom Drake. He's a genius, that little lad!'

'He's certainly remarkably gifted,' Beth agreed. 'He'll go far, given the chance.' She would always be proud, she thought, that she had given him his first chance by teaching him to read and write.

'And now Jake Tempest can read, there's no holding him, either. Never his head out of a book, even if he's read it twice before. And he helps my two a lot. He's a good teacher.'

'Shortage of books is the trouble now,' Beth said. 'I'm going to have a word with Mr Tiplady and Miss Herbert, see if something can't be done about it.'

How wonderful it would be, she thought, if she could discuss with Jake the books they'd read. She knew of no-one with whom she could talk about such things. Will, though he was able to read, wasn't interested. But she mustn't complain about Will, even to herself. Since he was back at work he was a changed man.

On the following Saturday afternoon Sally said to Jake: 'I want you to take me down to Batty Green this afternoon. I'm bored here. I want to see a bit of life!'

She had stayed in bed until after eleven o'clock, eaten a substantial breakfast, then spent the time since in trying on dresses and doing her hair. She was quite pleased with her reflection in the mirror and didn't see why someone other than the deadly dull inhabitants of Jericho shouldn't have the pleasure of seeing her.

'Of course I'll take you,' Jake agreed. 'As for being bored, why don't you find something to do? Why don't you make a start on making baby clothes, for instance?'

Sally pulled a face.

'I hate sewing. I'm no good at it.'

'It will have to be done, sooner or later,' Jake said. 'Perhaps we'll find some material this afternoon.'

'Don't rush me,' Sally protested. 'I'll do it when I have to – or more likely I'll get someone else to do it for me. Some women are quite clever at that sort of thing. I'm not.'

'Be ready in twenty minutes,' Jake said. 'We'll catch the tramway.'

'What I *would* like,' Sally said persuasively, 'is a new dress! I haven't a thing fit to wear. I suppose you *do* want your wife to be smart?'

'You always look good,' Jake said truthfully. 'And what's the use of buying a new dress now? It wouldn't fit you for more than a few weeks. But after the baby's born, *then* I'll buy you a new dress!'

'Oh the baby!' Sally said petulantly. 'I'm sick of hearing about the baby. It's all you can talk about.'

Jake bit back a sharp retort. With his failure in bed

added to the fact that she was carrying the baby, she had every right to be difficult.

They caught the tramway. At Batty Green they went first to Burgoyne & Cocks's stall where Sally, from her exalted position as a married woman, was condescendingly gracious to her former colleagues. Then, when they had walked around a little while, Sally wanted to go into the Welcome.

'I'm tired,' she complained. 'I want to sit down. And I'm thirsty.'

'What about the tearoom?' Jake suggested.

'I don't want the tearoom. I might see a few old friends in the Welcome. You don't grudge me that, surely?'

'Of course not!' Jake said. But when she chose to drink gin instead of the lemonade he suggested, he remonstrated.

'Gin is bad for the baby.'

'Oh, not the baby again!' she said. 'Always the baby! Well if you won't buy me a proper drink I know plenty who will!'

He ordered the gin, which she drank in one gulp then promptly asked the waiter, who was still at the table, for another. 'A large one!' she ordered.

After that Jake angrily refused to buy any more. While she was picking a quarrel with him he pulled her to her feet, took hold of her arm, and escorted her out of the inn.

'You're next door to drunk,' he said. 'We'll walk around until your head's cleared and then we'll catch the tramway home.'

It was while they were walking across Batty Green, he holding her arm, that they came face to face with Will and Beth Seymour.

Jake raised his hat.

'Good afternoon, Beth, Will.'

'Good afternoon, Jake, Mrs Tempest,' Beth said.

261

Will raised his hat to Sally while eyeing her with appreciation. She was a looker all right, he'd always thought so when he'd seen her on the stall, and now there was a becoming flush on her cheeks and a sparkle in her eyes. What did she see in a sobersides like Tempest? But then what did the rest of the women see in him? There was no accounting for women's tastes.

'You're looking very well, Mrs Tempest,' he said.

She flashed him a smile.

'Please call me Sally! I'm feeling very well. On top form!'

She spoke with slow deliberation, rather too carefully. Beth gave her a quick look, and then looked from Sally to Jake.

'My wife is rather tired,' Jake said. 'We're just going to get the tramway back to Jericho.'

'My wife,' Beth thought. Did he have to say that? Did he have to rub it in? And his wife was without doubt intoxicated.

'My husband and I still have some shopping to do,' she said, slipping her arm through Will's.

She was lovelier than ever. Jake's heart ached at the sight of her. Her hand on Will's arm gave him a swift stab of jealousy.

'Then we mustn't keep you,' Jake said politely. He raised his hat again and the two couples walked away in opposite directions.

'She's a toffee-nosed bitch!' Sally said.

'Stop it!' Jake snapped. 'I won't have such language!'

'Could it be that you have your eye on her?' Sally teased. 'Could it be that *she* could make a man of you? But if you have, you're wasting your time! I can't see that husband of hers letting her out of his sight. He looks at her as though he could eat her.'

'You're talking a load of nonsense,' Jake said. But he had observed Will Seymour's attitude towards Beth. It made him sick.

It was not until late that night that the encounter with Jake and Sally was mentioned in the Seymour home, though all evening Jake had been in Beth's thoughts.

'She's a bonny lass, that Sally Tempest,' Will said. 'He's on to a good thing there. When is the baby due?'

'How should I know?'

Will looked up in surprise at the sharpness of her voice.

'Women usually do know these things,' he said mildly.

'Well I don't. It's not my concern.'

Of course she knew. Hadn't she calculated almost to the day when Sally would have her baby? Jake's baby. Hadn't she imagined what it would be like, carrying it all those months in her body; feeling it move against her, giving birth, feeding it, clothing it. There were days when she was tormented by such thoughts, and having met with Jake and Sally face to face, today was the worst of them.

In spite of herself, her eyes filled with tears, which brimmed over and ran in slow drops down her face.

Will looked at her in consternation.

'Oh, love! I've upset you! It's the baby, isn't it?'

Beth nodded. It was more than the baby, but there was no way she could tell him that. He stepped towards her and put his arms around her, and for once she didn't push him away, but accepted the comfort he offered her.

'It was stupid of me,' Will said. 'I should have had more sense. I know how much you want a child, and believe me, love, so do I.'

He stroked her hair gently, and for a while there was a silence between them, which he was the first to break.

'Couldn't we . . . ? Couldn't we try again?' He was quiet, hesitant. There was something in him at this moment of the Will Seymour she had first known.

'Surely,' he pleaded, 'I've not to spend the rest of my life without your forgiveness for one mistake, however terrible? And I know it was terrible.'

She felt a sudden overwhelming pity for him. He had been punished enough, and wasn't she at the same time also punishing herself? The time had come to put Jake out of her life. He was lost to her, and she must face that, let him go. And perhaps, she thought, if I forgive Will, God will also forgive me, and send me a child.

'Please take me back,' Will urged.

'I will try,' Beth said.

Without a word she took his hand and led him to the bedroom.

It was no good. From the moment Will began to make love to her, from the moment his hands moved over her body, she felt herself stiffen. She felt sick, there was an ice-cold sweat on her face. She tried with all her strength not to show her feelings, her terrible anathema, and then it seemed that she succeeded, for Will, seemingly oblivious of her rigidity, went through with the act to the very end. When it was over and he lay on his back with his eyes closed, she got out of bed, crawled into the living-room, and was sick.

'I must say,' Phoebe said casually to Sally one Monday, 'you seem to be having an easy pregnancy.'

She was getting ready to take the children to Nazareth, picking up Elsie's brood on the way. Sally was still at the littered breakfast table – and it will still be littered when I get back, Phoebe thought. Madam won't lift a finger to clear it.

'I mean,' she continued, 'not a bit like mine. I was sick from beginning to end with my two – *and* I had indigestion, strange fancies, swollen ankles, the lot! You seem to escape everything!'

'Would you rather I was wretched?' Sally demanded.

She wished they would all shut up about her pregnancy. She was fed up hearing about it.

'Not at all,' Phoebe said pleasantly. 'I just thought . . .'

Another thought struck her. She was not sure where it came from. She left the sentence unfinished.

'I'm off,' she said. 'Elsie will be waiting.'

'I've had a strange thought,' she said a few minutes later to Elsie. 'Strange – but I'm sure it's true!'

'What?' Elsie asked.

'Sally Tempest. I don't think she's pregnant at all. I reckon it's been lurking in the back of my mind for some time, and this morning I was sure it was true!'

'Not pregnant?' Elsie said. 'Then why would she pretend she was? What would she gain from that?'

'A husband,' Phoebe said. 'I'll lay any bet that's why he married her. He's certainly not in love with her, that's as plain as a pikestaff!'

'You could be right,' Elsie said thoughtfully. Come to think of it, there had been a number of signs, small things which didn't quite fit. Nevertheless, it was strange.

'What shall you do?' she asked.

'Tackle her with it. I shall tell her that if she doesn't tell him, I will.'

'It's not our business,' Elsie pointed out. 'In any case, he'll find out in the end.'

In the middle of the morning Jake came in from work.

'You're late,' Sally said. She was still sitting at the table.

'I did a couple of hours' overtime,' Jake said. 'We can do with the money. As soon as I've had my breakfast I suggest you get dressed and we'll go for a walk. It's a lovely day. The fresh air will do you good – and the baby.'

Sally leapt to her feet, made a wide, impatient

sweep of her arm and knocked a cup and a plate to the floor.

'Damn the baby!' she shouted. 'Damn and blast the bloody baby!'

Jake stared at her.

'Whatever do you mean? Are you ill? Has something happened?'

'I'm not ill. More to the point I'm not pregnant! There *is* no baby!'

'No baby?' What could she mean? He didn't believe what he was hearing.

'There never was a baby. If it's anything to do with me, there never will be.'

'But you said . . .'

'I pretended. It wasn't difficult, you were as green as grass. If I hadn't said I was expecting you wouldn't have married me, would you?'

'No,' he admitted. 'I wouldn't.'

'It was what I wanted. I wanted to be married and I wanted to be married to you. Little did I know! I was a fool. I can see that now.'

And I am trapped, Jake thought. Now and for ever I'm trapped.

He turned swiftly and walked out of the house.

That same afternoon Phoebe was standing at the table, ironing, while Sally was sprawled in the armchair.

'Aren't you worried that Jake hasn't been home for his dinner?' Phoebe asked. 'He doesn't usually miss a meal.'

'He'll be all right,' Sally said calmly. 'If you must know, we quarrelled. He stamped out in a mad hig.'

'Quarrelled?'

'I'm sure you're dying to know what about. Well, I'll tell you. It'll come out sooner or later.'

Phoebe put the iron down, the better to listen.

'I think you'd more or less guessed I wasn't

pregnant. Well it's true, I'm not! I told him and he wasn't best pleased, so off he went! But he'll be back.'

Phoebe opened her mouth to speak, and at the same moment Elsie Drake, the children following her, came in at the door. Elsie could tell at once there was something going on, she could feel it in the air, even if Phoebe hadn't given her a meaningful look.

'Am I . . . am I interrupting something?' she asked tentatively.

'I'm sure Phoebe'll be pleased to tell you all about it,' Sally said.

Once again, before Phoebe could speak, the door opened and Jake came in. The three women stared at him.

'Have you heard the news?' he asked. His voice was tight with anxiety.

Phoebe found her voice.

'News?' Surely he wasn't going to mention Sally in this way?

'It's very bad. Smallpox! There's smallpox at Sebastopol.'

Sebastopol was the next settlement down the tramway from Jericho, not far from Batty Green.

'Smallpox?' Elsie said.

The three women stared at him in horror.

'A woman and her two children. Real bad, they say. They've taken them into the hospital at Batty Green. It could spread like wildfire! They say there's a suspected case at Batty Green.'

'What are we going to do?' Sally asked, shuddering. If you got the smallpox and you didn't die of it, it left you horribly disfigured. 'What are we going to do?' she repeated.

'First and foremost,' Jake said, 'you must none of you go near Sebastopol, or to Batty Green. And above all, you mustn't take the children there.'

267

# 15

Within the week everyone, in every settlement from Batty Green to Tunnel Huts, had heard the news that a third child of the woman from Sebastopol had gone down with smallpox and that the mother and all three children had died of the disease.

Terror gripped the population of Ribblehead and many, especially single men who did not find it too difficult to move on, packed their bags and fled.

'I'd like to do just that,' Elsie Drake said to Beth, 'but with four children where would we go – and who would have us when they knew where we came from? But you and Will could leave.'

Beth shook her head.

'Will wouldn't hear of it! He says if we're fated to catch it, we'll catch it, and if not we won't.'

'And what about you? What do you think?'

'I shall stay with Will,' Beth said. 'It's my duty. All the same, I think we should take every precaution, keep close to home, not mix with other people. And I reckon it would be wise, with our menfolk meeting with others at work, if we abandoned the children's reading classes for the time being. Just to be on the safe side.'

'I suppose you're right,' Elsie said. 'They'll miss it, though. Especially Tom. He won't know what to do with himself.'

'I shall miss Tom,' Beth admitted. 'He's a wonderful pupil. In fact, one of these days I know he'll outstrip me. But I'll tell you what I'll do. I'll lend him a couple of my own books in the hope that they'll keep him going until all this is over.'

Not for the first time since that awful day when Jake had brought the news, fear gripped Elsie's heart.

'Oh Beth, when *will* it be over?' she said. 'And what's to come before it is?'

Beth put her arm around Elsie's shoulders.

'I don't know, love. We must hope and pray.'

Thus, each and every family tried to keep itself to itself, within the confines of its own house. It was not entirely possible. Shopping had to be done, food to be bought, the men had to go to work and mix with others. And then there were a few, like Will Seymour, who seemed untouched by fear, who went about as always, mixed where they pleased.

But in spite of the precautions most people took, and probably because the infection had already begun to spread before anyone was aware of its existence, the disease went through the settlements like wildfire. Not one shanty town was spared. In Jericho a father of three was taken; in Nazareth a young woman, pregnant with her first child.

'They're building two huts at Batty Green just for the smallpox cases,' Jack Drake said one day when he came home from work. 'I reckon it won't be enough. I reckon they'll have to build more.'

Elsie looked at her children, three of them sitting at the table, Baby Joe asleep in the cradle. What more could she do to keep them safe? She would do anything in the world, she would give her life if need be, but what *could* she do? She had never felt so helpless.

'The people on this railway line have had more than their fair share of sickness and death, accidents and suffering since it started,' she said. 'And the innocent pay just as much as the careless and the guilty. What about that little girl thrown off the tramway when the engine was derailed? She only came to see her aunt at Sebastopol. She was killed before she'd begun her visit! And the man killed in the tunnel, and two at the viaduct? What about them?'

'Hush, love!' Jack said. He saw the older children watching and listening open-mouthed. 'Accidents will happen.'

'Far too many, if you ask me. If you want to know, I've begun to hate the railway. And now why does God have to send the smallpox?'

'More likely the devil sent it,' her husband said. 'We must pray to God that we escape it.'

Jake returned from work a day or two later with the news that there were two more cases at Tunnel Huts. Sally shuddered with horror at the thought.

'How do I know *you're* not bringing it home with you?' she accused him.

As far as she could, though it was next door to impossible, she held herself aloof from everyone in the house, constantly washing herself, laundering her clothes, cleaning the bedroom.

'They reckon we should whitewash the inside of the hut,' she said to Phoebe. 'It keeps the infection away. So why don't we?'

Phoebe shrugged.

'What has to be, will be. I reckon those who are most frightened of it will catch it first!'

'You only say that because you know I'm terrified,' Sally said. 'Well I admit it! Anyway, I'm going to whitewash our bedroom, or rather, I shall get Jake to do it.'

It would be safer, she thought, if she were to spend most of her time in there. Nothing could free her from sleeping in the same bed as Jake, though mercifully not at the same time, since he was still on the night shift and slept during the day. In any case he now made no move at all to be intimate with her. They were like strangers, forced to inhabit the same place.

'Go ahead,' Phoebe said. 'Though if you don't mind a bit of plain speaking I can think of better things to do in a bedroom!'

'You would!' Sally retorted. 'It's all you *do* think about!'

'And if you don't think about it a bit more, you stand to lose your man!' Phoebe warned her. 'Why would anyone be such a fool as to lose Jake Tempest?'

'Mind your own business!' Sally snapped. What did Phoebe know about it, anyway? And she'd certainly got the wrong end of the stick this time.

When she asked Jake about whitewashing the bedroom, he said: 'Since Phoebe agrees, all right. She's the landlady.'

'Don't I know it,' Sally grumbled. 'She thinks that gives her the right to say anything she likes to me. Oh, why can't we leave here? Why can't we move right away? I tell you, it's not safe!'

Jake made no reply. There was nothing to be said. Although in his worst moments he thought he would flee to the far side of the world, though not because of the smallpox, there was no way he would leave the area with Sally in tow. It was bad enough that he was tied to her, but while he remained here he had his job, his workmates and most of all, though she was unattainable, there was Beth. To know that she was nearby was enough to keep him at Ribblehead. Further than that his thoughts wouldn't reach.

During the rest of that spring, and into the early summer, the smallpox epidemic did not abate. Day after day the sad processions left the shanty towns and the hospital, making their slow way to the church at Chapel-le-dale where the vicar was kept busy reciting the funeral rites over the victims as they were interred in the small burial ground.

'They say,' Will Seymour said to Beth, 'that the

271

churchyard won't hold any more. The vicar's asked the Earl to let him have a bit more land, otherwise there'll be nowhere to bury the dead.'

The hospital at Batty Green had been doubled in size, and every known measure to contain the disease had been put into operation, but still the epidemic continued, until one day in early June, when the weary doctor to whom every awful day for several weeks had merged into the next awful day, so that all time seemed the same, looked up from the records he was penning after his round in the hospital, and spoke to the matron.

'Do you realize, Mrs Halifax, that we have some empty beds, and that the last death from smallpox was a fortnight ago?'

'I do indeed, Doctor,' Mrs Halifax said.

'Can we dare to think it's over at last?' he said slowly.

'I think we can. Almost over. The Lord's name be praised!'

'I could wish the Lord had acted sooner,' the doctor said.

'It seems our ordeal is behind us,' Mrs Halifax said.

The doctor shook his head.

'For some the worst is to come. They have to face life without their loved ones; children, fathers, mothers. However far they go back to their homes, they'll never forget the Settle–Carlisle railway.'


'I think we could start the reading classes again, don't you?' Beth said to Elsie Drake.

'I'd be glad of it,' Elsie said. 'My lot are fast what to do with themselves, and I know Phoebe feels the same about hers.'

Beth was glad to see the children back. With no lodger to look after, and Will out at work all day, and having been confined to Nazareth, time had hung heavily on her hands. At Mr Tiplady's party she had made friends with Miss Herbert who had given her much useful advice, and had lent her more equipment. Now that the smallpox was over, she would be free to go down to Batty Green, and to meet up again with the schoolteacher.

On the children's first day back at Nazareth she quickly discovered that they had fallen behind with their reading, which was no more than she expected. They needed constant stimulation. Not so Tom, of course. He stood before her now with shining eyes.

'I finished both the books you lent me,' he said. 'Then I'd nothing to do, so I wrote two stories.'

Beth prickled with excitement as he handed them to her. 'I'll read them as soon as I can,' she promised.

When she had settled the children down with lists of words they were to copy and learn, she started to read. From first word to last she was engrossed, and when she had finished she called to Tom to come and stand beside her.

'Are these the first stories you've written?' she asked.

'Yes, Mrs Seymour,' Tom said.

'And did anyone help you?' It was a silly question, she thought. Who was there to help him?

'Oh no!' Tom said. 'I did them on my own. I didn't show them to anyone else.'

'Well, I reckon they're very, very good,' Beth said. 'There are one or two mistakes, and I'll point them out to you, but nothing important. Thank you for letting me read them. I enjoyed them very much.'

He went crimson with pleasure.

'I'd like to be an author when I grow up,' he said. 'I'd like to write books.'

'And I don't have the slightest doubt that one day you will,' Beth assured him. 'Now wouldn't it be a nice idea, when you got home, if you were to read these aloud to your mother? Show her what you can do.'

And I must speak to Elsie myself, Beth decided. This child's gifts are too precious to be wasted.

'He really needs more education than I can give him,' she said later that day to Elsie. 'He's hungry for it. Will you let me speak to Miss Herbert and Mr Tiplady about him?'

'Well of course – if Jack agrees, that is.' She couldn't think how she came to have such a clever son. There was no-one in the family like that.

'I'm proud of him,' she admitted to Beth. 'Of course I am. But I'm glad he's a nice boy, a loving boy, as well as a clever one.'

'He's certainly that,' Beth assured her.

'What could the teacher and the Missioner do for him?' Elsie asked. 'Would they give him more lessons?'

'I don't know,' Beth said. 'What Tom needs is to go to a good school, a really top-class school where he'll be stretched. And it's possible Mr Tiplady might be able to arrange that. There are scholarships, and I'm sure he could win one, so you'd not have to pay.'

Elsie looked at Beth in dismay.

'You mean he'd have to leave home?'

'In term time,' Beth said. 'He'd come home for the holidays.'

Elsie shook her head.

'I don't think me and Jack would like that. We want him with us.'

'But it would be a wonderful chance for Tom,' Beth said.

'Well, I don't know,' Elsie said doubtfully. 'But I'll talk to Jack when he comes home.'

'Will it be all right if I walk across tomorrow evening, see what you both think?' Beth asked.

'Of course. But we'll say nothing to Tom for the moment.'

The next morning Beth suggested to Tom that instead of joining in with the lesson he might like to try to write another story. He jumped at the chance, and for the rest of the morning his head was bent over the table while he wrote, oblivious to anything else happening in the room. He ate his dinnertime sandwich while still writing, and by the end of the afternoon he had finished the story.

'Will you mind leaving it so that I can read it when you've gone?' Beth said. 'I mustn't keep you any longer. Your mother, and Mrs Grange, will be expecting you all home.'

In the summer weather there was no need for them to be accompanied by an adult. It was enough that Emily was in charge, mainly to ensure that they kept away from the shakeholes and to see that they didn't loiter. Beth stood at the door and waved them off and when they were out of sight she brought a stool out and sat down in the afternoon sun to read the story.

It was wonderful. He had a way with words and a natural rhythm in his sentences, and his main character, a boy of his own age, leapt off the page with reality.

She was still reading when Will came home, not pleased that his tea was not on the table.

'I'm sorry,' Beth said. 'I was carried away – and if you read that while I'm making the tea, you'll see why! I *must* do something for that boy!'

Will regarded her thoughtfully.

'It's not up to you, Beth. He's not your lad.'

'I know that!' Beth said.

'I'm going to the beck to have a good wash,' Will said. 'I'll be back in quarter of an hour.'

'I'll have your tea ready,' Beth said.

Will did not approve of her going to Jericho to talk to the Drakes about Tom, and flatly refused to accompany her.

'Leave people to bring up their own children,' he said. 'They know what's best.'

'I'm not sure that they do,' Beth said. 'I don't think that they recognize Tom's potential.'

It turned out she was wrong.

'We've thought it over,' Jack Drake said. 'Elsie's not totally sure, but I am. We should let the lad have his chance. We've got a good lad and we mustn't stand in the way of his future.' There was pride in his voice. 'So if there's anything you can do . . .'

'You'll not regret it,' Beth said. 'I'm certain of that. And he has a bright future.'

Next morning she was up early, served Will with his usual hearty breakfast, which he ate with relish. He scraped his plate clean, grunted with satisfaction, and rose from the table. As he turned, he winced.

'What is it?' Beth asked.

'Nothing much. A stiff neck; it hurts when I move it. It'll wear off.'

'Then you must wear a neckerchief,' Beth advised. 'The best thing for a stiff neck is warmth.' She searched in a drawer and brought out a clean neckerchief, red with white spots. She was about to hand it to him when she changed her mind.

'Come here,' she said. 'I'll tie it on for you!'

He stood there while she fixed it for him, adjusting the folds, carefully tying the knot. The feel of her cool fingers against his neck was balm to his spirit. He raised his hands and touched her shoulders and for once she did not flinch, or try to move away. After a second or two she stepped back and surveyed him.

'You'll do nicely,' she said. 'The neckerchief suits you. And if your neck isn't any better by the time you get back home I'll rub it with some camphorated oil.'

'That'll do the trick,' he said. 'You always did have healing hands.'

'When I've done a few jobs,' Beth said, 'I'm going down to Batty Green to see Miss Herbert and Mr

Tiplady about Tom. No point in letting the grass grow under my feet.'

'I've told you, love, you shouldn't interfere,' Will said. 'It's nothing to do with you. We should keep out of other people's business.'

'I don't agree,' Beth said. 'Not in this case. And I'm doing it for Tom's sake. It might not come to anything, but I mean to try.'

Will shook his head. There was no moving her when she set her mind to something, but he would say no more. Suddenly, this morning, they had had an easier relationship and he would do nothing in the world to upset that.

'I'm also hoping to get a nice bit of calves' liver while I'm down there,' Beth said. 'I'll have a good tea for you to come home to.'

'I'll be off then,' Will said.

Greatly daring, he leaned forward and kissed her lightly on the cheek. She did not return his kiss, nor did she rebuff him. When he left the hut she stood in the doorway and watched him walk – jauntily, and with a spring in his step – away down the moor.

As he walked Will breathed deeply, filling his lungs with the clear, moorland air. It was a perfect day, warm in the sun, but with a fresh breeze which rippled through the long grass away from the track and sent fleecy clouds scudding across the sky. He felt truly alive and full of hope. Things were going to change between himself and Beth. He could feel it in his bones. He began to sing, his clear, strong baritone startling a hare, which bounded away from him in long leaps. He sang all the way to the viaduct, not even ceasing when he passed people on Batty Green, not the least put out when they stared at him. It was a day for singing, and hadn't he something to sing about, whether the rest of the world had or not?

When he reached the pier on which he was working

he climbed the scaffolding to the top, twenty-five feet from the ground. He was still singing. Except for the stiffness in his neck, he climbed with ease. In spite of his long weeks in bed, he was in fine fettle again, his muscles strong, his body ready to do what he demanded of it.

His mate, Alf Reddy, was already at the top.

'You sound happy enough!' Alf said.

'And so I am,' Will said. He couldn't tell the other man what had made him happy; simply the fact that Beth had tied his neckerchief and had allowed him to kiss her cheek without turning away. It was such a small thing – but not to him. To him it was the start of something new, he was sure of it.

'Well, you'll not have much breath to spare for singing in this wind,' Alf said.

They were working on a king pier. Every sixth pier was a king, very much thicker than the other piers and designed so that if the arches, which would be built on them, were to collapse, only six would fall.

'I don't mind the wind,' Will shouted. They had to shout at each other, and even then they couldn't hear what was said. The wind carried their voices away. Though it might be no more than moderate on the ground, at this height it came in strong gusts.

'We should finish this one today,' Alf shouted.

They had reached the springing, where the arch would eventually be turned. The scaffolding would be taken down and erected again further along the line. It was said by some that there would be eighteen arches in the end, some said twenty-four. No-one seemed to know for certain.

Will paused for a moment to look around him before starting work. He did this every day, seeing the world from his vantage point high on the scaffolding. To the west was Ingleborough, rising up to a top as flat as a table. To the right of that he had a view of the narrow road from Ingleton up which, at this moment, a team of six great horses pulling a car heavy-laden with timber climbed the steep slope to Ribblehead. There were few buildings on the west side of the viaduct since the land was more than usually boggy.

He watched the horses for a while, admiring their strength. He felt that his own strength echoed theirs. Then he clambered around to the other side of the scaffolding from which he could view Batty Green with its huts, brickworks, stables, machinery, inns, people and, dominating everything, Whernside. It was only fractionally higher than Ingleborough, not as tidily shaped, but to Will it was all-powerful.

He was still staring at the scene when Alf called out to him.

'Well, are we going to start work today or not?'

'I'm coming! Anyway, don't nag. Rome wasn't built in a day!' Will spoke with good humour, smiling, as befitted this perfect day.

The smile was still on his face as he turned towards Alf, and as he tripped over a piece of scaffolding, lost his balance and plummeted to the ground. There was no scream, no sound at all from him as he fell as swift as a stone through the air.

When Will had left the house Beth completed her chores as quickly as she could, then changed into the new summer dress she had finished making only two days earlier – green-and-white, narrow-striped cotton with a white collar and cuffs and a deep band of tucking above the hem – dressed her hair carefully, bit at her lips and pinched her cheeks to make the colour come. She wanted to look her best for the occasion, if only for Tom's sake. Then she put Tom's three stories in her basket and set off down the moor.

Sheep, with fast-growing lambs still staying close, cropped at the lush green grass, flowers sprang underfoot. Beth breathed deeply, savouring the mountain air. It was a perfect day and she looked forward to the mission she was about to undertake.

When she arrived at the school, Miss Herbert saw her at once, and listened with interest while Beth told her about Tom Drake.

'I've brought the first three stories he's written,' she said. 'The first two he wrote at home with no prompting, the third he wrote in class but without help from me. It's only in the last few months he's learned to read and write.'

Miss Herbert examined the stories with interest.

'They're extremely good,' she said. 'Here's a child who'd be worth helping; but except in the very best of weather – and even then it's a long way for a nine-year-old – he'd not be able to do the journey to and from Jericho every day. In any case, I'd say he's streets ahead of my pupils. He'd need special teaching.'

'I thought so too,' Beth said. 'Then would you agree that I should speak to Mr Tiplady about the possibility of a boarding school?'

'If he were my child, that's what I'd do,' Miss Herbert said.

And if he were mine I'd leave no stone unturned, Beth thought. Nor will I, though he's not mine.

Mr Tiplady was equally interested, and even more impressed than Miss Herbert by the stories.

'And you say he's good at other things also?' he asked.

'At everything he touches,' Beth said.

'Then we must do something for him. It would be unChristian to let such talent go to waste. Will you leave it to me to make enquiries?'

'Gladly,' Beth assured him.

'Of course I shall call on him, and on his parents,' Mr Tiplady said. 'I must make sure what *they* want.'

'I know they'll be grateful,' Beth said.

She rose to go. Mr Tiplady saw her to the door. As she stood on the step making her farewells, the covered wagon, which was the ambulance, came tearing across the green from the direction of the hospital, the driver whipping up the horse to go even faster, while the man at his side violently rang a handbell. Those in the path of the ambulance scattered to right and left.

'Whatever—' Beth began.

'From the speed he's driving almost certainly an accident,' Mr Tiplady said. 'And in the direction of the viaduct. I must follow at once, see what I can do. Please excuse me!'

He ran into the street and set off in pursuit of the ambulance, as did several people who had been standing around.

Beth gasped in horror. The viaduct! Will! But even if the viaduct was the scene of the accident, why should it mean Will? There were dozens of men working on and around the viaduct. So she told herself as she ran with the crowd towards the scene.

The ambulance was there, also a police constable trying to control the crowd.

'Stand back there!' he shouted, waving his truncheon.

Beth, who attempted to run forward to where, several yards away, a man was being lifted onto a stretcher, was barred by the policeman's outstretched arm.

'I saw it happen!' a woman next to her in the crowd said. 'I was right here when he fell. From the highest bit of the scaffolding it was. I reckon it was a sudden gust of wind blew him!'

She paused for effect, then started again.

'His hat fell off, floated down on its own. It was slower than the man, tossed about by the wind. He came down fast, being heavy I suppose. He was wearing a red neckerchief. You could see it as he fell!'

She paused again, searching her mind for more revelations, but before they emerged Beth had already broken out of the crowd, dodged under the constable's arm, and was streaking across the space which separated her from the ambulance. The ground was boggy, the thick black mud covered her feet, but because she ran so fast she avoided being sucked in.

'A red neckerchief!' The words screamed in her ears. But didn't half the men in the area wear red neckerchieves? It didn't have to be Will.

She ran as fast as a hare, no-one could stop her. When she reached the scene the stretcher was being carried towards the ambulance, the body on it covered by a blanket. She tweaked back the blanket.

'It's Will! It's Will!'

'Stand aside, lady,' one of the stretcher bearers said. 'You're stopping us!'

'But it's Will!' she cried. 'It's my husband! He's dead, isn't he?'

'He's not dead, lady, but the sooner we get him to the hospital, the better. If he's your husband you can go in the ambulance.'

While the ambulance bumped and bounced over the uneven ground, she sat close to Will. He was unconscious, but breathing.

'Will,' she implored. 'Open your eyes! Look at me! Speak to me!'

'He can't hear you, lady! He's not conscious,' the ambulance man said.

She wiped the blood from his face with her inadequately small handkerchief until the man passed her a towel. Not until they reached the hospital and she was walking beside the stretcher, into the hut, did she notice that her new dress was soaked in blood.

Will died two hours later. Though she continued to call his name, begging him to speak to her, to open his eyes and look at her, he did not do so. He remained unconscious until the end.

Someone led her away, seated her in a chair, drew a screen around her; someone gave her tea which she could not drink. She remembered afterwards that at one point Mr Tiplady came in and spoke to her – and went.

She had no idea how long after it was – it could have been one hour or several – that the screen was pulled aside again and Jake was standing there. He held her by the hands, pulled her to her feet, and took her in his arms. When she came to her senses and looked at him, really looked at him, there was blood on him too.

Will Seymour was buried three days later, on a hot June day, not a puff of wind or a cloud in the sky. A surprising number of people walked behind the cart which bore the coffin the two miles to the churchyard at Chapel-le-dale; people from Nazareth and Jericho, drinking pals from the Welcome Home, workmates. The discovery that he had been popular raised Beth, for a minute or two, from her lethargy.

When it was over, Elsie Drake went back home with her to help serve the funeral tea, most of which she had also provided and made, since Beth could not bring herself to do it.

'I don't want a funeral tea!' she said.

'You've got to have one, love,' Elsie said. 'It wouldn't be respectful to Will, otherwise. What would people think?'

'It's barbaric!' Beth protested. 'Burying someone, then sitting down to eat and drink.'

'You're wrong there, love,' Elsie looked at Beth with compassion. 'It has healing qualities, the meal has. I don't quite understand why, but it helps to bring you back to normal. We have to go on, you know, choose how! But what I suggest is that you go to bed. There's no more to be done and it's been a hard day. I shan't be long before I turn in meself. I'll sleep in the other bedroom so as not to disturb you.'

'There's no need for you to stay the night.' Beth's protest was half-hearted.

'Oh yes there is!' Elsie contradicted. 'Just for tonight. Tomorrow I'll have to get back to Jack and the children.'

And what will I do tomorrow? Beth asked herself. No husband, no income. Will I even have a home?

But now she was too tired to think about it. All she wanted now was to sleep and sleep.

# 16

Beth's worries about keeping her home were solved within a week of Will's funeral.

It was a terrible week in which she could not summon enough strength even to leave the hut. The energy which had seen her through the funeral had quickly evaporated, leaving a dreadful lassitude. She cooked no meals; she didn't want to eat, and who else was there to worry about? She read nothing, not even the newspaper which Elsie brought her and which contained the report of Will's accident and death: she did no housework, went to bed early while the sun was still shining and stayed there until late next morning. Today, the sixth day, she was still in bed when Elsie paid her daily visit around noontime.

'I've brought you some broth,' Elsie said. 'You've got to eat whether you feel like it or not. It'll do you no good to starve. And as a matter of fact, you've got to bestir yourself, get up and get going.'

'Why?' Beth asked.

'I'll tell you why,' Elsie said sternly. 'Though it's not something I ever thought I'd have to say to you, of all people. It's because your house is getting mucky, you haven't washed a pot or dusted a shelf, and because you yourself are not too clean. Will you take a look in the mirror? When did you last put a comb through your hair?'

Beth made a movement with her hand as if she would like to push Elsie out of the bedroom.

'I can't be bothered,' she said.

'You've got to be bothered,' Elsie said. 'Oh, don't think I'm not sorry for you. Of course I am. Why do you think I come every day? And Phoebe, and Jake? Jake Tempest is sick with worry about you.'

Jake had been to see her twice since the funeral. She had nothing to say to him, she had nothing to say to anyone. He had spoken very little; just sat with her, held her hand, left quite soon because she clearly didn't want him there.

'So today I'm going to stay here while you get up, have a top-to toe wash, and put on some clean clothes. Then I'm going to help you put the house to rights. I'm not going to do it *for* you, I'm just going to give you a hand.'

'You can't,' Beth protested. 'You've got the children to think of.'

Elsie shook her head.

'No I haven't! Phoebe's taken the baby and she'll keep an eye on the others from time to time. Emily's looking after Tom and Ada, so they'll be all right.'

Elsie noticed the first flicker of interest in Beth's face at the mention of Tom's name. She seized on it at once.

'Tom did say he might walk over with the girls, later this afternoon.' It was pure invention, but it might work.

Beth sat up in bed, took a deep breath. Tom! She had been visiting Mr Tiplady on Tom's behalf when the ambulance had rushed by. From that moment to this she had not given him a thought. She had not even passed on to Elsie and Jack what Mr Tiplady had said of Tom's chances.

'It wouldn't be nice for Tom to see his teacher looking as you do at this minute,' Elsie persisted. 'Tom thinks a lot of you!'

'I'm sorry,' Beth said quietly. 'I'm sorry about all this, Elsie. You're quite right. I'll get up at once.'

'No need to be sorry, love,' Elsie said more gently. 'I only want what's best for you, we all do. I'll go and heat the water and bring the bathtub in. You can have a nice bath and wash your hair before anybody comes.'

Beth got out of the bed, then she turned her head and looked at it, and it was the sight of the bed which caused a great wave of guilt to sweep over her. I have not been a good wife to Will, she thought. I didn't try hard enough. Whatever he did, I should have tried harder.

It was this, she suddenly recognized, which she had been suppressing since the moment of Will's death. She had allowed no thoughts at all into her mind, pushing everything away, lying around in a near stupor instead of facing her true feelings. And even though she now recognized her feelings as guilt, added to anger for Will's sake that this should have happened to him in the prime of his life and after all he had gone through, she knew that in facing her emotions she would somehow come to deal with them.

She stripped the bed down to the bare mattress, in what felt like a stripping of herself, then she went into the living-room and stepped into the bath which Elsie had prepared for her.

'And while you're having your bath,' Elsie said, 'I'm going to make a start on the bedroom.'

When Beth was newly dressed in fresh clothes, her still-damp hair tied neatly back, the two women worked together throughout the afternoon until the hut was clean from stem to stern. Elsie looked around with satisfaction.

'I think we've earned ourselves a cup of tea and a slice of cake,' she said. 'And it so happens I brought some cake with me. Now confess it, love, you do feel better, don't you?'

'I admit it,' Beth said. 'Tired, but better.'

'And things will improve each day.'

Elsie said the words more from hope than from experience. She wasn't sure she believed them. She didn't know how she would face life if anything happened to her Jack.

'Tom didn't come,' Beth said when Elsie was about to leave.

'So he didn't,' Elsie said, sounding surprised. 'Happen he'll do so tomorrow.'

'I'll start the classes again soon,' Beth promised. 'Except that . . .' Her voice trailed away.

'What?'

'Oh, Elsie, how do I know how long I'll be able to stay here? Even if I can scrape up the rent money, which I doubt, will they let me keep the hut? Won't they want it for someone who works on the railway?'

'Meet that when it comes,' Elsie advised. 'In the meantime, if I were you I'd keep quiet. Say nothing until they do.'

Beth didn't have long to wait. Halfway through the next morning Mr Pennington called. When she opened the door and saw him standing there her first thought was one of thankfulness that the house, and she herself, were clean; her second one of frightening apprehension.

When his preliminary condolences were over he said: 'I've brought you some money – wages due to your late husband. It will tide you over for a bit. Four pounds six shillings.'

Beth took the money from him.

'Thank you.'

'And next we come to the question of the hut.'

Beth stood silent. She could think of nothing to say.

'Now as you know, Mrs Seymour, the Company's policy is to rent the huts only to someone who works on the line . . .'

'But Mr Pennington . . . !'

He held up his hand.

'Hear me out. We have two men, brothers, who've been working on number two contract, and now they've asked to work here, on number one. They're married men, but their wives aren't with them and they need lodgings. You've been a good tenant, Mrs Seymour. You keep things nice.' He glanced around with approval. 'And I fancy you keep a good table.'

'Oh I do, I do! I'd be pleased to look after them if you'd give me the chance!'

'Then we'll give it a trial, shall we? Their names are Alan and Charlie Miller. They'll be working in the cutting, south of the tunnel, so Nazareth will be handy for them. They could come tomorrow if that suits.'

'It suits me very well,' Beth said eagerly. 'I wonder . . . do you know what rent I should charge them?'

'That's up to you,' Mr Pennington said. 'As long as you pay your rent to the Company and keep a good house. Why not charge what you charged that other lodger you had? Tempest, wasn't it? What happened to him?'

'He got married. He and his wife lodge in Jericho.'

'Jericho?'

'With Mrs Grange.'

Did she imagine it, or did his eyes light up at the mention of Phoebe Grange?

Alan and Charlie Miller arrived next day, in the early evening after work. When Beth opened the door to them she thought for a moment that she was seeing double. Though they were not twins – later they told her that there was a year between them – they were as alike as two peas in a pod, both tall, strongly built, with bright blue eyes in faces deeply tanned from working in the open air, and when they simultaneously doffed their hats in a polite greeting, they both revealed thick blond hair.

'Please come in!' Beth said.

She liked the look of them, and over the next few

minutes it seemed they liked everything they saw, especially the room they would share.

'I reckon we'll be very comfortable here,' Alan Miller said.

'Very comfortable,' his brother echoed.

Beth quickly discovered that Charlie Miller echoed everything his elder brother said, always agreeing, never venturing his own opinion first.

'I'll cook you a good breakfast,' Beth said, 'make you sandwiches for your midday break, and give you a good meal when you get home from work.'

'That sounds very satisfactory,' Alan said.

'Very satisfactory,' Charlie repeated.

'And we won't be here at weekends, not unless we're working overtime,' Alan said. 'We only live in Skipton, so we can get home to our wives at the weekend.'

This time Charlie merely nodded in agreement. Beth wondered if, when he was in his own home, he repeated his wife's words or actually used his own. But he was amiable enough, they both were. She foresaw no trouble with them, they would be a source of both income and company in this lonely place.

'Well, I've been making a meal,' she said. 'It'll be on the table in half an hour if you'd like to be settling yourselves in, in the meantime.'

When they had eaten, both of them leaned back in their chairs, wide smiles of appreciation on their faces.

'That was very tasty, Mrs Seymour,' Alan said.

'Very tasty!' Charlie agreed.

'And now, if you don't mind,' the elder brother said, 'we thought we'd take a walk down to the Welcome Home.'

Oh no, Beth thought. Not drinking men! What would she do if they came reeling home? What if they did so every night? When she heard Alan's next words she realized her thoughts must have shown in her face.

'Oh, we'll not be long, Mrs Seymour! Two pints and that's our lot. We have a wife and two little ones apiece to provide for. It doesn't run to much drinking!'

When they had left, she cleared away, then started to lay the table. There was a knock on the door and when she answered it, Jake stood there.

'Come in,' Beth said.

He did so. They stood facing each other. He wanted to take her in his arms, to hold her close, never to let her go. He couldn't do it. What had he to offer her? She was free but now he was bound, that was the terrible irony of it.

'I wanted to see how you were,' he said. 'Are you all right?'

'All right,' he thought. What a feeble way of putting it! Of course she wasn't all right, and nor was he, and would they ever be?

'I'm fine,' Beth said. 'I have two new lodgers, did you hear?'

'Elsie told me,' Jake said. 'So where are they?'

'They've gone down to the Welcome.'

He gave her a sharp look. 'Then I'll stay 'til they return,' he said.

Beth smiled.

'It's kind of you, but you needn't. They'll be all right. They can't afford to drink much. And – admit it – it's livelier at the Welcome than it is here. They need it at the end of a day's hard work.'

All I need, Jake thought, is to be found within these four walls.

'But do stay a bit,' Beth invited. 'That is if you have the time.'

'Oh, Beth, you know I have the time for you! Always and for ever!'

'But you can't have,' Beth said gently. 'You have Sally.'

'Sally means nothing to me, nor I to her,' Jake said.

'Nevertheless,' Beth said, 'you *are* married to her, she is your wife.'

For several seconds they looked at each other without speaking. If he were to take me now, Beth thought, if he were only to put out a hand and touch me, I would be powerless.

'I was wondering,' Jake ventured, 'whether I might have more reading lessons?'

Beth shook her head.

'No. You don't need more lessons. You read as well as I do now. All we need is more books.'

Then, with a great effort, she said, 'Perhaps you shouldn't come here at all.'

'I can't promise that,' Jake replied. 'Please don't ask me to.'

He stayed with her until the brothers returned, which was not late, nor were they in the least the worse for wear, simply pleasant and affable. For twenty minutes the three men talked together about their work, while Beth sat and listened.

'It must be hellish in the tunnel,' Alan said. 'Give me the open air any time, no matter what the weather's like!'

'I've grown used to the tunnel,' Jake said. 'It's hard, but you can see it taking shape day by day. I'll stay with it until it's finished. I wouldn't want to work anywhere else.'

He looked forward, these days, to going to work; and when he had finished his shift, no matter how tired he was he didn't want to go home. The strenuous physical labour and the difficult conditions challenged him, suited his mood.

The following day Elsie Drake came to Nazareth, bringing a letter she and Jack had received that morning from Mr Tiplady.

'He's coming to see us tomorrow evening about our Tom,' she said. 'Me and Jack wondered if you'd be there. We'd be glad if you would; you know more about these things than we do.'

'Of course I will,' Beth promised. 'Oh, isn't it exciting?'

Elsie looked dubious.

'I'm not so sure,' she said. 'We'll have to see.'

The purpose of Mr Tiplady's visit was to tell them that he had the highest possible hopes of getting a place for Tom in a good boarding school.

'It's in York,' he said.

'York!' Elsie was dismayed. 'But that's a long way away!'

'Not really,' Mr Tiplady said. 'Trains run to York from almost everywhere in the country these days. It's not a long journey from Settle. He'll be home for holidays, probably even for half-terms – and you might be able to go and visit.'

'That's true enough,' Jack Drake said. 'We mustn't stand in his way, love. We've agreed on that.'

'And the school has agreed that I may have the entrance examination papers and he can take the exam in my house, with me acting as invigilator,' Mr Tiplady said.

'We'll need money for books, and new clothes – uniform and such like,' Elsie said. She knew in her heart she was searching around for reasons why he couldn't go. She was ashamed of herself for doing so, but she couldn't help it.

'If he gets the scholarship it will cover his books,' the Missioner said. 'And I'll try to find a source of money for the uniform.'

'No need for that!' Jack Drake was firm. 'We can manage that ourselves. Never let it be said we couldn't clothe our own children!'

A day or two later, early in July, Tom walked down to Batty Green, by himself, and took the examination in Mr Tiplady's home. After that he walked around the stalls, mingling with the crowds, and bought himself a glass of ginger beer with the penny his mother had given him, before making his way home.

Elsie, who had kept an almost constant watch for him, saw him walking up the hill and hurried to the door to greet him.

'Well, love, how did it go?' she asked.

'Quite well, I think,' Tom said. 'It wasn't difficult.'

'Your dad'll be pleased to hear that when he gets home from work,' Elsie said.

A week later Alan and Charlie Miller brought home the news that there was a new outbreak of smallpox at Batty Green.

'They say several cases, and pretty bad. It's all hands aloft at the hospital,' Alan said. 'We thought it was all over, otherwise our wives would never have let us come. Anyway, it means we mustn't go home until it's over. It wouldn't be fair.'

'Have you been in contact with anyone who might have it?' Beth asked. They went down to Batty Green at least twice a week, sat in the crowded Welcome Inn.

'How can we tell?' Alan asked. 'You don't know until it happens, and by then it's too late. But we shall stay away from the Welcome, that's for sure!'

Next morning Beth went early to Jericho to give the news to Elsie Drake.

'I know,' Elsie said. 'Jack told me.'

'Then once again I reckon we must stop the classes,' Beth said. 'Just to be on the safe side.'

'Oh, I agree!' Elsie said. 'Shall I let Phoebe know, or will you call?'

Beth hesitated. If she called on Phoebe now, like as not Jake would be there. She longed to see him, longed even to be in the same room with him, and knew she must not.

'You tell Phoebe,' she said.

'Very well,' Elsie agreed. 'I've heard they're desperately short of help at the hospital. Have you heard that?'

'I can well believe it,' Beth said.

On the way home, and for the rest of the afternoon as she went about her tasks in the hut, she thought about this. It would be women they needed; women to help with the nursing, to take on the cleaning and the laundry: there were so many jobs to be done. Almost every man in the area was employed on the railway and what women there were – by no means as numerous as the men – were wives, and usually mothers, who couldn't possibly risk working in the hospital. But I am not, she thought. I am neither a wife nor a mother. Come to that, of what great use am I in the world?

She had the Miller brothers to look after, of course, but what was the most important thing; what ought she to be doing?

When they came home at the end of the day, she asked them.

'What shall I do? There are so many hours in the day when I'm not occupied. I could help in the hospital, but what would you two do? How would you manage?'

She left them to discuss it with each other while she did other jobs. When she came back to them, Alan said:

'What if you brought the infection back here? We have to think of our wives and children. We can't take too many risks. We don't mind looking after ourselves for a week or two, it's just the infection.'

'I wouldn't come home,' Beth said. 'I would ask if I could sleep in the hospital. I daresay they'd be glad of that.'

So it was agreed, and the next day she presented herself at the hospital.

Elsie, when she called in and told her on her way down the moor, thought she was out of her mind.

'I shall be worried sick about you!' she said. 'Have you thought what risks you're running?'

'I've thought about it all night,' Beth admitted. 'I won't say I'm not the least bit worried, because I am. But I still think I ought to do it – if they'll have me, that is.'

'Well, I can see there's no changing your mind,' Elsie said.

'I'll see you all when it's over,' Beth said. 'And will you do me a favour? Will you tell Jake, tell him not to worry, and he's not to come to the hospital.'

'I'll tell him,' Elsie promised.

She opened her arms to Beth and the two women embraced. It was something they had never done before. When they looked at each other before parting there were tears in Elsie's eyes.

Beth was warmly welcomed at the hospital. 'Though I've no experience other than nursing my husband through his illness,' she explained.

'You're another pair of hands,' the matron said. 'We need all the help we can get. And the fact that you're willing to live in makes you even more valuable. But you have considered the possible danger, Mrs Seymour?'

'I have.'

'Well then, I'll be glad to have you, and the sooner you can start, the better.'

'I can start tomorrow,' Beth said.

'There are some things you can do to help yourself, to lessen the risk,' Matron said. 'Keep yourself clean. Take baths as often as you can, wash your hair and keep it covered. We disinfect everything we possibly can. Hygiene is the answer. It's the lack of hygiene in the shanty towns which allows infections to spread, but people won't believe that until it's too late.'

How tired Matron looks, Beth thought. But then, she'd hardly had time to pull round from the first wave of smallpox before the second one was upon them – and the second one seemed likely to be worse than the first.

Beth had never worked so hard in her life, never known that she was capable of doing so. As the days went by she discovered that under the direction of the other nurses, who were more experienced but far too few in number, she could do most of the tasks set her. Mostly they needed willingness, care, common sense.

All day long she washed patients, fed them, changed their clothing and their bedding, dressed their sores, fetched and carried bedpans. When the washing of bed linen was more than the two laundry maids – young and frightened – could cope with, she also took a hand with that.

Every day new cases came in, until the hospital was full to overflowing, and then beds only became free when patients either recovered and went home, or died. It seemed to Beth that far too many died. Not all the care and attention in the world could save them.

On Beth's sixth day in hospital Matron sent for her.

'I'm sorry, Nurse, to give you this further burden,' she apologized. 'It's something I'd rather have kept you from for a while longer, but we're desperately short-staffed. I'm asking you to help Nurse Proctor deal with two patients who have died this morning. It has to be done as soon as possible.'

Beth felt herself stiffen. I can't do it! I can't do that! she thought.

'Nurse Proctor will show you what has to be done, but I have to impress two things upon you. One is that the body of a person who has died of smallpox is extremely infectious, and you must take every possible care of yourself. The other is that you must go about this task quietly and soberly, treating the body of every victim, whoever and in whatever state they are, with decency and reverence.'

To behave so, Beth found, when for the first time she carried out the task with Nurse Proctor, came naturally. What she was not prepared for was the rush of pity which threatened to overwhelm her as the two of them dealt with the body of a young man in his twenties. As they sewed him into a blanket soaked in disinfectant, which acted as his shroud, she worked through a mist of tears. When the undertaker came with the coffin, liberally lined with sawdust doused with more disinfectant, she helped to lift the body in, and watched while the undertaker immediately sealed it with putty.

'And it won't be any easier with the next one,' Nurse Proctor said quietly. 'It's a little girl, four years old.'

Two days later, worse was to happen.

In the morning a young man, Adam Beck, was admitted. Beth knew him by sight, since he lived at Jericho, a few doors away from Phoebe Grange. He was desperately ill, barely conscious, and with a raging fever.

'I don't give much for his chances,' Nurse Proctor said, when they had done all they could for him.

In the afternoon there was another admittance. Beth was elsewhere when the patient was taken onto the ward. It was Nurse Proctor who told her.

'It's another one from Jericho. They must be in for it there! A child this time.'

Beth went cold. Six children she knew in Jericho. It could be any one of them. Or perhaps not, she told herself. There were others. But she had to know.

'Excuse me!' she said – and hurried off to the ward.

She knew which bed it would be. It had been made ready only that morning after its former occupant had gone home. Praying – incoherently – she approached the bed. Her prayers were not answered. The boy lying there was Tom Drake.

His face was flushed crimson with the fever, his eyes, when he opened them, were too bright. He moved his head uneasily from side to side. He seemed at first barely conscious, but when he saw Beth he recognized her and gave her a faint smile.

'Hello, Tom!' Beth said. 'How are you feeling?'

'My back aches, Mrs Seymour,' Tom said. 'And my head hurts something terrible. Please do something to stop it!'

'Of course I will!' Beth promised. 'I'll bathe it with nice, cool water for a start. You'll be my special patient, Tom love!'

She had already seen enough of the disease to recognize when there was a mild case or when it was serious. She knew just by looking at him that Tom was very ill indeed. She stayed with him a few minutes longer, then went to see the sister in charge of the ward.

'The little boy in the end bed, Sister . . .' she began.

'Tom Drake,' Sister Kenny interrupted. 'He's a very sick child.'

'I know him,' Beth told her. She explained the circumstances. 'I wonder whether, if I have any spare time, you'll allow me to spend it with him? I realize his mother won't be able to visit him because of the rest of the family – there are three more little ones. He'll miss her so much.'

The only access relatives had to the two smallpox wards was that on certain days and for a strictly limited period they were allowed to look through the window at their loved one. Even this was discouraged. It was best to keep well away from the area.

'I don't know about that, Nurse Seymour,' Sister said. 'You know how busy we are. You have your own duties . . .'

'Oh I know!' Beth said. 'I'll not neglect a single one. I just thought . . .'

Sister Kenny held up a hand to stop Beth.

'. . . And when those are completed it's your further duty to take what rest you can. You have to keep well for the sake of all the patients. We don't have time for special nursing.'

'It's just that . . .' Beth began. How could she explain what she felt about Tom? 'He's a very special little boy.' She felt as if she was pleading for her own child, the one she would never have, but then she thought of Elsie, and what her anguish must be. She wanted also to do it for Elsie.

'All children are special,' Sister Kenny said. 'Nevertheless, I take your point. So you may give him what extra attention you can, while not neglecting your other duties, and I will trust you not to overstretch yourself. Indeed, Nurse, that's an order, and I shall watch to see that it's carried out!'

'Thank you! Thank you very much!' Beth said.

Sister Kenny did watch, and saw that Nurse Seymour was doing far more than her strength allowed, but she did not interfere, not even when the night nurse reported that Nurse Seymour had come down to the ward in the middle of the night to sit with Tom.

'Don't stop her,' she told the night nurse. 'It can't last long, he's too desperately ill, poor child.'

Beth herself was aware that Tom could not go on much longer. He hardly knew her. Fever raged in him; his body was covered in spots, now turning into blisters as the disease took its course. She bathed him, changed his bedclothes, and when she had done all the practical things she sat beside the bed, day or night, it didn't matter, held his hand, and prayed. She had never been so weary, so desperately tired, but she knew she would go on to the end. Nothing would stop her.

Then one night – it was two o'clock in the morning – she was snatching some rest when she wakened with a sense of urgency, of being desperately needed. She went at once to the ward and when she saw Tom she knew that that was so.

She sat by the bed, holding his hand. It was not the time now to do anything more for him, to disturb him in any way.

She didn't know how long she sat there or who came and went, but in the end the days and nights of fatigue overcame her, and she dozed, slumped forward over the bed, Tom's hand in hers.

The first daylight creeping in through the window awakened her. At once, before she even raised her head, she knew that something had happened, something was different. Then she felt a hand on her shoulder and heard the night nurse's quiet voice.

'Nurse Seymour! It's all right! Tom's all right!'

Beth lifted her head and looked at him. It was true! Beneath the ravages of the disease, he was different. The fever had left him. He slept naturally, his breathing eased.

On the same day, four hours later, Adam Beck died. Though Beth's heart was sad as she helped Nurse Proctor to prepare the young man's body for the undertaker, she could not help thanking God that it was not Tom she was dealing with.

Sally stared at herself in the mirror which hung on the wall in the bedroom she shared with Jake. Everyone else in the house, including Jake, had gone to Adam Beck's funeral at Chapel-le-dale, except Phoebe's children who were being looked after by Elsie Drake.

Sally had flatly refused to attend the funeral.

'Why should I walk three miles to Chapel-le-dale to bury someone I hardly know?' she'd said to Jake.

'As a mark of respect,' Jake said. 'Everyone goes to a neighbour's funeral.'

'Well I don't,' Sally had said. 'There are too many funerals. It's gloomy.'

No-one could deny that. In this summer of 1871 death had been an all-too-frequent visitor to Ribblehead. No shanty town had escaped him. But Sally's true reason for not attending Adam Beck's funeral was deeper than the one she gave.

She was afraid. She was dreadfully and terribly afraid of the smallpox. She now went nowhere, never leaving the house and spending much of the time isolated in her room. Every day, sometimes several times a day, she looked in the mirror, as she did now.

She saw a beautiful face. She needed no-one to tell her she was beautiful, it was there before her; her flawless skin – though paler than it should be because she lacked fresh air – her sensual, curving mouth, her lustrous hair escaping in tendrils over her forehead. And her eyes, large, limpid, thickly fringed by black lashes.

It was her eyes she saw now in the reflection in the mirror. She stared at her eyes, and what she saw in them was terror. What if, in spite of all her precautions, she caught the smallpox? What if Jake brought it home with him, or one of the children? What if she died? She wasn't ready to die, she was too young. What if she didn't die but was horribly scarred? Looking in the mirror, she saw her face pock-marked.

'I can't stand it!' she cried out loud. 'I can't stand it another minute!'

And then she knew what she must do. It was the only thing. She would run away, leave this awful place for ever, go where she would be safe.

Into a bag she packed only what she needed for the journey. She wanted none of her clothes or other possessions. Who knew whether they would carry infection? She needed money, but she knew where Jake kept his savings because he made no secret of it. She took those, every last penny. He could earn more.

She glanced at the clock. If she hurried she could get a lift from Burgoyne & Cocks to Settle. It would mean setting foot on Batty Green, but there was no help for that.

Quickly, she found a piece of paper and scribbled a note which she left on the table so that Jake would see it the moment he came back.

She glanced at the clock again. She must be quick or they would be back from the funeral.

When Jake returned from the funeral with Phoebe and her husband he was surprised by Sally's absence. These days she never left the house. Then he saw her note, picked it up and began to read it.

'Is anything wrong?' Phoebe asked.

'Not really. It's Sally. She's gone to stay with her aunt in Settle. It's not a bad idea. You know how nervous she is about the smallpox.'

As the days passed with no word from Sally, Jake wondered if he should go to see her in Settle. It was easy to decide against it. She wouldn't welcome him, she would worry that he might somehow carry infection. In any case, he had no desire to see her.

At the end of a fortnight two letters arrived on the same day, one from Settle, the other addressed in Sally's writing, postmarked Bradford. He opened Sally's letter first, read it quickly, then, hardly able to believe what it said, he read it again.

Dear Jake

I will not be coming back, not ever. The truth is I am not married to you and never was. I married Matthew when I was 16 but it all went wrong and my mother packed me off to Settle. I have met up with Matthew again and I know he is my true love. My aunt did not know.

All in all I daresay you will be pleased.

Sally

He stood there, holding the letter in his hand. There was only one thought in his mind, and he was filled with it.

'I'm free!' He said the words out loud.

Eventually he picked up the second letter. It was of no importance to him, all he needed to hear was in the first one. Nevertheless he opened it. It was from Sally's aunt.

I want you to know, (she wrote) I knew nothing of all this. My sister never said. When Sally told me I sent her packing, never to darken my door again. I know you can report her for bigamy but I am begging you not to for my sister's sake even though she deceived me. You are a true gentleman and I hope you won't.

Yours truly
(Mrs) Jane Sutherland

He didn't bother to read it twice. It was not important. 'I am free!' he told himself again.

He left the hut and set off down the moor at a run, towards the hospital.

## 17

Nurse Proctor, her face gleaming with excitement, came into the ward. Beth was washing a patient.

'There's a man at the door, wants to see you. I was passing through the hall and the bell was ringing like mad. Eliot wasn't there. I don't know why we have a porter, he's never at his post!'

'So who wants to see me?' Beth asked. Who would seek her out at the hospital? She felt stirrings of alarm.

'He says his name's Jake Tempest. I wish it was me he wanted to see!'

Jake! What could he possibly want? Something must be wrong! Elsie – or Phoebe? One of the children? Surely not the smallpox? Please God not that! The thoughts raced around Beth's head.

'He said to tell you it wasn't bad news,' Nurse Proctor said. 'So you've no need to look like that.'

Beth's relief gave way to a slight annoyance that Jake should have presented himself at the hospital about something apparently unimportant when she had specifically asked him not to. All the same, she longed to see him. It was a longing to which she knew she shouldn't give way. He was not for her and that was the end of it.

'I can't see him,' she said. 'I hope you told him that?'

Apart from her own reason for not seeing him, it was not permissible. In the present circumstances of the epidemic no visitors were allowed into the building, nor was any nurse allowed to step outside to meet with one. The rule was strict. Before a nurse was free to leave the hospital, which she could only do in her rare time off, she must change out of her uniform, take a bath liberally laced with disinfectant, wash her hair and put on clean clothes. Even then she was not advised to mix with anyone; simply to take in a change of scene and breathe some fresh air.

'Oh, I told him,' Nurse Proctor said. 'He says he has something to say to you and he won't go away until he's said it. He'll wait outside until you appear. Aren't you the lucky one?'

'Except that I won't appear,' Beth said. 'And there'll be trouble if Matron sees him hanging around. There'll be trouble for you, too, if she finds out you answered the door. What in the world can he be thinking of?' She longed to know.

'You could talk to him through the glass,' Nurse Proctor suggested. 'He could write a note and hold it up to you. Oh, isn't it romantic!'

It was also feasible. It was the way patients and visitors communicated, since it was impossible, even when they shouted, to hear what was said through the thick glass of the windows.

Beth thought for a moment. 'All right, I'll do that. Then will you do me a favour?' she said. 'I'll be at the linen-room window in fifteen minutes. Will you ask Eliot if he'll show Jake Tempest where it is, and tell him to be there?'

'Oh, I will, I will!' Nurse Proctor said. Wasn't this a most welcome break from routine?

A quarter of an hour later Beth went into the linen room, closing the door firmly behind her. Jake was already at the window. She felt a quick surge of delight at the sight of him, and just as quickly squashed it. This was a stupid, mad thing to be doing and the sooner it was over, the better. What in the world would she do if Sister or Matron walked in?

Jake, looking remarkably happy, spoke words to her through the glass. She thought he said . . . it seemed like . . . but of course she must be mistaken. She shook her head vigorously.

'I can't hear,' she mouthed.

Then he smoothed out the piece of paper he was holding and held it flat against the window pane so that the words faced her:

WILL YOU MARRY ME?

She *had* been right. It *was* what he'd said. What could he mean?

She took the sheet of paper she'd brought into the room with her, wrote on it, and held it against the glass.

DON'T BE SILLY! Jake read. YOU ARE MARRIED!

Jake shook his head

'I'm not!' he shouted.

Then he turned his sheet of paper over and held it against the glass. It was Sally's letter. Jake watched the amazement on Beth's face as she read it, but when she came to the end she shook her head again.

'I can't,' she mouthed.

Jake looked at her in disbelief, then wrote again. WHEN ARE YOU OFF DUTY?

TOMORROW. TWO O'CLOCK, Beth wrote back.

I'LL WAIT FOR YOU AT THE GATE. I LOVE YOU!

The door opened and Nurse Proctor rushed in.

'Sister's on the prowl! She's asking for you.'

Beth gave a hasty wave to Jake, and hurried out after Nurse Proctor.

She went through the rest of her day's work as if in a dream, performing the tasks automatically, hardly knowing what she was doing. When night came she went to bed, but slept little. When morning arrived she counted the hours until she should see Jake. Yet though her heart should have been light, it was not. She was apprehensive about what she must say to him.

When she left the hospital he was waiting at the gate. He moved quickly towards her and she knew he would have taken her in his arms had she not sharply turned away from him.

'No!' she said. 'Let's walk. Let's get away from the hospital, away from Batty Green.'

She wanted to get out of the sight of the viaduct which, though still no more than half-built, dominated the scene. She was in its presence every day; every time she looked out of the hospital windows it was there. It seemed as though she always saw, standing out from the rest, the very pier from which Will had fallen. She pictured him hurtling through the air, his red neckerchief around his neck.

'Wherever you like,' Jake said. 'How long have you?'

'Two hours. I'm on duty at four o'clock.'

They turned their backs on the viaduct, walked a short way up the turnpike road which led to Dent, and eventually to Hawes, and then, turning right, left the road and began to follow a stream which ran down from the high hills to join the Ribble. The August day was hot, the way was steep. Except for the road which ran through the valley to Settle, every way from Batty Green ran uphill.

In a very short time they had left the bustle of the shanty towns behind. There was nothing now but birds and sheep, and the sound of the stream.

'Let's sit down,' Jake said. 'I have to talk to you. And first of all I want to know what you mean by shaking your head at me.'

Beth said nothing.

'Beth, I love you,' Jake said. 'I'm asking you to marry me.'

'I can't!' It was no more than a whisper, wrung out of her.

Jake grabbed her wrists and pulled her around so that she was facing him.

'What do you mean?' he demanded. 'Look me in the eyes and tell me you don't love me!'

She met his eyes, and remained silent.

'Say it,' he persisted. 'Say "I don't love you".'

'I can't say that. You know I love you.'

'Then why can't you marry me? I don't understand you!'

'It's Will,' Beth said. 'I feel so badly about Will.'

'I understand *that*,' Jake replied. 'It was a nasty shock, the way he died. You wouldn't have wanted that to happen, and nor would I. But—'

'It's not that! I feel guilty,' Beth interrupted. 'I feel guilty all the time.'

'Beth, love, you're not guilty,' Jake said gently. 'It was an accident. Not the first on the railway, and no doubt it won't be the last.'

'That's not what I feel guilty about,' Beth said.

'Then what?'

'I wasn't a good wife to him. I failed him.'

Jake looked at her in astonishment.

'You're talking nonsense, Beth. You were the best of wives. The boot's on the other foot. I don't want to speak ill of the dead, but if there's any guilt, it's Will's. Not to put too fine a point on it, he was a rotten husband!'

'He was not!' Beth said sharply. 'You knew him mostly when he was ill. He wasn't like that really.'

Jake opened his mouth to speak, then closed it again. He had known Will Seymour before his accident. He had been a selfish, grumbling, bullying man. He had never understood how Beth could have married him.

'You never saw him as I did,' Beth said. 'You didn't know him before we came to this place. It changed him.'

Had she forgotten what Will had done to her, Jake asked himself? But if she had, it wasn't in him to remind her.

'What he did to me,' she said, as if she could read his thoughts, 'was my fault. I drove him to it. I didn't love him enough. He was a decent man at heart, and he loved me.'

'Beth, you loved me when Will was alive. You love me now, you can't deny it. And I've loved you since the minute I saw you. We love each other. Fate, or chance, or whatever you like to call it, has spun the wheel so that we're free to marry each other. *We* haven't made that happen. It's meant to be, Beth!'

'I can't,' she said. 'Not yet at any rate. Not the way I feel.'

'What do you mean by "not yet"?' Jake said roughly. 'Do you mean you *will* marry me, but you don't know when? And in that case, when will you know?'

'Please, Jake, don't bully me,' Beth said. She was close to tears.

Jake was immediately contrite. He drew her close, and held her.

'My darling, I would never bully you. It's just that I love you and I want you so much and I can't see how anything can stand in the way of us being together.'

'And I can't marry you until I sort myself out. It wouldn't be a good start. But in any case, I couldn't marry you until Will's been dead a year. I'd still be in mourning.'

'I don't set much store by such rules,' Jake said. 'I wouldn't have thought you did.'

She drew away from him.

'I find that I do. Oh, Jake, there are so many things separating us at the moment. If we're to marry I want us to have the best possible start, nothing coming between us. But in any case, if everything else was plain sailing, I couldn't leave the hospital while the smallpox is on. It wouldn't be fair. I'm needed there.'

'That, at least, I understand,' Jake conceded. It was also what he dreaded. The thought of the risks she ran was never far from his mind. He wanted to pick her up and run with her, take her miles and miles away from the danger she was in.

'I understand that,' he repeated, 'but I'm terrified of the risks you run.'

'Until it's over we're all at risk,' Beth said. 'You don't have to work in the hospital to catch the smallpox. But let's not talk about that now. We don't have much time left. I'll have to turn back soon.'

They set off to walk further up the hill. For a while they walked in silence, then Jake said: 'I won't give up! I won't stop trying to persuade you!'

'Please don't say that,' Beth pleaded. 'We *must* wait. We must see how things turn out. A year isn't so long!'

'It will seem like a lifetime,' Jake said. 'But promise me one thing, Beth. If you're going to make me wait a year, promise we can see each other – and as often as we want to.'

'I promise that,' Beth answered. Would he wait for her, she wondered? Would he tire of waiting?

A year's a long time, Jake thought, but I would wait for her for ever.

The smallpox summer came to an end, though not before thirty victims, in coffins carried shoulder-high over the long track from the shanty towns, had been buried in the churchyard at Chapel-le-dale. It was now full, chock-a-block, not a single space for another coffin to be found there. Had the Earl not graciously given an adjoining piece of land to be consecrated, there would have been nowhere for the Reverend Smith to bury the dead. He, poor man, what with deaths by accident, in childbirth, from fever, as well as by smallpox, had been kept inordinately busy. Two or three funerals a year were more the usual mark.

When the last case had left, this time to return home cured, though scarred, the isolation wards of the hospital were thoroughly cleaned and disinfected, the rooms fumigated. Beth dropped formaldehyde and permanganate of potash into a bowl then escaped quickly, sealing the doors, before the noxious vapours should overcome her. No-one seemed quite to know what would befall her if she did not escape in time, but the warnings were enough to ensure that she fled from the room well before the mixture started to boil.

When it was all over, when every room, every closet had been fumigated, every surface swabbed, when Beth's hands were raw from scrubbing, Matron sent for her.

'I think we can congratulate ourselves that it's all over, Nurse Seymour,' she said. 'And you have played your part. Should you wish to stay on to nurse in the hospital you will be more than welcome.'

'Thank you, Matron,' Beth said. 'I can't really. I have two lodgers who've been shamefully neglected during the epidemic. It's my duty to get back to them.'

She would be glad to leave the hospital. Nursing had come naturally to her and in other circumstances she would have enjoyed it, but the horrors of the smallpox, the constant deaths, especially of the young, were something she would never forget.

Matron nodded.

'As you wish, Nurse. Thank you for what you've done. Should you ever wish to return you'll be very welcome.'

The summer had been wet. Walking anywhere, even from Nazareth to Jericho, was a case of looking out for small patches of dry turf so that one didn't sink ankle-deep in the mud. To go as far as Batty Green, if the tramway happened not to be running, was hazardous, and it was impossible, in the meadows along the river valley, to get the hay in until a sudden and brief dry spell allowed it. But now the rain had come again, turning the rock-like boulder clay, normally so hard that when a man drove his pickaxe into it the shock of the impact went through his entire body, into a cloying, thick soup.

'It's times like this,' Alan Miller said to Beth 'that the bog cart comes into its own. We couldn't do without it. It can go where horses would just sink into the ground.'

'There was a horse last week,' Charlie said, making a rare observation of his own, 'sank up to its middle in the bog. We had to fix ropes round it to pull it out, poor beast!'

'Whoever invented the bog cart was a clever man,' Beth observed. 'But you have to admit, it's a strange-looking object.'

She was glad to be back with the Miller brothers in her own home, living a more normal life, freed from the fear of sudden illness and death, though the memory of Will's death was never far from her. Time and time again she wondered why he had fallen; had he known he was falling to his death as he hurtled to the ground? Had he been afraid, or had he mercifully lost consciousness in the seconds before he hit the ground? All this she wondered about, but she also thanked God that on Will's last day on earth he had set off for work a reasonably happy man, with a spring in his step.

She had started the lessons again. Now she had eight children, including one more boy from Jericho and two extra girls from Tunnel Huts. It was more difficult to teach now because she had absolute beginners together with those who had progressed over several months, though two lengthy interruptions because of the smallpox had been no help at all.

There was no-one of Tom Drake's calibre. In September he had gone off to his new school in York. She missed him greatly. There had been discussion about how he would get to York, he who had travelled no further than Batty Green on his own. His father could not take the time off and Elsie, much though she wanted to be with him to the last minute, was too nervous to contemplate the journey. To add to that, she was pregnant with her fifth child and was far from well. The rocking of the train, it was reckoned, could prove hazardous.

'And supposing we got on the wrong train,' she said nervously. 'Supposing we got lost in York. They say it's a very busy place.'

'You wouldn't do either of those things,' Beth assured her. 'But if you're really not fit to go, why then, I'll take Tom to York and deliver him to his school. Though only if you want me to.'

She longed to do it. It would be almost like accompanying a child of her own. She held her breath for the few seconds it took Elsie to make up her mind.

'Oh, I'd be so grateful!' Elsie said. 'I'd know he was safe in your hands. After all, you travelled all the way from Surrey!'

And safe he had been. Though every mile of the train journey had been exciting – so much to see from the train window, so many stations which had been no more than names until then – they had arrived in York without mishap, and had had time for a cup of tea and a bun in a small café in Stonegate before meeting the school representative at the appointed place, which since it was no more than yards from the Minster was easy enough to find.

The parting had been swift.

'Say goodbye to your mother, Drake,' the schoolmaster said, but before Beth could open her mouth to explain she was not the mother they were off, a crocodile of a dozen small boys in their new uniforms. She had watched them until they were out of sight, and had then made her way back to the station.

That had been in the autumn of 1871. She had

written to Tom, and he to her, and then at Christmas he had come home for a week's holiday, travelling on his own. In his first term away at school he had changed and yet he had not changed. He had a new independence, a self-confidence which had been missing in him before.

'I like it there,' he said to Beth. 'It's interesting. And there's a whole library full of books!'

'That's good,' Beth said. 'That's very good. But some things are improving here, too. There's a new reading room opened at Dent, with newspapers and magazines, though of course Dent is a far step away. And we've had some good penny readings down at Batty Green. You'd have enjoyed those.'

'I know. Though I'd rather read for myself than listen to someone else. And I don't mean I don't like it here. This is my home.' He spoke politely, not wishing to give offence.

A strange home, Beth thought. Strange for all of us. Living in huts in hastily thrown-up shanty towns in the middle of a wild and bleak moor. And the minute the railway is finished, she wondered, will we all be driven away, thrown out? What will happen to us then?

In spite of the vagaries of the weather, the work was proceeding. One day it would be finished, the trains would run from Settle to Carlisle, over the viaducts, through the deep cuttings, into the tunnels through the darkness of the mountains. When that day came there would be no need of this army of men with all their skills.

She saw Jake frequently. She placed no limit on the number of his visits, though she made it plain that he must come when Alan and Charlie Miller were at home. It wouldn't be right if he came when she was alone.

'You mean you don't trust me?' Jake said.

Beth didn't answer. The truth was that she didn't

trust herself. She loved him so much, longed to be with him all the time.

'I daresay you'd be right not to,' Jake said. 'I'm not sure I could keep any promises I might make. Beth, why can't we be married? Why do we have to wait any longer? We're not children.'

'It's children who can't wait,' Beth said. 'I'll marry you in August – and oh, so willingly! But not before.'

He was back on the day shift now, had been for several months. His visits were confined to the evenings and to part of the weekend. With one part of her Beth did not like it that he crossed the pitch darkness of the moor, with its treacherous shakeholes and bogs, to visit her. With another part of her she rejoiced whenever she answered the door to his knock, and saw him standing there.

In the spring, on a clear, crisp Sunday in late March, they set off early to climb Whernside.

'I meant this to be one of the first things I did when I came here,' Jake said to Beth.

They had reached the summit, had scraped the snow from a flat rock from which they now surveyed the scene below them. The line of the railway, cutting along the valley, was no more than a narrow ribbon, carelessly flung down. The shanty towns and huts were like children's bricks. From this viewpoint the high hills, their tops still under deep snow, and the wide sweep of the land, dominated everything, reduced everything.

'It's taken me two years to get up here,' Jake said. 'But if I'd come when I intended I'd have been alone. Now you're with me. It was worth the waiting.'

Three days later Elsie Drake gave birth to her baby. To her great delight it was another girl.

'It was as easy as pie!' Elsie said to Beth as the latter stood by the bedside holding the small new creature in her arms. 'Just slipped out like a pea from a pod!'

'You're a fortunate woman, Elsie,' Beth said quietly.

'Oh, Beth, I'm sorry! I never think, do I?' Elsie was contrite. 'And of course I do know I'm fortunate.'

As she was leaving Jericho Beth met Jake, coming home from work. He was black from head to toe with the dust from the tunnel. He would have taken hold of her, and then remembered the state of him.

'Oh, Jake!' she blurted out. 'You shouldn't marry me! You know I can never give you children! Never!'

The tears were running down her cheeks now. Ignoring the dirt on him, Jake took her in his arms.

'I don't need a horde of children,' he said. 'All I need is you. You and me together, for always. That's all I want.'

'Are you sure, Jake? Are you quite, quite sure?' Beth pleaded.

'Quite certain. Just you – and the sooner the better!'

They were married in August.

Unknown to Jake, and secure in the belief that her wedding *would* take place, Beth had several weeks earlier sent away for a new dress. It was quite perfect – pale blue with white embroidery, and fitted her as if she had been measured by the highest couturier in the land. When she looked at herself in the mirror on the morning of her wedding day she was pleased by what she saw.

Almost all the inhabitants of Jericho and Nazareth joined the bridal party, which went on the tramway to Batty Green. There Jake had hired a pony and trap for himself and Beth, for Elsie who was Beth's matron of honour, and Jack Drake who was Jake's best man. The rest of the company walked, or rode on hired horses, behind them to the church at Chapel-le-dale. After the wedding, before they left, Beth, with Jake beside her, placed her bridal flowers on Will's grave.

Later in the day the pony and trap took the two of them to Settle, where they boarded a train for Skipton.

They were to have a two-day honeymoon and Jake had booked a room in an hotel.

The trap drew up in the main street. While Jake paid the driver, Beth gazed up at the hotel, with its imposing pillared portico. It was quite splendid; she had never in her life stayed anywhere like this.

'Oh, Jake,' she whispered when he rejoined her, 'are you sure this is the right place?'

'Of course it is, love!' he assured her. 'Why? Doesn't it suit you?'

She took his arm.

'Oh, Jake, don't be silly! It looks wonderful! Are you sure we can afford it?'

'Quite sure!' Hadn't he been saving for this for months? 'So as long as it pleases you, we'd better go in!'

They went together to the desk.

'Mr and Mrs Tempest,' Jake said firmly. 'We have a reservation.'

'Certainly, sir,' the clerk said. 'We're expecting you. Now, if you will just sign . . .'

Standing beside her husband, Beth felt a glow of pride as she watched him write her new name.

'The boy here will take you to your room,' the clerk said. 'If there's anything you want you have only to ring!'

There'll be no ringing from them, he thought as he watched them follow the boy towards the stairs. They'll have better things to do. You could always tell honeymoon couples, they stood out a mile. He envied this fellow; she was a tasty bit and no mistake!

The room was a small one, at the rear of the hotel. Its predominant feature was the high double bed, with scarcely room for any other furniture.

It was strange, Beth thought, that though she had been married before and she was by no means a stranger to what was so soon to take place in that bed, and though she knew that she was not the first woman ever in Jake's life, she felt herself to be, at this moment, totally inexperienced.

She turned away from the bed and looked out of the window. A barge, heavy-laden with coal, was being pulled by an old horse which made its slow, deliberate way along the towpath.

Jake came and joined her, putting his arm around her shoulders.

'Not the most romantic of scenes,' he said, 'but it means something to me. I was brought up on that canal. We'll walk around there tomorrow.'

'I'd like that,' Beth said. 'I want to see all the places you know. I want to see the house where you lived with your mother – everything!'

'So you shall,' he promised. 'Tomorrow.'

He drew down the window blind, shutting out the view, then took her by the hand and led her to the bed. She stood before him in silence while, with trembling fingers, he undid the twelve buttons down the front of her bodice and then, deliberately and not hurrying, took off the rest of her clothes until she stood before him naked.

He gazed at her, not holding her, not touching her. Then just as deliberately, she began to undress him. Everything they had worn lay in a heap on the floor.

He picked her up and laid her on the bed.

'We've waited so long,' he murmured. 'It's been so long.'

'But the waiting's over,' Beth said. 'It's over.'

Everything was new, as if they were the first lovers in the world. Yet everything was perfect, as if the act of love had been created only for them.

# 18

Batty Green was crowded, scarcely room to move, and the stalls were busy. Beth was there with Elsie, both of them doing their weekly shopping. It was a lively scene, though hardly comfortable. Horses, with or without carriages, brewers' drays, milk carts, butchers' carts, carts of every description trundled across the Green without the slightest discipline, splashing up the mud, frightening the lives out of dogs, small children and shoppers on foot.

'My word, it's a very different scene from when I first came here,' Elsie said. 'Just before you arrived, that was. All but three years ago now. Not so many people then – or vehicles taking up the road.'

Beth nodded. 'And scarcely any wives and children.'

She had been one of the few wives who had accompanied her husband. Living more than two hundred miles away, if she hadn't done so they might have been parted for a long time, which was not to be thought of. Most of the wives had arrived later, when the husbands had tested things out, reckoned it was all right for them to come. Some had never arrived, their husbands being all too pleased with their new-found freedom at Ribblehead.

'When you come to think of it,' Elsie said, 'most of the little ones and the babies have been born in the shanty towns. They've known nothing else.'

'It's better than it was,' Beth said. 'At least in some ways.'

There were more shops, more concerts and penny

readings, the Mission was well attended and, the greatest blessing of all to Beth, there was now a public library. She was no longer starved of books, no longer dependent on finding something cheap and suitable on the newsagent's stall. The riches of literature, or a hundred volumes or so and not nearly enough of them novels, were there for the borrowing in the library hut.

'In some ways, though, it's not all that different,' Elsie mused. 'In some ways it's no different. Just as many fights. Just as many drunks staggering around. Some folks never improve, and the more money they earn, the worse they are!'

While they waited their turn in front of Burgoyne & Cocks's stall, Beth gave a fleeting thought to Sally Roland, wondered where she was. No-one, it seemed, had had sight or sound of her since she had walked away. Jake never once spoke of her. It was as if she had never existed.

It was tedious waiting to be served. Beth was unusually tired and there was a niggling pain in her back. She shifted uneasily from foot to foot.

'I'll be glad to get to the library,' she said to Elsie. 'I can have a sit-down there.'

Elsie looked closely at her friend.

'You do look a bit peaky,' she said. 'I'll tell you what – get served here before me, and get to the library. I'll not go with you there, seeing as I can't read and I've a few more things to do. Wait there for me and I'll pick you up. We don't want to miss the tram back, do we?'

Beth sat at the table in the library with a small pile of books in front of her, wondering which she would take. She would like them all but it wasn't allowed. There was Jake to choose for as well as herself. Since he could now read as fluently as she, his head was never out of a book.

She was glancing through *Vanity Fair* by Mr Thackeray – which she had read before but it would be a pleasure to read it again – when the words on the page began to blur, then run into each other, until finally the page and the book and the table spun round in a black vortex in front of her, and then there was nothing.

When she opened her eyes again it was to see an anxious-looking librarian, together with Elsie Drake, standing beside her. Elsie was chafing her hands.

'She's coming to!' Elsie said. 'My word, Beth love, you did give us a scare! I came in at the door just in time to see you keel over.'

'I don't understand,' Beth said. 'I've never done such a thing in my life!'

'Well, lucky for you Doctor Stokes has a surgery at Batty Green this morning. I know he's still here because I've seen his horse tethered. When you feel fit enough I'm taking you across to see him.'

'Oh no! I'm sure that's not necessary,' Beth protested. 'I'm all right now. Or I will be once I'm home.' She felt weak and dithery, but there was no need for a fuss.

'Better safe than sorry,' Elsie said firmly.

Elsie sat in the waiting room while Beth, reluctantly, went in to see Doctor Stokes. In view of what he told her Beth was glad Elsie was not in the room. She could hardly take it in.

'So what's it all about?' Elsie asked when Beth emerged.

'Something and nothing! He says I'm overtired.'

Elsie looked at her keenly.

'You do too much. You should take it easy.'

'I'll try,' Beth promised.

She would not tell Elsie that Doctor Stokes had said he would come to Nazareth in the morning, give her a good going over.

He came as promised. When he had examined Beth and questioned her he gave his verdict.

'I haven't the slightest doubt about it, Mrs Tempest. You're pregnant. I can't be totally sure how far, because you seem vague about dates.'

Beth stared at him, speechless. This was what he had said to her in the surgery yesterday, but she had scarcely taken it in. She couldn't, because it was too good to be true, it couldn't happen to her. How could she believe him? Most of the night she had lain awake, tossing and turning, her head bursting with whirling thoughts. Much though she had longed to tell Jake, and had found the evening in which she had kept silent interminable, she had not allowed herself to do so in case it was a false alarm.

In the middle of the night he had been awakened by her restlessness.

'What is it?' he asked drowsily. 'Why aren't you asleep?'

'I don't know,' she lied. 'It's nothing. I'm just restless.'

He had grunted, turned over, and was immediately asleep again.

'I can't believe it,' she said now to Doctor Stokes. 'I was married to Will for four years. I'm barren!'

'You most certainly are not. Nor were you,' Doctor Stokes assured her. 'The difference is, you have a new husband. I've seen this happen again and again.'

She could say nothing. She was mute, bereft of words. All these years I've thought it was me, my fault, she thought. Will had never reproached her in words, but the silent reproach had been there. More than that, and far worse, had been her own guilt, eating away inside her. She had never felt herself to be a whole woman. She was lacking in what mattered most. And now, suddenly, everything had changed.

Doctor Stokes looked at her keenly. 'One of these

days the world might stop blaming the woman,' he said.

Beth found her voice. 'It doesn't matter any longer, at least not to me it doesn't,' she said quietly. 'But I won't ever forget it. But can't you please tell me when it will be, Doctor? When will I have my baby?'

'As near as I can say, around Christmas. I'll know better as time goes by,' Doctor Stokes said. 'And what better time than Christmas?'

Beth went through the rest of the day in a dream, hardly knowing what she was doing. When it was time for Jake to leave his work, she set off to meet him. Usually, since the cutting where they worked was a shorter distance away than the tunnel, Alan and Charlie Miller arrived home before Jake, but today she could not bear that to happen. She must give her news to Jake the moment she saw him, and she must see him alone.

How perfect the May day was for the bearing of such wonderful news, she thought as she set off. It was as if the weather had conspired with her. Although the breeze was present, there was warmth in the sun and, except on the summit of Whernside, the snow had gone. Flowers were appearing in the short grass and pushing their way through the cracks in the limestone. Larks rose high in the clear sky and a wagtail went to and from its nest in a niche in a stone wall. Soon now curlews would be back for the summer, raising their young in the meadows before the cutting of the hay drove them out. She had always paid attention to the comings and goings of birds, animals, flowers, but never before had they seemed so significant to her. She felt herself part of Nature's plan.

Halfway up the hill she saw Jake in the distance striding towards her. He was so tall, silhouetted against the sky, he walked so proudly. She quickened her step, and at that moment he recognized her and began to run down the hill. She stopped where she was and waited for him, and when he was only a few yards off she ran into his arms.

'Oh Jake! Oh Jake!'

'What is it? What is it?' Jake said. 'Is something wrong?' But that couldn't be the case. Although there were tears in her eyes her face was alight with joy.

'Oh no! Nothing's wrong. Nothing at all! But you're not going to believe me when I tell you because I couldn't believe it myself, but now I know it's true, and it's wonderful!'

He put two fingers over her mouth to stop the flow of words.

'Please tell me, love! What is it that's so wonderful – or am I supposed to guess?'

'You'll never guess! You'll never guess! Would you ever guess that I'm going to have a baby?'

Jake stared at her.

'There! You wouldn't have, would you? Well I am! It's true! I am going to have a baby!' She shouted it out loud, in pure triumph and the wind carried her words across the moor.

'Sit down!' Jake commanded. 'Sit down and tell me slowly.'

They sat on a rock and Beth told him, every detail. He listened in silence, then when she'd finished speaking he took her in his arms.

'Oh, Beth! Beth! This is the happiest day of my life! Of my entire life!'

'And of mine, Jake.'

They continued to sit there in total bliss, Beth with her head on Jake's shoulder, he with his arm around her.

'We must go!' Beth said at last. 'I don't want to, but Alan and Charlie will be home. I haven't given a thought to supper.'

'Who wants supper?' Jake said. 'I'd rather stay here.'

Beth jumped to her feet and held out her hand to him.

'Come along,' she said, smiling. 'We have to eat. What about me? I have to eat for two!'

Jake stood up.

'Of course you have, sweetheart! And I'm going to take the greatest care of you, beginning this minute!' He took her arm and began to lead her down the hill.

'Be careful how you go,' he warned her. 'You mustn't fall!'

She stopped dead, and turned around to face him.

'Stop it, Jake Tempest!' she said. 'I won't have it! I'm perfectly healthy and I don't need to be cosseted.' She spoke firmly, she meant what she said, but she loved his care for her.

'Try to stop me!' Jake said.

'I will,' she said. 'And I'll succeed. Or maybe you'll tire of it. We've seven months to go yet, remember.'

'I'll never tire of caring for you, looking after you,' Jake vowed. 'I couldn't bear it if anything happened to you – or to the baby.'

Beth laughed.

'Jake, love, nothing's going to happen to either of us! Now stop fussing and we'll go home and I'll make the supper. And by the way, I don't want to tell Alan and Charlie just yet, not just yet. I might tell Elsie, since she's my best friend, but no-one else at the moment.'

'I want to tell the world!' Jake said. 'But you can have your own way on this.'

The Millers were not in the hut when Jake and Beth returned.

'They'll have gone down to the beck to wash,' Jake said.

Like all the men who worked on the railway, the brothers came home filthy every day, not as blackened as Jake, from the tunnel, who looked like a miner emerging from the bowels of the earth, but usually thick with mud and dust from the cutting, weary from a day spent on a job which was all pick and shovel, digging out the heavy soil which would then be used for building up embankments on other parts of the line.

Jake went into the hut to fetch his soap and towel, then walked down to the beck to join the brothers, who were standing waist deep in the fast-flowing water.

'My word, you're a mucky sight,' Alan called out. 'You'll dirty the water and no mistake!'

'Then come out, both of you, and let me in!' Jake said.

In fact, the beck ran so swiftly, its water clear and sparkling from the high hills where it had its source, that the dirt of the day's work was swiftly carried away. The only drawback was the temperature of the water, seldom higher than that of the snow on the summits. Jake caught his breath as he waded in.

'You had a rough day, then?' Alan asked him.

'One of the best days of my life, actually!' Jake said, soaping himself vigorously. He longed to tell them the wonderful news.

The brothers stared at him in disbelief.

'Tunnel going well, is it?' Alan asked.

'Very well,' Jake said. In fact that was true. The work there was, for the moment, proceeding well and they were ahead of schedule. All the same, that had nothing to do with the gladness in his heart. His thoughts were not on the tunnel.

'Rather you than me,' Alan said. 'I couldn't stand to work in the tunnel.'

'I couldn't stand it, either,' Charlie said.

'I need to be able to look up and see the sky,' Alan said. 'I've never worked inside, let alone in a tunnel, in all my life.'

In fact, Jake thought, there had been many days in

recent months when his thoughts had run along the same lines. It was true that the tunnel was going well, but there was more to it than that. When he'd started on the job he'd quickly got used to the darkness, to working in flickering candlelight, to the moisture running in rivulets down the walls, to the air below ground, which, no matter what the Company did to freshen it by blowing fresh air down the shaft, remained stale; but now all these things irked him. He started off each day by hating the moment when he must step into the cage and be taken down into the darkness below. He lived for the moment when he was hoisted up again and could stand on the earth's surface. I'm like the Millers, he thought. I want to look up and see the sky, make sure it's there, and I'm not buried for ever in a dark hole.

He thought this as the Millers climbed out of the beck and began to dry themselves while he ducked under the water and began to wash his hair. But today was different. Today Beth had given him her news and the whole world was transformed.

'We'll be off then!' Alan called out. 'Don't be long. Don't keep us waiting for our supper. We're as hungry as hunters, me and Charlie.'

'As hungry as hunters,' Charlie agreed.

Jake completed his toilet, dressed in the clean clothes he had brought down with him, then went back to the hut. When supper was over Alan and Charlie went down to the Welcome, which was a relief to Beth and Jake because now they could talk about what filled both their minds.

Beth stacked the dirty dishes on the table, fetched a bowl of water and began to wash up. Jake watched her from his armchair. Even washing dishes, her sleeves rolled up, her hair none too tidy, she was so pretty, so graceful.

'A boy or a girl?' he said. 'Which?'

'I don't mind in the least,' Beth said pushing the hair out of her eyes. 'I just want a baby!'

'A girl then!' Jake decided. 'I think a girl.'

'Very well,' Beth agreed. 'A girl first – and then a boy.' There was no reason, was there, why they should not have a family as large as Elsie's? They were both still young.

'Remember what I said,' Jake told her. 'You're to look after yourself every minute of the day. Eat well – and rest. You'll have to give up the classes for a start.'

Beth stared at him.

'Give up the classes! Whatever do you mean?'

'Exactly what I say, love. It's hard work. It's not just when the children are here, it's all the time you spend preparing for them. It's gone a long way beyond just teaching three or four children to read.'

'But Jake, I love the work, I enjoy the children. There's no reason at all why I shouldn't do it. And it earns a little money.'

'There's no need for you to earn money,' Jake said swiftly. 'That's my job. Do I keep you short?'

Beth looked at him in astonishment.

'Of course you don't. You're most generous. But I like the idea of a little independence.'

'You don't need it,' Jake said. 'I'm here for you to depend upon.'

'I know,' Beth said. 'And I do depend on you for almost everything. I'm glad to. But everyone must have some small area of independence. It's not the money that's important. It's the classes themselves – what I do in them, what the children do. Surely you understand that, Jake?'

'What I understand is that you're having a child – my child—'

'And mine!'

'Ours. And that you need to save all your strength

329

for that, not waste it on other people. The other children can do without you; our child can't.'

His face was set in obstinate lines but, watching him, Beth felt her own feelings harden.

'Our child won't ever be neglected, either before she's born or after,' she said. 'She'll always come first. And I have enough health and strength to carry this baby *and* to keep on the classes. So I'm sorry, Jake, if you don't approve, but that's what I'm going to do!'

She took the dishes out of the water and banged them down on the table. She could hardly believe what she was hearing herself say, or the strength of the rebellion she felt inside her. They were quarrelling! It was their very first quarrel – and it was unbearable. Tears filled her eyes and splashed down into the washing-up bowl.

'Oh, Jake!' she cried. 'I didn't mean to be so harsh! I didn't mean it to come out like that! The last thing I ever want is to quarrel with you.'

He jumped up, spun her around and took her in his arms, kissing away the tears. With soapy wet hands she caressed him in return.

'And I didn't mean to be hard with you,' he said. 'It's just that I love you so much. I want to protect every hair of your head.'

'And I want that too,' Beth said. 'But please don't ask me to give up the classes! Not yet. I should hate it.'

'Very well then,' he said reluctantly. 'But later on, and the moment you start to be tired.'

'Later on perhaps,' Beth agreed. 'And I promise to take every care, take no risks. Please believe that, dearest.'

'Come to bed,' Jake said. 'I want to hold you in my arms properly. There's only one way for two people who love each other as much as we do to make up a quarrel.'

'But Jake, it's early! Alan and Charlie aren't home yet.'

'They don't need us to wait up for them. They're big boys now!'

'I must finish the dishes, clear away,' Beth said.

'No you mustn't. Come to bed!'

Elsie was overjoyed at the news of Beth's pregnancy.

'It's wonderful!' she cried. 'You'll make a lovely mother! Oh, I can't tell you how pleased I am!'

The words were not quite out of her mouth when the door opened and Phoebe Grange walked in.

'So what's this you're so pleased about?' she demanded. 'I must say, you look like two cats who've swallowed the cream!'

Beth and Elsie looked at each other.

'Well, I'm not telling the world, because it's too soon,' Beth said. 'But there's no reason why you shouldn't know. I'm expecting!'

Phoebe gave a whistle.

'And we thought . . . I thought . . .'

'And I thought so too,' Beth interrupted. 'I thought it was impossible I should ever have a child. Well it wasn't, and I am!'

What wonderful luck to be having a child by Jake Tempest, Phoebe thought. Especially what luck to experience what went before it. She had, however, though with a reluctant sigh, put the man out of her mind since he had married Beth Seymour. They were such a pair of lovebirds that it was quite sickening; it was a lost cause on her part. She recognized that, and she was never one for pursuing lost causes. They were a waste of her time and talent, and in this place, peopled with frustrated men and too few women, there were opportunities galore. Still, it was a pity about Jake. He was something special, and a man was at his most vulnerable as his wife's pregnancy advanced. It was a pity also, though not for her, that too many wives didn't recognize that.

'Well, I'm very pleased for you,' she said. 'Very pleased indeed. So, shall you be giving up the classes? I do hope not.'

'I shan't,' Beth assured her. 'Not unless and until I have to.' In her heart she saw no reason why she should abandon them even after the baby was born, but that was a point she had no intention of raising. 'It will be business as usual,' she added.

A week later Jake arrived home from work, put down his jock tin on the table, and said: 'Good news! I'm going back on the night shift from the end of this week. I was given the chance and I took it.'

'Well, if it's what you want to do, I'm pleased for you,' Beth said. For her part she wasn't sure. It would be good to have him in the daylight hours, but how would she feel at night without him beside her in their bed?

'It *is* what I wanted,' Jake said. 'Don't you see, if I'm at home days I'll be able to help you with the classes – since you're so keen on them.'

Though they had not argued about the subject again, Beth knew that he was not happy about it. In any case she would be glad of his help. He could read as well as she could and he had a rapport with the children, especially with the boys. Also, he was much better than she was at arithmetic, which she was only too aware the children ought now to be learning; that, and geography, which was also not one of her strong points. The City Mission had some months ago supplied her with a globe of the world, which was a help, and would have been even more of one had she had the slightest idea where to place her finger on foreign countries.

'I'd appreciate that,' she said. 'There's a real need for the children to spread themselves, and we

332

complement each other, you and me. What I can't do, you can, and you're every bit as good a teacher as I am.'

'I enjoy it,' Jake said.

In fact, he enjoyed his work with the children far more than anything he did in the tunnel, though he did take a pride in the building of that, in seeing it progress. They had turned the curve now and sometimes, especially when the day outside was bright, it was possible to discern the light at the northern end. He longed for the day when the gangs from the south would meet up with those tunnelling from the north. When that happened, or soon afterwards, Blea Moor tunnel would be completed, they would have conquered the mountain.

'All the same,' Beth said, breaking into his thoughts, 'we must work out a timetable. You must be sure to get your proper sleep.'

As the spring moved into summer and Beth's pregnancy advanced she remained well, though she began to tire more easily, and when a warm June gave way to an even warmer July, with herself and Jake and all the children crowded into the small hut, the heat began to worry her. Sometimes they took the children outside for lessons, but there were too many distractions in the open and not enough learning. Inside the hut the stove had to be kept going to provide means for cooking, and heating water. Beth, though she would not have thought it possible, was truly thankful when August came, and she could declare a month's holiday for the children.

'Not a moment too soon!' she said to Jake.

It was Saturday evening, Jake's night off from work. They were sitting outside watching the late sun going down over Ingleborough, the air still warm and insect-laden.

'I've had an idea,' Beth said.

'What?' Jake asked sleepily.

'I keep thinking how much easier it would be, both for us and the children, if we had a separate hut, if I ran it like a school . . .'

Jake wakened at once.

'Wait a minute!'

'No, you wait a minute,' Beth said. 'Let me finish! I think it's something the Company might be glad to do for us. It wouldn't cost a lot in their terms – a hut, desks, chairs, a stove for when the weather turns cold. I feel sure the Mission would do something.'

'Beth, stop it!' Jake interrupted. 'You're talking nonsense! Less than five months and you'll have the baby to look after. What's all this rubbish about starting what would turn into a school before you knew where you were?'

'I daresay it would,' Beth agreed. 'Turn into a school. But that's not rubbish. A small school of our own is exactly what we need on this part of the moor. And it's something I could do. We'd close for two or three weeks at Christmas, while I have the baby, but after that there'd be no problem.'

Jake jumped to his feet and stood in front of her.

'Will you just stop it!' he repeated. 'If you've any sense at all you won't start up the classes again at all.'

'Oh, but I must,' Beth disagreed. 'I'm not sitting around doing nothing until Christmas. The busier I am, the quicker the time will pass.'

'You're mad!' Jake stormed. 'I don't understand you! But I tell you this, you will *not* talk any more about getting a hut and starting a school. I absolutely forbid it and I would tell the Company so. They won't let you do such a thing without your husband's approval, and that you don't have. Do you hear me?'

'Quite well,' Beth said. 'There's no need to shout.'

He was right, of course. The Company wouldn't

334

consider it if Jake was against it. She was beaten, at least for the time being.

'Very well,' she said. 'I give up – for the present. Until after the baby's here.'

'By which time you'll find you have plenty to do,' Jake said.

'But when the holiday's over I want to go on with the classes. I'll be quite sensible, Jake. I'll give up when I'm tired.'

He put out his hands and pulled her up.

'Come here!' he said. 'Do you realize we almost quarrelled again? And we'd better go inside. The sun's gone. It's turning chilly.'

Arm in arm they walked back into the hut.

Beth started the classes again at the beginning of September, but by mid-November she knew the time had come to stop. She was slow and awkward, the child was so heavy. Also, she found it difficult to sleep at night so that in the mornings she was good for nothing.

'I'll have to give up at the end of the month,' she confided to Elsie. 'Jake will be pleased.'

'I should just think so!' Elsie said. 'I'm on his side in this. Start saving your strength. You'll need it when you go into labour. I can vouch for that!'

Beth's labour started on the twenty-third of December, and at ten in the morning of Christmas Eve the baby was born, Phoebe Grange acting as midwife.

'A lovely little girl!' she said. 'And not so little at that! A whopper, in fact.'

She wrapped the baby in a shawl and placed her in Beth's arms.

'You can have her for two minutes,' she said. 'And then I'll clean you both up and the new father can come in. I've found men like to wait until all's shipshape!'

When Phoebe called Jake into the room a little later it was to Beth he gave his immediate attention. She lay flat down in the bed, stretched out, immobile. Her face was pale, and there were dark shadows under her eyes, but the eyes themselves were shining.

'Oh Beth! My darling Beth! Are you all right, love?' Jake cried, bending over her, kissing her gently.

'Of course I am!' Beth said. 'Except that I'm bound up as tight as an Egyptian mummy! I can scarcely move!'

'It's for your own good,' Phoebe said. 'You want to get your figure back, don't you?'

She glanced at Jake. He was looking at Beth with worship in his eyes. What made me think I could ever get near him? Phoebe asked herself. The man's besotted!

'Don't you want to see the baby?' Beth said. 'Your daughter!'

'You can hold her for a minute,' Phoebe said. She took the child out of the crib and placed her in Jake's arms. When he looked at the dark, downy head and the crinkled red face – which was all he could see, for she was more tightly swaddled even than Beth – his eyes filled with tears.

'So what are you going to call her?' Phoebe asked.

'Mary,' Beth answered. 'What else would you call a baby girl born on Christmas Eve?'

'And Lily for her second name,' Jake said. 'My mother's name.'

The baby fell asleep as he was holding her, and a minute later so did Beth. He placed the child gently in the crib and tip-toed out of the room.

Beth was sound asleep when the knock came on the door. Jake rushed to answer it so that she shouldn't be wakened.

Armitage stood in the doorway. Wherever the snow could settle on his person it had done so; on his shoulders, on the top of his fur cap, thickly on his eyebrows, and on his trousers and boots.

Jake stared at him, hardly believing his eyes.

'Well, aren't you going to ask me in?' Armitage asked.

# 19

'Armitage! Good heavens! Come in! Come in at once – you look frozen!'

Armitage stepped over the threshold. Jake, overcome with joy and surprise at the sight of his friend, enveloped him in a warm embrace.

'This is wonderful!' Jake said. 'The last person in the world I expected to see – and no-one I'd sooner see!'

The two men stood there, beaming at each other. In the warmth of the room the snow was already melting from Armitage's garments, forming small pools on the floor.

'I'm sorry,' Jake said. 'You're wet – and you must be frozen. Take off your coat and things at once. Come to the stove and get warm. You look blue with cold.'

'It's a bit parky out there, I'll not deny it,' Armitage said. He removed his coat, unwound his long scarf, shook the snow from his hat. Then he stretched out his hands, white with cold as the snow itself, to the stove.

'Your boots as well. I'll find you some slippers,' Jake ordered. 'And then something hot inside you. There's soup in the pan. It'll not take me a minute to heat it.'

Though he longed to know the circumstances which had brought Armitage to his door on this cold Christmas Eve, Jake asked no questions until he had served the old man with a bowl of steaming soup, thick with vegetables, and watched him drink it to the last drop. Only when Armitage put down his spoon and leaned back in his chair, breathing a sigh of relief, did Jake frame the first one.

'How did you find me, Armitage? How did you know I was here?'

'Oh, that wasn't difficult,' Armitage explained. 'I spent the last two nights in Settle at Mrs Sutherland's house. She told me she thought you were still working on the railway, so I decided to risk it.'

'You walked from Settle? In this weather?'

Armitage shook his head.

'No, friend. My days for that, at least in the winter, are over. But there seem to be carts going back and forth quite frequently. It wasn't difficult to get a lift. When I got to Batty Green I asked questions in the Welcome Home. They knew you lived in Nazareth. It was God's grace that I knocked on the right door first. So here I am, and mighty glad to be so!'

'And I'm mighty glad to have you,' Jake said.

Now that he had time to observe him, Jake was struck by how much Armitage had aged in the last four years. When he had seen him last he had been a man to whom you wouldn't think of attributing any particular age; it would have seemed irrelevant. Now he was old.

'Mrs Sutherland said if I found you I was to give you her best respects,' Armitage said.

'Did she say anything else?' Surely she would have told him about Sally?

'Nothing,' Armitage replied. 'In fact, she seemed singularly quiet. I didn't get much of her usual entertaining gossip. Why? Was there something to tell?' He had not missed the note of apprehension in Jake's voice.

'Not at the moment,' Jake said. 'It can wait.'

'They did tell me at the Welcome Home that you were married,' Armitage said. Indeed, now that he had thawed out enough to look around him, he realized that everywhere in the room there were signs of a woman's touch; the pictures on the wall, the vase of dried flowers on the sideboard, the patchwork cushions and crocheted antimacassars on the armchairs, this was not what he would have associated with Jake, though of course he had never before seen him in his own domestic setting. All that was missing from the scene was the woman.

'I am indeed,' Jake said.

Armitage heard the warmth and pride in Jake's voice.

'So is your wife perhaps visiting a neighbour?' he asked. 'Will she be back soon? What will she say when she sees me?'

'She'll soon realize that you're the second most wonderful thing that has happened to us this Christmas,' Jake said. 'The first is that my wife's just given birth to our first child, our daughter! At this moment they're both fast asleep.'

A smile spread across Armitage's face, lit his eyes.

'Why, that's splendid, Jake! I'm very pleased for you.' And then, as suddenly as it had come, the smile left him. 'But you won't want me at a time like this, of course you won't. And I wouldn't want to disturb you. So with your permission I'll rest an hour, and then I'll be on my way.'

'And where would you go?' Jake demanded. 'In weather like this, where would you go?'

'Why, I'll go to the Welcome Home,' Armitage said. 'They'll find a bed for me. The landlord seems a decent sort. As for the weather, I've never given much thought to that. I've tramped these dales from west to east, from north to south, in every kind of weather you can think of. A few inches of snow hasn't stopped me.'

But that was when I was younger and stronger, he thought. When he had turned his face towards Settle a few days ago, determined to find Jake Tempest, he had faced the fact that those days were now over, that this was to be his last long walk. All the same, he wouldn't show it. If he really made the effort, he reckoned he could get back to the Welcome.

'So if you can spare the time I'll stay another hour or so, catch up on what you've been doing, then I'll be on my way.'

'Oh no you won't!' Jake said. 'I won't hear of it. And as a matter of fact, as it so happens, there's a bedroom spare. Usually we have two lodgers – brothers, name of Miller – but they've gone home to their families in Skipton for Christmas. They'd not mind you using their room.'

'And what about your wife? A stranger at Christmas – and she with a new baby?'

'You'll be no stranger to Beth,' Jake told him. 'I've talked about you often. She'd be cross with me if I let you go. And I certainly wouldn't want you to leave without seeing the baby. So as soon as you're ready I'll show you your bedroom and you can unpack your things.'

'Not that I have many,' Armitage said. 'You know I travel light – just what I can carry on my back.' But in the last year, no matter how much he threw out whatever he could dispense with, his backpack seemed to grow heavier. He would be glad to cast it aside for twenty-four hours, perhaps for a day or so longer if he was allowed.

When Jake showed him to the bedroom and he saw the bed he could have fallen into it. He was very tired, very tired indeed.

'Did I tell you . . . ?' Jake asked. 'No, of course I didn't, there hasn't been time. Beth taught me to read!'

Armitage straightened up from his unpacking and grabbed Jake by the arm.

'Why, that's wonderful! That's altogether mighty

wonderful! Didn't I tell you it was the one thing you should do?'

'You did,' Jake acknowledged. 'And you were right. It's opened up new worlds to me. More than that, we've taught a few children to read – Beth's done most of that, but I've helped.'

'And so the word spreads,' Armitage said. 'And so it will from them to others. Imagine a world in which everyone, man, woman and child, in every home in every country, could read. What would that do, eh?'

'Four years ago I couldn't have imagined,' Jake admitted. 'But I can now. Anyway, I'll leave you to it!'

When Jake had left the room, Armitage looked down at the bed, at its thick, soft pillows, its honeycombed white counterpane. Never had any bed looked so inviting. He would lie down for ten minutes, just ten minutes, no longer.

When the baby cried he didn't hear her. He was deep in sleep, though fully dressed. At the first sound from the baby Jake went in to Beth, and as he looked at her she opened her eyes, and smiled at him.

'Ah!' she said, 'I've had a lovely sleep. I do feel better!'

'She's crying!' Jake said.

'I know, love. I've still got my hearing!'

'What shall I do?' He was all anxiety.

'Nothing *you* can do,' Beth said. 'Except hand her to me. I daresay she's hungry.'

He took the baby out of the crib and when he held her against his shoulder she immediately stopped crying.

'You hear that?' he cried. 'She's stopped!'

'You're very clever, dear,' Beth said. 'You're going to be the perfect father! I still think you'd better give her to me.'

She wanted to hold her all the time. She wanted never to let her go. If she could, she would have kept

342

her in her own bed but Phoebe, who had turned out to be quite bossy in the circumstances, said it was not allowed.

'Aside from anything else, you'd neither of you get any rest,' she'd said. 'So make the most of your lying-in. It'll all be over far too soon!'

'We have a visitor,' Jake told Beth.

She looked up from the baby.

'I didn't hear anyone. Who is it?'

'Armitage!'

'Armitage?'

'I told you about him. I met him in Settle before I came here. He was the one who told me I should learn to read.'

'Oh, of course I remember, though I've never met him. So where is he now?'

'Fast asleep on Alan Miller's bed. When I told him about you and the baby he was all for going back to the Welcome, but I persuaded him to stay the night. You don't mind, love, do you? I'll look after him.'

'Of course not,' Beth said.

'He looks very tired. I doubt he's well.'

'Then he's welcome to stay three nights, until the Millers' return. And when he's awake, bring him in to see me and the baby.'

Armitage was awakened soon afterwards by Phoebe Grange's arrival on the second of the twice-daily visits she was making to Beth and the baby. She blew into the hut like a strong wind, calling out as she entered, closing the door noisily behind her, marching across to the bedroom.

Armitage opened his eyes, not sure for the moment where he was, then stretched his limbs and swung himself down from the bed. He felt refreshed from his short sleep but he was glad not to be starting the walk back to Batty Green.

343

'I'm sorry I fell asleep,' he said, joining Jake in the living-room.

'I expect Mrs Grange wakened you,' Jake said. 'She's looking after Beth and the baby. When she's left I'll take you in to see them both. Beth wants to meet you.'

'And I want to meet the lady who taught you to read,' Armitage said.

Later, he shook hands with Beth as she lay in the bed, then peered at the baby in the crib.

'A most handsome child,' he observed. 'And with a look of both of you.'

He believed that was the thing to say. He knew nothing of babies and was secretly pleased that he was not expected to hold it. He had been married – it was a long time ago now, he had almost forgotten what his wife looked like – but there had never been any children.

'You're very welcome to stay until my lodgers return,' Beth told him. 'And if you want to stay in the neighbourhood longer I feel sure we'll find a neighbour who'll put you up.'

She was worried by the look of him. He was older and frailer than Jake had described him to her. It was certainly not right that he should be tramping the country at this time of the year, and with January and February, the very worst months, still to come.

'You're a very kind lady,' Armitage said gratefully. 'We'll see what happens.'

What happened was that two days later the postman, trudging through the snow to the few people in Nazareth and Jericho who ever received letters, delivered one from Alan Miller.

They were not coming back to Ribblehead, Alan wrote, because their wives and families missed them too much and wanted them nearer home. 'So we have got ourselves jobs at the new limeworks near Settle.

There is plenty of work to be had and it will be easier to get home . . .' Beth turned the page. 'Hoping this finds you as it leaves us and thank you for your kindness, Alan and Charlie Miller.'

'So!' Beth said, handing the letter back to Jake. 'What a surprise! And I shall miss them. But now Armitage can stay a week or two. I don't want to take on new lodgers until I'm up and about.'

'There's no need to do it at all,' Jake said.

'We'll see!' But in fact, Beth thought, with the baby, and the classes which she fully intended to resume, she wasn't sure she wanted lodgers, not permanently, though Armitage was welcome for a while, until he was fit again.

The winter passed. Ice, snow, frost, rain, gales, and sometimes something of everything at once in the short days and long nights. Occasionally there was fitful sunshine and Whernside stood out against a pale blue sky, though the mountain itself was blanketed in snow. And then, though in January and February the change was imperceptible, when March came the days were seen to grow longer.

Mary thrived; put on weight, was rounder and rosier by the day; gave her first smile, which Phoebe said was nothing more than wind, but Beth knew better. In the early summer she was sitting up of her own accord, while every day out of her rosebud mouth came new sounds and gurgles, among which Jake swore she said 'Dada' while looking straight at him. She was a happy, healthy baby, the delight of her parents' life, the mainspring of their happiness.

It was not so with Armitage. As Mary grew in strength, so Armitage weakened. He never complained, except with exasperation that even a short walk now fatigued him, but from Christmas to May Day Beth, observing him with worried eyes, thought that he must have lost two stones in weight. His clothes hung on him. There were new hollows in his neck and below his cheekbones and his eyes were set deep in dark sockets.

'I don't like the look of him,' Beth said to Jake. 'He didn't look good when he came to us at Christmas, but he's worse now.'

'You're right,' Jake agreed. 'I reckon he should see Doctor Stokes, but he won't hear of it.'

'I'll have another go,' Beth said. 'I'll try to persuade him.'

The change came sooner than she had expected. Two days later, on a Friday morning, she answered a knock on the door and there stood Doctor Stokes.

Beth smiled at him, but spoke hesitantly.

'I didn't send for you, Doctor – though I'm pleased to see you, of course. Has there been some mistake?'

'Oh, no mistake,' he said. 'I was in Nazareth so I thought I'd look in to see how you and Mary were.'

'How kind of you! We're fine. And I'm particularly glad to see you, Doctor. To tell you the truth . . .' She lowered her voice. 'I'm worried about a friend who's staying with us. We couldn't persuade him to visit you, but . . .'

'Then ask me in,' Doctor Stokes said. 'I'd like to set eyes on Mary again, for a start.'

Armitage was sitting by the stove, trying to warm himself, though the room was like a hothouse.

'Doctor Stokes, this is our friend, Mr Armitage,' Beth said.

Armitage, while regarding the doctor with suspicion, extended a hand.

'He came to check on Mary, as he was passing,' Beth explained. 'Wasn't that kind?'

'Very kind.'

Doctor Stokes turned his attention to the baby.

'She seems in fine fettle!' he said after a few minutes.

'Then if you'll excuse me I'll just put her down in her cot,' Beth said. 'She's due for her nap.'

She went away, leaving the two men together.

'I trust you are well, Mr Armitage?' Doctor Stokes said civilly.

'If you must know, I'm not!' Armitage's reply was sudden and fierce. 'I wouldn't have troubled you, I've never had the need to see a doctor, but since you're here . . .'

'Shall we go to your room?' Doctor Stokes suggested. 'I expect you'd rather talk privately.'

Twenty minutes later the two men emerged from Armitage's bedroom. Beth looked up from her sewing, her eyes full of questions.

'It appears,' Armitage said, 'that all is not *quite* in order. But we know where we stand.'

'Not entirely,' the doctor said in a kind voice. 'Not until I've done a few tests. I'll do them as soon as I can, and I'll let you know.'

'Thank you,' Armitage said. But he doesn't need to let me know, he thought. He's as certain as I am. He himself had been certain for some time now. Wasn't that why he had made his way here?

Beth looked from one man to the other, but said nothing. It was clearly not the time. She wished Jake was here. He would know what to say.

'And your husband?' Doctor Stokes asked Beth. 'He's well?'

'Very well. He's on night shift so he would have been here, except that he's gone to Batty Green to buy provisions. I couldn't go. I'm expecting the children any minute now.'

Doctor Stokes nodded.

'I've heard all about your classes. You're doing a wonderful job there, Mrs Tempest. Just don't overtax yourself.'

'Oh I won't, Doctor!' Beth reassured him. 'It's

347

what I keep telling my husband. I'm as strong as a horse.'

'I daresay you are,' the doctor said. 'And I reckon it's better to do too much than too little.'

'If you meet Jake on your way back I'd be glad if you'd tell him that,' Beth said as she showed him to the door.

She stood in the doorway watching as he mounted his horse. They said his old mare knew every inch of the moor, from Ingleton to Dent Head. *She* would never fall down a shakehole, day or night.

Beth wondered what the doctor had said to Armitage, but there would be no time to ask him, even if she had the courage, because she could see the children approaching, uphill from Jericho and down the moor from Tunnel Huts. She had a dozen of them now, four days a week, and could have had twice as many except that there was not enough space. It was difficult to squash even twelve children into the small hut, and though she hated refusing the parents who wanted their children to come to her, Jake was still set against her asking the railway company to provide a hut especially for the purpose.

She stood there until the children from both directions saw her and started to race to reach her first. As they came near, shouting and laughing, she held up her hands to stop them.

'Come in quietly,' she told them. 'The baby's asleep!'

Armitage was sitting by the stove again and as the children streamed into the hut he moved farther back into the shadow, though there was no way he would leave the room when the children were there, especially as Beth had given him permission to stay.

'You don't trouble me in the least,' she'd told him. 'In fact I like to have you there. If there's a question asked to which I don't know the answer – and goodness knows there are plenty of those – well, you always do! It's true what Jake told me. You know something about everything!'

For his part Armitage was amazed at Beth's skill and patience with the children, considering how limited was her training. She was a born teacher, and so, for that matter, was Jake, who had had no training at all. 'When I watch the two of you with the children,' he'd told them, 'I can't believe you've ever done anything else!'

He himself was allowed to help on occasion. In the last twenty minutes of the school day he was permitted to read aloud a story, or tell one out of his own head; something about his travels, or the people he had met. This week he had been reading *Alice's Adventures in Wonderland* and would be reading a further episode this afternoon. He only hoped that he would not be too tired to do so. He never quite knew when the awful fatigue would strike him.

He planned, when *Alice in Wonderland* was finished, to start on *Through the Looking Glass*. He had sent away for the book. Would his strength last, he wondered – especially in view of what the doctor had said to him today – until he had finished that book? There were so many books waiting to be read.

Jake completed what he had to do on Batty Green and then, refreshed by a pint of ale at the Welcome, turned his steps towards home. Passing the viaduct he paused, as always, to look at it. The work was well ahead now and would soon be finished. The arches soared impressively, strong yet elegant, outlined against the summer sky. The whole edifice was like a great monument, and it *was* a monument, Jake thought; a monument to the hundreds of men who had worked on it over the last few years. From the look of it it would last forever.

He felt a stab of envy as he watched the men working high above the ground in the clear air, high enough to look down on the birds which flew in and out through the arches. Oh, he knew the tunnel was every bit as important to the running of the railway as was the viaduct. He had always taken pride in it, and still did, but apart from the inconspicuous opening at each end its life and function were hidden, secret; its strength and symmetry, the toil and skill which had gone into making it, were invisible to the world and in its darkness would never be seen.

There were days, more and more of them recently, when he felt like a mole or a beetle living in the dark. True, the tunnel was open all the way through now – the headings had met within three inches of each other – and a light engine ran regularly through its length bringing supplies. There was no more of men being lowered in a cage down the shaft, but daylight could not penetrate far – though the low-lying fog did. The fog reached everywhere.

In one way the tunnel was less dangerous; now that they were using dynamite instead of gunpowder there were fewer explosions. But he was weary of it. He had been almost four years in the tunnel, one of the longest-serving men there, for they came and went. Perhaps it was time he changed his job? What would it be like, he wondered, to work on the viaduct? He was a skilled man now, in charge of other men. It might be quite easy to find a job other than in the tunnel.

By the time he was back in Nazareth the children were on their last lesson of the morning, ready at any moment to break to eat the packed dinners they had brought with them.

Beth looked up and smiled warmly at him as he came in at the door.

'Right, children,' she said. 'That's all for this morning. Close your books, and as it's bright and sunny we'll eat our dinner out of doors!'

When the children had eaten she gave them twenty minutes to play their games. It was the season for skipping ropes, though the boys scorned this, preferring to kick a ball about. She sat watching with Jake and Armitage on a bench outside the hut, the baby in her arms.

'Was it busy at Batty Green?' she asked Jake.

'As always,' he said. 'I stopped on the way back to take a look at the viaduct. It's coming on famously. I began to wish I worked on the viaduct instead of in the tunnel.'

'Don't say that! Don't ever say that!'

Beth rounded on him, her voice shrill, almost a scream. Jake looked at her in consternation. This outburst was not like his Beth, not at all like her.

'I'm sorry, love!' he said.

She was not easily to be pacified.

'Haven't I already given one husband to the viaduct?' she cried.

'I'm sorry,' Jake repeated. 'It was thoughtless of me. Of course I won't do it!'

'Promise me! Promise me you'll never work on the viaduct!'

'I promise!' Jake said.

She calmed down.

'I know you've begun to dislike working in the tunnel,' she said. 'Don't think I don't notice, or that I don't sympathize. But it won't be all that much longer. Everyone says another year should see the railway finished and running.'

'I daresay that's true,' Jake agreed. And what will we do then, he wondered?

Beth put the same thought into words.

'What will we do then?' she asked.

'What would you like to do?' Armitage chipped

351

in. 'Think of that first; what would you really like to do?'

The three of them sat in silence for a moment while the children continued to play. Beth was the first to speak.

'I think I know what *I* would like to do. I'd like to have my own school, run it in my own way. Or even better, I'd like for the two of us, Jake and me, to run it. Yes, that would be my choice!'

Armitage nodded.

'I can picture you doing that. I reckon you'd do it well.'

'It's nothing more than a dream,' Beth said, 'and I mustn't sit here dreaming. It's time the children were in. As for you, Jake, you must get your sleep or you'll be fit for nothing when you go to work.'

All the same, she wondered as she called the children and went back indoors with them, what *would* they do when the railway was finished?

# 20

On a Monday late in August, the postman handed Beth a letter. *B. Armitage, Esq.* the thick white envelope said, in exquisite writing with many flourishes. *Care of Mr J. Tempest.*

She handed the letter to Armitage. What did the B stand for, she wondered? He was extremely secretive about his given name.

'Ah! Splendid!' Armitage said. 'I've been expecting this! It will be from my solicitor.' He had written to him a week ago and had asked for a speedy reply. He wanted no time wasted.

What can Armitage want with a solicitor, Beth asked herself as she watched him open the envelope and read the single sheet it contained.

'Yes, that's all in order,' he said. 'Now all I have to do is go to Skipton next Friday.'

'To Skipton?' Beth queried.

'I have to sign things,' Armitage said. 'Please excuse me while I fetch paper from my room. I must reply at once.'

'What do you suppose he's talking about?' she asked Jake when Armitage had left them. 'And is he fit to travel to Skipton on his own?'

'I don't know why he's going,' Jake admitted. 'He always was a bit eccentric, and no worse for that. But I agree with you, he's not fit enough to travel to Skipton and back on his own. He's an old man, and sick. I'd not be happy to see him do it.'

'Then we must go with him,' Beth declared. 'The

class is still on holiday and I'm sure Elsie will look after the baby. And as for you, you must take a day off work.'

'They won't like it,' Jake said. 'But you're right and I'll do so. I'd not be easy in my mind otherwise.'

Armitage, when he came back into the room and they put the idea to him, was delighted.

'I wouldn't have asked you,' he admitted, 'but I'm most grateful. I wasn't looking forward to making the journey alone.'

'But if it's simply a question of signing something,' Jake said, 'couldn't you ask your solicitor to come to Nazareth?'

'Oh I couldn't possibly do that!' Armitage was shocked at the thought. 'Mr Jepson is quite an important man. I couldn't expect him to come all the way to Nazareth for such as me. But if you and Beth will accompany me to Skipton then that will please me mightily. I'll write and tell Mr Jepson to expect us, and we'll make it a day out.'

Beth cleared the breakfast table and Armitage sat down to write. He wrote at length, and Beth wondered how he could find so much to say on what seemed a simple matter.

'There!' he said at last. 'That's done!'

He turned to Jake.

'Shall you be going down to Batty Green?' he asked. 'If so, will you take my letter to the post office? And I thought that I might hire a pony and trap to take us to Settle, and from there we can get the train to Skipton. Will you see to that for me, Jake?'

'I will,' Jake promised. It would cost money to hire the pony and trap, but since the old man seemed keen to do it he would make no protest. It would certainly be more comfortable for his friend than being jolted around on any old cart which happened to be going in that direction.

Elsie was more than willing to look after the baby.

'You know I love to have her, and she'll be no trouble at all. I'll come and fetch her on Thursday.'

'Bring Tom with you,' Beth said. 'We haven't seen much of him this holiday.'

'I will,' Elsie said. 'Have you heard the news about Phoebe?'

'What news?' Beth asked. 'Since there are no classes at the moment I haven't seen either her or the children.'

'They're leaving!' Elsie announced.

'Leaving?'

'That's right. Phoebe says Malcolm is fed up with the railway, but I reckon it's Phoebe who's fed up with Jericho. Too quiet for her. She's every inch a town girl.'

'Where will they go?'

'Bradford. Malcolm reckons he'll get work there. It'll certainly suit Phoebe better.'

'I suppose so,' Beth said. 'I must pop round and see her.'

She found Phoebe on her knees, packing a large tin trunk from an assortment of objects scattered around the room.

'I'm sorry to hear you're leaving,' Beth said.

'Thank you,' Phoebe said. 'I can't say I'm sorry, though. Four years and more we've been stuck in this place. I'm ready for a taste of civilization, a few new faces. Oh, I don't mean you, love,' she added. 'You and me have always got on well. And the children will miss you.'

'I'll miss them,' Beth confessed. 'They've done so well. But in Bradford they'll be able to go to a proper school. They'll learn much more.'

Phoebe shrugged.

'I'm not sure they need more school. They can read and write now, do a few sums. What else is there?'

'Quite a lot,' Beth said.

'Oh well, we'll see. I look forward most to when they're earning a penny or two!'

On Friday, since the driver of the pony and trap had declared it impossible to bring it all the way up the rough moorland track to Nazareth, they took the tramway down to Batty Green. It ran more often now. When Jake helped her into the trap, which was waiting for them at the tramway terminus, Beth was reminded of her wedding day, and she knew by the gentle squeeze which Jake gave to her arm as he helped her up that his thoughts matched hers. She had not been to Settle, let alone Skipton, since then.

The drive through Ribblesdale was enchanting, the trees and hedges thick with their summer greenery, the corn in the fields turning to gold. It would be an early harvest this year. They halted at Horton to let the pony drink, and Jake fetched her a glass of lemonade from the inn.

'Do you remember we stopped here when I first walked from Settle?' Jake asked Armitage.

Armitage nodded. 'I remember it well.' He had taken to Jake from the first. He had always known that their paths would continue to cross.

When they boarded the train at Settle station it was stifling hot. Jake opened the windows and Beth sat with her back to the engine so that the smuts should not blow onto her face or, worse still, onto her very best summer dress.

'This is exciting!' she said, smiling across at Armitage.

'For me too,' Armitage replied. 'I've made most of my travels on my own two feet, though I must say, walking is quieter.'

Most nights, when he blew out his candle, he lay on his back and took a walk in his mind. Each night a different walk, always one of which he knew every step.

He climbed the green fells, scrambled down the steep, shaly inclines, walked through flower-filled meadows and by clear streams. His back never ached, his feet were never sore; the sun shone, or in a brief rainstorm there was shelter. And if he was lucky, long before his journey's end came into sight, he fell asleep. He was glad he had done so much in his younger days. How else would he keep going on his memories?

Now he looked out of the window and marvelled at the speed with which the fields, the trees, the sheep and cattle sped by. All of forty miles an hour the train must be doing through the valley. Only the birds which flew past the window travelled faster. It was no time at all before they were in Skipton.

'Mr Jepson's chambers are in the High Street,' Armitage said. 'Jepson, Murthwaite & Jepson. We can walk there.'

'Are you sure?' Jake asked. 'Wouldn't you rather we had a cab?'

'Not at all!' Armitage said. 'I still have the use of my legs, at least for that distance!'

It was not his legs, but his shortness of breath which was troubling him by the time they reached the solicitor's premises, and the fact that Mr Jepson's own office was at the top of a steep flight of stairs was no help. Jake suggested that he and Beth should remain in the waiting room while Armitage conducted his business, but Armitage would have none of that.

'I want you with me,' he said.

He had told them nothing of what his business was, or why it had been necessary for him to take this journey when he would have been better resting at home. Whatever it was, Beth thought, it was clearly of importance to him.

They waited no more than a minute or two in the outer room before Mr Jepson came out of his office to meet them. He was a small thickset man with a round smiling face. He stepped, arm extended, towards Armitage, and shook his hand vigorously. He's not a bit like a solicitor, Beth thought, though true enough she had never met one before.

'Good to see you, Mr Armitage,' Mr Jepson said. 'And this lady and gentleman must be the friends you told me you would bring.'

He nodded happily towards Jake and Beth and when Armitage had introduced them the solicitor led the way to his office, seated himself behind his imposing desk, with the three of them arranged in front of him. There was a question in his eyes as he looked at Armitage.

'Have you . . . ?' he began.

'No,' Armitage said. 'Mr and Mrs Tempest accompanied me here out of the kindness of their hearts. They know nothing more.'

'In that case,' Mr Jepson said, 'they have a pleasant surprise in store.'

Jake and Beth looked at each other, and then from the solicitor to Armitage, who was leaning back in his chair, a satisfied smile on his face.

'The thing is that Mr Jepson has drawn up my will and I am happy to tell you that the two of you are to be my sole beneficiaries!'

Jake stared at Armitage. It was several seconds before he found his voice.

'But this is a total surprise, Armitage! I had no idea!' He looked at Beth for confirmation and, speechless, she nodded her head. She wondered, in fact, if she had heard aright.

'Are you sure about this?' Jake asked Armitage. 'Don't you think . . . ?'

'I'm quite sure,' Armitage said firmly. 'I've thought it all out. I've no kith and kin of my own and you've been exceedingly kind to me. This is my return.'

'Whatever we did for you, it was a pleasure,' Beth

said quietly, finding her voice. 'We had no thought of . . .' For a moment words failed her again, then she pulled herself together. 'I just hope – I'm sure Jake does – that it will be a very long time before any of this happens.'

She spoke the truth. She was deeply moved by the old man's gesture, though common sense told her that the amount involved would be small. Armitage was a poor man. He paid his way in the house but he never seemed to be left with two ha'pennies to rub together. All the more reason, though, to appreciate what he was doing.

'Well then!' Mr Jepson said briskly. 'I have drawn up the will exactly as you instructed, Mr Armitage. All that remains is for you to sign it in the presence of two witnesses, who cannot, of course, be the beneficiaries.'

He rang a bell, and from an adjoining room two clerks appeared. It took no time at all for the signing and witnessing to be completed and for the clerks to leave as silently as they had come.

'And now for my further business,' Armitage said to the solicitor. 'Have you made any progress there?'

'I have indeed,' Mr Jepson said with satisfaction. 'In fact I believe that what I've been able to find will suit you down to the ground! *And* the premises are empty. My chief clerk, Mr Feathers, has the keys and he will be pleased to accompany you.'

Armitage turned to Jake and Beth.

'You look confused,' he said. 'And no wonder. It's my fault. I should have told you earlier, but there it is, I didn't! The fact is, I'm interested in renting a property in Skipton.'

'A property? But why . . . ?' Beth began. 'What sort of a property?'

Why did Armitage want to leave them? she wondered. He had seemed happy enough in Nazareth.

What was more, was he well enough to look after himself? She didn't think so, and that was a worry. She had grown so fond of him.

'You shall soon see,' Armitage said. 'So if Mr Feathers is free . . .'

Mr Jepson rang the bell again and the chief clerk appeared; a thin, grey man clutching a bunch of keys in his bony hand.

'At your service!' he said.

Armitage rose to his feet.

'We'll be off then, Mr Jepson. And I'll let you know what I think in a day or two.'

'The property is no more than ten minutes' walk away,' Mr Feathers said to Armitage as they went down the stairs. 'But perhaps you would like me to get a cab?'

'We'll walk,' Armitage said. 'As I told my young friends earlier, I haven't quite lost the use of my legs!'

'As you wish, sir,' Feathers said. 'The property is just beyond the High Street, and therefore quieter. In fact, a prime position for the purpose.'

Beth looked at Jake. Why did Armitage need a dwelling in a quiet, prime position? her expression said. And could he afford it? Jake shrugged his shoulders, equally puzzled.

Feathers led them to the top of the bustling High Street. As they passed the hotel where she and Jake had spent their honeymoon, a thrill of delight, so strong that she thought it must be visible to everyone, shot through Beth's body. She squeezed Jake's arm and he drew her closer in response.

At the top of the hill, where the church faced down the High Street, they branched off to the right. The houses were larger here, with deep windows and solid front doors. They were not the least bit suitable for Armitage, Beth thought, not unless he simply intended to take a room or two in one of them, and they did not look like houses which let off rooms.

Mr Feathers halted.

'Here we are!' he announced. 'The Beeches.'

Behind an elaborate wrought-iron double gate a wide path, flanked on either side by a square of lawn, led to the front door, set in the middle of a square-built house, its golden stone lit by the summer sun.

'There is, of course, a larger garden at the rear,' Mr Feathers said. 'I daresay you would find that useful.'

Whatever for, Beth wondered – but was too constrained to ask.

Mr Feathers selected a key, unlocked the front door and let them in. They stood in a wide hall, doors opening on either side and a well-proportioned staircase rising to the upper floor. Armitage stood in the centre of the hall and looked around him, a quiet smile of satisfaction on his face.

'Capital! Capital! Very suitable, I'd say!'

Beth could contain herself no longer. Armitage had clearly taken leave of his senses.

'*I* must say,' she ventured, 'it doesn't really seem suitable. Isn't it rather large for you, Mr Armitage?' To say nothing of the cost, she thought.

'Bless my soul, I'd not need more than one or two rooms,' Armitage said. 'Small ones at that, and I'd be content at the top of the house. No, the rest would be for you.'

'For us?' Jake said. 'I don't understand. What would we do with a house like this?'

'Why, it would house your school, of course! Don't say you've changed your minds! Don't tell me you no longer want to run a school!'

Beth and Jake stood quite still. I don't believe this is happening, Beth thought. It's a dream and I shall wake up any minute. She struggled to find her voice.

'Of course we do, Mr Armitage! But we couldn't possibly afford a place like this. You know we couldn't!'

Jake turned to Mr Feathers.

'There seems to be some mistake here. I'm afraid we've been wasting your time.' What *was* Armitage thinking of?

Feathers looked anxiously at Armitage.

'I understood, sir . . .'

'And you were right,' Armitage reassured him. 'The mistake I made is that I didn't tell my friends here what I had in mind. I wanted it to be a surprise, you see. Perhaps that was wrong?' He addressed the question to Jake and Beth.

'Not wrong, Armitage,' Jake said gently. 'But not really practical. You see, there's no way Beth and I could afford to rent a place like this. Not until the school – if we were to have one – was up and running and making a profit. And there'd be a deal of money to be paid out before we reached that stage.'

'But it was a kind thought,' Beth put in. 'We appreciate that.'

'Oh, I didn't expect you to rent it!' Armitage said. 'That's *my* contribution. After all, aren't you my heirs now?'

'But we don't want to inherit for a long, long time,' Beth said. 'Do we, Jake?'

'Certainly not,' Jake agreed.

'It's good to know that,' Armitage said. 'It makes me a very happy man. But it doesn't mean that I can't use some of the money on your behalf, and whenever I like. You see . . .' he was suddenly hesitant, diffident, '. . . there's a fair amount of money. My mother left it to me, and then an uncle left me more still. I never spent much – what did I want with money, living my kind of life? And Mr Jepson invested it wisely for me, so that it just grew. So if you don't like this house, or you don't think it's suitable, well then we can look elsewhere.'

'Oh, it's not that. It seems wonderful,' Beth said. 'It's just that . . . Really, I can't believe this is happening!'

'Nor me!' Jake agreed. 'But let me say at once that if, by some chance, we go ahead, then as soon as the school is in profit we'll naturally pay you back every penny.'

'As you wish,' Armitage said.

'Then would it not be a good idea to look over the rest of the house?' Mr Feathers suggested.

They went from room to room. The more Beth saw of the house, the more excited she became, and Jake quickly caught the excitement from her. It was not that there were over-many rooms, just enough to house themselves, Armitage, their family – even though so far it was only one daughter – with two large rooms which would make ideal classrooms; but that the whole house was light and bright and welcoming, with white paint everywhere and large windows through which the sun streamed in. At the rear was the garden Mr Feathers had promised; large and square, roughly grassed over and with trees around its perimeter.

'The garden needs some work on it, of course,' Mr Feathers said. 'Flower beds. Paths.'

'Oh, we wouldn't want it too spick-and-span,' Beth said. 'It's perfect for children to play in!' She saw the whole thing in her mind's eye. 'Don't you agree?' she asked Jake.

'Absolutely,' he said. 'And I could put up a swing from one of the trees.'

When they had toured the whole house, including the two spacious attics from which there was a view over Skipton to distant green hills, they stood again in the entrance hall.

'Well?' Armitage said.

'It's quite perfect!' Beth said.

'I agree,' Jake said.

'You don't think we should look at one or two others?' Armitage asked. 'To make a comparison?'

Beth shook her head.

'No. We'd not find anything better. This house *feels* right. I can tell it at once.'

'The only thing is . . .' Jake said, 'can you really afford to lend us the money, knowing we can't pay it back quickly? And we'd need more. We'd need money to equip it.'

'The other thing is,' Beth said, suddenly serious, 'can we actually run a school? Do we know how? Of course it would be small, and we'd take only young children, but could we do it? And would we get pupils?'

'I think you would,' Armitage said. 'Skipton is a thriving place, with lots of families. And I'm sure you're competent. Think what you've achieved in Nazareth, with so few advantages.'

'Thank you,' Beth said. 'You give me confidence. And I think you're right. I think Jake and I could make a go of it between us.'

'As for the money, I can see to that,' Armitage said. 'But perhaps you'd like to go back to Nazareth and give it further thought?'

Beth and Jake looked at each other.

'I don't think we need to do that,' Jake said.

'In that case, Mr Feathers,' Armitage said, 'we'll return and talk to Mr Jepson!' He would be glad, he thought, not to have to make too many more trips to Skipton. He was quite tired.

Back in the solicitor's office Armitage quickly made arrangements with Mr Jepson about the renting of the house, paid a quarter's rent in advance and signed everything which needed to be signed. 'Just in case,' he said.

It was late afternoon when they took the train back to Settle and dusk was falling when the pony and trap which they had hired at Settle deposited them at Batty Green. To Jake's dismay, the last tram, which would have taken them as far as Jericho, had already left. Armitage was clearly not fit for the climb over the moor.

'I'll take you as far up as the horse can pull the trap,' the owner of the vehicle said reluctantly. 'But it won't be far. The way's too steep and the track's too rough. The trap would tip over in no time at all.'

'Just as far as you can, then,' Jake said.

They were well short of Jericho before it was clear that there was nothing for it but to walk the rest of the way. Jake supported Armitage as best he could, at times half-carrying him. Armitage was white-faced and silent with fatigue, though trying his best not to be a burden.

Reaching Jericho, they stopped at Elsie's hut in order to collect Mary, but also to give Armitage a rest.

'The baby's hard and fast asleep,' Elsie said. 'It's a shame to wake her. Why don't you let me bring her up to you in the morning?'

'I will,' Beth agreed. 'Come early. I've such a lot to tell you, you'll never believe!'

Jack Drake was looking at Armitage with concern. The old man looked all in.

'It wouldn't be a bad idea for *you* to stay here until the morning,' he offered. 'We can make you up a bed.'

'Oh, no!' Armitage protested. 'I must get home! I must!'

'In that case,' Jack said to Jake, 'you and me can carry Mr Armitage between us. You'll not object to that?' he asked Armitage.

'I confess I'd be grateful,' Armitage said. 'I admit I'm very tired.'

Elsie fetched a blanket and put it around his

shoulders, then between them the two men carefully, and with great gentleness, carried the old man from Jericho to Nazareth. Beth went before them so that by the time they reached the hut Armitage's bed was ready. They laid him on it.

'I'm afraid it's been quite a day for you,' Jake said. 'You've done too much.'

Armitage's face lit with a contented smile.

'It's been one of the happiest days of my life. I shall sleep well tonight!'

It was Beth, taking him a cup of tea, who found him in the morning. He was sitting upright against his pillows and at first she thought he was asleep, and wondered if she should let him be, he looked so peaceful; but then she thought there was a stillness about him which was not right.

Gently, she touched his hand. It was colder than a stone in winter, and as she touched him he slid sideways.

'Jake!' she cried. 'Jake! Come quickly!'

## 21

Jake came running.

Beth, leaning over Armitage, looked up at her husband with frightened eyes.

'He's . . . Oh, Jake!'

Gently, Jake eased her out of the way and felt for the old man's pulse. It was there; irregular, faint, hard to find, but still there.

'He's not dead,' he said. Though he looks it, he thought. His face was as white as snow, his lips a thin blue line, his breath barely discernible.

'We must get the doctor,' Jake said. 'I can run down to Batty Green faster than you, but will you be all right here?'

'Yes,' Beth said.

'He might . . .'

Beth interrupted him.

'He might die. I know. But please go! Quickly!'

'I'll tell Elsie on the way down, ask her to come round.'

Beth shook her head. 'Don't waste time!'

'I won't!' Jake said. 'I have to pass her door. I don't want you to be alone.'

Elsie, breathless, arrived within minutes of Jake's leaving.

'I ran all the way!' she explained. 'Oh dear, he does look bad, poor man!'

They stood on either side of the bed, watching Armitage for the slightest sign of movement. Then there came a moment when he took a great, shuddering breath, then slowly, almost silently, exhaled it – and was still.

'He's gone!' Elsie said.

Beth stood there, rooted, until a cry from Mary who had been asleep in her crib in the next room brought her to her senses.

'You go to Mary,' Elsie ordered. 'I'll see to Mr Armitage as far as I can, though we mustn't do much until the doctor's been. Then I'll make us a cup of tea.'

Minutes later she followed Beth into the living-room, and set the kettle to boil.

'He looks very peaceful now, poor gentleman,' she said. 'And he was a gentleman, wasn't he? You only had to hear him speak to know that.'

Beth nodded agreement.

It seemed a long wait before Doctor Stokes arrived.

'I was out on a case,' he explained. 'Jake had to find me. I'm sorry.'

'He died an hour ago,' Beth said. 'But I doubt you could have done anything. He was never conscious again.'

'It comes as no surprise to me,' Doctor Stokes said. 'Nor would it to him if he was aware of it happening, which I doubt. He knew it was coming, and sooner rather than later. I'd told him that. He wasn't afraid.'

'If only I'd known!' Beth said. 'If only I'd known earlier, perhaps I could have done something for him.'

'You couldn't,' Doctor Stokes said. '*I* couldn't. His heart was worn out. But you gave him exactly what he needed, a comfortable home in which to spend the last months of his life, a place in which to die with dignity.'

'He was always a dignified man,' Jake put in. 'In spite of the fact that he chose to live like a tramp.'

'A gentleman tramp,' Elsie said.

It seemed to Beth, a few days later, as they followed

the track to Chapel-le-dale, that she had walked behind more coffins in the time she had lived on the moor than in the rest of her life until then.

'We must write to Mr Jepson,' Jake said when they returned from the funeral. 'We must let him know.'

'We should have done it at once,' Beth said. 'It's just that everything happened so quickly. I'm sure he'll be shocked.'

It gave Jake a swift moment of pride that he was able, with no difficulty, to write the letter himself to the solicitor. Mr Jepson replied by return of post. His letter showed no surprise, and when, at his suggestion, they visited him at his office in Skipton, he expounded on that.

'Mr Armitage told me he had only a short time to live. It was the reason he wanted to put his affairs in order as quickly as possible, to make sure that his money – a not inconsiderable amount, as you will hear in a moment – went where he wished it to go.'

'We knew he wasn't well,' Beth said. 'But he never told us how ill he was.'

'He wouldn't,' Mr Jepson said. 'My late client was a most modest and unselfish man. He would not have wanted to worry you. And now we must get down to business!'

He rang the bell on his desk and Mr Feathers entered.

'Ah, Mr Feathers, I am about to read the late Mr Armitage's will, and then I'm sure there'll be matters to discuss. I wish you to be present.'

'Certainly,' the chief clerk said, bowing respectfully to Jake and Beth before he opened the file in front of his employer.

My goodness, Beth thought with surprise, they're treating us as if we were really important. But when Mr Jepson, in a solemn voice, began to read the will and then mentioned how much money Armitage had left, she was less surprised.

'It is not a fortune of course,' Mr Jepson said, 'but it is a tidy sum.'

'Oh, but it *is* a fortune, Mr Jepson!' Beth said. 'At least to us it is!' She looked at Jake.

'It is indeed,' Jake agreed.

'Over the years Mr Armitage spent very little. He saved his money and it accumulated, with the result you see.' Mr Jepson spoke with approval. He thought highly of clients who did not squander their money but trusted him to invest it wisely on their behalf. Mr Armitage had been an exemplary client in that regard.

'Now we come to the house which Mr Armitage was to rent on your behalf,' he continued. 'Will you still wish to pursue the idea of starting a school, or in the circumstances will you perhaps have other ideas in mind? I need to know because if you do *not* wish to rent The Beeches, the owner must be advised.'

Beth and Jake glanced at one another, but there was no need to consult.

'Our plans are the same,' Jake said.

'Except that we shall put them into practice sooner than we expected,' Beth added. 'There's no point in waiting.'

'Quite right!' Mr Jepson said.

'Do you think . . .' Beth began hesitantly, 'do you think we could look over The Beeches again while we're here in Skipton? There are things neither of us can remember. It was all such a surprise to us at the time.'

'Of course! Mr Feathers will accompany you,' Mr Jepson said. 'Should you have any questions I'm sure he'll be able to answer them. And I will be in touch with you both before long.'

They went over the house, seeing it with different and sharper eyes than on the first occasion.

'It's even better than I thought, though it's certainly shabby,' Beth said. 'We'll need to make a few alterations, some adjustments, do some painting, but there's nothing we can't manage between us.'

On the train journey back to Settle they discussed dates and times.

'Of course there's no way we can open for the September term,' Beth said. 'It's almost September now. It's a pity, that – but we'll open after Christmas. Oh, Jake, it's going to be so exciting! Did you ever think this could happen to us?'

Jake looked across at her, looked into her bright, shining eyes, alight with enthusiasm. But for the presence of other people in the compartment he would have taken her in his arms there and then.

'No, I didn't,' he said.

He gave his notice to the Railway Company at the end of the week, but was persuaded to stay on for another month.

'They weren't surprised that I was leaving,' he told Beth when he arrived home. 'It's beginning to happen with more than me. It won't be long before the railway's finished. People are getting anxious about what they'll do next.'

'I shall miss you,' Elsie said when Beth told her how soon they might be leaving. 'But Jake is right. Before long we'll all be gone. It stands to reason. There'll be no work left for us.'

Beth put her arms around Elsie's shoulders and drew her close.

'Oh, Elsie, I shall miss you so much! You've been such a friend to me. I couldn't have managed without you!'

'Nor I without you, hinny,' Elsie said. 'But I have to admit, I'll be glad to get back to Northumberland. I wouldn't want to live in Jericho forever. Shanty towns are no place to bring up children.'

'I agree,' Beth said. 'I hope my next child will be born in Skipton. A civilized place.'

'Beth! You're not . . . ?' Elsie cried.

Beth laughed.

'No, I'm not expecting! Not yet, anyway. But there's no reason at all why I shouldn't be, soon!' If it had anything to do with Jake and his love for her, she thought, she would be pregnant tomorrow.

'But surely, moving house, starting a school . . .' Elsie said. 'And Mary not yet a year old . . .'

'None of that worries me,' Beth said. 'There's nothing I can't do. Or at least there's nothing Jake and I can't do together.'

Phoebe left, gladly shaking the dust off her heels, and set her face towards Bradford, though the children had been tearful.

'I like it here,' Clarissa wailed. 'I don't want to go.'

'You'll enjoy it in Bradford,' Beth said. 'I'm sure you will.' From what little she had heard of Bradford she was not at all sure, but she tried to speak with conviction. 'You'll have a nice new school.'

'Aubrey and me don't want a new school,' Clarissa said. 'We like coming here.'

'Well, I shall be having a new school also,' Beth said. 'But it will be much too far for you to come all the way from Bradford.'

'All the same,' she said to Jake a day or two later, 'perhaps we should consider whether we'll take a few boarders. Not many, we wouldn't have the room, and not Clarissa and Aubrey, but it would widen the scope and I'd quite enjoy it.'

'We'll think about it,' Jake said. 'We'll not dismiss anything out of hand.'

The going of Phoebe and her family was the first of several farewell scenes and in early November it was the turn of Beth and Jake to leave.

'We shall stay on a bit longer,' Elsie said. 'Jack's been promised work until the spring of next year. They reckon the trains will be running by then; at least, the goods trains. In any case, I don't think we'd want to move further north with the winter before us, though God knows if even Northumberland is as cold and wild as Blea Moor.'

Snow already covered the summit and upper slopes of Whernside on the day Jake and Beth left.

'I shall miss my mountain,' Jake said. 'I'm glad I have my picture of it.'

'It shall have pride of place in our new home,' Beth promised. 'And we'll never forget it, will we? So much has happened to us here.'

On the day before they left Nazareth Jake had walked with her to Chapel-le-dale and they had visited Will's and Armitage's graves. Beth had no bad memories of Will now. The happiness which had been hers in the last two years had wiped out every unhappy memory of the past.

It had been arranged that on removal day their goods and chattels would be taken down to Batty Green on the tramway, and from there by cart to Skipton. Beth and Jake, with Mary, could also have travelled on the cart, but Jake decided against it.

'We'll go on it as far as Settle,' he said. 'After that we'll take the train. We have to remember that we're no longer poor, though I admit it takes some getting used to!'

'It certainly does,' Beth agreed. 'And we mustn't be extravagant. Setting up the school, getting it running, is going to take a lot of money. All the same, I think you're right about the train. I wouldn't fancy being bumped all the way to Skipton and I'm sure Mary wouldn't enjoy it.'

With Jake by her side and Mary in her arms, all of them ready to leave, well wrapped up against the biting snow wind which was blowing across the moor, Beth looked around the empty room.

'Goodbye, little hut,' she said. 'You've served us well.' She turned to Jake. 'I wonder who'll live here next?'

'No-one, I should think,' Jake said. 'They'll be taking down the huts as people leave. They won't be required much longer.'

He picked up the two bags he was to carry, and they left, closing the door behind them. Facing into the wind, the snow-covered mountain ahead of them, they walked towards the tramway.

'I swear,' Beth said as they walked from the railway station and up the length of the High Street towards The Beeches, 'that Skipton is as cold as Nazareth!'

It was almost dark and snow was beginning to fall as they reached the house, but when Jake turned the key in the lock and opened the door it was a different story. Mr Feathers had been true to his word. He had promised to engage a woman who would at least sweep the floors and light fires in the kitchen, in the main bedroom and in the living-room for their arrival, and she had done so. By now she had left, and the fires had burned down to a red glow, but the three rooms, though without curtains at the windows, or rugs on the bare floors, were a pleasant contrast to the weather outside.

'I'll see to Mary, then make something to eat,' Beth said. 'There's nothing more we can do after that until the furniture arrives. Let's hope it won't be long.'

She had brought provisions with her: bread, cheese, a slab of gingerbread, some apples, and candles for light. They sat on the floor near the warmth of the fire, and ate. It was almost two hours later that the cart drew up at the gate. The first thing the driver

374

demanded, before he began to unload, was a bucket of water for his horse.

'It's a fair step from Ribblehead to Skipton for my old Bess,' he said. 'She's a good strong 'un but she gets tired sooner than she used to. Don't we all?'

When he had watered the horse the three of them, by the light of one street lamp, unloaded the furniture and carried it into the house. There wasn't much of it; it looked lost in the high-ceilinged rooms.

'I must see to Mary's cradle first of all,' Beth said to the driver. 'She needs to settle down. Then I'll give you something to eat.'

'Nay, I'll not bother,' the driver said. 'I'd best get down to the inn and stable Bess. After that I'll eat. Though thank you all the same.'

When he had left, by which time Mary was as sound asleep in her cradle as if she was still in the familiar hut in Nazareth, Jake said: 'Let's not do anything more tonight except put the bed up. It's been a long day.'

Lying in bed, in the curve of Jake's arm, Beth looked towards the faint glow which came from the dying embers of the bedroom fire. The rest of the room was in deep shadow. It was as if they were held, the two of them and the baby in her cradle at the side of the bed, in a magic circle of warmth and soft light.

'Oh, Jake,' Beth said quietly, 'I'm so happy! Everything seems so right. Please tell me you feel the same.'

Jake turned her towards him. 'I'll do better than that,' he said. 'I'll *show* you how I feel.'

From the moment they were wakened next morning by Mary's usual habit of delivering a long speech in her own incomprehensible language while she sat upright in her cradle, for Jake and Beth the hours, days and weeks raced by. What had seemed ample time to do all that had to be done before opening their school in the middle of the following January proved not to be so.

'There's so much to do!' Beth said, taking off her cloak and bonnet on coming in from the December cold. 'I wouldn't have believed it possible that there were so many things we hadn't even considered.'

'Which just shows what amateurs we are,' Jake said. 'Also, we made our decisions in such a hurry,' he reminded her. 'If we had taken more time . . .'

'I didn't want to take more time,' Beth said. 'Neither of us did. You're not sorry, are you?'

Jake shook the flakes of snow from his coat and hung it on the row of high hooks in the hall. Beneath the high row a low rack of hooks had been fixed, ready for when the children should start. It was only one of several jobs the carpenter had done in the house. They had found Mr Lomax just a week after they had moved in and he had been working for them ever since, making simple desks, benches, stools, chairs; fitting extra shelves into the cupboards with which the house was already well endowed. Mr Lomax was a real find, Beth and Jake frequently told each other. He was skilled, amenable to doing what was asked of him, and not expensive.

'Of course I'm not sorry,' Jake answered. 'Far from it.'

'But shall we ever be ready in time?' Beth's voice was anxious. 'Only a fortnight to go to Christmas, and the opening two weeks after that.'

'Don't worry, of course we shall,' Jake said. 'What's more, we'll take time to enjoy Christmas. Our first Christmas in our first real home – for I never intended that we should live in a railway hut for ever!'

'And Mary's first birthday,' Beth reminded him. 'But we were happy in our hut, weren't we?'

'Of course we were,' Jake agreed. 'But it wasn't what I wanted for my two princesses.'

Every morning when he wakened, he was glad not to be working in the tunnel. Sometimes he missed the company of the other men, but less and less so as time went by.

They had already advertised the opening of the school in neat, attractive displays in the Skipton paper and in the *Yorkshire Post*. There was no point in making it known further afield since they had agreed that, for some months at least, they would take only day pupils. The house was not yet ready for boarders.

'And let's face it,' Jake said, 'we can never take more than a few.'

The advertisements had brought a dozen enquiries, and the board – 'Beech House School for children aged 5 to 11. Mr and Mrs Jake Tempest' – painted in green and gold by a signwriter and fixed close to the front gate, had yielded a few more. Beth and Jake together had interviewed several children and parents with the result that they would have a certain nine when they opened for the spring term.

'Though it's not nearly enough,' Beth said. 'We need at least twenty to break even, let alone make a profit.'

'There's still time,' Jake pointed out. 'And by the end of the first term we'll get more pupils from recommendations.'

'Perhaps the handbills will achieve something,' Beth said hopefully.

It was why they had been out this morning, to collect from the printer a batch of tastefully designed handbills, setting out what they had to offer. They had distributed them, though in discreet quantities, around the better-class establishments in the town.

'We must wait and see,' Jake said. 'And don't worry. It will be all right eventually, you'll see!'

On Christmas Day, in the afternoon, Mary took her first steps, walking confidently, as if she had done it since the day she was born, until suddenly, after a dozen steps, she lost her balance and fell with a thump to the floor.

'Now stand up, princess,' Jake said, holding out his hands to her. 'Stand up and try again!'

'How Armitage would have loved to see her!' Beth said. 'He was so fond of her.'

After their Christmas dinner they had drunk a toast to Armitage with a glass of port.

'But for him, we wouldn't be here,' Jake said. He looked around the room. 'We'd have none of this. He changed our lives.'

Jake was proved right about the children. In January they enrolled eleven pupils, mostly between the ages of five and eight, but before the summer term was due to start after Easter they knew they were to have twenty-three children.

'And it will be more when the new school year begins in September,' Jake pointed out. 'That's the time children start school, or change schools.'

In April they received a letter from Elsie Drake. The thoughts were hers, but the letter was written by Tom who was home from York for the Easter holiday.

We are still here though not for much longer (Elsie said). But more and more people have left. Most of the work is finished and the huts are coming down. Next week there is to be a special train to take the directors of the Midland Railway all the way from Settle to Carlisle. Just fancy! Whoever would have thought it.

'There were times when I wouldn't have,' Jake said. 'Sometimes I thought the tunnel would never be finished; that it would fall in, or it wouldn't meet in the middle!'

'It seems long ago and far away,' Beth said. 'Another life.'

'Another life,' Jake echoed. 'And in August, if we're to believe the *Craven Pioneer*, the goods trains will be running.'

'And by next year the passenger trains,' Beth said.

'When that happens we will go on the railway,' Jake promised. 'You and me and Mary.'

# Epilogue

Although passenger trains ran from Skipton to Carlisle from May 1876, it was more than a year later before Jake was able to fulfil his promise to take Beth and Mary on the train.

The reasons for the delay were twofold.

The first was that Beech House School was so successful that it never seemed possible to find time to go on the railway. There were now forty-eight pupils, most of whom, as Jake had envisaged, had come from recommendations. And there was a waiting list. Beech House School had become sought after.

A young girl, Florence Mason, had been employed to help with the smallest children, though not to teach them. All teaching was firmly in the hands of Jake and Beth.

The second reason for the lengthy delay was to be seen in Beth's arms as she and her family boarded the train in the late summer of 1877. His name was John Armitage Tempest and he had been born – conveniently – in the Easter holiday of that year.

'At four months old, and just having been fed, he will probably sleep all the way,' Beth said with a contented smile. 'He'll not know what he's missing!'

She settled into her upholstered seat – even the third-class carriages on this new route had upholstered seats, and if you travelled from London, and could afford the cost, you could travel in the Pullman coach with an armchair to yourself, comfortable enough to sleep in. Just like in America.

'I wouldn't like the Pullman coach,' Beth said to Jake. 'It's too public. I prefer this compartment, especially if no-one else gets in.'

She sat by the window, holding the baby. Jake sat opposite with Mary on his knee, pointing out to her the landmarks as the train raced through the countryside. They were going as far as Appleby. Carlisle was too far.

'You see that mountain there, which looks like a lion,' he said. 'That's Pen-y-ghent!'

'Not a lion,' Mary contradicted. 'I got a lion in my picture book.'

'But like a lion,' Jake said patiently.

It didn't matter. He was waiting for Ribblehead and the viaduct, for the sight of his own mountain, and Blea Moor.

The train slowed down, and stopped briefly, on the viaduct. Looking out of the window he could, because of the curve of the line, see the back end of the train. He had never thought of the viaduct being built on such a curve.

He looked straight ahead of him now, across Blea Moor.

It stretched into the distance, wild, empty, no sign of life, the grass blowing in the wind.

He lifted Mary high in his arms and pointed a finger.

'Look! That's where you were born! Right across there!'

Mary shook her head emphatically.

'No! No houses. Babies are born in houses.'

Jake smiled.

'And that's my mountain,' he said. 'Like the one in the picture at home.'

'Mountain,' Mary said, vigorously nodding her head.

'At least the mountain hasn't changed,' Jake said to Beth.

'I don't think the moor has changed, not really,'

Beth said. 'People like us changed it for a few years, but I reckon it's gone back to being itself.'

The train started again, with a jerk. Jake stood looking out of the window until Whernside was out of view, then sat back in his seat.

**THE END**

**THE BRIGHT ONE**
**by Elvi Rhodes**

Molly O'Connor's life was not an easy one. With six children and a husband who earned what he could as a casual farmhand, fisherman, or drover, it was a constant struggle to keep her family fed and raised to be respectable. Of all her children, Breda – the Bright One – was closest to her heart. As, one by one, her other children left Kilbally, Kathleen and Kieran to the Church, Moira to marriage, the twins to war, so Breda, the youngest, was the one who stayed close to her parents. Breda never wanted to leave the West of Ireland. She thought Kilbally was the most beautiful place in the world.

Then tragedy struck the O'Connors and the structure of their family life was irrevocably changed. Reeling from unhappiness and humiliation, Breda decided to make a new life for herself – in Yorkshire with her Aunt Josie's family. There she was to discover a totally different world from the one she had left behind, with new people and new challenges for the future.

0 552 14057 0

# A SELECTED LIST OF FINE NOVELS
# AVAILABLE FROM CORGI BOOKS

| 14060 | 0 | **MERSEY BLUES** | Lyn Andrews | £4.99 |
|---|---|---|---|---|
| 14229 | 8 | **CEDAR STREET** | Aileen Armitage | £4.99 |
| 13313 | 2 | **CATCH THE WIND** | Frances Donnelly | £5.99 |
| 14382 | 0 | **THE TREACHERY OF TIME** | Anna Gilbert | £4.99 |
| 13255 | 1 | **GARDEN OF LIES** | Eileen Goudge | £5.99 |
| 14095 | 3 | **ARIAN** | Iris Gower | £4.99 |
| 14140 | 2 | **A CROOKED MILE** | Ruth Hamilton | £4.99 |
| 13872 | X | **LEGACY OF LOVE** | Caroline Harvey | £4.99 |
| 14138 | 0 | **PROUD HARVEST** | Janet Haslam | £4.99 |
| 14220 | 4 | **CAPEL BELLS** | Joan Hessayon | £4.99 |
| 14390 | 1 | **THE SPLENDOUR FALLS** | Susanna Kearsley | £4.99 |
| 14331 | 6 | **THE SECRET YEARS** | Judith Lennox | £4.99 |
| 13910 | 6 | **BLUEBIRDS** | Margaret Mayhew | £5.99 |
| 10375 | 6 | **CSARDAS** | Diane Pearson | £5.99 |
| 14123 | 2 | **THE LONDONERS** | Margaret Pemberton | £4.99 |
| 12607 | 1 | **DOCTOR ROSE** | Elvi Rhodes | £4.99 |
| 13185 | 7 | **THE GOLDEN GIRLS** | Elvi Rhodes | £4.99 |
| 13481 | 3 | **THE HOUSE OF BONNEAU** | Elvi Rhodes | £4.99 |
| 13309 | 4 | **MADELEINE** | Elvi Rhodes | £4.99 |
| 12367 | 6 | **OPAL** | Elvi Rhodes | £4.99 |
| 12803 | 1 | **RUTH APPLEBY** | Elvi Rhodes | £4.99 |
| 13738 | 3 | **SUMMER PROMISE AND OTHER STORIES** | Elvi Rhodes | £3.99 |
| 13636 | 0 | **CARA'S LAND** | Elvi Rhodes | £4.99 |
| 13870 | 3 | **THE RAINBOW THROUGH THE RAIN** | Elvi Rhodes | £4.99 |
| 14057 | 0 | **THE BRIGHT ONE** | Elvi Rhodes | £4.99 |
| 14318 | 9 | **WATER UNDER THE BRIDGE** | Susan Sallis | £4.99 |
| 13951 | 3 | **SERGEANT JOE** | Mary Jane Staples | £3.99 |
| 14296 | 4 | **THE LAND OF NIGHTINGALES** | Sally Stewart | £4.99 |
| 14263 | 8 | **ANNIE** | Valerie Wood | £4.99 |